I0689486

VASYL SHKLIAR

Raven's Way

A novel

Translated by

Stephen Komarnyckyj

K L P
Kalyna Language Press Limited

First published in the UK in 2015 by Kalyna Language Press Limited
This paperback edition published in 2015

Originally Published in Ukraine as Chornyi Voron by Yaroslaviv Val, Kyiv, 2009

Acknowledgements

Kalyna Language Press wish to thank Volodymyr Pekarchuk and the Ukrainian National Federal Credit Union for their support with financing this project.

Cover Design by Oleg Ganzha

About the Author

Vasyl Shkliar is currently the most popular writer working in Ukraine and has been named the 'Father of the Ukrainian Best Seller'. His novels have received the most prestigious literary awards in Ukraine, but despite this he astounded the entire country when he refused the highest accolade that can be awarded to a Ukrainian writer, the Taras Shevchenko Award, for his novel Chornyi Voron, in protest against the policies of the Ukrainian government at the time. Some might say he cut off his nose to spite his face, but in reality he was simply continuing the fight for freedom and democracy started by his grandfather and other young men in the forest so long ago. This time by hurling words instead of grenades.

He lives in Kyiv with his wife, but has a great love for his childhood village of Khlypnivka. There, just near to his house, a river flows through the forest where he fishes and usually catches his dinner and inspiration for his books.

About the Translator

Stephen Komarnyckyj is a poet and translator who was born in Yorkshire, England and maintains strong links with Ukraine, where his family live.

In 1921 the four year long war that Russia had waged against the Ukrainian People's Republic was decided in favour of the invader and Ukraine's soldiers were interned within the barbed wire fences of their former Polish allies. However, an armed struggle continued for years on most of Ukraine's terrain. The insurrectionists of Kholodnyi Yar undertook a desperate resistance against the Russian occupiers. Their black battle flag bore the inscription:

A Free Ukraine or Death

The spring cuckoo
Coos happiness to you,
For me the raven caws sadly
Forget me, forget me.

A folk song

Part One

Chapter 1

1

Otaman Veremii was buried secretly at night in Hunskyi Forest. There was no valedictory salvo of guns or speeches. Two sombre men brought the conveyance with his coffin, while a third man guided a priest from a nearby village to the burial site. They dug the grave twenty steps to the east of an ancient oak tree, where the pale, pine wood of the coffin stood out against the darkness. Its freshly cut boards were still fragrant with life.

'Open the lid,' said the priest. He blew on the incense for some time and tried to strike some damp matches, which hissed, sputtered and did not want to ignite.

'What for?' asked the man who had brought the priest. His head, which was wide rather than long, and hooked nose gave him the resemblance of an owl.

'Because it's necessary,' said the priest. 'For all I know there could be a dog in there.'

'This isn't the time or place for jokes, Father.'

'That's why you should agree to open the coffin. I can tolerate everything apart from sacrilege.'

The two sombre men drew closer and, slowly and unwillingly, raised the lid. The screeching of an owl reached them from somewhere in the depths of the forest. If it is true that devils box each other in the dark of night, then the sound might have been their cries.

'Yes, that's him,' said Father Oleksii, 'I knew the deceased. But why have they stuck his straw hat on him?'

'Because that was his will. He wanted to be buried in his straw hat and embroidered shirt,' said the man who resembled an owl. 'That's how the otaman went into battle. Didn't you know that?'

'It was a stupid custom,' said one of the sombre men, 'the enemy could see him among us from afar. All they had to do was aim at the straw hat until they were accurate.'

'But we could see him from a long way too,' said the second

sombre man. 'We always saw that he was with us.'

'It was still a stupid custom,' repeated the first sombre man, spitting drily over his shoulder.

'It is none of your business,' said the owl-like man. 'Begin the service Father and, if possible, don't draw it out, it will soon be morning.'

'Good, they've taken off his boots,' said Father Oleksii. 'It will be easier for him to enter heaven like that.'

'Begin the service, Father.'

The spooky call of night birds echoed through the forest again and it struck Father Oleksii that owls did not screech like that. He began the service.

'God of spirits and all things, You vanquished death, destroyed the devil and made a gift of Your life to this world, so Lord, soothe the spirit of Your servant, Veremii, in a place of light, of flowers, of calmness, from which all pain, anguish and lamentation has fled. Forgive all his sins of thought, word and deed, as a sacred God who loves humanity, for there is no man who has lived who has not sinned.'

After the short service they lowered the coffin into the pit and threw in a few pinches of earth. They filled the grave without heaping the soil on top, but instead levelled the grass and covered it with fallen leaves.

'Understand us, Father,' said the owl-like man, 'no one must know of this place. They will seek him, even in death.'

'But they won't find him,' said the second sombre man, throwing his shovel into the cart. 'Even if they stumble across the grave, he won't be here.'

'Why won't he be here?' Father Oleksii asked.

'He will have been borne to heaven.'

Father Oleksii crossed himself and breathed in the cold, while the chilled autumn air blew down the collar of his garment.

'Remember, there were four of us here,' said the owl-like man, with menace in his voice. 'Apart from us, no one has seen this place. If anything happens we are the ones to blame.'

He was mistaken, however, because an ancient raven,

10

perching on the oak next to them, had been awake for a long time. He was watching the spectacle of this strange funeral gathering with one, occasionally blinking eye. The raven was already two hundred and seventy years old, but he had not tired of observing the strange proceedings of humanity and trying to understand them. Now he was sitting on an oak, which was still holding on forcefully to its reddening leaves, breathing the warm fumes of the censer in the tranquil silence. The pale, quarter-full moon did not reach him among the oak leaves, although it threw a strong light into the small clearing where the people were bustling around.

The raven, although blind in one eye, immediately recognised the priest and the man with the hooked nose. It was not the first time he had seen them. It is true that his hearing was bad, he was as deaf as a tree stump and he was half blind, but he saw and heard what he needed to. He was surprised to see that on this occasion Father Oleksii not only shortened the service but did not mark the grave, which was an Orthodox custom, by pouring soil onto the coffin to form the shape of a cross. However, the scene that was subsequently played out in the clearing was even more amazing to him. Other people came, talking in a harsh language from elsewhere; alien, horned people, or rather people in horned caps. They measured out twenty paces to the east of the old oak and began to dig. When they eventually reached the coffin and raised the lid, instead of the corpse of the otaman, they found only a piece of paper on which a few words were written, words that if you spent time pondering over them would drive you to distraction.

The raven laughed quietly to himself, smothering his beak in his feathers so he did not caw and be heard. He knew the horned ones, in their wrath, would probably try to shoot him. The raven was not afraid of death, but he was not fond of the smell of burned feathers and, in his more advanced years, could not endure the scent that emanated from gunpowder.

2

I am still unable to explain, even to myself, the delight that grips me before every battle. It trembles through my entire body like a living

11

thing. My heart sings, my pupils dilate and my palms tingle. If there is a firm resolution that we will go forth into battle today, or even tomorrow, I cannot find a place for myself. Something shakes me from the centre of my being. I saw that this feeling affected not just me, all of us were captured by this delight, but we all lived through it in our own way. One guy would strut like a rooster, another would clean his pistol, someone else would hum or whistle, and there was one man who would sit motionlessly, while his eyes burned with an evil flame. When we suddenly forswore the battle, I experienced a feeling as though a young woman had refused me at the last minute and I remained alone with my longing.

No, there was no fear in any of us. It had been scattered to the winds, along with hope and when hope leaves a man how can there be any fear?

The blind sorceress, Yevdosia, would have said that there was nothing to boast about. I went to her when everything began. She could gather pain from the human body and was able to heal the soul. I went to her one day and said, 'Take from my being two unnecessary things. Draw them out of my spirit so that no trace of either remains.'

'What unnecessary things?' she asked as she smiled with her unseeing eyes.

'Fear and regret,' I said. 'Draw the fear from me and then the regret.'

'Those cannot be removed from you; without fear and regret you would swiftly lose yourself.'

I have recollected her words many times when I have been decapitating people in a way that was no longer like war for me but had simply become an everyday occupation that made my hands ache at night. That is how I had become when we captured some Chinese soldiers. You can imagine the kind of captivity it was for them. There was no clemency in our hearts. We would put our prisoners to the sword immediately, without squandering bullets on them.

On this occasion we led them to the block and I ordered them to lay down their heads ready to be executed. I do not know, even now, why the Chinese who fell into our hands laid their heads under our swords so willingly. It was as if they were in thrall to some enchantment. There was no pleading for mercy and no whining, only a completely submissive compliance with a reality that they could not change.

When between ten and twenty heads had rolled and the grass had become crimson with blood, the last one came to the block. He was skinny, not very tall, and had bow legs. It seemed to me that if I had grabbed his knees and spun him he would have rolled like a wheel, who knows in what direction. He was a complete calamity. The front of his head had been shaved and the hair on the back was plaited into a pigtail. What was particularly interesting about this 'walking calamity' was that when he knelt down and laid his neck on the block he suddenly grabbed the pigtail and gathered it onto the crown of his head. This made me laugh. What was it about? Was he afraid of losing this 'beauty' and had moved it to prevent it from being separated from his head, or did he gather it from the nape of his neck to stop it being spattered with blood?

My hands descended. I did not know whether to laugh or what to do, but I saw clearly enough that there was not a drop of fear in his eyes; as if he thought he was heading straight for paradise and was only worried about ensuring his pigtail was whole, clean and well groomed for the next life. I grabbed him by that tail, pulled him sharply from his knees and turned his face towards me. There was still no shadow of fear in those dark, narrow eyes. As he looked at me with a quiet curiosity and understanding, he suddenly spoke, 'Chan fights for whoever gives him a bite to eat. If you give him something to eat, he will fight for you.'

I released his pigtail and instead of throwing his neck onto the block again I turned to the lads and said, 'Well, shall we take this *Khodya* with us. Maybe we could train him like a dog.'

I did not foresee that the dark hour would come when I would be alone in the woods with this Chinese man as we ate our first raw raven without salt.

3

Raven is an uncompromising and stubborn enemy.
He is approximately thirty years of age and
tall. He has a black beard, long, black hair and
deep-set eyes, with a heavy, slow expression

on his face. He is a politically literate, former Tsarist officer who subsequently joined the ranks of the Petliurite Army and wears protective armour. He is wrapped in a double swordbelt, which they say he was born with; his mother allegedly told him that his umbilical cord was wrapped around him in this manner. He now has the habit of constantly laying his hands behind his swordbelt because he is very slow, almost clumsy, in his movements, but he is an excellent horseman and a crackshot. He is the son of a forester and writes poetry.

Raven's detachment has approximately 300 infantry and 75 cavalry and heavily armed bandits. It mainly conducts its operations in the areas of Zvenyhorodka, Cherkassy, and Chyhyryn, particularly in the Kholodnyi Yar, Lebedyn and Shpola forests. According to the latest reports, he was either killed or seriously wounded in battle with the 102nd Battalion, which resulted in the loss to the battalion of the assistant commissioner, one scout, 23 fighters, one mounted gun and three horses. The battalion commander was also mortally wounded.

The Authorised Officer, Kakavyshnykov

From the report of the authorised representative of the Kremenchuk district government police in the Chyhyryn district, 4 November 1921

It was only in the morning, as a light snow fell, that Raven recalled his meeting with Yevdosia and realised the meaning of her words.

'Tomorrow you will breakfast on a white tablecloth,' she said, as her eyes, blue like those of a young girl, smiled quietly.

'But what kind of lords will I breakfast with?' Raven asked, raising himself on one elbow in the wooden bed that was a little short for his tall, *Hetman*'s stature.

'Not with lords, but with a lady, pure and white as the snow,' Yevdosia said, smiling inwardly.

Her house was situated in the depths of the forest among

the marsh that stretched along the sides of the slender River Irdyn. If you looked at the place from a distance it was possible to think this deceptively slow flowing, marshy rivulet caused it to slowly sink into itself, but the house was nestled on a hard clay islet and if it had sunk a little it was only due to its antiquity.

'I will soon cleanse you of all sickness and you will leave at dawn,' said Yevdosia. 'How much protection can I give you?'

A broad, oak vat stood in the centre of the room. It was half filled with brown bathing water which was redolent with the fragrance of the spirit of grass. On the floor two cauldrons, filled with boiling water, were steaming.

'You say that I will go directly to this white lady?' Raven asked.

'No doubt. Maybe you would like to shave your beard before then. I will give you a piece of scythe blade, it is sharper than fire.'

'The beauty for whom I would shave my beard has not yet been born.'

Raven took off his linen shirt and when he was wearing only his underwear he looked at Yevdosia and felt embarrassed.

'Take it off. Don't be ashamed,' she said encouragingly, 'I can't see anything but if I desire to do so I can look at that which I need to see.'

'Hey, if you can't see, how did you see my beard?'

'Only the beard? I touched all of you when I patched you up and found two beards.'

'How is it that there were two?' Raven asked, before biting his tongue and looking even more embarrassed.

'You are a little slow,' Yevdosia said, as a smile stretched across her face. She looked with her motionless eyes at where Raven was standing. He removed his undergarments, covered his modesty with one hand, and when he climbed into the vat he felt an unusual delight as the warm water embraced him up to his neck.

'How long have I been here, Yevdosia?'

'A little less than a month. Your horse carried you to me when you were unconscious.'

'Where is he? Where is my Mudei?'

'He is standing in the barn, chewing straw with Halka, the

goat. His ear was cut but he survived. Don't worry about him, think about yourself,' said Yevdosia, massaging his muscles with a sponge improvised from straw. 'Perhaps you need to stop mooching around in the forest and start doing something useful. I tell you, no good will come from your fighting.'

'That's what my sister, Maria, said to me.'

'And what did you do?'

'I drew out my sword because I wanted to hew at her ... but ... she is my sister.'

'Would you be able to strike me down with your sword?'

'Maybe.'

'You have become evil. Stale. They say that you kill your own men who seek amnesty.'

'Those who seek amnesty are not mine. The *Cheka* would destroy them anyway, after breaking their spirit and interrogating them. There is only one path for us, wherever it leads.'

Yevdosia fell silent, but, as she washed his hair with damp ashes, which sufficed for her instead of soap, said, 'If you do strike me down you will not have the gold of the night that I have made for you with my sorcery.'

'What do you mean by the gold of the night?'

'You will see. This very night a maiden, pure and beautiful, will come to you. You will share your renewed strength with her.'

… And she came to him, a maiden, beautiful and pure. She had the fragrance of Pontian azaleas and was breathing incense and the wild orchids that grow on the marshy banks of the Irdyn. A marsh that never freezes and preserves the vegetation that has grown there since before the last ice age; Yevdosia had thrown some of this into the water in which he had bathed. The maiden came and lay next to him. Raven did not see her in the dark; he only heard the rustling of her hair and felt her body that was given over to him as a sacrifice. He embraced her, this maiden born out of the volcano that had risen on the place where Kholodnyi Yar now rests one million years ago. He shared the revived vigour of his body with her, becoming the root of the azaleas and wild orchids, decanting his power into them and drinking strength from her body until they merged into a single, rotating circle.

'Speak just a single word to me,' Raven beseeched her, releasing her lips after a prolonged kiss. But she did not give voice to a single syllable and sighed lightly, like an orchid, instead. When she left him, he thought that she must have been a chimera, a dream-woman sent to him by Yevdosia, or maybe it was Yevdosia who came to him, borrowing her youth from the golden lustre of that night. Only she knew, but there was something evil about that untainted maiden because, long after she had vanished, a fragment of white light, shaped like a sheaf of wheat, trembled on the place where she had been.

4

In the morning Raven saddled Mudei, shortening the right stirrup leather for his wounded leg, which was a little shorter than the left. He spurred on his wise Don horse and as they went on their way through the snow, which, for the first time that year, engulfed the earth in indolent flakes over the Irdyn Marsh, he realised the meaning of Yevdosia's words about breakfasting on a white tablecloth. The winter was a woman all robed in white that stepped forth to meet them.

The impetuous Mudei broke into a canter, hurrying to pound the earth, and just as suddenly broke into a trot. It was such a graceful stride that the rider was able to straighten his spine and square his shoulders. There was still a Carbine hanging from Raven's back and the pocket of his tunic was stretched with a French Corn Cob grenade. He was surprised how, with all this load, Mudei had taken his unconscious rider to Yevdosia, but he knew Mudei did not need to borrow wisdom from others because the horse had saved him more than once.

He thought about how the horse had known to take his wounded body to the sorceress. The last thing Raven remembered from the battle was that he was on the ground, almost crushed and unable to raise himself. Mudei was next to him, neighing quietly and pleading with Raven to clamber into the saddle. During the skirmish they had only lost Raven's Astrakhan hat, which he regretted very much, not so much for the hat itself but for the black ribbon that had been embroidered by a girl's hand with four words, *Return With The Dawn*.

He was now sitting in the saddle with a bare head and the light, large flakes of snow fell onto his long hair, onto the quiet trees, and onto the unfrozen earth. The horse's shoes, which had been fixed in place with good Japanese nails, left tracks in the snow behind them.

Raven did not guide the horse for a long time because here, in the marsh, Mudei knew the path better than him. Indeed, the horse knew the firm ground from feeling it with his hooves and with his spirit. He was convinced that his equine comrade had a soul and therefore he was unable to believe that the *Hetman* of Kholodnyi Yar, Vasyl Chuchupaka, had perished because of a horse. All his comrades were agreed on this point.

Some people had accused Star, the *Hetman's* mare, of following her nature when she had torn away like a wild filly in heat as Vasyl had tried to flee the enemy. Some said that as he was doing so his lustful mare, hearing the neighing of horses from behind, had turned and taken her rider into the enemy cavalry. Straight into the teeth of the devil. Vasyl had fired and hit some of the enemy horsemen. He even had the chance to changed the magazine on his pistol and once he had discharged all his bullets had taken out his Browning and placed it against his temple.

Prokip Ponomarenko, whose nickname was Kvochka, had survived the battle and said that Vasyl's last cry had carried as far as the Motryn Monastery. 'Live-e-e,' Chuchupaka had bellowed with all his heart. It was not known to whom he had addressed this cry during his last moment on earth, his brother, his *Haidamak* band, or Ukraine. However, Raven would have bet that the otaman had not died because of his horse. His mare would not have been able to entrap Vasyl Chuchupaka in this way, even though, earlier on that April day, the mare had behaved capriciously.

Vasyl had gone to the otamans' council at Kreseltsi Farm in the forest. He was accompanied by his brother, Petro Chuchupaka, the Borovytskii otaman, Pavlo Solonko, Hryb, Kvochka and Yurko Zaliznyak. They were all in a happy mood, glad of the first true, warm, spring sunshine and were laughing at the slightest thing. They had laughed at the otaman's mare, who on feeling the spring warmth had lost all shame and reared up wantonly against Solonko's stallion, and the saddle had torn his trousers. In his anger he had told Vasyl to give her to a butcher because she would cause him some misfortune.

'I will be entering Kyiv on Star one day,' the otaman said as he laughed. 'We will patch up your trousers, take them off now.'

'I would rather ride a goat than your mare,' Pavlo Solonko replied, spitting angrily.

When they arrived at the house of Hrechanii, the forester, there was already an aroma of warm borshch, but they did not sit at the table to dine because other men were due to arrive. They played cards while they waited and, not content with having made Solonko tear his trousers, Vasyl Chuchupaka trounced him at the game. Solonko, for his part, looked dejected and ceased chatting with Vasyl.

Later, when a shot rang out from the sentries, the group scampered outside and saw that the forester's lodge was surrounded by enemy cavalry. The men threw themselves into their saddles, but not all managed to mount their steeds, and the terrified horses, which were tethered to the fence, pulled at the ropes for their lives. Vasyl Chuchupaka had to slice the cords with his sword to release Star. He was the first to reach the hill and could have broken away into the forest, but instead he glanced back and saw how the enemy had cruelly twisted and tied his brother and Pavlo Solonko.

Now stand, take off your caps and let us think carefully with our thick heads, Yevdosia would have said. Could someone explain to me this one small thing? How could Star have galloped from that hill to a strange stallion, against the wishes of her rider? Is it not possible that Vasyl Chuchupaka would have been able to leap from her or plant a bullet in the mare's head to avoid her carrying him into the arms of the enemy? Of course he could have done, but he saw how they were binding his brother and Pavlo Solonko. Solonko, who had just been fretting about his ripped trousers and loosing at cards, was about to wave goodbye to his life. Vasyl knew that neither man would be killed immediately. They would first be tortured by the *Chekist* murderers, who would gouge out their eyes and cut out their tongues. He knew this better than anyone, so, without any delay, he charged at the enemy of his own volition. He turned Star around and rode back to disperse the enemy line with his trusty Lewis and liberate Petro and Pavlo. I am even certain that Star bore him carefully, for a good horse always knows its rider and is able to feel the fire and delight of battle, believe me. When he could not disperse the enemy and when he could not fix the second magazine to the overheated Lewis he was closely encircled by the enemy cavalry; it was only then that he raised the Browning to his temple and his cry echoed from ravine to ravine, from Kreseltsi Farm to the Motryn Monastery.

When the short-arsed commander of the squadron, Mytryukha Gerasimov, approached him, he was already dead. Gerasimov, who was greatly regretting his failure to capture the otaman, was surprised to find that rather than a terrible bandit, he was looking at the corpse of a young man of twenty-five, with pale hair and blue eyes that were looking into the April sky, Chuchupaka was smiling as if enraptured by the first spring sunshine.

The commander could not restrain himself from kicking the body. He grabbed a rifle from someone and began to beat the smiling, beautiful face with its butt end. The mob who accompanied him saw his display of anger as a command and flew at the body. They were small men with twisted legs and big, red faces. With a savage cackling and cursing they also began to beat the otaman with their rifle butts. They beat him so fiercely that Fedka Pyeskov, who came upon the scene from Zhabotyn, a nearby village, and who had earlier showed them the road to Kreseltsi, soiled his trousers. He was frightened to death, even though he was unaware that within a week he would be swinging from a branch.

The *katsaps* were unable to hold back and who knows for how long they would have vented their fury on the dead man if a shot had not rung out. Mytryukha Gerasimov had drawn his Mauser and fired into the April sky.

'Stop it, idiots! Who will believe that this is Chuchupaka? It would be better to send this bandit back to his mother and let her look at him now.'

They tied the destroyed body to a horse and carried it as far as Melnyky. The cart that bore the shackled figures of Petro Chuchupaka and Pavlo Solonko followed in their wake. Petro sat as still as a man carved from stone, while Pavlo bit his lower lip as a slender rivulet of blood trickled from his mouth to his chin.

Just before the black path that ran through the forest Raven drew on the left rein, but Mudei stood motionless, as if dumbstruck. He stretched his ears and Raven noted, not for the first time, that the horse's right ear was not dead, useless flesh, it was alive, a little shorter due to the cut, but sensitive and alert. Nearby, a magpie began chirruping. It was apparent that it had seen the bare-headed rider and, perhaps, like Mudei, noticed there was someone else. For why else would his horse pause suddenly when he was being guided?

Raven took the Carbine from his back, pointed it ahead of him, and scanned among the trees until his gaze was hampered by the dense undergrowth of the alder forest. He saw no one and so he put his hand to his mouth and quietly cawed. Within a few seconds a caw was heard among the alders, but it sounded timid and weak, like a magpie copying a raven. He knew this was not a bird and gripped the lock of his Carbine more tightly.

'Raven, are you alive?' A voice called out as a rider emerged from the undergrowth. She was holding a sword and wearing a short coat and a tall, grey cap with a blue ribbon. Her horse was as insubstantial as a shadow. 'You are alive!'

It was Dosia Apilat, a young Cossack maiden from Hrushkivka who fought in the Kholodnyi Yar's *Haidamak* brigade with Vasyl Chuchupaka. Raven had seen her on three previous occasions, but never during battle. The lads said she was like Satan during a skirmish, hewing out with weapons in both hands and sending the heads of her enemy rolling onto the floor like discarded fruit. That, even in the densest of enemy swords, she would leave a trail of blood in her wake. Raven was a little sceptical of these stories because it was hard to believe that her tiny body concealed such demonic strength. Even if it was powerful and tautly sprung, it was still a thing of femininity and not made for violence.

The true beauty of Dosia's physique was her delightful, long hair, which was difficult to conceal, even in a Cossack's hat. She tucked in her silken treasure with the same special care that an Indian Fakir binds his tresses. The coil was of such beauty that Raven's mouth hung open when he saw it at their first meeting in the courtyard of the

Motryn Monastery.

'Shall I bind you with my hair?' her bright mouth had asked playfully, as she half closed her shimmering eyes in which two devils bathed in tar. He thought then that with such hair it would have been possible to fetter more than one world, but instead he said, 'Don't bother, I am already bound.'

The demons in her eyes were quiet with astonishment. She spun away from him on the heels of her new, shiny, high-legged boots, striking sparks with the spurs.

They saw each other on two subsequent occasions and during one she asked, 'Well, Raven, how is it with you? Are you still in harness?'

If she had asked him once more, he would not have thought about the cold but would have pulled her from the horse and there, on the white cloth of the snow, shown her whose sword was the liveliest. Only ... how had Dosia come to be here?

'There was a rumour that you were dead,' she said.

'I thought that at first.'

'You're not an illusion?' She drew closer to Raven, as if wanting to seek refuge in him, and two harmonious angels seemed to smile in her eyes. 'Can I touch you?'

'If you are not afraid.'

Dosia let her fingers wander through his beard and gently touch his lips. 'Where are you returning from?'

'The other world.'

'Well, it looks like you left your cap there, hey?'

'I made a gift of it.' Raven fixed his gaze on the angels in Dosia's eyes and asked in surprise, 'How did you end up here?'

There was nothing surprising in her presence. She always returned to Hrushkivka on this dark path, but on this occasion she was returning to her village for a long time, possibly until spring, because the forest rebels went underground in the winter and usually stayed there until mid March.

It would have been pleasant enough for Dosia in such surroundings, if a little uncomfortable and shameful, not because she was a lady but ... well ... 'Understand me Raven, I am a woman. After all, I have to wash and groom my hair, and certain other things ...

22

It's not as easy for me as it is for your brothers. Although I know it is difficult for everyone to live like a mole.'

'It's merry enough for me underground,' he said.

'Maybe so, if you are in a group,' she agreed, 'but surely you don't love it when a woman starts to smell like a goat?'

'Why not? But only if she smells like a young and clean goat.' Raven's nostrils flared because he sense a certain elusive, familiar aroma that carried gently to him from Dosia. It was a scent almost teasingly pleasant, yet one that he could not recollect.

'Well, couldn't the lads dig a separate underground place for you?'

'Or perhaps a joint one for me and you?' She smiled so flawlessly that it were as if someone had flashed a handful of pearls before him. It was a smile that summoned him for so long tears nearly came to her eyes. She suddenly stifled them and clenched her lips tightly.

'Dosia,' he said, 'forgive me.'

'For what?'

'I don't know.' Raven was so confused that even Mudei began shifting from foot to foot, reflecting his master's uncertainty. 'You are so beautiful.'

'Don't lie. Let us say our farewells in a better manner, hey Raven. Farewell until spring.' She raised her right hand and he did the same, their palms pressed against each other then locked in a friendly shake. This was a manly gesture of valediction, but Dosia had earned a warrior's glory and the right to partake in this Cossack custom. The pressure of her hand was firm. It was a hand powerful enough to bear a sword or pistol, and again Raven smelled that fragrance ... What was it? Something elusive, but familiar, a feminine scent.

'Until spring?' She looked deeply into his eyes.

'Until spring.'

Dosia touched her horse with her spurs and, as lightly as a shadow, began to gallop into the darkness of the forest path. After ten steps she drew on the reins and turned back towards him, 'Hey Raven! Catch!'

He could barely see the grey cap with the blue peak as it flew through the air and he had to stretch to his full height in the saddle to pluck it from above.

'That's to stop you from freezing to death in Kholodnyi Yar.' Her long tresses, liberated from under the cap, unfurled as if alive, fell around her neck, and dangled as far as the croup of her horse. She disappeared into the trees.

Raven was baffled and gripped the hat for a long time before putting it on his head, only to remove it and sink his face into its dark fabric, which was still warm inside. No, this could not be. He inhaled the fragrance of Pontian azaleas, of incense, of a wild orchid …

Chapter 2

1

Veremii's gang has reappeared in Hunskyi Forest
and comprises 80 infantry and 30 cavalry.
They have two Maxim machine guns and five Lewis
guns. The bandits made a sudden daylight
raid on Zlatopol, robbed the local executive
committee telephone exchange and captured the
chief of police, who is believed to work for
them. It is known that when the leader dies
it is the custom among the bandits for one of
them to take his name, but there is reason
to believe that the chieftain, Veremii, was
not killed and continues his bloody business.
Efforts are being made to confirm this.

The Authorised Officer, Diakonov

From the report of the authorised representative of the Kremenchuk
district government police in the Chyhyryn district, 6 December 1921

They travelled on the four-wheeled cart to the house at the edge of the
village near Kryvyi Uzviz where Veremii's mother lived with his young
wife, Hannusia. They asked, calmly at first, where the master of the
house was; had he told them of his location recently, and when did he
last visit? His mother and Hannusia swore with one voice that he had
not visited recently. He had disappeared during the Nativity Feast and
no one had seen him since.

One of the gang that had come to the house, a tall man who
wore a leather coat and had a thin, goose-like neck sprinkled with
blisters, told them that if the whereabouts of a man was unknown it
was essential to inform the authorities. 'Perhaps,' he said, 'Veremii has
forsaken the house, his wife and his mother, so you should also forsake
him. If you don't you will be answerable to the authorities, particularly
if he has joined with a band of brigands or a *Petliurite* gang.'

'How could we forsake him,' his mother asked, 'when we do
not know whether he is alive or if his bones are in the grey soil? It is a

great sin to forswear the dead.'

'Perhaps you have heard something about him perishing?' The long, goose-like neck of the man in the leather coat stretched from its collar with still more tension.

'We have heard nothing from him,' said Hannusia, shrugging her shoulders and briefly laying her hand on her womb, where she felt her baby already stirring.

In truth, she did not know what had happened to Veremii, although there had been rumours that he had perished in Hunskyi Forest and was buried there. People then said that it was a lie, the otaman was not one of those men who could be killed easily. He had only been wounded and had hidden in a secure place. He had deceived the enemy and put someone else's corpse in the coffin, dressed in an embroidered shirt and straw hat, so that they would stop searching for him and leave his wife and mother in peace. Some people believed the words of his adjutant, a man called Chort, who had received an unusual communication from Veremii. Chort had gone to the barn yard where he and the otaman had previously arranged to meet if ever they lost each other in battle, but instead of his chief he had found a piece of paper inscribed with a few words in the otaman's handwriting:

I will be buried in Hunskyi Forest, twenty paces to the east of an old oak tree.

Who could know in advance when he would die and where he would be buried?

Later people whispered that the Cossacks had buried Veremii in the dead of night in an old cemetery in their village. The burial place had been kept secret from even his mother and wife because their tears would have eventually revealed the whereabouts of his grave. Hannusia and his mother suffered in silence for a long time, not wanting to sully their souls with a transgression, but not knowing where he was buried was even harder to bear than the certain knowledge of his death.

One night they both went to the old cemetery, where there

had been no burials for a long time, and found a freshly dug grave among the sunken tombs and tilted, decaying crosses. The sinners began to dig and eventually reached the coffin. They were both in a cold sweat because of their fear as they opened the lid, but the deceased was not there. The coffin only contained Veremii's bloody, embroidered shirt.

'Aha, no one has heard of him,' the man with the goose neck said, as his leather coat squeaked. 'So, you are not going to forsake him? Be careful, if anyone does hear of him you have only yourselves to blame. Then you too will be buried alive.'

The vagabonds went, but Hannusia knew this was only the beginning. The *Chekists* would have devoured them long ago and only restrained themselves in the hope that Veremii would visit home and they would be able to capture him. She knew they would not leave them alone until Veremii was found, either dead or alive. Her heart told her that Veremii was alive, for who would have put his shirt instead of his body in the coffin? This deception was incomprehensible and evil in her eyes. Hannusia understood that someone was playing a cruel game and this someone was probably her husband. If so then he was alive, dead people cannot play tricks like that, even if they could do so when they were alive. If Veremii was alive there was a purpose to all his actions and eventually he would make himself known or send a sign.

As she stood by the side of the house and thought, Hannusia noticed that a raven was perched on the top of the acacia. The bird was a little puffed up and drowsy, but Hannusia saw an inauspicious sign in him and felt an evil foreboding that reached to her throat. She felt sick, but it was not the first time she had felt a heaviness in her loins and it was in vain that she blamed the raven for these sensations. The bird was so old that he was no longer able, and did not wish, to cause evil to anything. He simply observed the bustle of humanity from above because that was the only thing that continued to interest him in his apparently endless life. Futility upon futility, all is futile, thought the raven, looking at the cart that was travelling further from Kryvyi Uzviz. The wheels rolled one way and turned back later.

Whether he had cursed her she did not know, but the next

night someone knocked lightly at her window, like Veremii had once done, and both his mother and her were startled out of their dreams. It was not her husband, instead a stranger was looking through the glass. Without saying a word he handed Hannusia a note printed with the words:

If you want to see me, come to Vysoka Hreblia after sunrise.

2

I was never a marauder but, with a stupid tingling in my breast, I loved to secretly shake down strangers' pockets, cases and portfolios, especially if I thought there was a serious catch in their French dresses, skins and furs. Yes, there were often costly things to be had, but also papers that concerned our brothers, which were more interesting. I am not talking about Bolshevik propaganda leaflets, which were useless to us, but the orders and directives that were a revelation to me. These included the strict warning that I found in the briefcase of the leading Cherkasy Battler Against Banditry, Yasha Halperovych, who had dared to travel as far as Kremenchuk by car.

No one had even dreamed that this insignificant town would become a governing centre. We must bow to Kholodnyi Yar and its foresters because it was thanks to them that it had become imperative to create a new provincial hub near to this 'fiendish nest of bandits'. Many officials were drawn to this little town, such as members of district and party committees, police governors, war committee members, and all the other commies and committees engendered by the commune.

I am not interested in that though, I want to talk about Yasha Halperovych, who had dared to travel on such a dangerous road accompanied only by four police guards, if we include the chauffeur. He had only dared to make this triumphal journey in an open-topped American Pierce-Arrow because the main roads were swarming with regular detachments of soldiers from the Red Army, who arrived daily at Bobrynska Station. They streamed like ants in the direction of Chyhyryn, Kamyanka, Cherkasy, Zvenyhorodka and Znamyanka.

They were not tall men, these crooked-legged, arrogant, impudent Muscovites, accompanied by the taller Latvians, with ice-cold eyes, the wolfish and eternally hungry Chinese, who the villagers named 'the blind ones', and the ugly Chuvashes and Bashkyrs. All of them had one enigmatic and terrifying word on the tip of their tongues - *Khalodnyar*.

They thought and conjectured that Kholodnyi Yar must have an unusual power to have drawn them here from distant fronts, but no one could unravel its enigma. The Muscovites said that Kholodnyi Yar was the ancient fortress of Prince Dolhorukiy and that all the people there were long-armed giants. The Chuvashes and Bashkyrs believed that it was the name of a great war leader, like Genghis Khan, who was so opposed to any kind of restraint that he did not wish to acknowledge communism. The Chinese believed, until they saw the place, that it was surrounded by a great wall where, even though it was cold, there was an abundance of goods and food that its inhabitants did not want to share. The Latvians did not think anything, they were just gunmen waiting for their orders.

So, Yasha Halperovych bravely sped down the road in his open-topped Pierce-Arrow, with a forceful wind behind him, and had not gone far when, shortly after Holovkivka, some riders came to meet him. They were wearing horned caps with big, fabric stars on their brows. Yasha Halperovych ordered his driver to stop to ask the riders if they had heard of any opposition on the road ahead.

'Which military unit?' he enquired in a severe voice, noting how the riders surrounded the car. It was clear to him that they had never seen such a car before.

'Can't you see for yourself,' suggested one of the riders, bending over Halperovych. His face was almost sparkling with laughter.

'I said, which military unit are you from?'

'Special operation forces,' replied the impudent rider, adding, 'or do I look like a werewolf?'

I almost laughed out loud while watching this comedy because the rider was my ensign whose nickname was Vovkulaka, which means werewolf. I was sitting on my horse in the forest by the side of the road so I did not alarm the *Chekists* with my long hair and beard.

'Please hand over your documents.' Vovkulaka pointed the muzzle of his Carbine to the left breast pocket of Halperovych's jacket.

'How dare you?' Yasha Halperovych shrieked, as his face, which had previously turned the colour of a beetroot with anger, suddenly drained to a chalk-white hue. He saw that the riders, who were admiring the car on all sides, had, in a moment, trained their guns on him. A long, cavalry sabre was held to the chauffeur's throat and when the driver's Adam's apple twitched in agitation, a thread of blood trickled down his neck. Yasha understood everything and his intense, confident veneer suddenly withered away.

One of the *Chekists* did command my respect though. He raised his right hand to his breast pocket, as if reaching for his documents, and suddenly produced a gun as if it had just slipped out of his sleeve and into his palm. It was a small, toy-like revolver. He placed the Cobold to his neck and squeezed the trigger. The shot was almost silent; my Mudei breaks wind more loudly, particularly after a bucket of barley. But this shot was quieter than an ant sneezing, thank God, because the sound of a shot ringing out was not part of our plan. The head of the *Chekist* jerked and, startled but already dead, he fell back, tranquilly, onto the seat, calling forth both respect and approval in me.

So they did not besmirch such a wonderful vehicle with any more blood the lads pulled the dazed Halperovych from it, together with the two semi-conscious *Chekists*, and took them into the forest. Vovkulaka sat next to the chauffeur and ordered him to follow them in the car.

From my vantage point in the woods I had worked out who had fallen into our net and when I checked their documents my heart sang.

Halperovych, becoming a little acclimatised to the situation, asked me to step aside for a face to face chat. 'You are the Black Raven?'

'Well, there aren't any white ones,' I replied.

Yasha Halperovych nodded nervously and even tried to smile. Then he mumbled, 'My fellow travellers will have to be liquidated, but as the boss of the district anti-banditry unit I can be of use to you.'

'That's interesting. How?'

'We will think of a story for my people in which I miraculously escape from you. Later, following my release, I will be able to provide you with valuable information.'

'Give me an example,' I said, giving Yasha hope.

'When and where there is going to be an attempt on your life or which of your men are agents.'

The level of his stupidity impressed me, surely fear had clouded his mind because he was spouting nonsense.

'To begin with, liquidate your own men,' I said. 'Cut them up with a sabre.'

'Would it be possible to use a revolver?' he asked, moistening his dry lips.

'No,' I replied, 'we don't need to scare sparrows. You will cut them up with a sabre.'

'You know that I am not a cavalier. I can't wield a sabre.'

'Well, beat them with the blunt side,' I advised him, 'between the ears like rabbits.'

'Then make them stand next to one another with their backs to me.'

We walked over to the trembling *Chekists*, who were surrounded by a ring of my men, and I ordered them to stand in a line, close together.

'Comrade Halperovych has asked that he be allowed to finish you off,' I said, giving him the sabre. 'Turn your backs towards him and get down on your knees.'

'Judas,' the pop-eyed, ginger *Chekist* said between his teeth. He seemed like a convert to Christianity, but he was the first to turn around and kneel. He lowered his head, knowing that it was easier to die in that pose. The others followed suit, kneeling and bowing their heads with the humility that the situation called forth in them.

The pop-eyed *Chekist* was the first to be hewed, but Halperovych did not use the blunt side, instead he used the sharp edge of the blade, and I realised that this was not the first time he had held a sabre. He did not strike at their necks, but at the crown of their heads. The victims fell noiselessly onto their faces. The crimson soup from their broken skulls spattered his boots and breeches. Halperovych looked at me with canine devotion and a feeling of satisfaction that he had fulfilled an obligation. 'Well, how was that?' he asked.

'Judas, he is a Judas.' I sighed as I turned to him and said, 'I don't want to sully my sabre with your blood.' Then I nodded to my men, 'Hang him.'

He fell to his knees, pleading with us to listen to him and stammered something about a secret collaboration. He then scooped up a handful of soil, which was mixed with the blood and brain tissue of his comrades, shoved it into his mouth and began to chew.

'You don't believe me? I swear to you, I am prepared to eat the soil.'

'The soil is not yours to devour,' said Vovkulaka.

Yasha Halperovych continued to devour the soil and smeared it around his face with such gusto that it filled me with disgust. This grotesque phantom flew towards me with his eyes distended and as round as a chicken's eggs. Stammering some inanity, he grabbed me by my boots and began to kiss them with his blood-smeared lips. I waved at the lads, wordlessly signalling that they should not delay in assisting with his demise. My boys set about doing this in a fitting manner by attaching a noose to a suitably strong branch. They bent the young birch lower, stuck Yasha's neck in the noose, so that he was quite near to the top of the branch, and let him go. The springy tree did not straighten, instead it oscillated upwards and swung so vigorously that Yasha touched the floor with his legs and, from time to time, flailed at the ground, only to propel himself upwards and shake on the poor tree. He was a grotesque vision.

It was a shame to leave the Pierce-Arrow but we could not travel on busy roads and the vehicle was unsuitable for wooded terrain. We would have loved to have such a conveyance in the more accommodating conditions of the recent past. The otaman of Chornyi Forest used to yoke horses to a similar one and take girls for a ride. He even printed his own money in the district he controlled, and in Tsvitne, and in other villages, there were credit notes from his temporary government that were emblazoned with the *tryzub* and his signature, *Khmara*.

There were no such extravagances for us, the less flamboyant warriors of these harder times, we simply gathered a chest of Mills grenades from the car, together with a Shtaer pistol, a flask of good wine, a roast piglet and a loaf of bread. We also enriched ourselves with two Pistole Parabellums and three Starr revolvers, to join the German Cobold. We could hardly regard these as a trophies; they endowed us with barely enough fire power to commit suicide. I was more please with the contents of Halperovych's briefcase.

The boys threw the corpses into the car and untied Yasha from the birch so they could leave him with his departed colleagues. They drenched the bodies with petrol and rolled the Pierce to the road because we did not play with fire in the forest. The late Chuchupaka had ordered that anyone who damaged even a single tree would receive twelve strokes of the lash. We waited until we reached the road before Vovkulaka lit his cigarette and threw the match onto the petrol-drenched corpses of Yasha and his men.

'Burn to dry ash, carrion.'

We were some distance away when the petrol tank exploded and a column of black smoke wormed its way into the air above the burning car.

I found, among the other documents in Halperovych's case, a yellowed copy of a text that I liked very much; the contents of which had been known to me for a long time. Entitled 'Instructions for Communist Agitators Working in Ukraine', it read as if it had been written by Shymon Petliura rather than Leon Trotsky. It was a mother load of truths such as this one:

You need to remember that the Ukrainian peasant hates the commune, emergency units, food requisition groups and the soviet commissars from the depths of his soul. They have awakened in them the spirit of freedom, which has slept for centuries, inherited from the Zaporizhia Cossacks and Haidamak rebels. The fierce spirit that seethes like the Dnipro over the rapids and imbues the Ukrainians with miraculous courage. The same spirit of freedom has flowed through them, as a superhuman strength, for hundreds of years, when they fought their oppressors, the Polish, the Russians, the Tatars and the Turks.

This was an innocuous warning compared to the other directive I found in his papers. It did not reveal anything to me that I did not already know, but it did offer a few necessary words of inspiration to those Cossacks, exhausted with years of struggle and living in the forest, who might have begun to think about an amnesty. I had learned how to recognise them from a distance; the guy who frets, who paces like a dove, who does not eat or drink, and finds the world a harsh place. I do not waste my strength keeping anyone like that and release the exhausted and those who have lost faith to the mercy of fate. It was only forbidden to leave us of your own will if you did not warn us and you took weapons. If anyone asked those who had left, they told them that they had fought with a scythe. If anyone gave us away they knew that we would find them, even in the next world.

I continued to read the paper that bore the seal 'Top Secret':

In regard to those bandits of a nationalist tinge who have turned themselves in to be granted amnesty; do not shoot or take them under guard, on the contrary, vet them carefully and, if possible, enlist them in the soviet forces; in particular as militia, as agents, as confidential employees, or as informants on nationalist operations. They can reveal the details of the gangs that have remained in the forests and the underground. Regarding the amnestied leaders - they are to be sent immediately to Kharkiv, to provide further information and be liquidated after further interrogation.

When we returned to Lebedyn Forest I gathered the Cossacks and read the document to them, then passed it around the ranks of men so that everyone could see it with their own eyes. This ensured they all knew that only an imbecile would believe the Bolsheviks' offer of amnesty, but after the exhaustion of endless struggle without a glimmer of light it did its work.

The paper was returned to me, I screwed it up and ground it into the dirt with my boot. Later I said, 'I will repeat this to you once more. No one is forbidden from presenting themselves for amnesty. That is everyone's private, personal decision. I swear to you that I will remain in the forest for as long as there is a single Cossack with me. Let that be as God wills it.'

3

'Return With The Dawn'. A persistent melancholy had taken over Raven's spirit after he had met her. She who had shamed him, a brave officer with three Georgian Crosses on his breast, and awakened his sleeping sense of honour.

Raven, who was then known as Staff Captain Chornousov because the army required him to use the Russian version of his name, Chornovus, had already graduated from the Omsk School of Standard Bearers. He had been involved in the wars 'For Tsar and Fatherland' and the 'Spirit of Kerensky', and had requested to enlist with the 'Death or Glory' Battalion. He had been close to death more than once and was awarded his first medal because, while under fire from the Germans, he had freed three dead junkers from the barbed wire that ensnared them.

On the eve of the February Revolution fate rewarded him by his assignment to the second division, which was based in Uman, fifty *versts* away from his childhood home. When he arrived at the division's staff office he entered the chancellery and the duty officer formulated his documents. It was here that the event, which revived his spirit so fatigued and battered by war, was waiting for him.

There were two young ladies sitting in the room, who whispered to each other between spurts of laughter. One of them looked at the unfamiliar staff captain in such a way that he began to stammer when he spoke. Her grey, smiling eyes, her short, blond hair and ... well you do not need to ask any more! The neatly arranged blouse with a black cravat, the diaphanous mesh of her skirt and below ... restrain yourselves gentlemen officers. The rose-coloured, delicate stockings were tightly guarded by the stiletto heels of her shoes. Even the most fashionable ladies in Moscow would not have been able to compete with her beauty.

Staff Captain Chornousov replied in Russian to the questions of the lieutenant, stuttering as if confused, 'In Moscow I was assigned to the 8th Grenadier Brigade ...'

'One moment.' The wonderful apparition in rose-coloured stockings interrupted him. 'Why are you talking like a Muscovite? You're Ukrainian aren't you?'

The cavalier with the Georgian Crosses clammed up. Was she ridiculing him? Did they make these kind of jokes here? In his confusion he directed his gaze towards the staff officer on whose face a conspiratorial smile was forming.

'Well, if truth be told,' said the lieutenant in Ukrainian, lowering his hands onto the desk, 'our time has come. The army is being Ukrainianised. We have to seize the moment. Where do you want to serve, in Uman or maybe in Cherkasy?'

'In Cherkasy,' he replied after a moment's thought. He would be nearer home there.

'Well, that's good. There is a position in the 290th Brigade.'

'Thank you. On an occasion like this allow me to request that you partake in a glass of Champagne gentle ladies and lieutenant.'

He turned to the ladies but he could only see one of them and there was now a curious, rather than an amused, look in her grey eyes. Perhaps this was because he had requested to serve in Cherkasy rather than a prestigious town like Uman where beautiful, noble ladies were found; even in the headquarters of the military.

'Let me make your acquaintance,' he said, both excited and pleased that his native language was returning from his remote past.

'Afanasii Karpovych Kalyuzhnyi.' The lieutenant practically jumped from behind the chancellery table. He straightened his body and stretched out his hand as he clicked his heels. 'I have been wondering why my nose has been itching from this morning onwards. Yes, permit me to be presented to you and to present my staff. These are our ... err ... colleagues on the battalion staff.'

Manyunia, the lady with bright crimson lipstick and a fake beauty spot, made a gracious curtsey, lifting her slender wrist almost to his lips. He took her hand, but before he kissed it he asked, 'Manyunia, in other words Maria?'

'No,' she smiled, 'simply Manyunia.'

Oh, this was yet a trifling bit of banter, otherwise he would not have joked with her. He noticed the lady with the aristocratic eyes, in whose presence Manyunia disappeared, along with her beauty spot.

'Tina.' She offered him a slender, cold hand, which he clasped in his before asking stupidly, 'Tina, that's Valentina?'

'Tina, that's me,' she said.

In the evening they dined at Restaurant Sofia, not far from Sofiyivka Park, the famous park in Uman where Prince Potocki had once poured mountains of sugar so he could take his capricious Sofia for a ride on a sledge in the summer. Staff Captain Chornovus, for he proudly recommended using his Ukrainian name, reserved Abrau 'champagne' for the ladies, and for the gentlemen officers, a carafe of rye vodka. He asked the waiters to bring some roast meat and all kinds of delicacies.

'Yes, these ladies confused you with their names,' said Lieutenant Kalyuzhnyi, who had begun to break into Russian after his second glass of vodka. 'Take me for instance, according to my birth certificate, I'm Afanasii but my mother and other relatives always called me Fania. Just Fania.

'But we will call you Panas,' said Manyunia, looking at him severely. 'Maybe then you will remember about the Ukrainianisation of the army.'

'Yes, excuse me,' said the lieutenant miserably, 'call me Panas if you like it more and while we are seated for dinner, Fania.'

'No,' said Manyunia, taking issue with him. 'Fania, that's a name for an old lady, but you are an officer and will therefore be Panas. Let us drink to your christening and to your new name.' The dark beauty spot trembled on her cheek.

They drank rather too much and Lieutenant Kalyuzhnyi became so befogged that he looked more like Fania than Panas. The alcohol made him gregarious and, throwing himself onto his chair, he said with feeling, 'Oh, this is great my friends.' It was wonderful, if a little melancholy and strained, for him to meet a beautiful woman.

A melody was being played vigorously by a violinist in a black coat with white epaulettes and long folds like a bird's tail. His violin resonated with anguish and hope. An unearthly instrument through which he painted a world beyond the clouds with mountains of sugar and rivers of honey.

'Where is your family from?' The grey eyes looked openly at Chornovus from beneath a blond fringe.

'I was born in Lebedynskyi Forest beneath a walnut tree.'

This was true. His father was a forester and they had inhabited the forest. The old midwife, Perchytsia, the mother of blind Yevdosia, had brought him into the world.

'We are compatriots,' said Tina. 'I am from Shpola and perhaps even gathered walnuts from the tree under which you were born.'

'And I am from Kyiv,' Fania-Panas slipped in inevitably, like Wednesday slips into the middle of the week. 'From Shulyavki and I don't talk Russian, I speak the Shulyavskyi dialect. Do you understand me? We are all compatriots from the Kyiv district. So, my compatriot, let us raise a glass. We will drink to your service in Cherkasy.'

'Fania is the polyglot among us,' said Manyunia, praising him ironically. 'He is able to converse in Little Russian and the *Khokhol* languages, the Shulyavskyi dialect, and even Ukrainian when he is sober. Isn't that right, Fanichka?'

'That's exactly right, sweetheart,' agreed the lieutenant with delight, still speaking in Russian. 'Not only do I converse, I also sing. It's a shame there isn't a guitar.'

'Well, why isn't there one? Hey, musicians!' Manyunia approached the orchestral stage where the musicians and a harmonium stood. She whispered something to them and returned with a guitar. 'Look at me Panas and remember that I am responsible if you break any strings.'

Lieutenant Kalyuzhnyi glided his fingers over the strings, tuned them a little, and sang in Russian in a hoarse, sweet voice:

Oh, why did you kiss me,
Concealing this vain fire in my breast?
Beloved you called me
And vowed, I am yours, I am yours!
And now you sing on a restaurant stage,
For gems and for money,
You sell yourself to old men,
For the sake of sinful, vicious pleasure ...

'Bravo,' shouted Manyunia, as the beauty spot on her cheek fluttered its dark feather wickedly. 'Fania, you do sing the notes perfectly.'

'Only in female company,' responded the lieutenant.

Chornovus looked into the grey eyes, which did not sparkle with laughter; instead they stared somewhere far, far away.

'And you are not enamoured by our female company?' Manyunia asked him.

'Why do you ask that question?'

'Well, you don't want to serve in Uman.'

'I, by the way, can still change that.' Lieutenant Kalyuzhnyi looked ardently at Manyunia. 'We may be able to find a place for the staff captain in Uman.'

'It isn't worth doing that,' said Chornovus. 'It is what is destined to be.'

The evening had not finished in the sweet paradise that the strings of the violin had portrayed. He had anticipated that he would walk Tina home and, possibly, she would arrange an assignation with him in Sofiyivka Park, which was known as a place for secret trysts and first, tentative kisses among its dark grottos.

When they left the restaurant and tarried beneath a pallid gas light she gave him her slender, cold hand. 'Good luck, Captain. We will see each other again if God wills it so.'

***

The next day he was in Cherkasy where the thunder of revolution resounded; a thunder that woke Ukraine, which had seemed as if it would never wake again. The former officer of the attack battalion, Chornovus, had never dreamed he would become the commander of the Cherkasy 25th Cossack Squadron and, stopping an echelon from his former colleagues at Bobrynska Station, would make those officers with whom he had fought shoulder to shoulder, 'For the Tsar and the Fatherland', stand against a wall at gunpoint.

Unfortunately the Bolshevik propaganda was doing its work. Exhausted by war and browbeaten with promises of a plot of land, many soldiers had fled the front and returned home. Some threw themselves into 'stealing that which was already stolen', and flocks of deserters, our own men and strangers, which had been transformed into bandits and cut-throats, swarmed everywhere. Eventually, only twenty-seven Cossacks remained in Chornovus's squadron, cut off from the scattered army of the Ukrainian National Republic.

On one occasion, at Tsvitkove Station, a crowd of drunken Muscovite deserters, who had 'fallen off' the train in search of easy meat, dropped on them and with a savage cursing and barking began to tear the blue and yellow insignia from the Cossacks' uniforms. One of the savages, who was wearing an unbuttoned military shirt, perhaps their chief, to the accompaniment of the raucous laughter of his men, approached Captain Chornovus, touched the left sleeve of his uniform where a gold *tryzub* glimmered and asked, 'What's this?'

Chornovus wasted no time. He grabbed his sabre and swung it at the chief. Immediately, the stranger's forearm was severed and fell to the ground. The mob fell quiet at once. The previously mad and emboldened Muscovites gazed at the severed forearm, which still looked alive because the broken fingers continued to twitch.

'Everyone to the wagons,' commanded Chornovus. 'The station is surrounded. If you disobey you will be shot where you stand.'

The mob dispersed like smoke and fell back into the wagons. Their chief, who groaned stupidly with pain and fear, looked at the platform and set about gathering his useless forearm.

Mixing with louse infested *katsaps* brought misfortune on Chornovus and he contracted typhus. It was a protracted illness and days and nights passed in one long, delirious nightmare. When he saw her grey eyes he thought he was hallucinating, but no, there is no evil and misfortune without some corresponding virtue and good fortune. The cards had fallen well for Chornovus and he realised he was again in Uman, in the district clinic where there were already many Ukrainian soldiers. It seemed like a miracle that Tina was one of the nursing sisters who cared for them. But there was nothing supernatural in her presence, she had asked to help when she heard that the sick patients lacked care because so few people wanted to be around those contaminated with typhus. It was miraculous that she should meet the staff captain as he was lying emaciated and sickly.

'It is you,' his lips, rough, desiccated and burning with fever, moved.

'Look at us,' she said, smiling.

'Where am I?'

'In Lebedynskyi Forest beneath a walnut tree. This is the second time you have been born into this world, only now I am your midwife and will bear you into the world like a stork.' Tina had not simply brought him into being again, but torn him from the embrace of the bony bridesmaid of death who had frequently walked by his side.

The Muscovites had already reached Uman and were certain to attack the clinic. The first sign of their presence was the sound of stamping and shouting in the corridors. Later, shots rang out from the neighbouring wards. One, two, three. Tina ran to Chornovus, she was holding a roll of gauze and suddenly began to wrap his arms up to his elbows. 'You must tell them your arms are covered with ulcers.'

She had barely finished when two men with high cheekbones entered the hospital; they were carrying revolvers. The young Cossack, Petrus, who was in the neighbouring bed, whispered quietly to himself in prayer. He was unable to bear the situation and he covered his head with a bed sheet as if to protect himself. They went to him first.

'We don't want your head, you need to show us your palms.' They tore the sheet from him and grasped his hands. 'Aha, everything is clear. This is what you deserve,' the Russian said.

The pistol barked, Petrus's head jerked back onto the pillow and, with a hole drilled into his forehead, he fell into an eternal silence without understanding what they had seen on his hands. When the palms are chapped, coarse and calloused, it is clear they belong to a proletarian, whereas smooth, well-groomed hands are the sign of a bourgeoisie.

'What are these mittens for?' The murderer stared at Chornovus's bandaged hands.

'Plague,' replied Tina, in Russian. 'A fearsome rash covers his hands.'

'Is it anthrax?'

'Even worse. You should have put on a surgical mask to

protect you against infection before coming in here.'

'Screw your mother! Hey Yemelia, let's get out of here.'

The Muscovites swirled out of the building in a second, giving them some breathing space, but the corpse of Petrus was an arm's length away, and in the next room wounded men moaned with pain. As he looked at his hands, bandaged and useless, Chornovus was seized with shame. He was gripped by the cold feeling that he had exchanged his life for Petrus's death. He did not thank Tina for her quick thinking, which had been his salvation, but lay silently all day. In the evening he told her he had recovered.

'Will you help me get to Mokra Kalyhirka?' he asked her.

'Where?' Tina asked in surprise. 'You still need time to recover.'

'I am as strong as an ox.' He jumped angrily from the bed and drew himself up to his full height, almost touching the ceiling with his head. He stooped slightly, however, as he looked at the metal bar of the bedstead, which he gripped tightly in anger, and realised it had almost bent under the pressure of his hands.

'Well, what comes next?' Tina looked up at him and he continued to answer his own question. 'What comes next is that I am beginning a new war and no one will keep me here, not even you my little sparrow. Do you hear me? I am beginning a new war!'

On this occasion he did not say goodbye to her in a caring manner, instead he left quickly on foot, avoiding villages and crowded places as he made his way home. The noise of chaotic shooting, anguished cries, the voices of women and the lament of dogs echoed from the villages. At night the sky was tinged by the fires from the burning villages, which, at a distance revealed the places controlled by the Muscovite punishment squadrons.

In Zaiacha Balka, not far from Mokra Kalyhirka, the Cossacks of Simon Hryzlo met him and took him to their otaman so his identity could be established. The otaman was well built and a little squat, but the most surprising thing was his attire. He wore a blue *zhupan*, or Cossack tunic, embroidered with yellow lace, wide Cossack trousers and a Cossack cap from under which protruded his blond forelock. The sharp points of his moustache were twisted upwards and gave him a merry, youthful visage.

'Where are you from?' Hryzlo asked, measuring Chornovus with his eyes. 'Don't try to twist your story because my sabre can sniff out a lie.'

Chornovus had no reason to demean his spirit by lying and Hryzlo believed him. He could not disbelieve his compatriot when he could remember Chornovus's father and knew nearly all the foresters in the district.

'Join with my Cossacks,' Hryzlo proposed.

'I'm not opposed to that idea, however, please let me first contact my family and then we will decide how to continue.'

Hryzlo bowed his head, 'What kind of Cossack worries about his home? There is no time for discussion now, yesterday the Bolsheviks shot forty of our people in Mokra Kalyhirka and hung six Jews who had made our clothes and footwear. It is necessary to pay them back.'

'It is necessary,' said Chornovus, looking at the otaman's tunic with more curiosity. It did not seem plausible that Kalyhirka Jews could have worked on such a tunic.

'We are obliged to show the *katsaps* and our villagers who is the master here,' added Hryzlo. 'There is a considerable unit in the town, which, if we strike suddenly, could be defeated. Today I have three hundred cavalry at my disposal.'

'At night. We need to strike at night, Otaman.' A Cossack, with a broad mouth from which huge, canine-like teeth protruded, butted into the conversation.

'He loves to battle at night,' said Hryzlo as he smiled indulgently. 'That's why we have christened him Vovkulaka. Don't sweat, we will attack at night.'

Hryzlo sent reconnaissance parties to Mokra Kalyhirka. It was Sunday, market day, and Chornovus, dressed as a beggar, also went to the town with which he was a little familiar. In his childhood he had gone there with his father to get oil. He had been to the mill and the bazaar, where his father had bought him poppy cakes, gold honey cakes, biscuits, and long mint sweets wrapped in gold foil, which made his tongue stick to the roof of his mouth; two for one *kopeck*.

The most fascinating part of these trips was their visits to Ben at the inn. The inn had a smoky, boozy atmosphere that made his head swim and his eyes water. Ben would come out to meet them wearing a long lapserdak. He was a little hunched man with a red beard; a kind and honourable Jew who was a great friend of Chornovus the forester.

'Hey Yakov,' he said, standing a rotund, green flask in front of his father, 'that's a good boy you have there; the kind that will grow well, even in the forest.'

Then Ben, dexterous as a juggler, produced a dish full of buns from under his hump and gave them to the boy. They were so hard that the boy could not bite into them and had to suck them like sweets. In Ben's other hand, a string of dried carp appeared for Chornovus senior. They both drank glass after glass together, while Ben's busy wife, Benykha, marvellously muffled in a black scarf so that her pink ears stuck out, trotted to the table. She placed chicken giblets, fried in goose fat, on the table; a special meal for their dear guests. Benykha did not forget about the boy and poured him tasty cherry cider that made his nose and mouth tingle. Later Ben brought a small barrel, adorned with a painting of a playful maiden sucking on a long onion stalk. He opened it and, narrowing his eyes, inhaled the fragrance deeply through his nose. This was the high-quality tobacco that his father loved to smoke.

'From the Kohan factory,' said the innkeeper exultantly, although he did not smoke himself.

When Chornovus senior prepared to leave Ben often asked him to stay a while longer because Reful would be coming from Zvenyhorodka, with twelve other musicians, and there was going to be such a *Mayufes* that everyone would be covered in the dust scuffed up from the dance floor.

'I see how the fiery *Mayufes* is already here,' said Chornovus senior, pointing at the floorboards that were covered in sunflower seed husks and had deep indentations from the dancing heels of their previous visits.

Would the unfortunate Ben have been able to see the *Mayufes* that the Red cut-throats had prepared for him?

Propping himself up on the rugged crutch, which was part of his beggar's attire, Chornovus limped through the empty streets to the area where the bazaar was usually held; although he had realised a while ago that it was not being held that day and people were sitting at home. He looked furtively back and forth until he saw the inn, which had been destroyed and looked as if it had been shattered by a thunderbolt. There were black holes left by the broken windows and doors, the walls were stripped and broken glass fragments lay all around, together with scattered feathers from the ripped bedding. He soon saw Ben hanging with other corpses on the gallows in the bazaar. He recognised the old innkeeper by his red beard and his hump, which had not been straightened, even by the heavy burden of death.

Chornovus limped in the direction of the mill and encountered a group of men with horses by the mill dam.

'Where are you going old man?' asked a big-eared Muscovite, who was so drunk that he was gripping the reins of his horse with one hand, while the other was grasping the mane.

'I'm going to richer villages,' he replied in Russian, so he did not arouse suspicion.

'And you can't tell us where the good-time girls are to be found here?'

'I'm not a local man.'

'Would you like to drink?'

'No, I'd rather have something to eat.'

'Here you are,' the big-eared rider took out a sweet from his pocket, 'that's your dinner.' He gave vent to such a deranged belly laugh that he almost fell out of the saddle. Chornovus noticed that it was a mint sweet from Ben's inn.

Later that evening Chornovus saw Hryzlo's generous side when he gave him a Mannlicher pistol, a Colt, two grenades and a Don horse, through whose skin he could see the horse's sinewy muscles.

'I don't know what he is called,' said Hryzlo, almost excusing himself, 'I *borrowed* him from one of those horny-hatted invaders and forgot to ask his name. Oh well, let him be called Mudei. The name doesn't matter, the main thing is that he bears you well.'

'Who is this Mudei you have named him after?' Chornovus asked, excitedly taking the bridle of the horse.

Hryzlo shrugged his shoulders, 'Who knows, he's Mudei and that's all there is to it. Look here, take the riding crop.'

The horse was powerful, agile and long legged, and the otaman knew that he was ideal for a man of Chornovus's rangy build. Chornovus could not stop his hands trembling as he searched through his pockets. Eventually, he found and unwrapped the sweet before presenting it to Mudei in his palm. The touch of the horse's lips sent shivers down his arm to his breast, and his heart sang. He buried his face in the horse's mane and so did not see how Hryzlo's eyes lit up when he saw their rapport.

The operation began at four in the morning when the drunken Muscovites were snoring heavily in their stupors. They began quietly, liquidating outposts and guards by the school and the sugar refinery before striking with all their power. The Muscovites jumped through doors and windows, fleeing unthinkingly in all directions, still in their underwear and dazed with sleep. Whoever saw them would have noticed the gleam of their underpants, which provided an excellent target, as they jumped across fences, stiles, orchards and gardens. How smoothly the Maxim and Lewis guns fired, how merrily the Corn Cob grenades burst, how the warbling of the bullets sang as sweetly as a nightingale. The terrified horses neighed and many of them, already riderless, stampeded through the streets, colliding with their own men and strangers. Screams, groans, curses and filthy Muscovite abuse flowed into a communal lament that smelled tantalisingly of the enemy's blood.

At dawn, when things became visible, they could see what a blow they had delivered to the Muscovites. The town was strewn with corpses, prone and twisted in the dust and weeds, under fences and in gardens and meadows. One unfortunate wretch hung from a fence and was in such a state that it was painful to look at him; another had lost his head somewhere (clearly due to a sabre) and lolled in a pool of his viscous blood, as dark as tar, and another was on a heap of manure with his intestines dangling from his body. Chornovus liked the way Mudei, his new comrade, stepped calmly over the enemy corpses, only snorting with anxiety when he saw a dead horse. He passed by the equine corpses, turned his head away and then continued with a firm, springy step.

They worked like a threshing machine, clearing the town of

the enemy, but this meant little to Hryzlo, 'Lads, we haven't finished the job yet,' he cried, wiping the blood from his battered brow, 'many are hiding in the undergrowth. Let's capture every last one of them. Do you hear me? All of them!'

The Cossacks did not need pressing. Burning with the heat of battle and awakened with the scent of enemy blood, they poured over fields and Steppe valleys and through belts of woodland, looking into every nook and cranny. Hryzlo seemed to be everywhere and the air over the fields was filled with his delighted cries, 'Every last one of them. Do you hear me, lads?'

The right-hand side of the otaman's moustache was crimson with the blood that flowed from his brow, but the spirit of youth still played across his features. Chornovus's mouth hung open when Hryzlo drew a shrivelled Muscovite from the bush and hewed him across the body with such force that his head flew off, accompanied by his arms and shoulders.

'Well done,' Chornovus cried to him, turning his horse into a ravine covered with a shallow growth of blackberry bushes. He had already descended to the bottom when Mudei paused and flapped his ears warily. Chornovus pulled sharply on the reins and smacked his lips, but the horse only looked towards a narrow gully, yearning to go there. Chornovus saw two people hiding by the opening into the gully. The big-eared Muscovite, who had thrust a sweet at him for amusement the previous day, and next to him a shivering, half-naked girl. Her pock-marked face was fleshy and full lipped and the heat of her body was almost palpable. You big-eared rascal, Chornovus thought. The earth was falling from under the Muscovite and he had taken a bitch with him. He wondered what had gone through the mind of the girl.

'What were you thinking when you fled with this big-eared fellow?' he asked, pointing his Colt at them.

'He forced me to go with him.'

'That's not true, she said she loved me and wanted to come,' the big-eared man spoke rapidly in Russian through his chattering teeth. 'Don't shoot, we are going to marry and go to Penza.'

'You are going,' said Chornovus, 'but further than Penza. Thank you for the sweet darling.' The gun jerked in his hand, but the bullet still flew directly to that place in the forehead where Raven thought the devil branded the Muscovites with his star. 'And you, whore, come here and pull up your petticoat,' ordered Chornovus, 'I'll thrash your arse so that you remember how to behave.'

The tubby girl crawled out of the gully, came to him and obediently pulled up her skirt, beneath which her naked body glowed. He flourished the whip and Mudei suddenly jumped, thinking that the rider was raising the whip to him. Chornovus steadied the horse and looked at the girl on whom he must purge the whip, before a resounding, enigmatic peal of laughter poured from his mouth as he released her. Her toes flashed through branches on the other side of the ravine. She stooped almost to the earth as she cleaved through the blackberry bushes like a wild boar; the brambles whipped the air above her.

The news of the glory of the rebels' victory in Mokra Kalyhirka flew rapidly to the surrounding villages. Villagers from every corner of the Zvenyhorodka district flocked to Hryzlo to bring weapons, victuals and horses. The otaman wanted to make Chornovus his chief of staff, but then things changed. It is better for partisans to operate in small units. Easier for them to manoeuvre, hide, throw off pursuit and obtain provisions, but the more people that arrived, the harder it became to do all this, so Hryzlo decided to divide his squadron into two units; one of which, led by Chornovus, would establish itself in Lebedyn. If it became necessary they would join and advance on Kyiv.

When Chornovus formed his unit the nocturnal desperado, Vovkulaka, asked to join with him. Hryzlo was not offended, 'Let it be so,' he agreed. 'It's hard for me to part with such a courageous man but he will be a good foundation as you begin to build your unit.' The otaman became a little pensive and then an enigmatic smile played on his coiled moustache. 'Do you know why Vovkulaka came to the forest?' he asked.

'Well ... err,' said Chornovus, nonplussed.

'Reading Shevchenko. I often ask the newcomers why they have come to me and in the past heard from one that the Muscovites had raised his house to the ground, from another that they had plundered his possessions, and from another that they had raped his girl. We never do anything until some misfortune strikes us. This one said to me, "I read *Kobzar*". Have you ever heard anything like it? That a man should read Shevchenko and become a bandit. Now there is power. I tell you this so that you know you will sometimes need to read aloud to the Cossacks. It works better than any military drill.'

Hryzlo gave Chornovus one more valuable tip; if he followed the path of rebellion, he would need an alias or the Muscovites would avenge themselves on his family. Hryzlo had not adopted a false name because here, in the Zvenyhorodka district, everyone knew him as the leader of the free Cossacks. Even the mongrel dogs on the street could tell you who Hryzlo was and against whom he fought.

It was October 1920, in an autumn as warm and clement as summer, and cobwebs glittered in the air. Chornovus stared into the endless, unreachable blue of the sky and saw, on top of an elm, a huge predatory bird, so black that an azure lustre rippled down its feathers.

' Raven,' he said. 'If you hear anything about the Raven, Father, it will be me.'

Chapter 3

1

In the evening, after the sun had set, Hannusia wrapped her scarf around the lower part of her face, so she would be harder to recognise, and threw on an old cloak and some well-worn boots. She now looked like a typical grandmother as she stuffed a basket with a few victuals; a slice of *salo*, bread, some fried potatoes, and even a pot of borshch. At the last moment she remembered to grab a candle and some matches before hurrying off to her assignation at Vysoka Hreblia. The fact someone had summoned her there awakened the hope in her heart that she would see Veremii because this was the place where they used to meet.

The boundary of Vysoka Hreblia was situated three *versts* from the village where the windmill owned by Veremii's Uncle Trokhym, who had also joined the rebels in the forest, stood on a hill top. There was something alluring about the isolated structure and it had a quality that had drawn Hannusia there as a young girl. She had listened to the wind's mesmerising murmur in the blades, watched the huge stone rotate, and listened to the whispering, fragrant torrents of flour. The huge wheels of the mechanism rotated their wooden teeth, gripped the power of the parts, and made everything vibrate with a remorseless motion. She could never explain to herself how the secret voice of the breeze, as it played in the blades of the windmill, transmitted such power to the rotating wheels. Once, Holy Mother of God, she had caught sight of someone who gripped the blades and was spun in a circle, balancing on the tremendous height. He had spun with the blades until they went out of sight in the whisper of the air. Uncle Trokhym had become scared, grabbed the rope, which acted as a brake, and pulled. The mill juddered to a halt.

Hannusia recognised the hare-brained idiot who had battled with the power of the air. It was Yarko, the strongest lad in the village, who lived near Kryvyi Uzviz. She regularly heard the stories people told about him. How he bent horseshoes with his bare hands and pounded pegs into the ground with his fist; how he could stand on his head for ages, bend himself into a wheel and roll as far as he wished and, on one occasion, how he had crawled beneath a bull before gripping its front legs and lifting it off the ground. The bull was so frightened that afterwards people said it even avoided cows. However, that was all just empty chatter compared to the unforeseen transformation of this strong, but empty-headed, boy. The boy became the wind and dissolved into it. He became the hurricane and the chaos, and for a good reason was named Veremii, Yarko to his close friends.

He stooped, slipped off the blades of the mill and onto the ground. He stared foggily at Hannusia and suddenly asked, 'Would you like some warm flour?'

'I would.' She ate the warm flour from his hand, like a foal.

'If you like, we could go to the banks of the stream and drink spring water?'

'I would.' She drank the waters from his cupped hands.

'Would you like to spin through the air with me?'

'I would.'

That evening she had become one with the wind. A sweet terror tingled through her body as if she were swinging over unfathomed depths with a soul as insignificant as a poppy seed.

Yarko promised that when they were married and could afford it he would buy the mill from Uncle Trokhym. However, soon afterwards, he was conscripted into the army and did not return for six long years. After his service on the German front he fought in the cavalry-artillery division of the Ukrainian National Army under the command of Colonel Almazov. When, in November 1920, the *Petliurites* retreated beyond the Zbruch, Yarko decided to return home rather than going with ignominy into a foreign land. He returned intact with a not particularly large wound in a place that would only be seen by Hannusia.

'Good Lord,' she said, slapping her hands on her thighs when she saw, 'what if ..?'

'I had shot myself with a cannon,' said Yarko.

They married and started building a house. They had got as far as the roof when Admiral Denikin's White Guards came and burned it to the ground. Yarko was so angry that he took to the forest. 'I'm not far away, don't cry,' he said to Hannusia. 'We will see each other again.'

Before long everyone had heard about Otaman Veremii. He moved rapidly, like the wind itself. One day he was in Hunskyi Forest and the day after at Fundukliivka Station examining the documents of the Bolshevik commissars; then near Zlatopol, crushing a military unit, which was responsible for deducting victual tax, on its way to strip off the skin from every peasant's back. He rarely visited home, but once he visited her with a stranger, a man who resembled an owl.

'Don't be afraid Hannusia, this is Chort,' said Veremii. 'He's a bonny lad, only a little sombre.' Chort tried to smile, but only succeeded in looking more terrifying.

Having taken his supper, Chort went outside to guard the otaman, who stayed overnight with Hannusia. That was four months ago. They had made love passionately, and shortly afterwards she realised she was pregnant and accepted this as being due to the grace of God. It was terrible that so much time had passed and Veremii knew nothing of her pregnancy.

Near Vysoka Hreblia, Hannusia ascended to the windmill, which glimmered forlornly on the hillside. She felt an ever increasing anxiety with each step. What would she find there? Would the men in skin coats, who had visited the house, be waiting for her? Had they decided to mock her and to test if she knew of the death of her husband? If she had known of his death, would she still have come?

The windmill stood cold and rigid. It had been a long time since flour had been ground there. The lock had been torn from the door and the blades were a blank cross, tilted to one side. Hannusia stood next to the wooden steps that led to the door; they groaned so dramatically that an icy sensation ran through her body. If Veremii was here he would have seen her from far away, even if he had been peering through a cranny in the wooden walls of the mill. He would have called out to her rather than waited until her heart was pounding with fear. Maybe he thought she was just an old *babusya* who had wandered there. He is not here, thought Hannusia. 'But who told you that he would be waiting for you rather than you waiting for him, sweetheart? Enter, look in the windmill, don't be afraid. If a stranger was watching you, you would not be able to escape anyway,' she talked quietly to herself to stop her fear.

She ascended the creaking steps to the door and wrenched it open. The prolonged groan of the hinges pierced her spirit and a draft of cold air, which stank of mice and bird's droppings, blew over her from the darkness. It looked as if no one was there, neither her own people nor, thank God, strangers. If Veremii had left some sign in the mill, how would she see it? Hannusia lowered her basket fearfully, groped inside it for a candle, took out the matches and had just kindled a flame when something pattered and tapped in the loft. She tensed and stood without breathing until she realised the light had disturbed something that slept in the darkness; a bat or an owl perhaps. Overcoming her fear, she looked up and saw a pair of turtle doves with half-closed eyes, which were sitting meekly.

Hannusia extinguished the candle, picked up her basket and went outside where it was less frightening than in the darkness of the mill. All she could do was wait. Perhaps Veremii would still come, or maybe on the way here something had made him wary or frightened him away. Hannusia hurt her eyes peering into the darkness, she listened to the night until she understood that he was not coming. After lingering for a while she wrapped a crust of bread and some cold potatoes in a white cloth, looked in the mill again, and left the bundle of food on the doorstep. She closed the heavy door, which screamed on its hinges, and departed.

She did not notice the bird perched on one of the blades of the mill. It was a raven. He stared after Hannusia and, although he was blind in one eye, he could see everything that piqued his curiosity. Suddenly, he twitched his neck and his wings in a strange manner as if he were shrugging his shoulders.

2

Nothing strangles the spirit of a man more than the absence of hope. That feeling first peered into our eyes in the autumn of 1920 after the truce between the Polish and the Russians. The Ukrainian army had yearned for it and hoped it would drive the Muscovites from our country; they had crossed the Zbruch, but the Polish, our former allies, had thrown them into camps and made them hang up their weapons. We did not know this at the time; we were not told the full truth. They fed us legends, and later even some of our own people began to dream up tales. It made life easier. I only believed in one legend, the one that we leave to our successors. The longer we resisted the occupier, the greater the belief in the future success of our struggle would be. If we laid down our arms once, then we would be lost eternally.

If we had known the truth about our army and government, and the confusion of our leaders, then maybe things would have worked out differently. We might have joined and marched on Kyiv. We lacked a *Hetman*, the Cossack chief, who would have stifled anarchy and prevented arbitrary action; perhaps someone like Vasyl Chuchupaka, who would not have endured chatterboxes with tongues that were longer than their sabres.

I will never forget how, once, at a noisy council at the monastery, he struck the stock of his Browning against the table and such a silence fell on the room that you could have heard the woodworm wriggling in the old beams. He loved order, obedience and good tobacco. When the abbess's room, where Vasyl based his staff headquarters, was awash with the smoke from expensive cigarettes, and a crimson box of Camel with a picture of a one-humped dromedary lay on the table before him, everyone knew that the otaman of Kholodnyi Yar had recently crushed a squadron of Denikin's White Guards.

Perhaps we would have advanced on Kyiv were it not for the blind faith in the return of our army. In September 1920 three brigades of Kholodnyi Yar Cossacks, which were at this point under the command of Derkach, gathered in Moshny. They were joined by the Steppe Division of Kost Blakytnyi and the brigades of Lyutyi, Holyi and Mamai. We had thirty-thousand troops gathered in a single spot. How many more of us must there have been throughout Ukraine?

So, we gathered. But what came out of this brief unity? We seized Cherkasy, which was full of Red Army troops with armoured train carriages, Hotchkiss machine guns and long-range artillery. There were even armoured boats firing from the Dnipro, but we still completely annihilated them. It was a victory, even though more than one of our horses lost its tail. We acquired vital supplies, such as salt, soap, matches and tobacco; then we returned to our separate nooks and crannies, rather than staying together and marching further.

Oh, what is there to say now? It's too late to talk about and reflect on lost opportunities. Trokhym Holyi spoke the truth when we paused for a smoke before setting out on the road home, 'My soldiers are like a grey, country horse. If he wants to be led, you can lead him, if he doesn't want to be led, you can't shift him. These boys just grab some goodies and then hurry home to make a gift of them to their wives. You can see that they are more accustomed to waging war within sight of their own thatched roofs and if …' Holyi stared dreamily into the sky and saw two intact wires attached to telegraph pole. He drew his Mauser and fired twice and the wires hung uselessly. The otaman loved to show off and Trokhym, who was as relaxed as if the shot had been effortless, blew into the barrel of his pistol and cried to his Cossacks, 'Forward lads!'

So, Holyi's boys came to Horodyshche, which was strewn with Muscovite nests, singing their favourite ditty:

Oh the lads go forth, oh
From Ukraine.
Releasing their horses,
Into the valley …

They sang as if Ukraine was only Horodyshche and the surrounding villages and they were returning home from the wild field. They had flown, like hawks fly, to Cherkasy to make merry and would now let their horses graze. That was a time when everything seemed possible, a time that gave way to the hour when expectation became nightmare, despair and utter fatigue.

Then emissaries came from abroad and swore that, beyond the banks of the Zbruch, a new Ukrainian army was being formed and that a call for an insurrection across the whole of Ukraine would soon resound over the broad pastures of our country. That is how they kept up our spirits, but sadly the hope of victory faded away when our army did not arrive. I think that if it had not been for the inescapable futility of our situation fewer of the rebels would have been broken in spirit, handed themselves over for amnesty and betrayed the forest. Their nerves could endure no more and, indeed, my own spirit was not cast in iron. I could no longer suffer those emissaries from abroad, who came to encourage us, and I wanted to shoot them as agents provocateurs.

In the spring of 1921, another wise guy came to us and drew a document from the lining of his jacket. It gave his credentials, printed on a piece of linen, as a representative of the revolutionary staff of Yurko Tiutiunnyk, in Poland.

'The balloon will go up this summer,' he said. 'The Ukrainians interned in Polish camps have armed themselves and are eagerly awaiting the command to rise up. In August, planes will twist in the skies above Ukraine, making loops, and that will be the signal for a mass uprising.' He raised his finger into the air and quietly, as if whispering God knows what secret, said, 'Be vigilant and remember the planes will loop the loop.'

'Listen to me,' I butted in, 'we don't need your fairy tales and uplifting words. We have waged war for three years without your help and, thank God, have survived to battle on. If you are so well educated, sod off and teach someone else or I'll have you arrested.'

'How can you act like this Mr Otaman?' he said challengingly. 'You are sowing pessimism among our troops.'

'Because,' I replied, 'I will never lie to them.'

'I have already met Otaman Zahorodnii, Holyk-Zaliznyak and Hupalo and they all listened to me with understanding.' The emissary continued to spout nonsense.

'You will lead us to a bad end with your lies, but I will not lead my men to disaster by lying to them. In the name of God, go from here or I'll show you exactly what a loop is with a rope dangling from that stout oak over there.'

I drove him from our camp like a diseased sheep. Later, I regretted my action somewhat and wondered if I had been wrong to vent my frustration on him. It is hard not to credit promises when they offer everything that you have yearned for and expected for so long.

Raven's mob have impudently assaulted the Lebedyn sugar factory. During a cultural propaganda action in the factory's club, the bandits attacked and organised a nationalist orgy. The mob massacred the workers who had organised the action, spilling their blood and leaving many men killed and wounded.

The bandits have also taken 100 litres of alcoholic spirit from the factory and 250,000,000 roubles from the cashier's office. It is difficult to capture them because the active core of the Kholodnyi Yar gang is divided into small groups. This is a deliberate strategy to allow them to evade attack by fleeing in different directions. They have successfully evaded a co-ordinated assault from several directions by sections of the 74th Brigade of the 467th and 68th units. The bandits are again regrouping, using densely wooded terrain and extremely rugged countryside around the Kholodnyi Yar forests. Each group comprises 40 to 80 people that, when required, band together to form larger units.

Government Informer Antropov

From information collated by the Kremenchuk secret police department, 28 August 1921

As he breathed he caught the fragrance of Pontian azaleas, wild orchids and incense. Something very strange had happened to him that night and he could not understand what. Yevdosia? Dosia? Two sorceresses were united in a single entity. It was only now, in the aftermath of his encounter with Dosia, that Raven considered this. Two she devils, one old and one young. The old woman had borrowed the gilded, nocturnal beauty of youth from Dosia, or perhaps the young maiden had beseeched Yevdosia for her magic that night, or how could she have come to him in the darkness of the Irdyn Marsh?

Raven had been taken there by Mudei after he had been

physically crushed in the battle for Starosillia. He had been saved by the horse, but he had seen how his comrades each fell in turn; mowed down by bullets ... Makovii, Yizhak, Dobryvechir. Vovkulaka had been catapulted from his horse after a grenade exploded near him. He had got to his feet quickly, run to his slain horse and fallen to his knees. It was clear that he had been confused because he cried and stammered something incomprehensible as he tried to wrench the saddle from his dead steed.

'Leave it.' Raven shouted at him. 'Come with me.'

Vovkulaka did not hear, either because the explosion had deafened him or because he had become crazy, and he persisted in wrenching at the saddle. Raven turned Mudei around and was hit for the first time in the leg. A searing heat engulfed him. His body was wrenched from within and lights, like the flames of one thousand candles, danced across his eyes. He fell over the neck of his horse and grasped his mane. He could see nothing, but through the darkness he heard the trampling of horses' hooves near him or perhaps above his body. When he next opened his eyes he was in a forest, lying on the ground, and was badly injured. A dense pain, which engulfed every fibre of his being, told him he was still alive, but he could not get to his feet. Mudei was lying next to him.

Everything had started so happily. A small squadron, comprising only thirty-five Cossacks, had almost paraded into Kapitanivka. They were adorned in the uniforms of the communist army and Vovkulaka had led them, brandishing a red flag. You really had to be there and see his self-satisfied face and wolfish teeth to appreciate the effect. That red flag really suited him. Vovkulaka did not release it from his grasp, even when he was using his sabre to carve up the Muscovites who were guarding the grain store. They had greeted what they thought were Red Cavalry men, even if they were a little confused.

'What's the special occasion? Why has no one told us?' they asked.

'The first of May,' replied Vovkulaka.

'What the devil do you mean May? It's autumn.'

'Well, all right, we are celebrating the October Revolution,' said Vovkulaka.

58

'What a strange man, that is still a long way off.'

'A long way off for you,' said Vovkulaka, 'our October has lasted four years and there's still no end in sight.'

He wound himself up so much by talking about the soviet festivals that he could restrain himself no longer and, without waiting for the otaman's signal, drew his sword and slashed the guard with it. The other lads joined in and six of the guards were dead before they could cry out a warning. One sentry did manage to slither between the false Reds and took to his heels.

Vovkulaka again amazed Raven. With barely a second's thought, he lifted the pole to which the flag was attached and threw it like a spear into the back of the fugitive. The flagpole flew, twisted like a serpent with the crimson tail of the communist banner, and pierced the wretch in the nape of the neck. He fell face down, buried his nose in the dust and tried to fool them into thinking he was dead, but Vovkulaka resurrected him with a prod from his sword and made him get to his feet. He ordered him to shake out the banner, which was now covered in dust, and only then sent the wretch into that world where there are no holidays or flags, but only peace and eternal benediction.

'Did you serve for a time in the Don regiments?' Raven asked Vovkulaka.

'Why?'

'The Don troops use their spears brilliantly in battle.'

'Against whom?' asked Vovkulaka.

'Against us, obviously.'

'No,' he replied. 'I didn't serve in their ranks. It's not difficult to use a pike in battle though. A savage can always use a spear.' Vovkulaka showed his fangs in what Raven later realised was a smile.

In Kapitanivka they burned down the district executive committee's building, after they had confiscated the 'citizenry taxes' from its head; one hundred and ten roubles, one hundred and eighteen silver roubles and five gold roubles. On the way back they also burned down the *Komnezam*, the so called 'committee of poor peasants', and dispatched its head to the heavenly chancellery. There was, however, too much tell-tale smoke from this conflagration, so they headed away from the scene of the crime almost as far as Starosillia.

They were still in a festive mood and there were a few comic moments on their journey home. After ten *versts*, our 'Red Army soldiers' stumbled across a cavalry division of the militia that were searching the roads, together with a flying squadron of the anti-banditry unit. They thought it was better to roll up the flag and hide it before they began to head towards Zaiacha Balka Farm. Unfortunately, the enemy realised that there was something strange happening and opened fire before giving chase. Raven's men wriggled away from the frying pan only to fall into the flames, as two cavalry squadrons fell on them from the other direction. The flying squadron was coming at them from behind so they had no choice but to head towards the farm that was concealed in a gully.

Things started to get really interesting. The brave communist cavalry, seeing the 'phoney Red Army soldiers' fleeing towards the farm, followed by a rabble crying, 'Hurrah', began to fire at the real Red Army who were pursuing the fakes and they were stopped by the fire from the flying squadron. The communist cavalry dismounted and knelt on the ground before opening fire on their comrades. The comrades fought each other for about five minutes before they realised that something was not right. Once they understood what was happening their rage was tripled and they threw themselves into the pursuit of the Cossacks, who at this point were standing, staring at the Reds. Instead of fleeing to the forest as fast as they could, our boys feasted their eyes on this comedy. They planned to wait until the Red Army had finished slaughtering each other and then fall on the survivors. Vovkulaka was even preparing to unfurl the banner to make things even merrier because an attack under the communist banner, accompanied by cries of 'Glory' might frighten even Lucifer himself.

The Muscovites quickly regrouped, split in half and began to encircle the gully in a pincer movement. While Raven's men made it to higher ground, the Red Army soldiers advanced for about two hundred paces. It is not the partisan's job to engage in battle at the enemy's behest in an open field without cover. The Cossacks attacked unpredictably and suddenly; their trump card was surprise. They scattered over the field to make it more difficult for the enemy to fire accurately at them, and then flew towards the forest, which was just a dark strip in the distance. But their horses were fatigued, their legs faltered and they snorted with exertion. The dark strip of woodland grew clearer as it became closer, but the enemy was breathing down their necks. They fired their revolvers rapidly while retreating, without thinking about the accuracy of their shots, but Raven still managed to remove the two liveliest cavalry men from their horses.

They heard the sound of a machine gun and Makovii threw his arms into the air and fell to the ground. Tussocks of grass and divots of soil flew into the air on either side of Raven. The bullets no longer whistled; they hummed and flew with an awful 'dum dum' sound, the sound which means if they pierce their victim there is no chance of survival.

Yizhak's horse fell. He lay by its side for cover, placed his Carbine on the corpse and fired a couple of times before falling silent. Then Dobryvechir fell from the saddle, his leg caught in the stirrup and the terrified horse dragged him along the ground. Vovkulaka, who had reached the woods, turned his horse around and rode to join his colleagues. 'Fly, I will cover you,' he cried to Raven, standing tall, almost upright, in the stirrups and hurling grenade after grenade at the enemy.

Neighing dementedly, the horses bounding at the front of the retreat reared and threw their riders, while the horses behind spun around and kneaded the earth with their hooves as they rotated aimlessly. One of the enemy cavalrymen replied to Vovkulaka's bombardment with a grenade, which hummed through the air and exploded under the Ukrainian soldier's horse. The horse fell, kicked its legs and began to beat its head on the ground. This confused him and instead of running to the forest, Vovkulaka started to wrench the saddle. It is hard to say now whether they cut him down where he stood or captured him alive to kill him with their brutal interrogation methods later. Raven could see his almost deformed, yet kindred, face, which resembled some kind of terrifying mask with its broad, bare eyelids and the bald eyebrows that Vovkulaka had scorched when sitting near the fires they lit at night.

If there was no work during the hours of darkness, Vovkulaka loved to sit by the flames and blow into them, until he singed his brows and lashes, and inhale and gulp the smoke deeply until he had to cough. Perhaps it was the fire that had tanned his face, leaving it immobile, ruddy coloured and as shiny as a copper kettle.

Vovkulaka would not have swapped his characteristics for anyone else's face, however beautiful. It terrified some people more than the grenades in his hands, particularly when he first appeared on the scene.

There was one occasion when they had attacked the Lebedyn sugar factory, where a vaudeville that the devil would have envied had been arranged. The news had spread by word of mouth that the following Saturday, at the factory club, most, if not all, of the local bigwigs, including the top brass from Shpola, Zvenyhorodka and Kalnyboloto, would be gathered to celebrate the harvest. They had fulfilled the monthly plan of bread requisitions by deducting the August victuals tax. There would be a concert and the local amateur theatre group had prepared a staging of *Shelmenko-Denshchyk*, after which there would be a raucous banquet.

Raven felt a sickly, excited feeling in his stomach, where the cold flames of expectation danced like they danced whenever he had a presentiment of interesting work. He loved rich banquets and always prepared conscientiously for them. On this occasion he had instructed his men not to make any forays in the next few days and to stay in Lebedynskyi Forest until Saturday. Only the nocturnal spies were allowed to gather intelligence in the hours of darkness. Vovkulaka was one of their number and acquired, not only some significant news but a book by Kvitka-Osnovianenko. He would sit for long periods by the campfire at night, reading its pages as avidly as if it were a detailed plan of their assault on the sugar refinery. After reading the book something odd happened to Vovkulaka's speech, it was as if his tongue had turned on itself.

On Saturday morning he said to Raven, 'I, Your Excellency, am *Shelmenko-Denshchyk* and will say that I do not love untruths to permit a sin. I live truthfully on this earth and will pour that truth in their eyes, like sand.'

'Well, pour away then,' Raven said as he smiled.

'Also,' Vovkulaka continued in his newly acquired, grand, archaic style, 'thus, truly I say unto you, Your Excellency, that it may have been thus - It was not necessary for us to burn the foreign vehicle, it could have been better used as a conveyance on which we could have rolled to the club as if we were a military emergency unit with one of the checking operations. If it is not beyond possibility to resurrect the burned remnants we could travel there on a Phaeton. Someone could ride atop the aforementioned Phaeton and a few souls could ride with the coachman, bold as brass, into the festivities.'

Indeed, they had a vehicle that was truly suited to the task. A carriage with an open top that had been used by the late chief of police, Kosovorotkin. They had assigned the chief of police, politely, to the other world when they met him in Balakleya, but had retained his carriage. The covering of the carriage was extremely suitable for the current climate because, since the early morning of that day, the clouds had gathered, heavy and dark with rain. Raven's men even began to worry on behalf of the local dignitaries, hoping that the weather did not ruin the festivities. The rain would make their operation easier. The one hundred troops guarding the factory, a mixture of Muscovites and Chinese, might have drunk enough by the afternoon; after all, there were enough spirits to drown in at the sugar refinery, and to ensure that it would be easier to talk to them. Raven decided that twenty Cossacks would be a sufficient number to conduct that conversation, to draw less attention to the gateway from Lebedyn, and that they should be organised in small groups to attack from a number of directions.

By the afternoon when the ceremonies were due to commence, the heavens, already swollen with rain clouds, thundered as if heralding the coming storm. In defiance of the weather, carriages, vehicles, two-wheeled carts, and riders passed through the factory gate in the yard near the factory club and were greeted by the brassy roar of the orchestra. The guests were well nourished from their lunch. The proper festivities were due to commence in the evening and, red-faced and fattened up, they were languishing in their parade-ground jackets, creaking boots and sword belts. They saluted each other idly and merrily shook hands, shouted out of necessity, due to the clamour and their inebriation, and walked slowly onto the club's verandah. There were two soldiers by the door who were wearing white naval-style coats and examining people's papers. They stood to attention and saluted some of the bigwigs.

The hall was capacious and it appeared that the guests just

collapsed into whatever seats they chose, but everyone knew their place. Some sat close to the stage and others, who had not achieved a high enough rank even to sit in the centre rows, sat at the back or stood. So, without jostling or making excessive noise, the guests filled the hall to the brim, took off their caps and wiped their sweaty faces with them. It had become very hot before the thunderstorm and they were exhaling such vapours that the bugs flying overhead suffocated in the humid air and fell onto the floor, stunned.

The chief of the Zvenyhorodka division of the *Cheka*, Sienia Katsman, an attractive, albeit skinny, youth, with a squint in one eye, was seated in the front row. He was dripping with sweat like the other guests, but he did not take off his cap and coat because he had heard rumours that the amateur theatrical troupe had such a beauty in their midst that he would have to restrain himself in order not to surrender to her charms.

The barrel-shaped chief of the district provision committee, Syromyatnikov, was seated to the right of Sienia Katsman. His mouth exhaled a foul stench, similar to that emanating from a beet-pulp pit. On Katsman's left, the chief of the revolutionary committee, Dolbonosov, twisted his duck-like head in every direction. His chisel-like nose was as flat and long as a duck's beak. Officer Krasutskyi was sitting near to Dolbonosov. He crossed his legs loftily and sat with them thus, waggling the tip of one of his new shiny jackboots ostentatiously. He was a generous spirited but cunning *Khokhol* and well groomed, but with the fragrance of eau de Cologne similar to all secret drunkards.

Sienia Katsman hated all three men from the depths of his soul because they worked blindly, without grasping the requirements of what might be called 'the political moment'. These boors had planned this 'breadless parody' of a harvest festival when they had requisitioned everything. They had even taken the seed grain from the crops the *Khokhol* peasants had cultivated this year. Well, the time would come when Sienia would remind them how they had troubled the malleable peasants and brought dishonour on the Soviet Union. At the moment he was sitting between them because he was obliged to do so in anticipation of the performance, which maybe would warrant this idiotic gathering. Of course, it was not the performance itself that stimulated his interest so much as the beauty who would soon take to the stage.

Sienia held the ragamuffins that were sitting at the back in even lower regard; all the poor peasantry committee, party members and activists, who had previously been nobodies. Idle bastards who wanted to become all important only so that others would think the sun shone out of their arses. Well, the time would come when he would line up these roaring boys against the wall. They would be dealt with first, followed by Krasutskyi, then Dolbonosov and Syromyatnikov. No, on the contrary, he would deal with Syromyatnikov first and the foul stench he exuded, which made Sienia turn away, gagging with nausea.

The Red Army soldiers were seated in the back rows, behind the activists and the bare-footed rabble. They were holding their pistols between their knees and had been driven here to stand guard over this worthy gathering. They were indifferent to the place, the festival and the performance, but were forced to sit on guard so that even an insect could not fly into the hall without authorisation. Sienia would not shoot these guys, but they would shoot others in fulfilling his orders. The rest of them would go to the wall.

Suddenly a cry rang from outside, 'Fire!'

Sienia jolted because there really was a commotion coming from the yard. The danger that seemed to have been predicted by the storm clouds had started.

'Is there a lightening conductor on this club?' Syromyatnikov asked anxiously.

'Don't be scared,' replied Sienia, looking at him askance, 'you are safe here. Nature greets us with the sky's fireworks. It's time to start.'

The rebels' carriage arrived at the club to the accompaniment of a streak of lightning and heavy drops of rain exploding on the ground. Four late, but extremely severe looking 'chiefs' jumped out from under the shelter of the carriage. One of them sported a beard and the guards in the white naval coats asked to see his documents.

'Get out of here,' Beardy thundered at him, 'can't you see that we are from the government police? I will personally check who is gathered here.'

'But ...'

'Get out of here, both of you,' said Beardy in such a tone that the white naval jackets went rapidly, but somnolently, to their barracks, which were also under the control of the omnipresent emergency military unit.

The one hundred troops guarding the factory were cleverly and precisely disarmed and surrounded effectively, as if for a special circumstances investigation. Three 'police chiefs' quietly entered the hall and another ran from the corridor and towards the entrance to the stage. They would have attracted more attention if the spectators had not begun clapping loudly to demand the start of the performance.

Then everything began. The curtains swung open and a soldier appeared on the stage in an antiquated, Tsarist uniform, a white sailor's cap, white trousers and a blue tunic with a red cape.

'*Shelmenko-Denshchyk*,' murmured the spectators in Russian. 'Look! What an ugly rascal.'

The only frightening thing about the soldier, however, was his grotesque face. Laughter rippled through the hall when he began to speak. 'I am *Shelmenko-Denshchyk* and will say that I do not love untruths to permit a sin. I live truthfully on this earth and will pour that truth in their eyes, like sand. Therefore, I will speak unto in the manner of which the book is written. I request everyone to hand over their documents.' Shelmenko bared his teeth and rolled his eyes over the crowd in such a comical manner that everyone laughed. Even the soldiery seated in the back rows chuckled as if on command; although they had not yet worked out the intentions of this comedian in a costume.

'I am not, however, the Denshchyk that you imagine me to be,' the deranged Shelmenko continued. 'I am the Denshchyk of the chief of the district secret police and, being with him in this hall, order you again to produce your documents.' He ceased speaking and, while the bewildered crowd looked at one another, produced a grenade from his pocket, and while brandishing it, barked in Russian, 'Throw all your weapons to the ground. The club is surrounded and will be attacked with grenades if anyone disobeys.'

After a command like that everyone seated in the hall cast their eyes towards the door, but no one moved from their place. The three unknown arrivals were standing by the exits, each with a grenade in one hand and a revolver in the other.

'Follow the orders,' barked Beardy, gripping the safety catch of his Browning.

The hall fell silent for a moment until Dolbonosov cried, 'Stop these stupid jokes.' He jumped to his feet and stretched his right hand to his holster, but a shot rang out. The crazed Shelmenko had planted a bullet between his eyes. Sienia's dream was beginning to come true. Dolbonosov jolted, became floppy, and slumped heavily into his seat. His dead, duck-like head fell onto his breast and his long, beakish nose pointed towards the floor where everyone had been told to lay their arms.

'Maybe someone still doesn't understand,' said the crazed Shelmenko in Russian, waving the barrel of his Colt to and fro in the direction of the front row.

Sienia Katsman, Syromyatnikov, Krasutskyi and the rest of the vainglorious brethren rapidly undid their gun-belts and threw their weapons to the floor, ostentatiously pushing them further away with their feet. The Red Army soldiers in the back rows also threw their rifles to the floor, unwittingly hampering each other because the barrels clanged together. Their long, three-line rifles could not be laid in place neatly and easily by their legs. To hurry them along, one of the rebels, who now controlled the situation and was keeping a vigilant watch on the hall, Petrus Makovii, went to the back rows and waved a grenade. Within seconds the Muscovites had lowered their heads and covered their ears with their hands, as if they were more afraid of the deafening explosion than the shrapnel.

'As you were,' shouted the irrepressible Shelmenko. 'All of you, uncover your ears, our amateur choir will now perform the glorious national anthem *Ukraine has not yet perished.*'

He waved his hand, in which a Colt glittered gallantly, and between ten and twenty choristers poured onto the stage. It was apparent they had intended to perform a comedy because they were dressed in their costumes; one in an old-fashioned coat with a knotted cravat, one wearing an officer's uniform in the style of the old regime, and one in a tattered, peasant's jacket. The wondrous, aristocratic beauty was resplendent in her laces and flounces. The choristers arranged themselves in three rows, assuming a very serious stance due to the pomp and circumstance of the occasion. Shelmenko, however, took his desire to celebrate nationhood still further, 'I order everyone in the hall to rise and, together with the choir, truthfully and honestly, sing our national anthem. Anyone who is unable to, either because they don't know the words or due to some stupid principle, will be shot immediately.'

After such a blunt warning everyone rose to their feet, apart from Dolbonosov, who had already been taken care of by the devils who were his kith and kin. Observing the compliant behaviour of their leaders, the Muscovites in the back rows also rose to their feet. Even with their ears uncovered, they were only dimly aware of what the madman with the wolfish grin wanted from them, but when people talk about shooting you even a deaf person can figure out what the words and gestures mean.

The madcap Shelmenko turned to face the choir, waved his Colt like a conductor waves his baton, and they thrashed out the anthem:

Ukraine has not yet perished,
Neither her glory nor her freedom,
Fate shall smile upon us once more,
Brother Ukrainians!

The walls resonated with the powerful song, the ceiling lifted high into the air, and the thunder outside joined the choir. Every person in the hall sang or moved their lips and stretched their mouths, vigorously miming if they did not know the words. They were afraid to look like they were not singing, even when a pause was appropriate. It was amazing to see how amicably they sang. How clumsily they chewed on the incomprehensible words, lustily gulping the air as their Adam's apples bobbed rapidly. How they roared, stammered, hummed and bellowed, but all the noise flowed into a single melody, weirdly united in a victorious, 'Hosanna'. Perhaps this harmony would not have emerged had the choir not sung so melodiously over the raucous crowd as they smoothed out their dissonances, and had there not been someone behind the scenes singing the anthem truthfully with

68

their body and soul.

Sienia Katsman could only remember the first line of the song, but knew that it was a fearsome subversion of authority which must be cauterised with a heated iron. However, he did give the appearance of singing. It was fortunate that he was standing in the front row near the choir, so no one could see what was really happening. He opened his mouth, swung his head, raised his slender eyebrows, rolled his eyes, one of which squinted, and saw that Syromyatnikov also moved his lips and Krasutskyi gave vent to every word with deep emotion.

The bare-headed Muscovites made an amazing and moving vision. There was something so absurd in this crowd of mingled humanity, some small, some with jug-like ears, some naive, but all so inspired by fear that the spectacle of their singing might have moved someone to tears. All their mouths distended into an 'O' shaped hole and there was an unnatural feeling, as if the weak, anguished, beetle-like droning emerged from a hollow or a rat hole.

Raven almost felt compassion for them. An inane desire to prolong their lives for a minute or two awoke in him. Let them dance more, these gophers who would soon perish like dew evaporates with the dawn, but he knew it was risky to put off things any longer. They could not hold so many people in thrall for long, even under the hypnotising power of the anthem and a few grenades. So when Sutiaha and Kozub came into the club he waved his Browning vigorously as if to tell them it was time.

Vovkulaka remained on the stage and continued to conduct the choir and the people in the hall. Meanwhile, Makovii and Koliada began to lead the honoured guests into the yard. They took three or four at a time and led them to a store with a cement floor. The rain hammered down and the thunder pealed and, together with the thick walls of the store, ensured that any shots fired in there would be either inaudible or sound like someone, some distance away, had cracked a whip.

'Are you going to sh ... shoot us?' Sienia asked in his trembling Russian voice, while he was led out in the first trio, with Krasutskyi and Syromyatnikov. 'That would be a big mistake. You could barter us.'

'You barterer.' Koliada shoved him between the shoulder

blades with the muzzle of his revolver. 'Are you Dzerzhinsky or what? They wouldn't give a dog's tail for you.'

Sienia suddenly broke away and ran while crouching over. He bounded like a hare. Koliada did not hurry, he slowly swung his Shtaer in his outstretched hand, narrowed his eyes and, after allowing Sienia to bound for five more steps, squeezed the trigger. The thunder pealed, simultaneously drowning the sound of the shot, and Sienia fell, face first, into a puddle.

'Did the thunder kill him or what?' Koliada shrugged his shoulders. 'My grandmother told me that you shouldn't run in a thunderstorm because it will kill you. Hide quickly in the store lads.'

'If you knew where you would end up,' muttered Krasutskyi. He had already made peace with his death. 'You go to see a performance and come out ...'

'A performance, heh,' said Koliada sympathetically. 'Let's go, you are getting drenched.'

***

The same fate that had sent Raven to his previous meeting with the woman who had woken his slumbering honour played a part in this scene. She was different now, utterly different, only recognisable from the ironic smile, which he remembered from their first meeting, now trembling in her grey eyes. Tina saw how, before he came to her behind the scenery, he took out a handkerchief and dabbed his hands and forehead. She checked that no one would see them together.

'Am I dreaming?' he asked.

She was fiendishly beautiful, this director of the amateur theatre troupe and chorister. Her lace blouse and puffed sleeves made her seem ethereal; her high collar opened onto her untouchable, white neck and her aristocratic eyes looked at him from under the nimbus of her short fringe in such a way that he spoke deferentially to her.

'Where have you come from, Milady, Tina?'

'From somewhere. Every time closer to you, Sir Otaman. I am teaching in Lebedyn now.'

'In Lebedyn? Teaching?'

'You probably don't know about my education.'

'What do I really know about you?' he asked. 'Although you once taught me a lesson that will serve me well for all of my life. Tina, Tina, why does God bring us together only for a moment?'

'Well, at least he does bring us together.'

'If I had known you would be here ... Forgive me. There may be some unpleasantness for you now.'

'That's OK. You made us do this, didn't you?' Again, that ironic smile.

'Say that you sang under the fear of death. Perhaps it would have been so if ...'

'But what?'

'If you had refused ... Farewell Tina, it's time I left.'

'Farewell, Otaman,' she said coldly but informally. 'We will see each other again if God wills it.'

That was exactly how she had parted from him by the restaurant in Uman. He turned and as he was leaving swiftly he heard her call, 'Otaman, don't put on airs and graces.'

He turned and raised his eyebrows in surprise.

'I see that you comprehend nothing,' she said.

'But what?'

'I planned all this,' she said. 'This performance and this gathering.'

'Oh! How?' Raven did not understand her at first and when he realised the importance of her words, he stood as rigidly as a fence post. 'That's why everything went so smoothly.'

He vented his fury on the remainder of the Red garrison that defended the refinery. Then the lads, having dealt with the Muscovites, led the Chinese to the block. They held them at gunpoint in the pouring rain and they stood silently as the rain drenched them and their teeth chattered. One of them was distinguishable by his scalp, the front of which was shaven, and a pigtail that had been painstakingly plaited dangled down the nape of his neck. He proudly held up his head, which was as round as a melon, and he did not stagger or slip on the treacherous mud as we led him to his death.

Chapter 4

1

The next day was a Sunday. Hannusia could barely wait for the evening when, again, she would make the journey to Vysoka Hreblia. Perhaps something had startled Veremii yesterday and he would come today. It was easier for her to walk across the field to their trysting place than to sit at home in ignorance of his fate.

Stealthily, looking in all directions, she ascended the hill to the windmill, sensing her gorge rise as a sickly, isolated feeling travelled through her breast to her throat. She paused, breathing heavily, and caught herself feeling afraid of looking through the doorway of the mill to see whether the bundle of food she had left was still there. She opened the door, waved her hand over the threshold, and lit a candle. There was no trace of the bundle she had left. If some beast had eaten it or a bird had pecked it there would be some remnants. It must surely be a human who had taken the food. Hannusia overcame the blind wave of delight that had initially engulfed her when she thought that Veremii must have visited here in the night, instead she allowed her common sense to whisper a painful, 'No,' to her heart.

The dark bowels of the mill exhaled the same stench of mice and birds as she stood to consider who could have been there. Veremii would not play with her so callously. But why had a stranger thought up this idiotic game of hide and seek? If they had wanted to catch and torment her they could have done so yesterday. Perhaps someone had looked in the mill by chance and taken the gift of food. But then who had written to her? Who had summoned her to the place that was so significant to them both?

She felt estranged from herself as she set off home. When she arrived there was no light in the house. Mum was not yet asleep, she was sitting on her bed, which was placed above the stove, and staring as intently as an owl into the darkness.

'You have been to the mill?' she asked.

'Yes.'

Hannusia changed her clothes as quietly as a shadow passing over the wall and went to Veremii's mother to sit with her and feel the warmth. They sat silently, looking at the darkness of the wall. Mum, without waiting for what Hannusia had to say, spoke first, 'Tanasykha came this evening, she said that a man who looks like Yarko has been seen in the bazaar at Chyhyryn. He was disguised as an old man wearing rags and had a profuse beard and shaggy hair. It was cold and he, the poor wretch, was barefoot and wearing a straw hat.'

'Who saw him?' Hannusia asked.

'Oh, just people, anyone. They saw how he asked for alms from passers by.'

'And do you believe them, Ma?'

'Well, Tanasykha says that someone recognised him. They wanted to ask him something but he disappeared quickly and ... no one knows where he went.'

'Yarko would never beg for alms,' said Hannusia.

'That's true, but people are saying things.'

'They haven't said enough to us.'

'And the hat, as you see, has ended up here,' Mother moaned softly. 'I thought that, perhaps ...'

'Oh, I don't have the strength to listen to this.'

Day after day, new rumours reached their ears. It was said that Veremii had been wounded and sent to Poland to recuperate. It was rumoured that he was in the Cherkasy interrogation cell. Someone swore that they had seen him in the Onufriivskyi Monastery, garbed as a monk. Other people insisted that the otaman continued to wage war against soviet power, but far away from his home and under another name, Vovhur or Bosyi or Tuz. This was enhanced by a story about how the Cossacks of Bosyi, who, rumour had it, were now led by Veremii, had halted a train between Bobrynska and Tsvitkove. They had slaughtered the military personnel on board and examined the documents of the civilians.

Hannusia had forgotten when and how to laugh, but all this gossip warmed her heart with the hope that Veremii was still alive. She had recently dreamed that four sturdy men had carried a coffin containing his body into the snow-covered yard of their house. The body was dressed in Veremii's straw hat, a bloodstained embroidered shirt and his Cossack trousers, but his feet were bare. Hannusia had wanted to fall on him and weep, but Veremii had suddenly moved and sat upright. She yearned to lie next to him, to rest and gently hold him against her breast, and to feel his heart still beating.

The next morning snow fell heavily, frost gripped the yard and there was a white muffling blanket like in Hannusia's dream. She grabbed ten eggs and ran to the wise woman, Khtodykha, so she could help her to understand the meaning of the dream. Grandmother Khtodykha did not spend too much time thinking before she said, 'Although it is often the case that dreams mean the opposite of what they seem to mean, in this case your dream is true, your Veremii is still alive. There is blood and, I will not lie, this means he has been caught or is injured somewhere, but death has not taken him.'

Hannusia flew back home on wings of delight, eager to tell Mother about the dream and Grandmother Khtodykha's opinion. When she arrived home what she saw was like someone smacking her in the stomach with the haft of an axe. A harsh voice crowed in Russian, 'Come with us sweetheart and recognise the corpse of your beloved bandit.'

There was a vehicle parked by the gate and two soldiers grabbed Hannusia, shoved her in, and drove her to Matusiv, where they were obliged to show her the corpse. They were certain it was Veremii and understood there were orders requiring that a family member, friend or acquaintance had to testify to the identity of the deceased. The two military men warmed themselves with home-brewed vodka and laughed raucously, jabbering something in Russian at her as they travelled. She did not speak a word to them, but sat, as if carved from stone, without feeling the cold. It seemed as if her womb, where his child slept, was slowly petrifying, along with her soul. She did not notice how long it took to travel to Matusiv. Time had now stopped for her and she was indifferent to everything on the earth, even the hope that had warmed her heart so recently.

They came to a halt by some stables, not far from the local government buildings, and Hannusia saw something that made her hair stand on end. There was a man standing. He was drawn up to his full height, with his back pressed against the side of the stall. He was unclothed, with bare feet and a bare head. There was only a bloodstained shirt offering some scant protection against the cold.

His face was already frozen, his eyes were closed and their lashes were two glittering stripes of hoarfrost.

'Yarko!'

Some time passed before Hannusia realised the man was no longer alive. His body had been all night in the frost and had grown as rigid as a piece of oak. The devils had deliberately stood him on his feet and fastened him to the wall to give her false hope. It was apparent they had mocked the dead man and pelted him with frozen dung, which was now heaped against the side of the stall.

'Yarko, this isn't you.'

She could not determine whether it really was him and, drawing closer, looked fearfully into the face of the corpse. It was a face deformed by death and violence. She was able to ascertain for herself that this was not Veremii. There was a resemblance, but it was not him. 'No, no,' Hannusia said to herself, 'this is some other man.' At the same time something whispered to her that she might be mistaken. She had seen more than once how death transformed the features of a person. A death due to torture could often render someone unrecognisable. She looked into his face to seek some familiar feature. She examined his neck, his hands and his fingers, but saw only the marks left by the derision inflicted on the corpse.

'What do you say to that, darling?' jeered a Russian voice.

Hannusia had no certainty whether the corpse was Veremii's. A whole mob of Muscovites had gathered by the stall. 'Maybe you could look under his knickers,' cried one of them, 'you'd recognise that quickly!'

Hannusia blocked out their savage laughter. 'Well,' she said, 'I will look. Only bear him into the stable.'

'No way. You will rape him there,' the *katsaps* brayed again.

'As you were,' cried one of the senior officers, who was wearing a white jacket rather than a military greatcoat. 'This is an identification process. Take the bandit into the premises and conduct the identification according to protocol.'

They took him from the wall and laid him on the straw in the stable. Hannusia asked them to leave her alone with the corpse. Barely a couple of minutes had passed before she emerged. 'Yes, that's him,' she affirmed.

'OK, well done. We will take you home now,' said the man in the white jacket. 'Sign here.'

Hannusia scrawled her jagged signature on the paper, with a hand that seem to be made of wood, and felt how slowly the blood oozed through her veins. Something sharp moved in her womb, the nameless child would live and there was a vision, a hope in the fact of life itself.

The scar on Veremii's body, which only she should see, was not visible on the dead man's body.

2

Satan himself conceived the New Economic Policy that grasped us by the throat. We began to lose that bulwark of resistance to the occupation, the villagers who had begun to breathe freely and had been allowed to become the masters of their own land and to live with unfettered hands; perhaps still in thrall to foreigners, but able to chew the meat from the bones of well-nourished animals. Until recently, the villagers had greeted us like their protectors, with sacks of bread, *salo* and poultry, and given us their best sons for our army. Now things had changed, 'Forgive us, boys,' the old guys said, hiding their eyes, 'times have changed. It's time you started doing some proper work, nothing good will come of you holing up in the forest. Go back home, farm the land and live like human beings.'

These words drove me over the edge. There was one occasion when exhausted, famished and rain drenched, we were returning to Lebedynskyi Forest after an assault on the store of the peat manufacturers near Ivanova Hat. We had crawled into a barn to rest and dry, and had barely bothered to look around before we slept on the straw. Such a heavy fatigue had settled on us that it almost knocked us off our feet.

In the morning a cunning bloke, a typical crafty peasant, came to the barn, which smelled of manure and tar. His eyes swivelled over us rapidly. It was obvious that he was afraid to speak but he could not remain silent. 'Who asked you to come here?' he began in a weak, fearful voice. 'Do you want to drive me into the grave? Think with your heads. When you leave this place someone could find out that you stayed here overnight.'

'Are we waging a war to save your hide?' Koliada asked severely.

'To hell with your war. You came here and you will go and tomorrow they'll hang me,' the peasant cut in. 'Things have changed, you are no longer our representatives but the scourge of God on our heads. More than one person has been dispatched to the other world because of people like you.' He paused for a second, reflecting whether he had gone too far then, to placate us, said, 'Wait, I'll be back soon.'

He left the barn and returned quickly with a bowl of *varenyky*, they were cold, probably from yesterday evening, but they were white, plump and made with good flour. I saw how the Adam's apple of our Chinese man, Khodya, bobbed up and down with delight. We had not eaten so much as a grain of sand for more than twenty-four hours.

'Enjoy yourselves lads, but don't bother the dogs,' said our affiable peasant. 'Do you hear me? Do what you like, but don't bother my dogs.'

As he was speaking the doors flew open with a squeal and a hairy muzzle was thrust into the barn. A handsome, grey mutt looked at us with his luminescent, intelligent eyes and, instead of barking, he licked himself.

'Who told you that we would hassle your dogs, Uncle?' asked Koliada. 'We are more willing to be friends with dogs than we are with people like you.' He took the bowl of *varenyky* from the peasant's hand and placed it in front of the dog. The dog sniffed and took one in his mouth. He did not eat it, but looked enquiringly at his master. We no longer had the strength to laugh; hungry and angry, we gave vent to our fury later when we raided the grocery store in the village.

The circle that defined the scope of our activity continued to tighten like a noose. Soon we could not even permit ourselves to engage in such limited actions as the one at the store that we had carried out to obtain supplies. The same Satan who had conceived the N.E.P. conceived of a new weapon to use against us. The institute of those responsible for warranting the loyalty of the village to the state. The Bolsheviks would shoot villagers who had dealings with the forest rebels or who were even suspected of engaging in such disloyal acts.

The most 'responsible' people fell onto the blacklist of the 'institution' and the hostages had to answer for the loyalty of the whole village. At this time they were still known as *Desyatykhatnyky*.

It was from this point that we tried to avoid the villages and only ventured into them out of dire necessity. I saw how the spirits of the boys began to sink. It is frightening even to think about what the absence of hope does to people. Chatterboxes became silent. Happy-go-lucky types grew anguished. Dare-devils became cowards, and certain people turned into traitors. Who would have thought that the otamans of Kholodnyi Yar, such as Derkach, Vasyl's cousin, Simon Chuchupaka, Panchenko, and with them one hundred *Haidamak* rebels, could have been broken? It was shameful and bitter to see what the mangy looking *Chekist*, Ptitsyn, or Ptichkin or Kanareykin or whatever the hell he was called, had done to them. The young, green, fledgling *Chekist*, who had gained his adult plumage early on in the Latyskyi unit of the Cheka Sveaborg, which in September 1918 was guarding - Who do you think? Lenin himself, in Gorky.

Having wandered among the *Chekist* garbage for a while, Ptitsyn finally ended up in the Kremenchuk district accompanying a squadron that had entered the village of Melnyky. Here, a permanent military garrison was established on what had been the base of the 25th Rifle Division.

Melnyky, the native village of the Chuchupaka brothers, was five *versts* from the Motryn Monastery and Ptitsyn was beside himself when he occasionally heard the peal of the bells carrying over the dark wall of the forest. He was aware that the bells told the rebels when enemy forces had entered the area, and the strength and the direction in which they travelled; albeit they did not signal an intention to engage in battle. The *Haidamak* rebels were not equipped to venture out of the forest; engaging in head to head confrontation with regular military units was not their business, and it was extremely dangerous for the Reds to enter the forest.

After establishing himself as an uninvited guest in the spacious house of the local priest and the priest's rather gorgeous daughter, Ptitsyn initially ordered that a proclamation be hung around the village and on the fringes of the forest. The announcement was written in ugly, bedevilled Russian:

Citizens of the Kholodnyi Yar District

An extraordinary congress of the Ukrainian Soviets has declared amnesty for everyone who ceases to struggle against the authority of the workers and peasants and hands over their weapons. In the villages of the Chyhyryn district, in the Kholodnyi Yar area, the bands, led by the atamans Raven, the Chuchupakas, Derkach and Poltavets, wait and hope for something, but ahead of them lies only the certainty of death.

Vast armies have been assigned for the liquidation of gangsterism in Kholodnyi Yar; after which a firm hand will restore order. Those who have strayed and been deceived will be allowed the chance to return to peaceful work. Between June 26 and July 2 an amnesty will be granted to all atamans and members of their gangs who voluntarily hand over their weapons and declare the termination of any further struggle against authority. Everyone in receipt of amnesty will be provided with a document stamped with the appropriate insignia. Those who have been granted amnesty will not be arrested. Bandits will be received in the premises of the garrison at Melnyky village during the entirety of daylight hours.

Representative of the Kremenchuk
Gubchrezvichtroiki, Ptitsyn
Chief of the Military Garrison, Shterenberg

A leaflet quickly appeared in reply to Ptitsyn's announcement that called on the peasants not to believe the Muscovite hangmen and to fight the soviet commune at every step.

After a few days a boy brought a note to the staff headquarters addressed to Ptitsyn:

If everything you say is true, come to us in the forest. We will talk. We guarantee your life. Come, if you are not a coward.

Ptitsyn was not a coward, but before venturing into the forest he took hostages and placed the relatives of the Chuchupaka brothers under arrest, stipulating that they were to be shot if he did not return. He went unarmed into the forest, carrying only a mandate that gave him the right to grant amnesty. Before he knew what was happening, he was surrounded by three Cossacks who blindfolded him and led him in circles before they arrived at their underground garrison.

Raven, who was waiting to receive him, was surprised to see such a pallid man who was younger than he had imagined. Ptitsyn frequently blinked his beady, bird-like eyes, either because it was dark and smoky or because it was a habit he had been born with. Raven scowled at Derkach, Chuchupaka and Panchenko and wondered why they had led this lousy scum-bag into the camp.

The underground lair was bursting with about fifty people, almost all of whom were sitting on benches at long tables, which were covered with an abundance of food and drink. The present stunt of allowing themselves to play at being best buddies with a *Chekist* was another idiocy in which the otamans had allowed themselves to indulge. Raven did not like it when Ptitsyn entered and everyone became quiet and would not take their eyes off him; as if he really was a big cheese who demanded their undivided attention. So, this was what they were like, the eagles of the *Cheka*, he thought.

Derkach led the way. He tried to speak sarcastically, but without success, 'That's interesting ... and how do we address you?'

'Pyotry Ptitsyn,' said the worthy and duly-empowered *Chekist*, in Russian. 'Don't judge me by my Russian surname, I am *Khokhol* by the way.'

'Then why don't you speak our tongue?' Derkach asked in Ukrainian.

'Because Odesa is my native city. My grandfather's family name was Ptakh. So I don't speak Ukrainian, but I understand it. You may speak that language and I'll be really pleased. It is an amazingly melodic language.'

Derkach looked simple-mindedly at Raven, astounded by what he had heard.

'Do you drink *vitka*?'

'What is *vitka*?' enquired their guest.

'Diluted spirit.'

'I don't drink alcohol. I have problems with my stomach.'

'We will dilute it for you with ten parts spring water to one part spirit,' Derkach soothed him. 'There can be no chat without it.'

'OK, just a little to have a better chat,' agreed Ptitsyn.

'Great, well sit then,' said Simon Chuchupaka, frowning.

They chatted for a while and Raven became even more surprised when he saw where Simon had seated the mongrel. He was almost in the corner, between himself and Derkach, and Panchenko was making himself cosy at their side. If Vasyl Chuchupaka had known what was going on he would have jumped out of his grave and had all three of them lined up against the wall and shot.

Ptitsyn sipped his drink cautiously between his teeth. It was apparent that he was either genuinely ill or wary of getting drunk among the camaraderie of these cut-throats. He eventually drained his glass and, blinking his tear-filled eyes, set about eating the *salo*, as if trying to remind every one of his grandfather's Ukrainian name.

While he tasted his ancestral cuisine, Ptitsyn cast his myopic gaze into the corners of the room and was clearly surprised that the walls of the subterranean house were whitened with lime. The top of the traditional shrine in the corner of the room was adorned with the image of the Mother of God and her Son, and lower down there were two unfurled linen flags. The blue and yellow one of Ukraine, and the black battle standard of Kholodnyi Yar, on which was embroidered, with silver thread, 'A Free Ukraine or Death'. Ptitsyn's gaze was riveted to the inscription; he stopped chewing and, as if puzzled by it, read each word obsessively, letter by letter.

'Let's have another one,' said Derkach, as he poured another measure.

'Hold on, we won't have time to talk,' said Ptitsyn.

'We have plenty of time.' Chuchupaka pushed his glass towards Ptitsyn's, encouraging him to partake in the toast. 'We're not ready for a serious chat yet, the main thing is that you weren't afraid to come here.'

'Why should I be afraid? I came here to conduct negotiations, not to seek marriage.'

'Well, don't sit there like a nervous bridegroom,' said Derkach. 'Cheers!'

Ptitsyn wrinkled his nose and downed the second glass with more aplomb and courage. His pale face became stippled with rosy blotches after the third glass. He weakened and cast his eyes along the tables, looking at the forest fellowship.

Raven liked the fact that the lads had long ceased gawping at Ptitsyn and were talking amongst themselves in the midst of a thick fog of home-grown tobacco. It were as if a curtain of smoke separated them from the *Chekist* and the otamans who were drinking with him. Ptitsyn, by now visibly inebriated, could not work out if the room was that smoky or if his eyes were fogging up with alcohol.

'Everything is really great. I mean drinking vodka,' he said, 'but I have to get back to the garrison headquarters in the evening otherwise Shterenberg will be worried.' He assured them that there were hostages currently sitting under arrest in Melnyky and they would be shot by the guards if he did not return later in the evening.

'Write a note to Chief Shterenberg to tell him that the negotiations have been prolonged until tomorrow. This isn't a simple job, there is a lot for us to ponder over,' Simon Chuchupaka advised him.

'Really, write him a note, the boys will take it to him,' said Derkach, joining in and at the same time pouring more into his glass.

Ptitsyn drank and picked up a gherkin, but rather than eating it, he inspected it from all sides, as if he had never seen such a fascinating vegetable before. 'Oh lads, what a life is about to begin,' he uttered dreamily. 'You should be sowing and ploughing, but you … it's as if you can see nothing but the azure distance of the Arctic.'

Ptitsyn put the gherkin on the table, propped up his bird-like head, which was now too heavy for his flaccid neck, with his hand and stared into a pale distance at something that was visible only to himself. This vague, grey perspective swam, oscillated and slipped still further away from his foggy gaze. Then one of the lads, intoned a note and quietly, in a hoarse, sweet, soft voice began to sing:

Oh, the grey cuckoo called,

Early in the morning at dawn …

A second and third joined him, until eventually all were caught up by the song. They sang in unison because they were all familiar with *The Cuckoo* and this was not the first time it had resounded on their lips, but now the song seemed to have another meaning.

Oh, the lads, the youths wept,
Oh, in a foreign country, captive in a dungeon …

Their voices were different too, as if the black anguish of their souls was singing through their throats, not about the Zaporizhia Cossacks of yore, who were punished by their harsh captivity, but the fate of these landless wretches, sitting at the coarse, timber tables, concealing their eyes and faces with their palms; not looking at one another and only feeling their own immovable anguish. These wretched Cossacks wept and grieved as they summoned up the image of the quagmire of their own destiny; a destiny that had forsaken them long ago. They beseeched the tempestuous breeze to liberate them from their fate, while their tormentors forged still stronger manacles to hold them captive. There was nothing and no one in this world now, apart from the song sung by Cossacks, otamans and officers. They sang until they forgot themselves, utterly, surrendering to the sorrows of it.

They did not notice how, in response to the song, the expression on the face of their guest was transformed. He had been left by himself for a few minutes while they sang and he suddenly became calm, pricked up his ears for a second, grabbed his head, which was slumped on his chest, and grew rigid. A slight tremor ran over his shoulders and, at first, Raven thought that the monster was laughing, but Ptitsyn wept. These were inebriated tears of course, but he did not hide them and wiped his face as the song finished.

When the last notes faded and silence fell, Ptitsyn was the first to speak, 'We used to sing that song at home,' he said, wrinkling his nose, 'I feel so sad. Oooh.'

Raven was taken by the mischievous thought that Ptitsyn would leap to his feet and declare in Russian, *Lads, I'm staying here with you, forever. Don't believe those Bolshevik fairy tales. We will fight*

83

until the end. But he knew that this was an image painted by his capricious imagination.

'My grandfather, whose surname was Ptakh, often sang that song, he said.'

He was fooling everyone to such an extent with tales of his grandfather that Simon Chuchupaka, already softened up with alcohol, began to reminisce about his own family, 'Well my grandfather, or perhaps my great grandfather, who had been in the Tsar's army, loved to belt out the odd *katsap* song. If he was in the pen with the swine he would warble to them in the Muscovite tongue, "Chu-chu, you nasty things."'

'What? What?' Ptitsyn interjected.

'Chu-chu,' repeated Chuchupaka. 'That's how we called out to the swine when they were doing some damage or misbehaving. Well, my grandfather, or perhaps my great grandfather, would say to them, Chu-chu, you nasty things, and because of that people began to refer to him as Chuchupaka. From then we all had the surname, Chuchupaka.'

'Interesting,' said Ptitsyn. 'Very interesting. So he only spoke to the pigs in Russian?'

'Well, who else could he speak it with?' Simon Chuchupaka replied in surprise. 'There was nobody else in Melnyky who spoke in the Muscovite tongue.'

'And did they understand him?'

'Who?' said Simon, not comprehending what was being asked.

'The swine.'

'Well, as much as I understand you.'

'It's amazing.' Ptitsyn shrugged his meagre shoulders and hurled down another glass of *vitka* without waiting to be asked. He swallowed hard but he could not hold it down and gagged as the drink rose in his throat. Ptitsyn jerked and suddenly covered his mouth with his hand as red vomit spurted between his fingers. They took him in their arms, because he could barely move his legs, and led him outside. When they brought him back underground, he presented an appalling spectacle; he had now turned a bizarre, earthy, green colour.

Before he put the *Chekist* to bed, Derkach sat him at the table with a pencil and a scrap of paper. Ptitsyn, thought for a moment then, with an amazingly firm hand, wrote the following note in Russian:

'Top Secret' - To the Chief of the Garrison, Comrade Shterenberg

Taking into account the importance and confidentiality of these negotiations, they have been prolonged until tomorrow. Please do not be concerned.

Ptitsyn

'Well, that's good, the note will be in your staff headquarters within an hour,' said Derkach. 'Perhaps we could celebrate that fact with more *vitka.*'

Ptitsyn did not hear him, like a marathon runner who with his last strength bore the glad tidings to the preordained place, he had slumped head first, as if dead, onto the table and was snoring loudly. The men lifted him from the table and threw him onto the straw in the corner of the room, where he slept until morning.

Who would have imagined that the next morning this carrion would wake up a completely different person. After washing himself with cold water, he refused breakfast and the hair of the dog that was proffered to him. He quickly gathered his wits and readied himself to speak. He asked them to bring everyone who was prepared to listen to him. When the room was again crammed with people, Ptitsyn fired forth such a sermon that it held everyone's attention.

Raven also listened and became more assured of the fact that any otaman who permitted a foe to deliver propaganda in his own camp should be shot. He was compelled to watch how the *Chekist* agitator conducted his propaganda speech with such fine words, while portraying such a bright and strong presence in front of these people who were fatigued with the extremity and hopelessness of their predicament.

'Soviet power,' he said, 'is not interested in persecuting those who have been granted amnesty because it needs people like you. Strong people. All doors are opening in front of you today.' He pointed his finger at the throng before him, as if he had a particular individual in mind. 'I know that you long to return to your wives and children and that you wish to till the soil. You will indeed farm the land again because only you know the price of a peaceful existence. I know that you,' he pointed his finger at the other side of the crowd, 'want to serve in the Red Army, and you will serve as a commander in its ranks because you have a wealth of military experience. I know,' he pointed at someone else, 'that you're not opposed to the idea of working for the militia. You will be a superb police officer because you understand crime and how to fight it. Isn't that a better choice than the certain and futile death you now face?'

He spoke for three hours without shutting his mouth for more than a moment. The crowd did not interrupt him and when he had finished they began to question him. They asked if it was true they would not be persecuted? Would the tax they paid on the sale of produce be the same as everyone else's or would they pay more? Would people who had been granted amnesty be deprived of the right to a vote? Would they be able to go to large towns and work in the mines or would their movement be restricted? Ptitsyn, of course, assured them that they would be permitted to do everything. A new life in a new Ukraine awaited them. 'He who wishes to chose this new, happy existence must appear before the authorities and hand over his weapons within one week.'

'Think again,' cried Raven, who was unable to endure any more. 'Who are you listening to?' He leaped from the bench, drew himself up to his full height, almost banging his head against an oak beam, and drew close to Derkach. 'You forget that you are in Kholodnyi Yar.'

Derkach was silent and hid his eyes.

'Have you forgotten your brother?' Raven said, turning his leaden gaze to Chuchupaka.

'Let's not trouble the dead,' said Simon quietly.

'Oh, so good health to you then!' Raven exclaimed ironically.

He left and was on the point of returning to Lebedyn Forest but decided to wait and see how things panned out. He stood by the shrubbery, playing with a whip that he held anxiously, and was unable to settle himself. He did not notice Panchenko approaching him.

'I know they will not let me live,' he said, 'but, after three years of this miserable existence in the forest, I am so fed up that I would die for the chance to live like a human being for three days and to sleep in a warm bed.'

Raven played with the whip in silence.

'Forgive me,' Panchenko spoke again, 'but if at some point in the future you want to kill me then I will not be offended, but let me say farewell to you, for I feel in my soul that we will see each other no more.'

Raven looked into Panchenko's downcast eyes, their gaze met and they embraced.

'Farewell ...'

***

Sitting among the branches of an old lime tree, Raven saw everything as if it were laid in the palm of his hand. The riders tore along the road from the forest and in their wake other, horseless rebels followed on foot. There were nearly one hundred of them. The forest partisans did not cross Kholodnyi Yar from the direction of Melnyky because it would have been too shameful for the *Haidamak* rebels to pass through their capital city in this humiliated state. Instead, they passed nearer to Holovkivka. They waded through the stream with their heads lowered and, without looking at each other, they descended lower and lower to the bottom of the ravine.

When they arrived at the village square there was a table covered with a crimson cloth on which rested an inkstand, a pen and some paper. Near the table, a flag, bearing a hammer and sickle, streamed in the wind. Ptitsyn was standing and shifting from foot to foot. He was accompanied by Shterenberg, the battalion commander of the Third Moscow Brigade, Kozlodoiev, and the local leadership. Nearby, on either side of the table, were empty wagons. The square was surrounded by troops.

There were many spectators, including children, who were transfixed by the scene, and crazy Varfolomii was wandering around nearby.

Varfolomii lived in the asylum at the Chyhyryn Svyato Troiitskyi Monastery and always appeared when there was a special occasion and more than a few people were gathered. He was emaciated, a bag of skin and bones, and whether it was summer or winter always wore a long, black mantle with the hood thrown over his head. Almost no one had seen his face, no one knew his age or could work out how old he was. Even old people remembered Varfolomii as being in the state he was now, a homeless, crazy vagabond whose presence was considered to be an evil omen. The villagers were afraid of him and said that misfortune came in his wake, that it was as if he gave it added power. In reality he only acted as an omen of inevitable misfortune. Since ancient times it has been known that when God deprives a man of his sanity, he compensates him with the special power of prophecy.

'Nevermore will you hear the bells,' proclaimed Varfolomii, shaking his fist at the sky. 'They fall to their feet, but not yours. Everything falls into ruin because stars on the forehead suit only cattle.'

The cloud of dust kicked up by the partisans drew ever closer to Holovkivka.

'There they go. There they go,' cried the children.

The riders, led by Derkach, Simon Chuchupaka and Panchenko, arrived first. When they dismounted they were each approached by two Red Army soldiers. One led the horse aside while the other showed the rider to the empty wagon where he had to throw his weapons. The swords, rifles and revolvers of Chuchupaka, Derkach and Panchenko flew into the first wagon. Then a strange event occurred. Ptitsyn, who was so affected by this solemn moment, returned the weapons to the three otamans and stood each of them by his side. Chuchupaka, Derkach and Panchenko were so surprised and confused by this that they trod on each other's toes in their agitation. A stream of rebels on foot washed into the square. They too threw their weapons into the wagons and, at the shouts of the Red Army commanders, lined up to face the table, the fraternal flag and the indifferent otamans who stood in the place of honour with bowed heads.

When the process of 'hanging up' their weapons was

completed, Ptitsyn spoke. He sang the same tune that he had sung during his propaganda speech at the dug-out, but on this occasion he did not make a long speech; there was no need for that now the rebels had surrendered.

Each of the forest rebels went in turn to the table. Their names were written on the forms for amnesty, which had been prepared and stamped in advance. None of the soviet functionaries handling the papers checked anything; they simply wrote down the names the partisans told them and handed the documents to them. After this process, each of the rebels was a legitimate citizen of the Soviet Union. They were free to leave the square when they wished, apart from the otamans. Ptitsyn explained that, as the commanders of the rebels, they had to provide a report on the activity of the units under their command.

'I knew that,' said Panchenko, completely resigned.

Later that day he was led, together with Simon Chuchupaka and Derkach, in a convoy almost as far as Kremenchuk. They were never heard of again. The wretched Panchenko did not get to sleep in a dry, warm bed in exchange for his surrender.

Ptitsyn did not stop with the abject capitulation of the rebels and undertook a further action that alarmed Raven more than the scene on the square. Immediately after granting amnesty to the rebels, the Reds flocked to the Motryn Monastery. Their ranks stretched along the forest road from Kreseltsi Farm to the plateau where the monastery rested. The troops to the rear did not even know where the monastery was, while those at the front were beginning to thrash around in the devil's nest.

Crazy Varfolomii ran ahead of them. He banged his fist on the gate and bellowed with such vigour that his cry echoed down the ravine, 'Hide, those of you who can. Lucifer is coming, with a star on his brow and horns on his head. He will strangle you all.'

Entangling himself in the folds of his long mantle, Varfolomii ran into the centre of the monastery courtyard, 'Woe unto you. Woe unto you who would marry Christ. The horned serpents come. They will violate you. Flee!'

Nobody inside the monastery thought of escaping from the

soldiers. The nuns placed their trust in prayer and the grace of God. Mother Yepystymiia, the tall, elegant mother superior, emerged from her chamber and said that if it had been adjudged that someone should suffer an execution and be a martyr, then that was the will of God and should be accepted as a benediction.

'Indeed,' said the lame dwarf, Onysia, who always followed in her wake, 'I'll thrash them with this cane and make sure they remember Onysia.' She waved her walking stick.

'Good girl, Onysia,' said Mother Superior. 'You can keep anyone in their place.'

Mother Yepystymiia's roots were in Tomsk, but it was known that twenty years ago she had been in an unhappy love affair and the monastery had offered her sanctuary not, as she loved to say, through the hands of the Cherkasy Episcopal Mykolai but through the will of God. She had only made peace with the rebels of Kholodnyi Yar because they protected her establishment from the various warring groups who had previously arrived and tried to get hold of the monastery's property.

'Indeed,' said Onysia, 'I have a long cane and a very short fuse.'

'You're a good girl. They are afraid of women like you,' said the Mother Superior, still striving to maintain a playful tone. Onysia noticed that her voice trembled.

Even the revelations of Saint John the Evangelist had never portrayed such terror to the nuns as that which now stood on their threshold. A malodorous flood of soldiers engulfed the yard. They cursed savagely amid torrents of raucous laughter and cackling. They were obeying their sole order, to remove the monastery's bells. They would destroy the main information system of this rebel country once and for all; this accursed Kholodnyi Yar Republic with which they were compelled to wage a harsher and more prolonged war than they had endured against the Polish, Germans, Denikin, Vrangel or Makhno.

While the nuns lamented and wailed, the soldiers pulled down the monastery bells to take them to Kremenchuk and then to Kharkiv as evidence of their victory over this new *sich* that had raised a sword from the ancient ramparts of Ukraine. The soldiers became

90

enraged by the great effort of removing the bells and the weeping of the nuns, and in their anger they burned down the bell tower of the Church of Saint John Chrysostom. A terrible pillar of flames roared upwards with ominous blood-red tongues.

'Animals,' Varfolomii cried, stretching his emaciated arms imploringly towards the sky. He had tilted his head so far back that the hood of his coat fell onto his shoulders, revealing a face that was as desiccated as a mummy's. 'Yet another star will fall on your one-horned heads.'

He bustled among the godless soldiery, grasping at their hands and garments until one of them struck him in the face with a rifle butt. Varfolomii fell and lay supine. The Muscovites trampled over the relic of his body. They stamped on his head, breast and belly with their cloven hooves, as if trying to level him into the soil. After a while it seemed as if he had been trampled to nothingness and that only his skin remained, covered by his black, crumpled mantle. Suddenly, a wave of soil lifted his remains and Varfolomii raised his bony hands to the sky. 'Death, throw yourself onto the stars and horns. As Melkhysedek said to me, you love only those who fear you.'

The soldiers no longer heard Varfolomii because they were deranged. They had been driven into a frenzy by the fire and the women's laments. The vagabond troops threw themselves, one after another, into the stores, vaults and chambers, grabbing everything that came to hand as they ran. They gulped down sweet mouthfuls of sanctified wine, so it trickled down their chins in crimson streams, and crammed their mouths and pockets with the communion bread. They tore into the Holy Trinity Monastery Church, grabbed anything that glittered, gold crosses, triple candle holders, silver discuses, offertory trays and chalices, and stuffed their coats with their finds.

The blessed abbot of yore, Melkhysedek, and the ancient Cossacks, Ivan Honta and Maksym Zaliznyak, looked in silence from where they were portrayed amidst the saints and icons, tightly sealing their lips on this orgy of sacrilege. Zaliznyak was depicted in a monk's cassock and held a sacred knife in his right hand. It was inscribed with the words *For You*. In his left hand he held a rosary. Above his right shoulder, three lines of notes from a song were inscribed, *There is no place where life is easier and better than among us in Ukraine.*

However, Zaliznyak, like his knife, was only a painted image and was powerless to prevent the ravenous predators from smashing the icons and seizing, breaking and throwing all that was precious into the depths of avarice and oblivion.

The intruders stumbled on the book collection. The stiff paper pages were unsuitable for rolling cigarettes so they tore the gold and silver fastenings and adornments from the books and hurled the husks into the flames that engulfed the bell tower. They had no regard for anything sacred and even burned *Margaret of the Sacred John Chrysostom Convent with words of instruction beneficial for human souls*, a book with a leather cover, printed in Ostroh in the summer of 1595, and the *Evangelists* of 1600. One breathless *katsap* carried the five-hundred year old chronicles of the Motryn Monastery to the fire.

Yepystymiia was petrified with fear because until now she had placidly watched over all who had endured misfortune and come to her. She ran to intercept him and tried to take the manuscripts before they burned. The *katsap* who jostled against her lowered the hand-written texts to the floor and started cursing and laughing. He had inflamed himself to such a crescendo that he threw her to the ground and shoved his paw under her habit. Little Onysia flew to protect Mother Yepystymiia. She beat the rapist on his fat behind with her cane and accompanied her blows with shouts of, 'Here you go.' Her actions only inflamed his desire and made him more rabid as he clawed at the nun's garments, and there was now nothing that could stop him from violating her.

A mighty dwarf-like creature charged at Onysia as if he was going to grab her stick, but instead he bundled her into his arms and bore her to the stable.

'Save me, Sister,' screamed Onysia, kicking her legs futilely in the air, but there was no one to save her because the other sisters had fled elsewhere. The Muscovites had pursued them, vying with each other to catch them first, but there were not enough nuns for them all and they could not bear to wait in line to take their pleasure in the women.

Varfolomii appeared before them again. His fists were as sharp as gnarled wooden pieces, 'Stand to, you inhuman ones. The hour will come when star will fall on star and horns will shatter each other,' he yelled.

Two Reds, who flitted here and there as they searched for an unclaimed victim, leaped blindly onto him, 'You carrion, are you still alive?'

Enraged, they grabbed Varfolomii's arms and legs and cast him, as easily as if he had been a feather, into the green flames beneath the bell tower that burned with renewed vigour. Varfolomii fell into the midst of the fire, which leaped upwards with green tongues and darted in all directions with streams of sparks. They were suddenly extinguished where the old man had landed, either because they were smothered by his mantle or through some strange miracle. All around Varfolomii the fires raged so intensely that it was impossible to draw near without the infernal heat searing their faces. The two soldiers who had cast him into the flames ran back and stood, stupidly watching to see what would happen next. A group of soldiers gathered by their side; having failed in their pursuit of the nuns they now had to wait their turn.

'Look, the flame does not burn him,' said a pock-marked Muscovite, as he looked through his white lashes at the flames while casually scratching his crotch and chewing communion bread. 'Vanya, have you ever seen anything like that anywhere?'

'He doesn't burn in flames, that's interesting. Will he drown in water?'

'Don't worry, he will ignite in a moment. It would be great to pour some fuel on him.'

It was at that moment that something crackled on the apex of the bell tower and the huge top of the structure collapsed and fell on Varfolomii. The sparks from the impact spurted almost as far as the onlookers, who drew back but then stared into the fire with bulging eyes for some trace of the black mantle.

'Oh shit,' yelled the pock-marked Muscovite, who was still chewing the host.

'He held on for a long time. He was some kind of magician.'

'He must have been. Vanya would you be able to hold on for so long?'

'Well, no. I can't wait any longer. Let's go look for somebody.'

'Is it true that they are still virgins?' asked the pock-marked

93

Muscovite as he gulped down his drool and took another piece of communion bread from his pocket.

'True, true, but you are a little late. Just a minute late.'

'Are even the older ones virgins?'

'That is not a question for me. Let's go or we'll be stuck with that lame dwarf.'

The invaders ran, some to the stable, some to the orchard, and some to the nuns' chambers. When the pock-marked one returned from the orchard with Vanya, fastening his trousers as he walked and eating the next piece of the host, he nearly choked with surprise. A nightmarish apparition in a long, black mantle, with the hood thrown over his head, was coming to meet them. At first he thought it was death coming for their souls because the spectre was clutching a scythe in his hands.

'Look, Vanya …'

But Vanya had already seen the spectre and was staggering, almost falling, as he took his rifle from his shoulder and screamed, 'On shit, it's the black monk.'

'And the stars will roll into the hyena of fire,' bellowed the figure in the mantle.

'It's that cursed sorcerer. He's alive,' the pock-marked soldier said in wonder.

'I can't understand it.'

Varfolomii waved the scythe and, shouting something incomprehensible, headed straight towards them. The agitated and unnerved Vanya jumped to one side and struck the scythe so hard with the butt of his gun that it flew one way and Varfolomii flew in the opposite direction.

'So, you don't burn in flames.' The pock-marked soldier stepped on the breast of Varfolomii with his boot, 'Who are you attacking with that scythe, you witch's offspring? What should we do with you for this? Speak idiot!'

'There's nothing to think about,' whimpered Vanya. 'The fire doesn't burn him, let's see if we can drown him. There's a pond nearby.'

They took Varfolomii by his legs and dragged him down the forest path towards the *Haidamak* pond, which glimmered in the gully

94

just beyond the monastery wall. They dragged him in such a vicious way that his head bounced off the bare tree roots, but Varfolomii did not make a sound. When they reached the bank of the pond, they took him by his legs and arms again and hurled him some distance into the water. The almost weightless Varfolomii fell so soundlessly that he barely caused the surface to ripple. As if he were not a man but a piece of drift wood. He fell inaudibly and lay supine on the water, not even giving a hint of drowning. His cowl and cloak, swollen with air, buoyed him on the surface, but perhaps his ancient and desiccated body would not have sunk, even without them.

'I see there is no ending to this,' said Vanya, again taking his rifle from his shoulder and drawing back the lock.

'Perhaps it is better not to do that.' The pock-marked soldier hesitated. 'If he's not killed by the bullet I'll go mad.'

'Oh come on.'

Vanya aimed, squeezed the trigger, *chk*, there was a click, but no bullet left the gun.

'Let's get away from here while we are still alive.' The pock-marked one pushed the muzzle of Vanya's gun abruptly to the side.

'It's just a malfunction.'

'That's doubtful. He was and still is a sorcerer, and here is another bad sign – The bells were removed.'

'But there was an award promised for them – for the bells.'

'You're an idiot Vanya. Just go and don't look back. Let him bask quietly on the water without bothering us.'

He took Vanya by the elbow and dragged him forcefully from the pond. When they had gone twenty steps Vanya cried in a voice that was not his own, 'Oh God's mother, I can't bear it.' He tore his rifle from his shoulder, turned towards the pond, aimed and fired. The cloak, still swollen on the surface of the water, trembled and began to settle. It slowly began to shrink into the liquid membrane, but still did not sink below the surface. It oscillated gently for a long time with the waves.

Ptitsyn had triumphed, the nest of bandits at Kholodnyi Yar had been destroyed. He informed the people's commissar, Balytskyi, that the Motryn Monastery had been taken and its bells had fallen at the feet of soviet power. The only thing that soured his mood was the report about how the soldiers of the Third Moscow Brigade had conducted themselves, but what could he do? It was war. He could understand the situation. Although ... they were cattle of course.

There was yet another worm of anxiety awakening in the depths of his mind. Ptitsyn considered that if there was a directive to remove the monastery bells in perpetuity, was it certain they would not ring again? But generally he was in good spirits. After a celebratory evening with Shterenberg, he had returned to the priest's house, where he needed to spend one last night. He thought about his spirit of service and how he had surprised himself with his dedication. He had lived for two weeks in the priest's house and had hardly seen the priest, his wife or their beautiful daughter. Who would value his sacrifice in the name of the revolution? Who would believe that he, Ptitsyn, who was over twenty years old, was still pleasing himself with his own hands? This manly decisiveness only displayed itself in his squalid, nocturnal fantasies. Which of the women around him had he not enjoyed in his fecund imagination, especially in Gorky where, in the chief's personal protection unit, Babusya Krupska was not the only woman he had seen? So here, in the priest's house, he imagined that the priest's daughter came to him every night, dressed in a long, white shift, even though he had never seen her. That is what dedicated service was like. He returned home when rural people were already asleep and had his own separate entrance because the priest's house was a substantial dwelling with two verandahs.

Ptitsyn lit the gas lamp and sat at the table to write a report about how successful the conduct of the operation had been. After a short while he felt that something was oppressing him and preventing him from concentrating, but he could not understand what it was. His thoughts roamed over the details of yesterday's events as he tried to find a reason for his anxiety, which had come upon him unawares, as if it were waiting for him just around the corner. He regretted that he had not been to the monastery today; instead he had left everything to the battalion commander, Kozlodoiev. He thought about his personal guard who patrolled this little corner of the village every night.

His thoughts continued to trouble him, like a needle poking out of a sack. If it was certain that the bandits would not return, why had they removed the bells? Ptitsyn assured himself that everything was in order. It was necessary to destroy the symbols and the sacred things that were the signs of the enemy. He had fulfilled a valuable task, but still some little demon whispered in his ear, 'Why ruin the bells if you knew that Kholodnyi Yar would not rise again?' His thoughts continued to awaken the anxiety in his soul. He racked his brains for a long time before his professional instinct sensed that it was the room that was troubling him. Something about it was not quite right.

Judging by appearances nothing had changed, but, on his life, there was something not quite right here. He looked at the tightly shut window, at the cumbersome wardrobe, and at the broad, oak bed, over which hung a green felt rug decorated with a picture of two zebras. On the wall by the door the long, weighted pendulum of a clock ticked sonorously. Ptitsyn was unable to get accustomed to the sound; the ancient mechanism began to hiss menacingly, then growled, and at last sounded the hour - bong, bong, bong. The hands pointed to two o'clock. Ptitsyn rose, went to the clock, and stopped the pendulum swinging. He sat down again at the little Viennese table, which was slightly skew whiff, took out his Luger from its holster and placed it on the table before him. Something struck his consciousness as sharply as the brass mechanism of the clock ticking the hours. He was suddenly warmed to the tips of his boots when he realised what it was that would not let him rest. The rug. The felt rug. It was like the one on the wall but a quarter of the size and placed under the table. Why was it there? He felt it should have been placed by the bed, in the middle of the room, or by the door. Why had he not paid attention to this small detail earlier?

He stood, moved the table to one side, and lifted the rug; beneath it was a trapdoor. Ptitsyn knew that in some rural settlements there were cellars that could be entered directly from the house, but why was this entrance disguised by a rug? He took his Luger from the table and with his left hand he grasped the small, metal ring that was attached to the trapdoor. It was heavy but he managed to lift it and discovered a black pit beneath him, which exhaled a blast of cold, stale air. It was hard to see anything in the murk and his curiosity was provoked further by the sense of something invisible. He took the gas lamp and, adjusting the wick for a bigger flame, shone it into the dark, cold obscurity below.

The darkness began to reveal the customary features of a cellar. There were small barrels, vats, flasks, pots and other utensils, but he saw something in the corner that made his heart skip a beat. He blinked so he could try to focus on what it was, as if a dazzling flame was burning in the vault. He saw a table and on it he noticed an interesting object. It was similar to the keyboard of an accordion and faced upwards. He realised that it was a rare and unexpected object to find in a priest's cellar. He hesitated as he thought about what to do with the object because he realised there was no ladder leading to or from the cellar.

Placing his lamp near the trapdoor, he stuffed the Luger into his belt, put his hands on either side of the aperture and lowered himself into the darkness below. It was only a short drop to the floor and he landed gently on his feet without noticing the impact. He slowly withdrew the Luger from his belt, looked around him and cast his eyes to the corner once more. Everything was calm. The only thing that grabbed his attention was the doorway. It was plain to see that there were some steps by the door, which the owners of the house used to enter the cellar. He put his ear against the door but heard nothing that might alarm him. He grasped the handle and pulled the door, but it was firmly bolted. Before he went to the table, he again looked over his surroundings. He even looked into the barrels of fermenting liquids, the vats and pots. He felt the potatoes in the basket, as if, instead of a potato, he might find a grenade.

Finally, he went over to the quietest and most secret place in this bandits' hidey hole; the small table on which rested an American Underwood typewriter. Ptitsyn blinked rapidly, as the opening lines of his coming report about this discovery spawned themselves in his small, bird-like head - *As a result of persistent and time consuming investigations, a bandit's typewriter has been found in the very hot-bed of Kholodnyi Yar.*

Such a report was in no way an exaggeration because there was a stack of printed leaflets next to the typewriter. Taking one of them, he went into the shaft of light that fell through the trapdoor and recognised the same typescript as that used for many of the leaflets he had seen displayed. It encouraged people not to believe the Bolshevik hangmen and their offers of amnesty. He read this fresh appeal:

Brother Peasant

The Russian stampede has made a mockery of our sacred Motryn Monastery. The godless soviet Antichrists have taken the church bells that unite us with God's voice and summon us to struggle against the Muscovite torrent. They have brutally violated the sisters of this sacred place, ruined God's church and burned the bell tower. However, retribution for these acts will not pass them by, for the punishment of the Lord and the vengeance of our weapons awaits them.

Brother Peasant, do not delay, slay the evil Muscovites whenever you can. Let he who is still strong enough to hold arms go to the forest. Don't believe the promises of the Muscovites and the mercantile ones who sell out Christ. Do not lay your neck under the katsap yoke. Our biggest rebellion is ahead. A new flame will shine forth from Kholodnyi Yar. Glory to Ukraine!

Otaman Raven

Ptitsyn ran his eyes over the appeal, while sitting on the stool and facing the door, and recollected some lines from the operational guidance. *Raven is an extremely subtle and unpredictable enemy noted for his great cruelty, even towards his own men.* He also recalled how he had arrived at Kremenchuk on the train from Kharkiv and seen a placard on the platform. It depicted a huge, black bird that bore a tiny Red Army soldier in its beak and one twisted in its talons. The inscription below the image had read, *'Your enemy is merciless towards you. Avenge yourself on him'.* Ptitsyn had never seen a more stupid example of political agitation. The artist had been impelled by the desire to amuse those bandit otamans, who loved to adopt such pseudonyms as Eagle, Buzzard, Raven and Hawk. He had glorified the hapless Red Army soldiers by depicting them falling, like feeble poultry, into the rebels' claws.

Well, this piece of work from the provincial draughtsman was not surprising, but where were those who looked over the scene from behind the propaganda and had reserved this work? Which way was the *Cheka* looking? The placards had only been removed after Ptitsyn's reprimand.

His thoughts again turned to the monastery bells. Even though they had been removed, it followed that there was no certainty they would not ring again and this discovery proved that the rebels still posed a threat. His temples again throbbed with the thought. He knew that it was necessary to do something decisive about this underground printer, but there was no need to hurry now, it was worth waiting until morning or longer. Maybe it was worth keeping this building under surveillance and then dealing with the whole of this subversive organisation at once. The impudence of them, setting up a printing operation right under his bed. Well, they would have a printer and they would have their 'new flame' all right, he thought.

Ptitsyn thought about which of the barrels it would be best to place near the trapdoor so he could return to his room, but realised he could not leave the cellar without leaving a trace of his presence. He could not leap high enough to grab the sides of the opening and haul himself up, and if he moved a barrel to stand on, who would put it back in its place? He would have to deal with the printing operation in the morning.

Suddenly, he heard a noise. He pricked up his ears as the sound of quiet footsteps came from behind the door, and the bolt squeaked as it was drawn back. He drew back the safety catch on his revolver and held it in his outstretched hand at eye-level.

5

Even though many bands and their leaders have handed over themselves for amnesty, the situation remains volatile. Dozens of organisations and mobs refuse to lay down their weapons. In the Chyhyryn and Cherkassy districts alone there are a few thousand bandits with a strikingly nationalistic tinge. It is necessary to considerably expand the network of informants and secret employees by recruiting people from those granted amnesty. These are people who have a good knowledge of the situation and can contact the bandits as and when necessary. It is suggested that the chairman of the district Cheka, Comrade Mozdrevych, moves immediately to strengthen the information gathering apparatus of the Chyhyryn district by using resources from other areas and recruiting new agents.

The morale and military efficiency of the Red Army units leaves much to be desired. It is necessary to bring a halt to the violence inflicted on the peaceful citizens because this provokes a hostile attitude from the local population.

During the winter period, because of the problem of water freezing in machine guns and the lack of glycerine, it is suggested that the machine-gunners are given spirit. To prevent them from drinking it, poison will be added.

Government Division Commander of the 21st Division, Poniedielin
Military Brigade Commander, Yegorov
Staff Commander Shelkman

From the order to the Kremenchuk government division, 26 November 1921

Mudei walked with soundless steps. It was apparent that the equine rascal was dreaming because he did not usually walk at such a lazy pace. Raven held back on the reins, unsure in which direction he should turn the horse. He wished he had been able to return to his nest in Lebedynskyi Forest sooner. He wanted to see which of his boys had escaped unscathed from the confused battle near Starosillia and to make his presence known so he could dispel the rumour that he was dead. Dosia had not believed in the evidence laid before her when she had seen he was alive, and in her delight she had made a gift of her cap to him. He remembered the cap, with its fragrance of wild orchids and fumes of incense, Dosia and the night that had passed. She was a real lascivious minx.

The road to Lebedynskyi Forest was before him, but a desire to make an excursion around Kholodnyi Yar overcame him. He could, perhaps, cast an eye over 'Old Motryn', as the partisans called the monastery, and see if the lone wolves, those rebels who had no family home in which to pass the winter, had gathered there.

Raven had not asked Dosia where the rebels were constructing their underground networks for this winter. They would need to dig new ones after some otamans had broken cover and more than a few Cossacks had sought amnesty. Those rebels who would not pass the winter underground did not need to know the locations. Indeed, someone might catch a bullet just for being interested in them, even if they meant no harm. Perhaps Dosia did not know where the Kholodnyi Yar rebels were going to ground for the winter or, the devil, maybe she did know. What kind of being was she that she was able, during one night, to be in Kholodnyi Yar and the Irdyn Marsh, in the house of blind Yevdosia? She had left no trace of her presence. Raven could not see the hoof prints left by her horse, though she had passed over the snow and the marsh with him. There was only the wild and bitter fragrance that still lingered on his lips and in the folds of her cap.

He took out his tobacco pouch and rolled a fat cigarette with the same tobacco Vovkulaka had given him not long before the battle at Starosillia. It was good weed that warmed his body deep inside. Raven still had some because he had not smoked for over a month, indeed since before Yevdosia had brought him back from the other world of death. He struck a match and drew deeply on his cigarette, feeling a pleasant, buoyant dizziness. He was no longer accustomed to the rich smoke of the home-grown leaves but he wanted to break the sinful spirit of that enchanted night.

He thought about Cossack Vovkulaka, who knew good tobacco, the nocturnal fires and the secrets of death. Raven already knew that a secret, which would not let him sleep, was hidden in Vovkulaka from the time when he was in Hryzlo's unit.

Not long ago, when they had gathered for another 'tour of wealthy villages' with their red flag, Vovkulaka had confided in Raven as they were sitting by the fire. It was as if he had felt an augury of death and wished to confess.

Vovkulaka's younger brother was the most handsome youth in all Zvenyhorodka. It is sometimes the case that two brothers, or two sisters, resemble each other and are clearly from the same stock, but in this case one was like a beautiful painting and the other was like a godforsaken thing. They said that Vovkulaka had been born at night when the moon darkened and that he had become a being that was only fit to howl at the moon. He loved his younger brother greatly, perhaps even more than he loved himself. He was his nurse, his mother and his protector, and they had joined Hryzlo's squadron together.

Despite being handsome Kuzemko was not a spoiled brat. He knew how to handle a sword, sat on a horse as if he were moulded into the saddle, and was not afraid to stare into the eyes of death. He could have chosen any girl he desired, but he was indifferent to their charms. His spirit was rendered arid with an unworthy passion for a fury of a woman. He fell in love with Tsilia Borukhova, the daughter of Borukh, the owner of the barber's shop by the Vynokur hostelry.

Tsilia was a fascinating, Jewish girl, as slender as a needle, with breasts that looked as if she had borrowed two melons and placed them on her chest. They regularly threatened to burst out of her velvet blouse. Her full lips stretched almost to her ears in a sensuous curve. If you looked into her soft, dark eyes their gaze would pin you helplessly to her skirt, which was the latest fashion, long and woven from fine, blue material.

Kuzemko had barely come of age when Vovkulaka observed his regular visits to the barber's to get his hair, which had just been cut, cut again, and while doing so straining his eyes to catch a glimpse of Tsilia's billowing dress. It was obvious that she had cast a spell on him.

There was one occasion when Borukh was not at the barber's shop and Tsilia, as if joking, had asked Kuzemko to let her cut his tresses. The fool sat in the chair and she threw the apron over him, touched his neck pleasantly with her fingers, and started cutting his hair. Then, unexpectedly, he felt those two springy, soft melons rest on his shoulders and he fell helplessly under her spell. After cutting his hair, she offered to shave him. It was the first time that he had been shaved and he nodded his head meekly, never before realising that the cold touch of a razor on his throat could excite him so much.

He would have never crawled out of the barber's but times changed. The Reds came to Zvenyhorodka, followed by the Germans and the *Hetman's* troops, then Denikin's men, then the *Petliurites* and finally, Budyonny's cavalry rolled through. They had been suddenly thrown into battle towards the Vrangel front in Crimea with orders to gather supplies on their journey through Ukraine. All these armies made demands of the unfortunate Jewish population and the air around their businesses seemed to echo with cries of give, give, give. The situation did not degenerate into an utter pogrom, but feathers flew over the Vynokur hostelry, the Likhter grocery, the Shaievich manufacturers and the Borukh barber's shop, none of which were hampering the troops in anyway.

A time like that rapidly changed people. Kuzemko and Vovkulaka had already joined the ranks of Otaman Hryzlo when a Jewish self-defence brigade, called the Red Hawks, was formed in the town. Tsilia tied a bright red, three-cornered kerchief around her head, changed her blue dress for a rusty green one and her velvet blouse for a leather jacket. She acquired a Mauser and joined the ranks.

Although Perchyk Nykhym was in charge of the brigade he did not enjoy the same authority as Tsilia Borukhova. She was able to force open the doors of the *Cheka* bosses with her knees, as well as those of the military committee and those in charge of the requisitions and the supplies committees. This was easier for her because most of them were not opposed to the idea of crawling under her jacket to check if her breasts were truly as fabulous as the curves of her blouse suggested. But even these ruthless and powerful men were scared witless of Tsilia. When she rode down the main street on her white colt, with patches of black on its hide, people stealthily crossed themselves and turned away because they all knew about her torture house.

In the cellar of Likhter's grocers, where the headquarters of the self-defence brigade was based, Tsilia personally conducted the interrogation of her enemies. They were mainly hostages who had family members in the ranks of the woodland rebels. She would summon someone's father, mother, or sister and issue a simple, unadorned demand - If your son or brother doesn't appear by a certain time, you will be shot. If the rebel did not appear, the hostage was shot in the quarry near Tikych and if the rebel did appear then the hostage was still shot, but they were joined by their renegade son or brother.

Eventually, Kuzemko's mother was summoned to the cellar, but curiously Tsilia only ordered her to call her younger son from the forest; although she knew that both brothers were roaming in the woods with the rebels. Kuzemko, without telling Vovkulaka the true purpose of his trip, journeyed to Zvenyhorodka under the pretence of visiting his mother. He did not utter a word about Tsilia.

Well, not a word means not a word, but he returned to their quarters as if he were drunk. What he had been drinking was not apparent, but it was something unusual; something dark roamed through him, clouding his mind and his heart. Vovkulaka did not know then how Tsilia had led his brother to the cellar underneath Likhter's and, instead of interrogating him, had opened her greedy lips, unbuttoned her jacket, cast off her rose-coloured bloomers and let him stuff her dumpling.

Kuzemko returned to the forest and after a few days had passed he asked if he could go home again to freshen up, change his clothes and visit his family. Hryzlo would often let the men go home if they needed to spruce up, providing there was no urgent work for the Cossacks. He liked his boys to be well groomed and said that everyone needed a stock of clean linen so they did not become infested with lice. However, Kuzemko requested these home visits so frequently that Vovkulaka began to be troubled by dark thoughts about his sibling. He asked his brother how things were at home, but Kuzemko just shrugged his shoulders and said that everything was fine there; the same as usual.

Things soon took a turn for the worse when they were jumped on by a punishment battalion in Popivskyi Forest, but they managed to get away after a struggle. Then the Red Army found them in Demuryne and they had to flee to the Moryntsi ravines. While they were moving from place to place, Hryzlo's squad became surrounded near Topylne.

They came under such a hurricane of fire that it stripped off the bark from the trees, sparks flew close to their eyes and bullets ricocheted off the trunks with a loud crack and flew into the branches. It was like the sky was pouring streams of lead onto their heads. The Reds attacked them with machine guns and grenades, blowing apart trees and ploughing up huge divots of earth in the process. It was an ever decreasing circle of death that only half the Cossacks were able to break out from after scattering into small groups. Kuzemko survived with only a small wound and Vovkulaka saw him with one of his arms bandaged above the elbow.

When they again gathered by Husakove, Hryzlo summoned his officers to one side and informed them that there was a traitor in their ranks, someone who was continuously leading them into the clutches of the Reds. 'We won't be able to find a comfortable, secure place for ourselves until we have exposed him. We need to set up guards around the camp using the Cossacks we have checked carefully. Let no one leave until we sort this out. We need to pay special attention to those men who soon ask permission to leave the forest or try to leave of their own accord.'

The description of what to look for in a traitor left an unpleasant taste in Vovkulaka's mouth, awakening the suspicion that the miscreant was Kuzemko. When he returned to the main camp from the council of senior officers, he found his brother sitting alone, leaning against a tree and re-bandaging his wound. He was gripping one end of the torn linen with his teeth and clumsily winding the other around his wounded right arm with his left hand.

'Why didn't you wait until I was here to help you?' Vovkulaka asked.

'Let it be. It's just a scratch. I'll survive until my wedding day.'

'What? Are you planning to get married?' Vovkulaka looked at him in wonder.

'No, it's just a saying.'

'Did it scrape the bone? Maybe you should go to the doctor's in town and get it checked out.'

'Why do I need a doctor?' Kuzemko responded warily.

'Why? Dr. Filitz would give you a jab, apply some antiseptic ointment and so on. It may yet become infected.'

'Whatever will be, will be,' said Kuzemko. 'But what are you up to?'

'Nothing, I'm just thinking about you. Do you know where Filitz lives? He's between the chemists and the Likhter grocery.'

'Why are you hassling me?' Kuzemko responded angrily.

'Okay, I won't trouble you again. Do what you like. You know best.'

Hryzlo's men did not kindle any fires that night and had a supper of rye bread and *salo* before going to sleep on beds improvised from leafy branches. Vovkulaka was within an arm's length of Kuzemko, but kept one eye open and did not sleep a wink. How could he sleep when he had as good as told Kuzemko that he knew everything and that he should flee before it was too late? Vovkulaka decided it was best to see what happened next, but knew that he needed to know the truth.

It was apparent that Kuzemko knew what Vovkulaka had meant by his earlier remarks and he was still twisting around for a way to escape from the net. Vovkulaka heard his uneven breathing and how he moved or crushed a bug that had tickled him near his ear. However, he did not move until the morning and the event that Vovkulaka was so afraid of did not happen. He began to warm himself with the faint hope that his evil thoughts about his brother had been unfounded.

***

Mudei suddenly quietened his steps, then stood still, only moving his wounded ear to try to catch some sound. Raven also pricked up his ears and heard a vehicle rumbling somewhere in the forest behind them. He moved away from the road and waited until the wagon drew level with him so he could see the passengers. Two mousy-coloured horses were drawing the wagon. An old man in a cap with ear flaps was sitting at the front. At the sides, with their legs over a ladder, holding guns on their laps and shaking as the cart bounced through potholes, were two police officers in greatcoats and berets with red edges. It was obvious they were carrying freight of some kind because there were two wooden receptacles and three bulging sacks on the wagon. Initially, Raven wanted to let them pass unhindered but then reconsidered the situation. It was a long time since he had experienced a merry adventure. Why shouldn't he amuse himself? He might even hear something new.

'Good health to you,' he shouted to welcome them as he emerged from the forest. 'Where are you from and where are you going lads?'

At first the police officers felt drawn towards the locks of their rifles, but they realised this was an idiotic reflex when they saw that Raven was not aiming his rifle at them. They waited tensely to see what would happen next.

'Good health,' said the old man, drawing the reins to himself. 'To Melnyky, from Kamyanka. Where else can I go?'

'And what are you carrying?' Raven asked, curiously looking over the wagon.

'We are taking goods to the cooperative shop,' the oldster explained, as if he were in charge and knew more than the rest of them put together. 'They've opened a new one at our spot and it has no stock yet, so we're taking this salt and sugar,' he said, gesturing towards the sacks with his riding whip. 'In the wooden containers there are bars of soap, matches, cigarettes, etc.'

'If you want to take something you'll have to give us a receipt immediately,' said one of the police officers, speaking with a nasal tone. 'We are the ones responsible for it, not him,' he continued, nodding at the old coachman. 'Chattering away as he does ... matches, cigarettes ...'

'I will talk with you in a respectable way,' said Raven, 'I can't write a receipt because my ink has dried out, but at the moment I won't take anything from you. I just want to ask what's happening at the monastery now?'

'What?' the old man said, again leaping in before the others could speak, and pushing his cap further back on his head with his whip. 'Nothing, you might say is happening there. There are just a handful of sisters left after the serpents scared them off. In truth they say that there are about eight more novices ready to take the veil. It appears that the Episcopal of Cherkasy, Mykolai, gave his consent for this at the request of the abbess.'

'And is there any kind of garrison there?'

'Garrison? There's no one there,' said one of the police officers.

'The anathema who scared off the sisters has moved on and our …' the old fellow turned, blinked at the police officers, and corrected himself. 'The bandits,' he bit his tongue because he knew who was standing before him and realised that he really should not have said anything like that.

'Well, well,' Raven said, feeling encouraged and hiding his smile in his beard. 'Are there any bandits there now?'

'There is no one there now apart from the nuns and the novices with permisson to take the veil,' the old man continued, trying to put his sinful mistake of referring to the bandits as 'ours' further behind him. 'The abbess is still there, and Ivan, the old priest. He doesn't venture past the threshold now.'

'I wasn't asking about them,' Raven interrupted him, looking sharply at the police officers.

'The old man spoke the truth,' confirmed the nasal-voiced man, 'there's none of those or any others there now.'

The second police officer sat and tensed his lips without breathing. His little face was as swollen as a hamster's when it hides food in both cheeks.

'But they will return in spring, don't doubt that,' the old man replied, determinedly thrusting his cap further back on his head with his whip.

'Who will return?' asked the nasal-voiced fellow in confusion.

'Who?' The old guy hesitated, caught in the crossfire and not knowing what to do. 'Whoever needs to do so will return when spring is in the air.'

'Let's go. The horses are freezing,' the nasal voice spoke again when he realised the old fellow was happy to sit and chat until the evening.

'Are you really so kind to animals?' Raven asked, smiling. He was a little disappointed that the chat had been so peaceable.

'I have work to do,' he said menacingly. 'The day is short now and we don't have time to waffle on.'

There was no need for him to speak like that. Raven wanted

to say goodbye but he did not like the tone this man had adopted, 'So, you're not going to treat me hospitably now?' he said, changing the angle of his rifle.

'Well, it's started ...'

'I won't pass up the chance of a few smokes.'

Nasal reached into one of the receptacles and pulled out two packets of coarse tobacco. 'Here you are. You've probably not smoked anything like this before, it's Kremenchuk Vosmorka.'

'No, I haven't,' agreed Raven, 'neither have my boys. What will you give us? Is that for two smokes? Give me ten more.'

The police officer reached into one of the receptacles and counted out eight more packs.

'You're a miserable miser. I said ten, and more matches.'

'I have to hand over a list of these items,' he mewed. 'What will I say when some are missing?'

'What you always say. Bandits robbed you, and thank God that there is an old man with you or I would take everything and the wagon. I have to return to my boys with gifts. Give me soap so that we can wash the ropes when we hang the Muscovite toadies.'

Raven packed the tobacco, matches and soap in his saddlebag. He took a packet of roubles from his pocket. 'Are your lot still using this crap?'

'But what?' The nasal one looked warily at Raven. 'Well, there was hryvnia and we use this too, but it circulates in millions because of inflation.'

'This should be enough for you.' Raven held out the packet of banknotes and the nasal man, after hesitating for a second, seized them fearfully.

'Well, if it's so, why?'

'You have seen and heard nothing.' Raven looked merrily at the 'hamster'. He leaned forward and pulled down the police beret over his nose, 'Do you understand?'

The 'hamster' coughed weirdly. He opened his mouth and a few seeds fell out. 'Move along now,' he said to the wagon driver.

When the wagon had travelled for about thirty yards, Raven cupped his hands around his mouth and bellowed after the old man, 'They will return in spring. Do you hear me, Dad? They will certainly return.'

The old man heard him and he pushed back his cap still further with the end of his whip and shook it, as if giving some special sign.

Raven unwrapped a packet of tobacco and smoked. It was not Bakun, but it produced a nicotine infused fog. He turned his horse around. If there were only the sisters living in 'Old Motryn', then why go there? Without hesitation he steered Mudei in the direction of Zhabotyn with the intention of going past there and heading for Smila. It was a long journey, but he did not have any more adventures planned so he should be in Lebedyn by the evening. He rolled another fat cigarette with the tobacco that Vovkulaka had given him and took two long, richly-flavoured drags. He soon felt a soft fog circle through his head.

***

So, let us finish the tale about Kuzemko. He did not gather himself to flee from the camp, although Vovkulaka had more or less told him many times that he knew where he was going so frequently and why he was going there. Vovkulaka would later be tortured by the thought that he had incited his brother to escape.

The next evening he saw that things were going badly for Kuzemko. His wounded arm, which was now bandaged and in a sling, was turning blue, and the poor wretch's teeth were chattering due to the fever.

'Hey, brother,' said Vovkulaka, 'you're burning up, get to Filitz quickly, you don't want to lose your arm, or possibly your life.'

Kuzemko hesitated, 'No, no,' he said, 'it's changing, you'll see, I'll be much better in the morning.'

Vovkulaka ran to Hryzlo to tell him that his brother had a fever and needed to go to the doctor's because it looked bad for him. Hryzlo ordered him to go immediately, but again Kuzemko was immovable, 'I'm not going and that's the end of it.'

'Well, I'll drag you there,' said Vovkulaka. 'I'll tie you like a sheaf and take you to Filitz or to the devil, but I won't let you die here.'

'You don't believe me,' said Kuzemko regretfully. 'You want to take me under guard to the doctor.'

'As you please, just get a move on,' replied Vovkulaka.

His brother, shaking with fever, said, 'Just come with me to the edge of the forest and I will make my own way from there.'

Kuzemko was barely able to get his foot in the stirrup, so Vovkulaka helped him mount the horse and they went as far as the edge of the forest before they parted. Vovkulaka produced a gold, ten rouble coin, on which there was an image of the Russian Tsar Nicholas II, from the lining of his coat. He pushed it roughly into Kuzemko's hand. 'Give Filitz my regards. Let him give you a jab, clean and bandage the wound, and then you need to lie in the attic at home for a few days.'

They separated and after a few days had passed, Vovkulaka asked Hryzlo about going to see how things were with his brother, 'My spirit is troubled with unease. I'll jump to it and be there and back in a flash, once I've found out if he's alive or if Filitz needed to amputate his arm.'

'Go,' said Hryzlo without hesitation.

Vovkulaka saddled his steed and rushed to Zvenyhorodka, which was about ten *versts* away. He travelled stealthily, passing through Vilkhivets and Ozirna and going down to Hnylyi Tikych. To pass unnoticed he used the willows that dotted the meadows for cover and eventually arrived in his own village of Pisky. The August night was almost fluorescent. There was no moon, but the heavens were strewn with so many stars that he could see for many *versts*.

There was a secluded spot in Pisky, near a birch tree and a modestly sized barn, which seemed as if it did not belong to anyone, even though it was always full of hay that had been gathered from the nearby meadows. Vovkulaka had spent the night there several times. On this occasion, however, it was obvious that the barn was already occupied because he saw two saddled horses, standing motionless, near the structure. Vovkulaka wanted to stay away from the place so he could avoid an encounter with potentially dangerous strangers, but something held him back and he did not know what. It was an unpleasant sensation that gripped him; a foreboding of evil like that which had grumbled in his soul when he had said farewell to Kuzemko. It coiled tightly around his chest. He first saw a colt, which was white with dark swatches, before recognising his brother's crow-black steed. He tied his horse to a weathered willow sapling that was near the haystacks, but he was unsure what to do next. That is to say he did not know where to begin because he was afraid of what he would find and what would happen. An invisible force was pushing him in the back whispering, 'Go on, go on, you knew about this long ago.'

Vovkulaka approached the doors of the barn. The colt and his brother's black horse turned their heads towards him and one of them snorted quietly. Although it was midnight it seemed to him that everything was clearly visible because of the extraordinary luminescence of the August stars. The more brightly the light glittered off the pale bark of the birch, the greater the darkness in his heart became.

The doors of the barn would not open because they were bolted on the inside. Vovkulaka was pleased that he had a little time to think and that the moment for decisive action would come later. He turned away from the barn and sat under the stack where his horse had already begun to munch hay. He took a grass stalk and chewed it while he meditated. Maybe he could wait until morning when someone would emerge from the barn, but he was not the type of man who could sit and wait. Before it was light he might end up in an unforeseen predicament and, as a soldier of the night, he did not like to undertake any action during daylight that could be accomplished under the cover of darkness. Banging at the door and calling his brother would also be stupid because he did not know if the doors would be opened or who would open them.

There was only one thing he could do, pull apart the thatch on the roof, steal quietly into the barn and then see what there was to see. The whole purpose of night is to frighten drowsy chickens on their perches. He considered setting fire to the barn to see who ran out, but that would cause a commotion, the Red Hawks would run to the blaze and Vovkulaka would not have the chance to talk to his brother, and he had something very important to say to him. Otherwise it would have been easy to wedge the doors shut from the outside, strike a match, leap on his horse and let everything burn to oblivion.

Vovkulaka reflected on his options as he chewed on the grass stalk. He was getting ready to go to the barn, to undo the sheaves and pile the straw against its wall, and was considering which side would be the most suitable for his purposes, when he heard someone scrabbling around inside. He barely had time to run and hide around the corner of the building before someone came outside. He took out his gun and looked along the barrel with one eye. His lower jaw hung open and his thirty-two vulpine teeth shone with a pale blue nimbus against the night sky. What he saw next turned him into a pillar of ice and froze his soul.

Tsilia came out of the barn. Her leather jacket was slung over her naked body. Her long hair cascaded over her full breasts, which swung slightly and were painted a soft, blue tone by the night. He noticed that below the waist she was wearing only rose-coloured bloomers that were short and scant. Vovkulaka had never seen anything like them. It had never occurred to him that women dressed like that. When Tsilia raised her arms and stretched sweetly, her jacket rose from her body. It seemed to him, for a second, that her pants would also fly from her, but no, the next moment she pulled them down to her knees and revealed her swollen pudenda covered with glittering hair. She squatted and a sinewy stream rustled so loudly that the black and white colt and his brother's black horse raised their heads and pricked up their ears. Perhaps they thought a viper was rustling in the grass.

Vovkulaka was confused. He did not know how to conduct himself in this situation. He knew that looking was shameful, but turning away was stupid. Tsilia, oblivious to his presence, sent her stream warbling into the grass for what seemed an eternity. It was as if she were trying to flood a gopher out of its hole. Eventually, she pulled up her drawers as Vovkulaka waited motionlessly. He was still uncertain what to do. She went to the doors and opened them a little. Vovkulaka leaped on her and clasped his left hand over her mouth, which was so large he could barely cover it with his palm. With his right hand he held his gun against her belly and pushed her before him as he entered the barn. Tsilia was unable to comprehend what evil power held her in its clutches.

'Good evening, brother,' said Vovkulaka, who could hardly breathe when he saw Kuzemko by the weak radiance of the gaslight.

He was sitting next to a pillow, on a sheet covering the straw, and was naked except for a blanket that covered him to his waist. But this was not what shocked Vovkulaka, he already knew he would find his brother here; he had known since he saw the black steed tethered by the barn. What stunned him was something else, so terrifying and incomprehensible that he was not able to gather his wits to comprehend it. Kuzemko, his handsome brother, looked at him with surprise. He showed no fear. It was more a look of resignation that Vovkulaka saw in his anguished eyes, as if he knew that his brother would eventually come and find him. A Browning laid by his side, next to Tsilia's Mauser, which peeked out of its holster, but Kuzemko did not move towards either of them, he just looked sadly at his brother who was holding Tsilia in his powerful embrace. Then Vovkulaka realised what was incomprehensible. What had astonished him when he had seen Kuzemko. It was as if he had been stabbed in the chest and it stopped him breathing. Kuzemko's bare right arm bore no bandage and there was no sling. It was as strong, suntanned and slender as his healthy, muscular left arm.

Tsilia let out a cry from the depths of her soul. She could barely move, but she wriggled in Vovkulaka's embrace and tried to break free. He gripped her mouth more forcefully because this fury would not prevent him from saying to his brother what he wanted to say, 'What's this brother? Have your friends helped you?'

Kuzemko was silent. He gulped and beseeched, 'Just don't kill her.'

Vovkulaka aimed the Colt and fired. Kuzemko's body jerked and then lay prone on the sheet that was now soaked with blood. The bullet had hit him straight between the eyes. Vovkulaka released Tsilia, threw her within an arm's length of Kuzemko, and fired again. Then he lit a match and ignited some dry straw before freeing the colt and his brother's crow-black steed.

When he reached Ozirianska Hill and looked back there was such a ferocious fire roaring through the birch trees that its crimson lustre illuminated his face. He watched with his long, vulpine fangs exposed and it was difficult to know whether he was laughing, crying, or in shock.

'Well, OK,' said Raven, as he pulled a baked potato from the embers of the fire, 'he would have been able to bandage a healthy hand to fool you into thinking he was wounded, but how could it have turned blue. If the hand was OK, what caused his fever?'

'Treachery. It is treachery,' protested Vovkulaka, 'cunning and inventive. If you live an honest life it would never occur to you to think in that way, but when you begin to twist and turn you make things up as you please.'

'Maybe he could have stained his hand using elderberry or something?'

'I don't know whether it was lilac or something else blue. Maybe that whore provided him with some device we don't know about, and maybe some sort of powder to make his teeth chatter.'

'Well, if you really want to you can make your teeth chatter without using anything,' said Raven.

'I don't know what was going on, however, I can swear to it that she conceived this scheme and persuaded him to collaborate with her. But how? I am indifferent now. Such indifference has settled in me here.' Vovkulaka touched his chest. 'It is as if I am bearing a huge rock in my heart. There was a time when I yearned to weep but I could not. Perhaps you can explain this to me, you are a literate, educated man, with more than a smattering of science if truth be told.'

'Science,' said Raven, shrugging his shoulders. 'After agricultural school my father sent me to Moscow to study mathematics, but what use is it now?'

'Well, I can ask you, as a learned man, what causes someone to shed tears? Why can one person pour them forth like shelling peas while another can shed none?'

'I can't tell you about that,' said Raven, bowing his head, 'however, I know for sure that you cannot weigh agony by the volume of tears someone sheds, just as there is no way that you can measure delight. But should we worry our heads with this? It's better that you tell me how you explained things to Hryzlo.'

'What?' asked Vovkulaka tensely.

'That your brother was never coming back.'

Vovkulaka stirred the fire with a stick. He was silent for a moment and then said, 'I lied to him for the first time. You cannot imagine how hard it was for me to do, but one lie soon leads to another. I told Hryzlo that my brother was ambushed by the Red Hawks and that he had been able to dispatch a commissar into the next life before they dealt with him.'

'And Hryzlo believed you?'

'I don't know, but no one apart from me knew the truth. I live by truth in this world,' said Vovkulaka, blinking his scorched lashes. 'That was the first time I felt the need to lie.' He extracted a potato from the coals and began to clean it. The skin on Vovkulaka's hands was so hardened that it was impervious to heat. 'Don't be angry Otaman, but I speak truly to you. That is the reason why I left Hryzlo and joined your unit. It had become hard for me to look him in the eyes, and I wanted to get as far away from home as possible. There is no door open for me there now.'

'There was no need,' said Raven. 'You ...'

'It's not necessary to try to make me feel better,' said Vovkulaka. 'I simply wanted to share with you the burden that I am tired of carrying alone. I wanted to tell the whole truth.' Vovkulaka again stirred the coals, sending crimson ripples of light scampering over his face, 'Tell me this Otaman, if the human spirit does not perish, why does no one ever give us a sign from the world after death? Do you know?'

'No.'

'I think that when the soul does not die it must speak, even if only to its relatives to give them hope. Could the soul become deaf to what happens in this life? It cannot be so and because of this I think that some entity prevents spirits from speaking to us. Someone forbids them.'

'Correct,' said Raven. 'Humanity may not know everything. There must be some great secret of life and death or all things lose meaning and substance.'

'No, that's not correct,' Vovkulaka disputed. 'I need to know. Remember Otaman, if you are not opposed to the idea, when I perish, when I die ...'

'What, are you getting ready to die?'

'Well, hypothetically. When the time comes, when I no longer exist, I promise you that, if you are not against the idea ... I promise you …'

'Well, just say it without promising,' said Raven smiling.

Vovkulaka leaned towards him and whispered quietly, as if he was afraid to eavesdrop on himself, 'I will give you a sign from the other world.'

'But what?'

'I cannot say yet, for in truth I do not know how it will be. However, you will certainly know who it is that calls to you. So you will see.'

Chapter 5

1

Hannusia had not visited the village recently because she could no longer listen to the fanciful rumours about Veremii and was afraid of people's prying eyes. It was apparent, even to a blind man, that she was carrying a child. Once she would have been proud of her swollen belly. She would have mixed with people deliberately to show them the sign of her womanhood, but now she knew that it was better to hide her pregnancy.

One day Tanasykha, who was deceptively agile for her years, flew into their house. She was wringing her hands over her breast, swinging her head, which was wrapped in three scarves, from side to side and lamenting as she crossed the threshold, 'They have borne him. Borne Veremii into the village.'

Hannusia and her mother-in-law both felt faint and stared at Tanasykha. They failed to understand her words.

'They have brought him here. Dead,' said Tanasykha, and pronounced sonorously, as if she were standing over his coffin, 'his poor, cold hands and bare, lifeless feet will no longer trample across blue cowslips ...'

'Where have they taken him?' Hannusia interrupted her.

'Where?' Tanasykha blinked her dry eyes, 'Through the village on a sleigh, to show everyone that he has been slain. They were shouting, "Go and take pleasure in your bandit" and "How fearsome and gallant he is now." They have almost reached our street.'

After quickly putting on their outdoor clothes, Hannusia and her mother-in-law ran out of the house. Tanasykha followed in their wake as she pronounced, 'Oh, you are travelling a distant road, our falcon, to where the wind does not howl, the sun does not warm, birds do not sing and stars do not shine.'

The body had been laid on a sleigh to which some good, sturdy horses were harnessed. It had bare feet and a bare head, but the body was clothed in a bloodstained shirt and underpants. To show, more convincingly, that this was Veremii's body, a straw hat had been placed near him.

Although the ground was gripped by frost, the sleigh was smeared with dung, as if it had been recently used for carrying manure. The corpse was on the bare boards without even a wisp of straw as token comfort. His head was lolling over the back of the conveyance, so that if the dead man had opened his eyes he would have seen an upside down view of the curious crowd trailing behind him. By his side there was a tablet on which was inscribed - *Otaman Veremii - This fate awaits every bandit!*

The driver, a member of the committee of poor peasants, who was as swollen as a well-gorged owl, was sitting on the sleigh and at either side marched two Red Army soldiers, like guards of honour. From time to time, the peasant shouted, just as Tanasykha had said, 'Go and take pleasure in your bandit. See how fearsome and gallant he is now.'

Several curious people had poured onto the street and some followed the sleigh, not wanting to miss this novel site. People came from their gardens and all, whether they were close by or further away, looked over the slain man, trying to work out if it was Veremii or just someone who resembled him. They initially followed the body with their gaze, then bowed their heads in silence. How long can you spend trying to recognise a badly beaten corpse that had lain for God knows how long on the frost?

Hannusia and Veremii's mother ran to the sleigh and looked at the body for a long time. No, no, this was not their Yarko. Hannusia recognised the same man she had been shown at Matusiv, but she knew she needed to weep for the dead man in front of other people so she did not arouse suspicion. Fortunately Tanasykha mourned for the unknown man in a way that rendered superfluous any show of grief from Hannusia. She ran after the procession, as if on cue, pushing aside people who stood in her way. She approached the sleigh, bent low over the partisan, wrung her hands on her breast and lamented in a weak, anguished voice, 'Oh, our son, child, it would have been better if we had looked on you in war rather than dispatching you into that distant murk of death. Already the orchards will bloom without you, the cuckoo will call, the nightingales will warble sweetly and we will be crushed by anguish.'

Tanasykha lamented over the slain man with such anguish

120

that it not only caused Hannusia and Veremii's mother to weep but all the women gazing over the sleigh. The men doffed their caps and the children became silent. 'Where will we look for you now, our falcon? In the mountains and valleys or in your burial mound? In a deep ravine or a distant country?'

The obese poor peasant and Red Army guards began to exchange glances. It was not meant to be like this. They were bearing the corpse of the slain otaman through the village to terrify people and hold him up to scorn, but instead this affair was developing into a proper ceremony. It was as if they were simply bringing him to his native village so that everyone could pay their respects to him as he travelled on his last road.

Suddenly, one of the armed guards walking by the sleigh gathered his wits. He leaped towards Tanasykha, grabbed her by the shoulders and wrenched her so violently that she rolled head over heels in the snow.

'Stop this counter-agitation!'

The Reds and the fat poor peasant whipped the horses with such wrath that flayed stripes of skin started to swell on their gleaming croups. The horses broke into a gallop and took the guards towards the neighbouring village of Zelena Dibrova, in compliance with their orders that Veremii's corpse should be displayed in all the villages in the area.

Tanasykha rose slowly, shook the snow from her clothes and, seeing how rapidly the sleigh moved into the distance, announced in a despairing voice, 'Oh, who have you abandoned us to? To what unknown country do you journey? A dark and cold country where there is no sound of bells or human voices.'

She lamented and spoke with such despair that a nearby raven was almost disturbed. He had been sitting on a chimney for a while to watch the proceedings. The dry heat it exhaled tickled his plumage pleasantly. He felt he could quite easily remain seated until the arrival of night. The raven loved to watch funerals; he regarded them with blissful indifference, but something here made his eyes fill up as if, in his dotage, he had acquired the ability to empathise.

The raven was not unduly preoccupied with any feeling of grief and it was really the smoke from the chimney that made his eyes water. He looked through a screen of tears at the sleigh bearing the lifeless body of the familiar partisan into the neighbouring village. The raven knew of him and knew too that the reds were taking the corpse into the area from where the dead man had hailed. He knew that the foresters would steal the corpse of their comrade and lay him to rest as they pleased. Whenever the raven predicted how things would pan out he was never wrong.

2

The field staff of the secret police, led by Comrade Mykhailov, have managed to persuade 76 bandits to hand themselves in for amnesty. They achieved this success following intense espionage work and the expansion of a network of informers. All were members of the Kholodnyi Yar insurrectionist committee and included Petrenko, Temnyi and Chuchupaka. The biographies of these atamans is typical, they are former Petliurite officers and teachers. Some were even members of the Tsarist bodyguard, who despite their imperial past support their 'native mother' Ukraine with all their hearts and souls. All are literate and well educated. It is necessary to state that, judging by appearances, the atamans are in a bad way; their clothes are shabby and they are physically drained. Any criminal act in their environment was punished in the most severe way, which included execution.

In Kholodnyi Yar there are smaller, individual gangs pursuing extremely criminal objectives. They are of various nationalities, including Russians, Saratovians, Uralians and Siberians. Many are deserters from the Red Army. There is a resentful element which owes allegiance to no social class and will disappear of its own accord after the general improvement of conditions in Kholodnyi Yar. Nevertheless, the facts expose their adventurous and most insurrectionist nature.

According to intelligence sources, gold

and diamonds to the value of hundreds of millions of roubles are buried in the woods. We are attempting to locate these caches.

As a rule, the bandits refuse to leave their native areas. Therefore it is strongly suspected that amnesty is simply a temporary respite, compelled by their harsh circumstances. It is anticipated that they will subsequently continue the struggle.

From the report of the clandestine information section under the authority of the council of people's commissars in the Ukrainian Soviet Socialist Republic, No. 154

The temperate, early arrival of spring 1921 gave us added strength and inflamed our hopes. As early as the beginning of March the sun burned with such heat that the melting snow fell from the trees in drops and stitched the sparse, white covering on the earth with holes. The partisan movement awoke with the forest after the long silence of winter. The lone wolves, who always dwelt in the forest, revived. The other rebels, who wintered in their village homes, returned and our ranks were swelled with new members. We struck the commune right between its satanic horns again, carving up Red Army units and striking like thunderbolts amidst soviet institutions, sugar refineries and supply posts. We acquired arms, provisions, clothes and general items. We successfully undertook a number of joint operations with the otamans Khmara, Zaharodnii and Honta-Lyutyi.

But what happened next? Well, the Bolsheviks quickly licked clean their wounds and swelled the ranks of their punishment squads, while our forces declined in number and strength. The Ukrainians beyond our border did not hurry to help because the realisation of their promise of the return of our army was severely restrained by the coils of Polish barbed wire behind which our soldiers were interned.

The disbelief in the success of our struggle stole into our hearts again. It is hard to believe that some of the people who handed themselves in for amnesty included the otamans Petrenko, Dzyhar and Oleksa Chuchupaka, Vasyl's youngest brother. They were all met by a military orchestra in Zhabotyn, where the 'Internationale' played, and the lost sheep of our groups were greeted by the Kremenchuk *Chekists*, Kerkener and Mikhailov. Only our 'friend', Ptitsyn, was absent.

***

When he heard the latch squeal, Ptitsyn raised the Luger in his outstretched hand to eye-level, but the very next second he was ashamed at such haste. A beautiful girl was standing in the entrance to the cellar. It was the girl who came to him every night, albeit only in his daring fantasies. He had not seen her for real before, but she was just as he had imagined her, young, fresh and virginal, with meek, but fiery, eyes. She did not enter in a white shift, like in his dreams, instead she wore a short overcoat even though it was clement summer weather outdoors. It was clear that she had equipped herself to spend a long time in the cellar.

'Good evening,' the girl greeted him, peering slowly down the slender barrel of the Luger.

Ptitsyn lowered the gun steadily, 'Goo … ood …'

'How did you happen to be here?' she asked, as if she had not seen the open trapdoor overhead.

'By chance.'

'And what are you doing here?' She asked her absurd questions in the heat of the moment.

'It's simple curiosity,' replied Ptitsyn, while containing himself. He approached her, looked through the door to check if anyone was there and shut it firmly. 'You are alone?' he asked in Russian. 'Enter. To tell the truth I didn't expect to see you.'

'What comes next?'

'What next? Sit in your usual place and we will talk.'

She went to the table and sat on the stool with her face towards him.

'This is your work?' He indicated the typewriter with a flick of his eyes.

'Yes, it's mine.'

'Why are you doing this?'

'Because I hate you.'

'You are too young to understand what hate is. Someone set you to work on this. Who was it?'

'I did it myself.'

'I don't believe you. Somebody gave you this typewriter and this text and made you type these leaflets, didn't he? You did it because somebody made you.'

'I don't understand what you are saying.'

'You don't understand Russian?'

'I don't understand everything.'

Ptitsyn searched for other words and asked again, 'Who ordered you to print these letters?'

'No one. I did it myself.'

Ptitsyn noticed that her whole body was trembling. He thought that this must be a terrifying situation for her, extremely terrifying, and she was trying, with all her might, to restrain herself and conceal the cold shivers that raced through her body.

'What are you going to do with me?'

'I don't know. I am obliged to arrest you.'

'Then what are you waiting for?'

'I don't believe you,' said Ptitsyn. 'You should tell me the whole truth. Maybe then I will help you.'

Ptitsyn was quite certain that something unusual was at work here. Something long forgotten and inopportune at a moment like this, but beyond his control. It was the same feeling he had known as a youth, when he first touched a girl. It was a feeling that roused something in him, summoning a powerful, masculine force. It had not visited him for a long time when he was in the presence of women, but it awoke suddenly and the more he tried not to think about it, the more it made itself known. This girl, with her terrified and beautiful face, was in his hands; he would be able to do with her as he pleased, but he did not know how to take matters further. He instinctively drew close to her, lowered himself into a squatting position, and looked deeply into her fearful eyes. 'What is your name?'

'Yulia.'

'Such a beautiful name. Listen, Yulia, we will put everything in order. It's wrong that such a beautiful girl should lose her life in such an idiotic and futile way because of a silly misunderstanding. Those who made you do this thoughtless act should be held responsible. Do you understand me?'

She nodded. It seemed that after her sudden fear, which had called forth involuntary aggression, the girl had calmed down. He put the Luger in his belt and took her hands in his. They were very cold.

'Who ordered you to print these letters?' Ptitsyn asked, surprised that she did not resist.

'Raven.'

'Personally?'

'Yes,' she said, looking to the side of Ptitsyn.

'So, he came into this house today?'

'Yes, he came here. I am afraid of him.'

'Has he threatened you?'

'No, but he did murder his former colleagues after they left the forest.'

'Don't be afraid of anything, I will protect you. Poor girl.' He caressed her hair. He felt sorry for her and was prepared to do many things on her behalf. 'I will protect you, Yulia. I won't let anyone hurt you.'

She did not refrain from showing her tenderness towards him. Ptitsyn stood, rooted to the spot when she lowered her head onto his shoulder. 'I want to live,' she said, sobbing.

'Of course, of course you will live.' Ptitsyn again caressed her hair, inhaling its delicate aroma, which was the fragrance of grass.

'Really? You are not deceiving me?' She raised her head and looked at him with her meek eyes.

'Of course not Yulia. Of course not.'

Suddenly her gaze glided past him. She grew tense and cast her eyes towards the door, 'It seems as if someone is there.'

Ptitsyn took the Luger from his belt, went to the door, listened and then threw it open, 'There is no one here, calm down,' he said, closing the door.

A little irritated that he had released her from what was almost an embrace, he returned quickly and saw a strange smile trembling on her lips. It stretched wider and wider and then she laughed loudly and flashed her white teeth. Although nonplussed, he grew tense as he failed to comprehend the reason for her mirth. The thought that

126

she was laughing at his masculine indecisiveness flashed through his mind.

'And you also are not very gallant,' she said, sobbing with her nervous laughter, 'you ran to the door immediately.'

He was confused and while he was standing, wondering about the fear of which she spoke, she suddenly stretched out her hand to him. The wrist turned upwards, as if she were playing a children's game and she was secretly giving him a thimble.

'Take it.'

She did this so quickly and spontaneously that he did not notice what was in his palm. He thought it was just a trifle or a curio and did not have the chance to reflect that his hand was wrapped around something heavy, cold and larger than a substantial potato.

'Raven sends you this,' she said.

He looked down and just had the chance to see the pin from the grenade in her other hand.

***

Our ranks diminished rather than increased and we no longer even considered ways of reversing this. We kept watch for provocateurs that had been sent to join our units, and were afraid of the treachery that closed around us ever more tightly. What is there to say about the informers who had been enlisted from our former soldiers, considering that entire Bolshevik units appeared and pretended to be partisans? They travelled around the villages asking the courageous to join the struggle against the commune and then killed those who went with them in the nearest forest. Dereza's squad were particularly frightening because they had been formed using the turncoats from our ranks who had gone to serve in the *Cheka*. These mongrels, who knew our language and slogans, did a large amount of harm before we followed their trail to Murzynskyi Forest.

Dereza was ruddy faced and healthy, and often had a curved pipe in his mouth. He had conducted propaganda in the village of Murzyntsi and had led seven young men into the forest where they waited for someone to seat them on horses. These boys were the three Momot brothers from the village, and four others who were their

127

second and third cousins. In Murzyntsi half the village was called Momot. All seven men had similar facial features, swarthy and round, each with a nose like a duck's beak, and glittering eyes.

Dereza put them on the horses that he kept specially for new recruits and, drawing on his pipe, led the squad to its forest *sich*. The new recruits would barely have time to recover from such happiness before they met the death that awaited them. However, soon after they had entered the forest Red Army troops charged out of the undergrowth and surrounded them. The Momot family were the most scared. Their seven round faces stretched and became sombre and long as the colour drained from their swarthy complexions, and their noses grew sharp and cadaverous. They had not yet borne arms and would lose their lives in vain.

Dereza was relaxed. He drew on his reins and said hoarsely, in Russian, as the pipe fell from his mouth, 'Stand to, we are yours. Don't shoot.'

Nobody was about to shoot. The riders encircled Dereza's squad in an ever tightening noose and only then, as they encroached ever closer, did anxiety grip his heart. The uniforms of the Red Army soldiers and their unshaven faces aroused an unconscious fear in him. Every moment was crucial now. In a few seconds he would realise the meaning of the foreboding that was beating in his breast.

'Drop your weapons or we will shoot,' I ordered.

'You will answer for that with your head,' Dereza said, still threatening us. He looked haughty, but his commander's honour was extinguished. He drew his revolver from its holster and threw it on the ground.

After that his entire squad, as if on command, threw their weapons down. We would, thank God, have these trophies as well as the horses. Yes, fifteen serpent-lithe steeds, if you included those on which the seven stunned members of the Momot family were now seated. The poor wretches had no weapons to throw at our feet and could not comprehend what was happening, but only stared vacuously through their terrified eyes.

'And now dismount,' I barked and, when all these godforsaken *Chekists* slithered off their horses, said in our Ukrainian tongue, 'Now, self-appointed comrades, we will lead you to a complete clarification

128

of your present circumstances.'

Dereza was overwhelmed by fear. His red face froze and grew motley with pallid blotches, and his lips jerked. The *Chekist* wanted to say something, but his tongue would not obey him, it had swollen and become so numb with fear that he was unable to move it properly. Finally, he regained his composure and looked towards his mob of cut-throats. 'We have f-f-f-fallen into the hands of bandits.' He forced out the words with hatred. 'It's my fault comrades. They have deceived us.'

The Momot family's feeling of panic increased even more. So that is how it was. The Cossacks were Muscovites and the Muscovites in the horned caps were Cossacks. The world had been turned on its head.

When I told them that nothing would happen to them, and they had been fooled and could immediately return home, they revived completely and their eyes sparkled. 'Maybe, we could join you,' one of them suggested hesitantly. It was clear he was the oldest of the family and had been the first to regain his wits. His face had already resumed its plump appearance and the red, swarthy hue, characteristic of his family, again played on his cheeks.

'With us? No lads, you don't get to join us that easily. First you have to show that you are capable of becoming partisans.'

'Give us weapons,' yelled another of the Momots, the one who was middle in age. 'We will show you our worth with these mongrels.' His arms, which only recently had been dangling uselessly at his side, flexed from the elbows and transformed into powerful pistons.

'A fool could use weapons to deal with them,' Vovkulaka said, cooling him down. 'You try to sort them out with your bare hands. Do you have the guts to do that kind of job?'

'What do you mean, do we have the guts to do that kind of job?' blurted another, just a boy really and obviously the youngest of them. 'You don't know us.'

'You don't know us,' they shouted in unison and, thrusting out their shoulders, stood bristling with anger. Their arms bent at the elbows to form piston-powered hammers of steel. 'If it has to be with our bare hands, let it be our bare hands,' they said together, 'but lead us to Tikych.'

The Hnylyi Tikych was a stream that flowed through the

forest. It had acquired the adjective Hnylyi, which means putrid, after its waters had become filled with Tatars' blood following a battle nearby. I was therefore confused as to where the Momot brothers wished to go. They had grown up in Tikych and knew the landscape and the river well; where it had troughs and whirlpools and where the crayfish wintered and the toad gave her teat to her young.

We led Dereza's squad to Tikych and I was again amazed by how these arrogant, impudent butchers meekly went to their deaths. They knew there was no chance of resistance succeeding and their submission left them with a nightmare remnant of hope. It was quiet in the forest and the cold breath of autumn wafted over the river bank. I ordered our captives to take off their boots and undress. They flinched at the sharp, cold wind as they stripped down to their underpants. I became confused when I saw that some of the Momot brothers were also undressing.

'Just you, bitch guts,' thundered the oldest Momot brother at Dereza who, in his white underpants and without his pipe, was indistinguishable from the rest of the turncoats and tried to hide behind them. 'Come on, we'll see who's better.'

Dereza did not take up Momot senior's proposal for a test of strength. He knew his card had been marked and, even if a miracle occurred and he somehow overwhelmed this village bull of a lad, his hopes of rescue would decrease still further. Momot senior grabbed him by the scruff of the neck and dragged him into the river, which, even by the bank, covered him up to his chest. There was no delay in Dereza's demise and it was only when the steel piston of Momot's hand pushed his head into the water that he struggled. His body jerked, his arms and legs thrashed and then his neck became tense in Momot's grasp. It was a good minute before it softened and relaxed with death as he exhaled the few last bubbles of air from his lungs. Dereza distended like a piece of snapped elastic and slowly drifted deeper into the water to wander among the bustle of crayfish and the toads who wondered when they would be suckled.

After that all the Momots jumped to it. They worked energetically with their piston-like fists, grabbed their enemies by their necks and drowned them one by one. One of the *Chekists* managed to break away and tried to swim towards the far side of the river. The youngest Momot dived after him, grabbed the fugitive by an unseen part of his body and left us all feeling anxious as they both disappeared under the water. The other Momots were about to jump to his aid when Momot senior raised his hand in front of them, 'Don't move,' he said.

We looked tensely to where bubbles were bursting on the surface. I had already thought to myself that we were futile in allowing ourselves this amusement. The boy might perish before our very eyes while we stood by uselessly. At the time we were not looking to the side and therefore did not notice another naked person leap into the water with his, not inconsiderable, manhood waving before him. It was our Chinese guy, Khodya, who could endure no more. After a while young Momot's head broke through the surface, greedily gulping mouthfuls of air, then, moments later, a head with a pigtail appeared. No one else's head broke through the glassy surface.

When they clambered onto the river bank, I saw that young Momot's body was scratched. There was even a reddening welt on his neck. Khodya's pigtail was sodden and stuck to the nape of his neck, but otherwise he was intact. 'That was a lively bathe,' he said putting on his trousers.

The Momots, soaked and blue with cold, looked at Khodya with curiosity and good-natured suspicion.

'Well, what now?' asked the oldest brother. 'Are you going to accept us into your ranks?'

'Take off your underpants and screw them up,' I said, 'if you come with us, you can't be ashamed of anything.'

That was how my squad filled up with an entire section of the Momot family.

***

That was a time when we were still able to deal with the enemy, and I do not mean just rabble like Dereza's mob; we could even tear apart sections of the regular military forces. For example, there was the time when we joined with Otaman Honta-Lyutyi for a battle by Zvenyhorodka and we annihilated over one hundred Reds. We lured many of their cavalry into Khlypnivskyi Forest and used a well-planned ruse we called, 'tying the horse by the tail'. This involved one of our cavalry units teasing the enemy, tempting them to pursue the unit as they fled into the forested area that was at either side of the road. When the Reds pursued the unit into the forest, our men 'tied the horse's tail'. It was only then that it became clear it was not just a few cavalry men they had followed, but a full Cossack infantry that were lined up in the trees, with pistols and a good stock of bombs. Our infantry trapped the enemy cavalry so tightly that they could not turn around because of the veritable 'wall of fire' that was our troops. They had no stomach for advancing because the Cossack cavalry who had been fleeing them had wheeled around to charge the reds.

After this defeat the Bolsheviks talked about an amnesty again and the commissar of the 145th Division requested that we visit his staff headquarters in Zvenyhorodka for discussions. Everything was arranged according to the strictest rules of diplomacy. They sent us hostages from their senior officers, who had to sit under guard until we reached an agreement with their leaders.

Four of us went to Zvenyhorodka. I was categorically opposed to these talks, but finally I decided that it was better to go myself rather than sending anyone else because I was familiar with the Bolshevik propagandists that could blind anyone with their fog of lies.

Otaman Honta-Lyutyi did not want to go to the Red's headquarters and sent Captain Boiko and Cossack Chykyrda, and I, wanting to bring this affair to a rapid conclusion, took Khodya. I had wanted to take Vovkulaka, the great diplomat, on this important mission, but he flatly refused to return to his home town in the role of a worthy parliamentarian and I understood and respected his wishes. He felt a certain disquiet whenever we went near Zvenyhorodka, so I took it on myself to ordain Khodya for this role.

After we had captured Khodya at the Lebedynskyi refinery, during the performance of *Shelmenko-Denshchyk*, he had, without any special training, acclimatised wonderfully to life in our unit. That was how he was. The boys had picked a small and rapid steed for him, which had a lot of stamina. It was a Steppe horse of Mongolian origin and Khodya sat on it with his bowed legs sealed snugly against the curves of its torso as if he had been poured into place. He looked like a Tatar Prince sent by the Crimean Khan to aid the Cossacks.

As he rode he probed everywhere with his short sword, brandishing it so dextrously and vigorously that the blade glittered like the rapidly circling wheel of a watermill. When we first saw how Khodya juggled the sword from hand to hand we thought he had been a circus performer and was not really fit for proper work. However, we were assured that this was not the case when we saw him in his first battle and realised he was a virtuoso of hand to hand combat. We were amazed when we thought about how easily he had surrendered to us and wondered why he had meekly laid his head on the block and gathered his pigtail ready to be beheaded. It was regrettable that we could not ask him because although Khodya had learned quite a few Ukrainian words he could not string them together, but he understood everything we said to him. He was like a well-trained dog.

Khodya had one other serious defect; he was a ferocious glutton and could never have enough of anything that we ate, whether it was gruel, potatoes, *salo* or boiled corn flour. He was continuously seeking out anything in the forest that he could throw into his cavernous mouth. He tore leaves from the trees, especially lime and mulberry, and ate roots, bark, acorns, snails, and birds' eggs, and probed the grass in search of wild sorrel and dwarf mallow.

Before we set off for the Red Army's headquarters Khodya washed his head in the Hnylyi Tikych, plaited his pigtail and dressed himself in a fancy, long coat. It was a good quality, quilted coat with a masculine cut, which he had acquired on Tsvitkove Station. The unit we had captured there provided us with quite a quantity of uniforms, footwear, ammunition and many other good things. Some of the Cossacks even cast off their rags and donned the new outfits on the station platform. I had forbidden them to do this because if night came, and with it a Red onslaught, we would end up shooting each other. The men only had my permission to quickly change their footwear for new boots so they did not have too much to carry. I picked out some new cavalry boots and a few pairs of clean undergarments for myself, but I cannot tell you in which container Khodya found that coat and a pair of soft slippers. I only saw how, shortly beforehand, he had crept up to a guard who was standing as stiffly as a concrete post on the square in front of the station, and how his sword had flashed. I did not see the coat until later when Khodya, as shiny as a new coin, modelled it for us in the camp.

Now, when preparing for such a significant and responsible role in the meeting with the Red commanders, he had decided to wear his aristocratic jerkin made of glittering, dark red, silken cloth. The coat was too large for him and reached his toes, but Khodya rolled it up to his ankles, cinched in his belt, rolled up the sleeves, and soon resembled a Chinese grandee. When he laid his palms on his chest and bowed politely I thought that leading such a courteous warrior to the meeting was too great an honour for the Red Army commanders.

However, we had decided to attend, and what a delegation we were. We must have looked like true parliamentarians. There was me with my hirsute physiognomy and shaggy mane, which reached my shoulders; I was wearing pale green field clothing and cavalier boots, which reached above my knees; Khodya, with his plait and Bordeaux-coloured tunic that he had tortured into fitting him; the hatchet-faced Captain Boiko in the parade ground kit of an Austrian officer, complete with his cruciform medals, also Austrian, adorning his breast, and an ornate swagger stick in his right hand; and finally, Cossack Chykyrda, who was wearing billowing Cossack trousers and had a talismanic pendant, which contained a few herbs, dangling from his neck. He had a long, old-style Cossack forelock, which he had coiled fantastically behind his ear. Most of all I loved the image of Khodya on his Mongolian horse, with the comical look of the slippers thrust bizarrely into the stirrups.

We were guided by a taciturn Red Army student in a rust-coloured cap with a half-broken peak. He was baffled by our Ukrainian *Khokhol* and looked at us with fear and suspicion for the entire journey.

At noon we headed for Zvenyhorodka from the direction of Hudzivka, near to which a small hill, like a stuck out belly button, protruded. Its outline was so regular that I wondered if it might have been built by hand. It was called Zvenyhora and had been raised by human hands that had heaped soil and rock before the era of the princes of Ukraine. It resembled a huge burial mound. In the past there had been a bell on its summit to sound the alarm when enemy forces approached. We made quite an impression on the people there. No one ventured onto the street and there was no bustling crowd, but from behind fences, ears pricked up and several pairs of eyes followed our weird procession which headed proudly for the Red Army's headquarters. Even the dogs were silent. They tucked their tails between their legs and curled up. The guard by the fire nearly fell over in astonishment when he saw Khodya.

We were soon welcomed into the divisional headquarters, which was located in a spacious building that had previously been a senior school. We were greeted pleasantly enough by Commissar Dybenko and Commander Kuziakin.

'Good health,' Dybenko greeted us in Ukrainian, and I noted that he too was adorned with a black beard, albeit one that was much less profuse than my own.

'Welcome,' said the long-faced Kuziakin. His shaved pate shone.

We dismounted our horses with dignity, except for Khodya, who hopped onto the ground with one bare foot because his right slipper had become tangled in the stirrup. However, calmly and without missing a beat, he reached under the horse's belly and pulled the slipper from the stirrup before he emerged from under his steed, crossed his hands on his breast and bowed.

Dybenko and Kuziakin were confused and bowed their heads respectfully as they formally announced their names and titles. Dybenko added, 'I am also a Cossack. I am from Brianshchyna where half the village are *Khokhols*.'

I presented the members of our delegation, 'Colonel Boiko of the army of the U.N.R.,' I announced solemnly, while instantaneously promoting Lieutenant Boiko's rank. He tapped himself in the chest with his swagger stick, making his Austrian medals chime. 'Chykyrda, Ensign of the *Haidamak* unit.' Chykyrda, instead of nodding, briefly swung his head with such vigour that his Cossack forelock unfurled and hung down almost as far as his belt. 'The representative of China in the U.N.R., Chan Khun Mun.' Khodya crossed his hands on his breast, bowed in three directions, and in correct Ukrainian, albeit with a heavy, Chinese accent, almost shrieked, 'Ataman Hraven.'

The Red Army commanders looked at one another and I was

certainly a little confused. After Khodya's manoeuvre I did not know what to call myself, so I simply said, 'Leader of the Ukrainian military delegation.'

'We know a little about you,' implied Dybenko, pleasantly. 'We invite our dear guests to dine with us.'

We led our horses to the hitching posts and followed Dybenko, Kuziakin and two other Red Army bosses, who were clearly *Chekists*, to the commodious schoolroom that served as a dining hall. We were astonished to see a massive table, as long as the room itself, groaning under the weight of the abundance of food and drink. Perhaps they thought our entire unit was coming or they were waiting for someone else, but there was enough food for fifty people, or ten gluttons of Khodya's capacity. I saw how his almond eyes darted everywhere and how his jutting Adam's apple bobbed up and down.

What a feast there was. Fried chicken, goose, carp in sour cream, dumplings, cold cheeses, sausages, blood pudding, jelly ... all that was missing was rice and bird's nest soup, things that Khodya had not been lucky enough to enjoy in his new homeland.

The four Reds and the four members of our delegation seated ourselves on opposite sides of the table. Dybenko poured everyone some home-brewed vodka from a huge, glitteringly faceted carafe. It was obviously strong because it left a ring around the glass. He spoke first. He did not speak Ukrainian too badly, as one might expect from a person from Brianshchyna, but his speech was tedious and long winded. He spoke of how Ukrainians could live like human beings for the first time and said that in the not too distant future our land would flow with rivers of milk.

On hearing this, even Khodya, with his limited Ukrainian, lowered his gaze and looked at Dybenko with narrowed eyes. His gut had gone into spasms because of the aroma from the food, and he suspected that the Bolsheviks had conceived a terrible punishment for us and were planning to torment us by presenting the feast only to tell us to either come over to their side or wave the victuals goodbye.

'And where will these rivers of milk flow?' I interrupted. 'Into the Volga?'

He became confused as he thought about what answer he could provide, until one of the *Chekists* hurried to his aid, 'He means the famine at Povolzhye.'

'A free Ukraine is only possible in union with Russia,' said Dybenko, 'so we will help the hungry.'

At this point Khodya's belly groaned so loudly that it derailed the train of Dybenko's thoughts. Khodya lowered his eyes guiltily and Chykyrda suggested it was time to have a bite to eat. He said that it was hard to reach an agreement on an empty stomach because the well-fed man was not a starving man's comrade. Chykyrda pushed his Cossack's plait behind his ear and raised his glass in a toast, 'To all our good health.'

Everyone raised their glasses and drank, except for Khodya who pushed his aside and started eating everything that was nearest to him. He ate it all rapidly and chewed cold cheese, jelly, carp and pickled cabbage simultaneously. So frantic was his feeding that he hurled a chicken leg, drowned in sour cream, into his mouth, complete with the bone. His teeth were sparse and small, but they ground the chicken's thighbone with such a cracking sound that we were unable to talk while it was happening.

Finally, I spoke on behalf of our delegation. 'You see,' I began, 'the issue is that Russia started war against us after the proclamation of the Ukrainian People's Republic. I say again that our independent state had been proclaimed and recognised internationally by Germany, the Austro-Hungarian Empire, Turkey, Bulgaria ...'

'And China,' said Khodya, suddenly sticking in his nose.

I looked at him in astonishment, Khodya never participated in serious conversations and here he had hit the nail on the head. He even ceased chewing and looked so firmly and beseechingly at me that I added in defiance of the facts, 'And China. And now you come to me, in my country, dictating your demands.'

Dybenko leaned towards Kuziakin's ear and began mumbling like an interpreter until the other man waved him away and said in Russian, 'Don't bother, I understand everything.'

'If you understand,' I said, raising my voice, 'then give a straight answer to my straight question. Has there ever been an occupying power that entered foreign territory for the purpose of doing good?'

'What is he saying?' Kuziakin asked Dybenko.

'He says that everything will be paid back,' Dybenko translated.

'No,' I said, answering myself. 'Any occupying power cudgels its way onto foreign soil to plunder and profit from others.'

'What is he saying?' Kuziakin asked again.

'He says that we are too demanding,' Dybenko whispered.

'Therefore, I wish to raise a glass for the establishment of historical justice,' I said. 'Let all the vagabonds and devourers of life perish.'

'Bravo,' echoed Khodya in Chinese and hurled down his glass of vodka without waiting for a toast.

'What is he saying?' Kuziakin asked again, cupping his hand around his ear.

'Who, the Chinese man?' Dybenko asked, not managing to follow the conversation.

'No, the otaman.'

'He says, let's drink to historical roots.'

Commander Kuziakin smiled in a friendly manner and raised his glass to me. Home-brewed vodka really is like fire and rapidly swarms into the blood. 'Since we have common roots, we cannot be driven apart from each other. So, we need to make peace Comrades,' he said, crunching on a gherkin. 'We will give you an official document and ask that you make all your people acquainted with it. It is a new proclamation of amnesty signed by Trotsky, Yakir and Balytskyi.'

One of the *Chekists* took a sheaf of paper from his briefcase and handed it to me. I ran my eyes over the printed text. It was the same old song about the delights and privileges of amnesty that soviet power was yet again 'making a gift of' to all those who were prepared to lay down their arms and return to a peaceful life.

Lieutenant Boiko read this legally worthless, poorly composed document after me, followed by Cossack Chykyrda, and I was again astonished when Khodya put out his hand for it. He looked for a long time at the primitively drawn hieroglyphics that were incomprehensible to him. He then stammered 'Bollocks' loudly as he handed me the paper, which was covered with his greasy fingerprints.

I also wanted to wipe my hands on the paper, but Lieutenant

Boiko, with his Austrian crosses jangling, took it from me, folded it into quarters, and placed it in the breast pocket of his uniform. It was interesting that the Red commanders now directed all their attention to Boiko, as if he, rather than I, were heading the delegation.

'Whether things are as stated in this document or otherwise, we are obliged to show it to everyone,' he said respectfully. 'Each individual has the right to make this decision for himself.' A sharp crack drowned out the next words he spoke because Khodya had set about devouring a goose's leg and produced such terrible sounds that it was like listening to a mammoth's tusk being turned to powder in an industrial grinder.

'Stop that,' snarled Boiko. He turned crimson with wrath and struck the table with his stick. 'It's impossible to say a word with that infernal noise.'

Khodya gulped at the air in surprise, but did not manage to catch his breath, he choked and then the poor, wretched man snorted, sending small chips of bone flying onto the table. He continued to wheeze and cough laboriously.

'Let the man eat,' I reproached Boiko, 'we can always find time to talk more nonsense.'

'OK, OK,' he agreed, gently tapping Khodya between the shoulder blades. 'Breathe through your nose. Shall we give you something to drink?'

Khodya nodded guiltily as Chykyrda handed him a pot of curdled milk. He took it by the ears as if it were a small goblet rather than a three litre pitcher. He peered into it like a dog staring at a bone, wrinkled his stunted nose, and began to gulp it. Chykyrda looked in wonder with eyes as hairy as a bee's velvety skin.

Dybenko then produced a silver cigar case, opened it and pushed it across the table, 'Shall we smoke?'

Lieutenant Boiko and Chykyrda each took a cigar, but Khodya, while still continuing to gulp the milk, extracted two. I rolled a cigarette using my own tobacco and began to smoke, casting my eyes over to the two *Chekists* who had been sitting silently for long enough. The *Chekist* who had handed us the useless proclamation of amnesty caught my glance and spoke, 'I don't know why you are drawing this out or what you are hoping for. Clearly the war is over, your people have decided to cease battling and to work peacefully.'

'Who told you that the war is over?' I demanded to know. 'Even the negotiations that we are engaged in at present demonstrate that the war is continuing.'

'This isn't war, it's something else.' Dybenko waved his hand dismissively. 'How can there be a war without an army?'

'There will yet be an army,' I said, 'or, more precisely, the army exists. It will begin its advance at the preordained time. You can be assured of that, if you live until that hour.'

'What is he saying?' Kuziakin asked again.

'He says that everything is ahead.'

'Well yes, he speaks correctly,' agreed Kuziakin, 'all possibilities are open to them in the future.'

Suddenly, his long face grew half as long again and I looked towards where his bulging eyes were focused. There was nothing strange there except that Khodya, instead of smoking the cigars had torn them open, poured the tobacco into his palm and, after throwing it into his mouth, began to chew vigorously. It was certain that Commander Kuziakin had never realised tobacco could be used in this way. Although people did not generally chew cigar tobacco, during a time of war it had to suffice.

'It's clear now that you don't know anything yet,' said Dybenko.

'Let me explain everything,' the *Chekist* who had handed us the worthless document butted into the conversation. 'You became really wild there in your forest. You lost contact with the world and don't know anything about your own army. Not so long ago, the miserable remains of the Petliurite Army made a substantial advance from Poland. Due respect should be given to those courageous men because they almost reached Kyiv, but the day before yesterday they were defeated by the army of Kotovsky.'

'It cannot be so,' bellowed Chykyrda, 'we didn't come here to listen to lies.'

'It's a fact,' said the *Chekist*. 'Almost no one is left alive. Oh, yes, your so called General Tiutiunnyk ran from the field of battle like a hare. A fact is a fact, there is no longer an army that can engage in battle. But why am I warbling like a nightingale? Please, read for

140

yourselves.' He extracted a newspaper from his briefcase and passed it over the table to Lieutenant Boiko. It was the *Red Military Epistle* and the black headline on the first page jumped out at me and made my vision grow dark:

The Remnants of the Petliurite Army Have Been Destroyed by Kotovsky's Heroes!

We lunged at the newspaper so anxiously that our foreheads banged together. It was true, there really was an article about how the *Petliurite* forces, who were interned in prisoner of war camps, had been stirred up by the western bourgeoisie and crossed the border in their blind faith, to bring down the government. They had been surrounded by Kotovsky's cavalry near the village of Mali Mynky and destroyed.

We read this report while our eyes darted from one another and back to the paper. We did not want to believe in this utter catastrophe, which brought with it the complete desolation of our hope. Chykyrda moved closer to Boiko, who was seated opposite me, and plunged his gaze into the paper. His lips moved anxiously as he read. Khodya, who was seated to my right, tried to look at what was written, but he was unable to read the text so murmured 'Bollocks' gently.

'You're right there,' I said.

Lieutenant Boiko mechanically folded the newspaper over eight times with the intention of putting it in his breast pocket, together with the fake proclamation of amnesty. However, I took the paper from him, ostentatiously tore off a strip, and began to roll myself another cigarette while looking unflinchingly at Dybenko.

'I think,' said Dybenko, 'that it's time we drank.'

'Yes,' said Commander Kuziakin, having completely understood him. 'Definitely!'

We all drank and the commanders began to drone on about how only people set on committing suicide would remain in the forest and how those who did not hand themselves over for amnesty were heading for certain destruction, while the phrase, 'Utterly ... the army is destroyed,' echoed in my head. I swallowed these words along with the smoke and such utter despair seized me that I yearned to wail like a stricken animal. How could this have happened? Why was there no signal for a general uprising? Why were we not informed of the army's incursion over the border? It was as if someone had deliberately prepared this catastrophe.

Then I heard a genuine wailing sound, a delicate monotonous drone rippling from somewhere at my side. It was so drawn out and filled with sorrow that it moved me immensely. The despairing resonance pierced me like a needle and it was some time before I realised the sound came from Khodya. He had become quite drunk and was humming his own song, or more precisely a melody that I had never heard before. Khodya did not sing a single word, he simply hummed his musical motif. This was the first time I had heard him sing and perhaps that is why it seemed so sorrowful and moved me so profoundly. He sang with closed eyes, as if he thought that no one could hear or see him, and his voice trembled and broke apart into countless tiny, needle-slender notes.

I do not know how his song affected each of us, but while he sang no one spoke. Even Commissar Dybenko, Commander Kuziakin and the two *Chekists* sat and listened passively.

It was only when Khodya fell silent that Dybenko suddenly awoke, 'So lads, maybe we could belt out some of our own *Khokhol* songs?' And without waiting for anyone's consent he sang in a prolonged, dense and beautiful baritone, 'Oh! Oh on the mountain, the reaper's harvest …' Dybenko jumped onto the table and wrinkled his eyebrows at us, urging us to sing, but no one joined him and, having sung as far as *the Cossacks pass through crevasse and valley*, he lost his enthusiasm.

I had no interest in these discussions from the beginning and after the news of the fatal retreat of our army I had no wish to stay here for a moment longer. Of course, the Bolsheviks and their newspaper may have misled us substantially, but I felt the truth of our army's tragedy in my heart.

'Let's go,' I said to Lieutenant Boiko.

'Before the wind gets up,' added Cossack Chykyrda, as we got ready to leave.

Commissar Dybenko and Commander Kuziakin began to urge us to stay until the morning, although nothing had been agreed during the negotiations. They promised to fill up the bath, bring some merry lasses, etc., etc., but I declined.

It was obvious that Dybenko was offended, both because we would not sing with him and because we had ended the talks so swiftly. As we were leaving the building, he approached me and said, with a stupid smile, 'You stole this Chinese guy from us.'

'Since when did Chinese guys start coming into *katsap* land?' I asked.

'Well, yes, I understand what you mean,' he said in Russian.

We reached the camp of Honta-Lyutyi by nightfall and at dawn I went with my squad to Smila, where there was some urgent work waiting for us.

3

From information given by an agent on 08/01 -

Raven's gang is now to be found in the Lebedyn district, approximately 23 versts from Novomyrhorod. Their arms comprise 90 swords, one Maxim and two Lewis guns. The bandits are sworn to wait for their ataman until there is firm news whether he is alive, and say that they will not lay down their arms and surrender until all the Muscovites and Communists have been slain. When we offered them the chance to surrender, with a guarantee of clemency, we obtained a written response from them in the name of the Chief of the 5th District. I have attached a copy as evidence below:

Comrade Nechyporenko

We are extremely grateful for the amnesty offered to us, but we will not present ourselves to you because it is necessary to first kill all the soviet military emergency units, (the words are illegible) katsaps presently seated in the soviet peasant labour power, who oppress the people in ways that Tsar Nicholas could not have even dreamed. So, who is a bandit in your terms?

He who comes from Muscovy and in daylight steals every house, or he who is driven from his home and has to go into the forest to defend his country? And to you, you Muscovite arse crawler, I say this directly to you - If you don't want to endure the same fate as the Lebedyn police boss, Borvik, and his comrades, who all bit the dust together, join us in the forest. Perhaps we could grant you amnesty and together we could destroy the commune and make a stand for truth. We do not love untruth to permit a sin, we live truthfully on this earth and will pour that truth into your eyes, like sand.

The signature below is illegible, but the surname, from the letters that can be made out, is something like Vovkodav or Vovkura.

A more substantial gang of bandits recently appeared in Zhuravka village and, amazingly, disappeared into the forest without leaving any traces of their presence. It was as though they had passed above the snow.

The chief of the district criminal investigation department Kozytskii, Secretary Smulson

From information collated by the Cherkasy branch of punitive search units from 15-23 January 1922

Raven passed through villages, forests and fields to reach Bohunovii Farm, which was just on the the outskirts of Lebedyn Forest, by evening. It had grown dark early because while he had been resting at Yevdosia's, Saint Barbara had increased the night but not extended the day. The silver German watch that Raven removed from his pocket indicated it was only 5pm. Night had already begun to fall, but this route was familiar and he could find his way to the winter den with closed eyes; so could his horse, who felt the road with the beat of his hooves.

While he had been with Mudei he had only lost his way in the darkness once. He still could not explain what power had guided them through the autumnal murk of that night. A dense fog had fallen and he could not see beyond the end of his nose. It was the time when Raven had chosen to allow those of his Cossacks who were closer to home to visit their families, and he had set off to see his own.

Although there was an impenetrable wall of rain that obscured all before them, Mudei swiftly bore him over the field to Vodianyi and beyond to where Tovmach was situated, but the village was not there. Such a dense wall of mist surrounded them that it hampered his breathing and Raven could not see further than the mane of his horse. He realised that Mudei had lost his way and was walking in circles, blinded by the murk that had erased the fields from sight. He could not whisper anything to guide the horse, but instead he tugged agitatedly at the reins and urged Mudei onwards. He could not see any point by which he could guide himself; no tree, shrub or sapling. Wandering, half blind, he hoped to chance on some familiar place near the villages of Skotareve or Kapustyne that would enable him to plan a direct route to Tovmach, but there was nothing. Some force stubbornly led them around the field which was awash with the dense, misleading fog. There was something deceptively occult about his surroundings.

When Raven halted Mudei again, so he could listen to the soundless night and determine which way to turn, he heard a noise, almost like lips smacking, behind him. It was the kind of noise that people make to drive a horse onwards and at first Raven thought he was dreaming or it was the ground below him, which had become invisible, being churned under the horse's hooves, or even the sound of a nocturnal bird calling. When he stopped the horse again he heard the same sound, but on this occasion it was coming from somewhere ahead of him. He longed to cry out into the sepulchral fog that challenged him like a sentient nightmare, but then he realised what force led him and had tried to make him panic. It was not fear but wrath at the lack of a sure way to regain his route. He was ready to turn back but did not know in which direction to guide his horse and he heard the distinctive noise of lip smacking several more times.

At the time Raven did not know that his steed, as if instinctively aware of danger, was attempting to save his life by prolonging the journey. Raven adopted the only wise resolution available to him in the darkness and placed his faith in the horse's will. A force that could not be swayed by superstition, conceptions or intention. It was only when he put himself at the mercy of the horse that he relaxed and it seemed that Mudei had ceased trotting in circles and headed in a direction he knew well. The horse trotted for a long time, but they still did not reach Skotareve, Tovmach or Kapustyne. Ahead of them was only fog, fog, and more fog.

When visibility improved slowly Raven began to recognise some of his surroundings and realised they were travelling across a field of maize when severed stalks crackled under Mudei's hooves. With a sudden flare of enlightenment he understood that he was circling around an area one *verst* from his parent's home and the way to reach Siryi Forest, where they dwelt, was now clear to him. It was now too late to go there because it would soon be dawn and a mounted patrol might be roaming in the half-light, so he hurried back to Lebedyn Forest before the fog dispersed.

Mudei now maintained an even, merry gallop, as if they had not recently been blundering through a nightmarish fog, and Raven reached the camp by morning. He did not tell any one about his nocturnal wanderings. What could he say? That he had been lost between two bushes by a house. That some evil presence had spent the night smacking its lips to confuse him.

He would have never told anyone about his wanderings if it were not for his discovery a few days later. On that same foggy night an ambush had been waiting for him near his home. The Reds had known the time when most of the forest rebels would visit their homes and had chosen to wait for Raven on the same night as the strange events occurred. Raven did not know to whom or to what to ascribe this salvation. Perhaps it was the foresight of his steed, who had sensed the presence of danger and purposely wandered to lead him away from the deadly menace to his life, or perhaps this force was in his parental home. It seemed to him that it was the same force that had saved Raven before when he was returning home.

Despite his mysterious protector, shortly after he had arrived home on a subsequent visit, the Reds suddenly emerged from Tovmach to seize him. Two of them charged into his parents' house so quickly that Raven did not have time to hide or present himself before they threw his father onto the bench, took out their whips and

146

shouted in Russian, 'Tell us where your son is.'

Raven appeared from a neighbouring room just as another executor, their commander, ran into the house. The commander stood on the threshold and, as if transfixed, looked carefully at Raven, then screamed at his men, 'Get out! Get out of here!'

Although they were confused, they obeyed the order and ran out of the house. Raven realised their commander was the former Staff Lieutenant Kalyuzhnyi, Fania, Panas, with whom he had become acquainted in Uman before they had dined together with the two enchanting ladies. Something had awoken in the soul of this turncoat from Shulyavki when he was confounded before the former Staff Captain Chornovus. He began to proffer his hand, became unsure and confused, darted out of the house with his soldiers, and dispersed like smoke.

There is no evil without a corresponding good, thought Raven, who was now entering ever deeper into the dark belly of the forest and hoping, anxiously, that no misfortune had driven his Cossacks from their base. But how many of them would remain underground this winter?

Frost gripped the night and it crunched under Mudei's hooves and crackled on the tree trunks. The harsh noise echoed through the forest like the spring call of a corncrake, as Raven passed through valley after valley and gully after gully. He only paused occasionally to listen to the deafening silence, which was sometimes pierced by the crackling of frozen branches and tree trunks. As he approached yet another place overgrown with dense shrubbery, he felt how rapidly his heart beat. There, below the hawthorn bushes, two of their underground homes, each of which could accommodate at least fifty people, were concealed. The Cossacks had also dug an underground stable nearby for over one hundred horses. These three dug-outs were linked by tunnels so they did not have to go outside unless absolutely necessary, and could move effortlessly from one to the other without opening doors and letting out the heat.

There was a time when the Bolsheviks would not dare to show their noses in the heart of the forest because they would not risk venturing into an unknown and remote, densely wooded area, even with a substantial force. They usually wandered by roads and through open fields, and checked out villages and homesteads for opposition. They rarely based their garrisons next to the forests like they had done at Kholodnyi Yar.

That was the situation before the Muscovites established a wide network of informers, which included some of the rebels who had been granted amnesty. It was hard to say what thoughts deterred them from entering the woodlands now, or whether they did consider venturing into the wintry forest where the rebels would be easier to detect, particularly when their numbers grew ever sparser.

Raven halted his horse and listened. He was surprised that he had not yet encountered a guard. Suddenly, he caught sight of two green specks shining in the darkness about thirty paces ahead. He realised that an animal was looking at him warily. Only the eyes of a grey wolf could shine with such an unearthly light. He was certain there were no dogs or cats here, and a fox or marten would have fled as the rider approached. Mudei shook his head and snorted as Raven unfastened the holster of his revolver. He waited for the wolf to dart off and disappear under the trees, but it continued to glare insolently with those luminescent eyes testing his endurance. Suddenly, the shadowy wolf shape yelled, 'Password,' with a human voice.

Raven could not believe his ears, not because the wolf had spoken to him with a human voice but because it was the familiar voice of Vovkulaka of whom he had expected to hear no more.

'Is this your sign from the other world?' he asked, 'Have you transformed into a wolf?'

'Otaman, I'm alive-e-e!' Vovkulaka ran towards him out of the darkness. He and Raven, who had already dismounted, held each other in a soldiers' embrace.

'I waited and looked for you every night,' said Vovkulaka, his fangs glittering in the darkness.

'Truth to tell, I thought I would never see you again,' said Raven. 'Where did that whirlwind of a battle cast you to?'

'You'll never guess what happened to me ...' Vovkulaka began to narrate his story. It seemed that, after yet another grenade had exploded, he had fallen at the side of his slain horse. He was so besmirched with blood and was such a terrible sight that it looked

148

as though he had been killed. One of the Reds looked, turned and fired at him, but the bullet hit the corpse of his steed. Vovkulaka was motionless and dreaming until everything was quiet, then he rose and looked around. Finding the corpses of Makovii, Yizhak and Dobryvechir, he buried them in a ditch in the forest.

'Hmm …' Raven bowed his head. He wanted to enquire further of Vovkulaka but was unable to do so because he suddenly became aware of two green eyes flaming in the darkness, accompanied by a quiet whining sound. He saw a modestly sized puppy run to Vovkulaka and watched as it squealed piteously while rubbing against his old comrade's legs. 'What's this? Have you acquired a dog?'

'It's not a dog, it's a wolf,' said Vovkulaka. 'Although I have given him a dog's name, Sirko. Let's go at once to the base. They have waited long enough for you. And do you know what we will do? You will first go to the stable with Mudei and then steal into the quarters and surprise our comrades. I won't say a word to anyone.'

'Good, good,' agreed Raven, trying to gather his thoughts, which had suddenly dispersed into pulverised motes and fragments after this surprise encounter. He was delighted that Vovkulaka was alive, but still could not believe how easily he had fooled the Reds.

They went to the entranceway that led to the stable, which was about half the height of a horse. Raven threw a heavy, felt cover on the ground to protect Mudei and the horse lowered himself onto his knees and wriggled through to his underground stable.

Part Two

Chapter 1

1

Hannusia's labour pains began two weeks earlier than she had anticipated. Prior to them starting a sleigh had pulled up outside her house again and the same two men, who had previously travelled on it, entered her home to enquire again about Veremii. They were the goose-necked man, on this occasion with his neck swaddled in a dirty flannel, and the other rascal with glassy eyes. The glaze-eyed rascal was clothed in a dead animal's skin, which was shabby and clearly canine in origin because a nauseous fragrance of dogs wafted from him.

'Who did you identify, bitch?' The goose-necked man snarled bestially at Hannusia. 'Who are you playing hide and seek with, bitch?'

'Ask me,' interjected Veremii's mother, 'you can see the state she is in.'

'It will be your turn soon old witch. And not only yours.' He cast his insolent eyes at Hannusia's round, pregnant belly. 'An angel got you pregnant too?'

'It happened a long time ago,' Hannusia replied quietly.

The goose-necked man continued to lament, harangue and threaten her, and from his tirade it became apparent that they had found the grave in Hunskyi Forest, twenty paces to the east of the old oak. They had scraped the frozen soil away, dug to the coffin, opened it and found, instead of the wretch's corpse, a straw hat, an embroidered shirt and the mocking inscription that had made the *Chekist* feel as if he had received a heavy blow to his innards - *The angels have stolen him.*

Hotsman, the goose-necked man, was so furious that he personally shot the amnestied rebel, a sombre man, who had led them to the grave. He then ordered his men to put the corpse in the freshly dug soil so their labour would not be in vain. He felt the prank with the grave and Veremii had been aimed at him because he had found Veremii slain. Had not the corpse been recognised by the villagers, Veremii's mother and this pregnant woman? Had they not taken him, as appropriate, through the villages for the praise and panegyrics that were due to the dead and to terrify the rebels? And how had this affair concluded? The dead man had indeed been stolen, obviously not by the angels, but by his own men.

The *Haidamak* rebels had fired on the vehicle transporting the corpse near the village of Zelena Dibrova. They did not usually venture out of the forest in daylight during winter, but on this occasion they had emerged from an unseen nook. Having stolen the corpse, they replaced it with the five severed heads of the Red Army troops and the obese poor peasant who had been accompanying the body. Unaccompanied by a coachman, the horses had pulled the wagon and the heads to Matusiv, striking fear into the whole area. There was, however, another aspect of this enigmatic event that was even more chimerical. The next day, when a punishment squad heading towards Zelena Dibrova found the decapitated bodies, there were no tracks leading either to or from the fields or the forest. The bandits had again passed over the snow and left no tracks behind them.

Hotsman knew a lot about their cunning tactics and was aware that in winter the forest rebels usually fought on foot. To sweep away the tracks they left in the snow, they would walk in a single file, towing a branch in their wake to smooth the snow behind them, thus obliterating any trail. He was inflamed by the bandits' mocking contrivances. He was a young but already hardened *Chekist* whose portfolio glittered with a silver tablet inscribed, 'To Comrade Hotsman from the Praesidium of the Cherkassy Extraordinary Commission, for the exposure of *Petliurite* bands'.

'So, the angels stole him?' He screamed at Hannusia again. 'Who did you identify in Matusiv, bitch? I won't permit anyone to strike me in the face. If he doesn't come to us and surrender within the next month, I will personally discharge my gun into your *Petliurite* womb.' He drew his revolver from its holster and poked Hannusia in the stomach with its muzzle. 'Do you understand me?'

Hannusia felt how sharply her insides moved and she instinctively put her hands on her stomach to protect her baby. She staggered and fell on the bench, but the rascal with the glassy eyes grabbed her by the shoulders and pulled her to her feet.

'Stand when the authorised agent is talking to you.'

The nauseating canine spirit drew the breath from her lungs and Hannusia vomited. Hotsman wrinkled his nose disdainfully and holstered his gun before walking towards the door. He paused on the threshold, glared at her and said, drawing out every word, 'If he doesn't come to us within the next month the angels will really sing to you and your child. I say this to you as your Tsar and God.' He gave her a thin-lipped, insane smile, for what seemed like an eternity, and then left. His companion, who smelled like a decomposing dog, departed with him, leaving behind an oppressive stench that followed Hannusia even when she went outside, desperate for a breath of fresh air.

The troublesome aroma was like poison piercing the depths of her soul. It left her unable to find any respite in her home or elsewhere. She went to bed without eating supper, but dreams and slumber abandoned her. She spent the night breathing restlessly and turning from side to side in a cold sweat. The child in her womb also grew tense and at dawn began to beseech her to come into the world. Hannusia seized her stomach with both hands, more from fear than pain. It seemed to her that an external force was pulling the baby from her, tearing her stomach and pulling out her innards.

Her mother-in-law heard her groans, jumped out of bed, lit a gas lamp and ran quickly to Tanasykha's to ask her to get the midwife, but Hannusia's labour was over swiftly. Tanasykha did not fetch the midwife, she ran to look at Hannusia herself and found the baby already lying on a warm bed on a shelf above the oven. He had come forth into the world and been momentarily stunned by the miracle of life beyond the womb before he began to cry.

Instead of getting help when she saw that the baby's umbilical cord needed to be cut, Tanasykha decided to deal with it herself. Hannusia and her mother-in-law could only exchange alarmed glances as the aged, skinny Tanasykha began work. It was as if she regularly cut and tied the navels of new born babies. Shouting at Yarko's mother to prepare a bath in a trough with sacred water, Tanasykha took charge as if she were in her own home. She quickly located the tailor's scissors in the cupboard on the wall and cut and dextrously tied the navel with sewing thread, as if dealing with the end of a sausage and not a child. When she put the anguished baby in a bowl and bathed and sprinkled him with holy water, she spoke these words as if they were written in a script, 'We will pour gold and silver onto our child to protect him from all harm. We will wash our Cossack with sacred water to protect him from the devil, so that the cunning devil, the female Judas, does not swap him for a changeling before he is christened.' She continued talking to the baby, 'You are a Cossack among us, eh. Oh Cossack, you are so like Veremii and you roar like a bull. Roar with your vigour, let your voice break and deepen to a man's voice.'

She seized the crying baby from the water, wrapped him in a linen swaddling, rubbed the dampness from his body, and laid him next to Hannusia. Then she wrapped the scissors that had cut the baby's navel in thread and placed them under the new mother.

'What's that for?' Hannusia asked in a weak voice.

'Because it's necessary,' said Tanasykha. She did not know why women who cut umbilical cords put the scissors under the new mother either. It was what she had seen others do, but she had never asked why. They were sorceresses whose actions you did not question.

'You are already a grandmother.' Tanasykha turned to Veremii's mother. 'Give me a candle, a wax rather than a tallow one. I will light it and go by the river in search of fragrant resin to fumigate the house so the angel of God will come more swiftly and protect the child from the devil.'

No one had yet fumigated the house but it seemed to Hannusia that the canine odour had already dispersed. Perhaps the sacred water helped, or possibly the angel of God had already appeared to her child. He had flown to the house and hidden somewhere by the stove so he could not be seen.

Hannusia could not say whether the angel had come to the new born child, but the raven who was close by did not consider this possibility. He had perched on their chimney, which had been the first in the village to heat up that day, to warm his aged bones. The bird did not see the birth, although he observed many things from on high and divined all that happened. He saw how they took the water from the well by the house early in the morning before anyone else, and how they had poured it onto the snow when it was reddened with blood. The raven flapped his wings sadly when Tanasykha, the poorly-trained midwife, buried the umbilical cord. She did not cover

154

it with soil, which was already frozen, but made a kind of soil wall around it, like a chicken would, and in a prominent place where it might be discovered. That's a bad sign, thought the raven sadly.

2

The year 1922 brought us both disenchantment and the gift of hope. To begin with an emissary from the government in exile in Poland, Colonel Manzhula, visited us and, instead of the usual idiotic encouragement to falsely raise our spirits, he poured an entire River Dnipro of icy water onto us. He said that the government of the U.N.R. was calling on the forest rebels to cease all military activity and refrain from any insurrection because the time for such action had passed. He said that further struggle was senseless and, in the present conditions, meant self-destruction. It was apparent from everything he saw that we would not defeat the communists now and therefore it was necessary to preserve our people until better times came. Partisan units were required to disband.

At first I felt as though I had crumbled to dust and when I managed to pull myself together I placed my right hand on my holster.

Colonel Manzhula continued, 'This does not mean that we are defeated,' he said, 'we have to wait for the hour when the entire world learns and understands the essence of the Muscovite commune and then our people will take up arms again. Then we will acquire new allies from outside Ukraine and fresh military force from within. Our struggle will recommence. I ask that all the otamans instruct their officers and Cossacks to take the responsibility for organising the disbandment of their units. It is necessary to help the rebels who are going to other countries with documents and money and to enable those who do not desire, or are unable, to establish themselves on their native soil to cross the Polish or Romanian borders. We will meet them there. Believe me, our government does care about their subsequent fate.'

Colonel Manzhula's eyes met mine for a moment. He fell silent and, tight lipped, nodded his head sadly. 'I understand your condition,' he said, 'perhaps, if I were in your place, I would reach towards my holster, but I am not your commander, I am just an emissary of the government of the U.N.R. passing on their directives.'

I took away my hand from my revolver and looked with heavy eyes on the stunned otamans, Larion Zaharodnii, Honta-Lyutyi, Denys Hupalo and Holyk-Zaliznyak. What would they say? As for me, my voice was so desiccated and my feelings so numb that I was unable to speak.

The sturdy, massive-headed Honta-Lyutyi coughed into his fist. It was clear that he too had a throat made arid by his feelings. He spoke in a hoarse but level and measured voice, 'Thank you, Colonel, for bringing this message, I will pass it onto my men unaltered but will let the choice of whether to disband be left to the judgement of each individual. We will not compel anyone to remain in the forest by force unless it is their will. Personally, I will operate according to the situation as it develops in my unit.'

Colonel Manzhula nodded carefully and looked at Zaharodnii. Larion stepped forward, threw his weight onto his left leg, which had become lame after he had been severely wounded, and nervously stroked his black beard. His face was almost green after he had been poisoned by a gas attack on the front, but his eyes smiled, even now when he was angry, as he said menacingly, 'You should have told us earlier that there is no hope of assistance from over the border and that our army is in some squalid camp nourishing Polish bed bugs, then we would have acted differently. But what now? If we live long enough we'll see.'

'That's understandable,' said Manzhula, shifting his gaze to Hupalo.

Denys Hupalo scratched the roots of his Cossack forelock and said furiously, 'Right, I'll leave everything now and just go home then.'

Mefodii Holyk-Zaliznyak, as skinny as a ladder, derided the politicians, 'As far as our governors are concerned, stick a pinion up their arses, there are seven Fridays in the week.' Before the war Mefodii had worked on the railways and often inserted the word pinion into conversation when he was angry. 'Let's reflect on this until autumn and we'll see who stays here under cover and who crosses the border.'

I sighed softly. There was darkness in my soul but the unity of the otamans warmed me and gave me hope. When Colonel

Manzhula looked at me, I said in a polite, fraternal tone, 'Pass on my greetings to General Tiutiunnyk. I expect that it's his fruitful idea to disband the units?'

Manzhula left my question unanswered. It seemed that he held the same view of our governors as Holyk-Zaliznyak. He listened to us with wonderful serenity and restraint and had a total absence of the pride that we had seen in other emissaries when they fed us stories about the signal for an uprising. Now there was not even a crumb of hope left that the signal to rise up would ever echo over Ukraine.

Though we needed to live until then to hear it, the summer would be illuminated by the call to rebel. A call that was issued without planes looping the loop, church bells sounding, or rockets exploding signals in the air, but, aptly enough, quietly and secretly.

3

With the approach of spring the bandits have revived again and raised their heads to terrorise soviet power. On March 24 a gang of up to 15 horsemen, who resembled Red Army cavalry, entered Zhuravka village, which is about five versts from Lebedyn, in daylight. It is necessary to note the particular impudence of their leader (probably the Raven, who we have already buried on three occasions, because the tall, sombre ataman had a black beard and long hair). He visited the Auto-Cephalic church in Zhuravka before the robbery commenced. While he lit candles for the deceased and for good health he participated in a prayer and, apparently, had a brief conversation with Father Oleksii, who has been suspected of having communications with the Petliurite underground for a long time.

After the ataman had prayed, the bandits immediately entered the village and shot the militiaman, Pasechnyk, the previously amnestied guerrilla from Yablochko's band; killed the chairman of the village soviet, Kovalenko; beat to death the chairman of the poor peasants' committee, and destroyed all the paperwork. When they left they took away three wagons with horses, having loaded them with 50 poods of barley and ten poods of rye.

The terribly good spirits and playfulness with which the bandits finished off the representatives of soviet power compels indignation. According to the testimony of an eye-witness, the ataman, having cornered the amnestied bandit, Pasechnyk, asked, 'This bullet of mine is a bit like a bee, where should I let it sting you, in the heart or in the head?'

Pasechnyk replied obediently, 'The head.'

'Well, that's appropriate because you swore once that Ukraine was in your heart.'

From the report of the secret agent 'Ne Pytaj' to the head of the local division of the G.P.U., Comrade Bergavinov, 29 March 1922

No, it was not Father Oleksii with whom the otaman had a conversation in the Church of Saint Illia. A woman was standing and praying before the icon of the Saviour and Raven felt her closeness to him with every nerve in his body. She was silently moving her lips in prayer before the crucifix and when he approached she sensed he was near and raised her head. For a brief moment their eyes met. An invisible lightning bolt passed between them, an electricity that no one save themselves could impede. He also approached the icon of the Saviour, made the sign of the cross, and stood behind her, listening to her tremulous voice:

Thy kingdom come,
Thy will be done,
In earth as it is
In heaven.
Come on Thursday evening
to Liashchiv Farm.
Give us this day our daily bread;
And forgive us our trespasses,

As we forgive those who trespass against us;
Come to the barn at dusk.
I will wait for you ... You can come?
Lead us not into temptation
But deliver us from evil.
For thine is the kingdom,
The power and the glory.
I will come, for ever and ever,
Amen.

***

That day Raven bathed carefully and with such relish that it could have been Maundy Thursday. On the stove, with its long bunk and iron sides, which were held together with bricks borrowed from the Lebedyn Monastery, he heated two cauldrons of water. He crawled with them into the underground stable and, in a wooden vat, washed away his sins. He found a piece of fragrant soap in his saddle bag, a trophy from a raid, and bathed, washed his hair and beard, and dressed in fresh linen. He wanted to splash himself with eau de Cologne, which was also part of their trophy stock because they sometimes used it to sterilise wounds. However, on reflection, it was laughable that a man who reeked of earth, blood and horse sweat should try to mask the smell of a warrior's soul with fragrant liquid.

He did all this due to the joy and anticipation of being close to the woman he had not expected to meet again. After so many failures and so much disillusion, Raven had driven away any feeling of expectation. They were false feelings that only confused the course of his life. Eventually, he donned his sheepskin coat, which was capacious enough to allow him to contain an entire institute of noble maidens in its folds, because the nights were still cold, and saddled his horse.

The ruined Liashchiv Farm was in a gully adjacent to Hrafskyi Forest. Raven had once known its now dead master well, a wealthy widower named Onysym Liashch. Onysym had always allowed in the men from the forest and did not begrudge them chickens, eggs or *salo*. He even gave them entire combs of honey from his hives. But how could he have done otherwise? Four of his sons had fought in the ranks of Otaman Zhujvoda's squad (the otaman was known as Chew Water because of his manner of speaking as though he chewed water) and three of them had died in a battle with Kotovsky's men at Nosachiv Field. Their squad had been unable to escape from the enemy forces who had surrounded them and so were compelled to engage in battle with the regular military. The otaman, seeing that there was no chink through which they could wriggle and escape, ordered his men to deluge the enemy with bullets and show them what the Cossacks were capable of. It was obvious there was an evil foreboding in his breast for he fell silent. He chewed wordlessly for a moment, seeking the appropriate thing to say, and then added unexpectedly, 'Let whosoever lives to see a free Ukraine, give her my greeting.' Zhujvoda ran the tip of his thumb down the bare blade of his sword so that the blood flowed.

The next day the nuns of Lebedyn Monastery gathered the bodies of more than one hundred fallen Cossacks from Nosachiv Field and buried them in a ditch in the forest. Only a few had been fortunate enough to escape the enemy forces and Onysym's youngest son, Zinko, was among them. When he went to his father and told of the loss of his brothers, old Liashch was silent for a moment and then asked, almost reproachfully, 'And how did you get out?'

'The horse bore me beyond the enemy,' replied Zinko

'Didn't they have horses?'

'Their horses were killed.'

'What a pity,' sighed old Liashch.

He did not know that within a month the local branch of the anti-banditry unit would begin to trail his remaining son. It came to pass that on his farm a terrible event would occur, stripping him of any feelings of reproach and suspicion of his youngest son.

The young man visited his home in the night and whether someone sold him down the river or the battlers against banditry successfully tracked him, the house was surrounded by troops who wanted to take him alive at all costs. When they opened fire Zinko returned it until dawn came. He aimed his rifle through the windows and then his revolver from the veranda, and threw the occasional grenade from the attic. Meanwhile Onysym acquired a sawn-off shotgun from somewhere and aimed it through the smashed glass at

160

anything that moved. The Muscovites assumed they were not alone, that there must be an entire group of partisans in the house, and were in no hurry to advance.

'You are surrounded. Come out,' they cried into the night. 'Surrender and we will not shoot you.'

No one emerged, but eventually there were fewer and fewer shots fired from the house until it finally fell silent. Zinko flicked out the drum of the revolver, saw there was only one round remaining, and looked guiltily at his father. Onysym Liashch was sitting on the bench holding the empty sawn-off shotgun. He had his back pressed against the wall and his immobile face now began to cloud over. 'You sod,' he said, 'didn't you think about me?'

'Maybe they'll let you go Dad,' said Zinko. 'I'll go out to them now, then they'll let you go. Farewell Dad. Farewell and forgive.'

'God will forgive you,' said Liashch.

Zinko left the house and blinked at the bright dawn light. His last remaining brother, his Shtaer, accompanied him. He wordlessly beseeched the gun not to betray him, for he knew it was often the last bullet that stuck.

'Don't shoooooot!' A commanding voice resounded. All guns were aimed at Zinko from every nook, cranny and tree. 'And you. Drop the revolver.'

'Okay,' said Zinko, 'just don't kill the old man. Now watch how people die for Ukraine.' He raised the gun and placed the barrel into his open mouth before squeezing the trigger. His brother did not cheat him, the bullet roared deafeningly with a regretful sound and Zinko felt no pain. His knees folded and he descended slowly to the ground, where his body stretched out as if he were still alive, but his eyes began to ice over and become like glass.

When the Muscovites approached the dead man, their commander, probably not realising what he was doing, took off his cap, leaned over Zinko and covered his eyes. 'He was a redoubtable soldier,' he said. 'It would be apt to bury him properly in a cemetery.'

They looked at the house where thick coils of smoke and fire streamed through the broken windows. It was obvious that someone had poured fuel over everything before lighting a match. They drew back from the flames, which seared their faces, and ran to the gate to wait and see what would happen next, but no one emerged from the house. The flames travelled from the thatched roof to the barn where the livestock was kept, the pig-pen and the livery. The yard was completely burned and all the goods and chattels passed away into the smoke. Only the barn nearest to the field remained intact.

According to word of mouth, old Liashch had not burned. They said that the blackened body that was found was one of the forest boys who had stayed overnight with Zinko. It seemed the old man had made it out alive. Later it was said that he, or perhaps his spirit, appeared at the farm and searched the ground, looking for something in the scorched waste and ashes, and sometimes stayed in the barn. Who, if not him, called mournfully with an owl's call from its roof?

Not every woman would have dared to choose this place for an assignation, thought Raven, as he steered his horse towards the farm. If Mudei had been able to speak he would certainly have asked him where she could have met him now, in the Lebedyn school perhaps or the local government building? Raven would have told the horse that he was only poorly acquainted with this brave lady because he had only met her three times previously; in the Uman staff quarters, where she had shamed Captain Chornousov into using his Ukrainian name; at the clinic, where she had saved him from death; and at the Lebedyn sugar refinery. He still could not believe she had organised the performance.

Be silent, the horse would have replied. You, my man, simply don't know where to go with your agitated feelings and end up thinking who knows what nonsense. So, you saw that black stork carefully looking for something among the scorched morass at night and, remembering the legend about the man, reflected that if Liashch had remained alive he would probably have been changed into a long-legged stork. Why would the old man call like an owl presaging evil when the evil had already happened?

Raven wondered if he had really heard those words interspersed with the Lord's Prayer or if the *Chekists* were waiting to ambush him in the barn. He suddenly felt ashamed for harbouring such a suspicion, but justified the feeling to himself by reflecting that treachery stalked him even where there was not a shadow of faithlessness.

More than one Cossack had lost his life because of a woman. The time had come when he might have to trade his own life for someone else's death, like a scrap of soap for five grammes of tobacco. No, his soul whispered, there is no stink of treachery here. His anxiety was not as a result of sensing danger. It was not a despicable melancholy chill that had overcome him, but a feeling as if, in the emptiness of his chest, his heart had been stripped naked.

The smell of burning around the farm had not been displaced, even by the fragrance of the spring evening. Raven rode to the barn, jumped from the horse and looked around again. There were no pretty women in sight and the black stork was not searching through the ashes. There was just an infinite silence hanging over the fields, but with something of death about it. It was unlike the active stillness one felt in the forest. Perhaps that was why the doors creaked so loudly when Raven opened them and stepped into the standing pool of murk in the barn that smelled of straw. It was then that he caught the tantalising fragrance of a woman's body. A glimmer from another, long-vanished and forgotten world about which he had tried not to think, though it sometimes troubled him in moments of weakness or when he was half asleep.

He looked on her like a deception of the half light, unable to find any words. Tina spoke first and said the most wise and practical thing that could have been said at that moment, 'Lead your horse to the barn.'

It was more secure, particularly as she remembered what had happened to Otaman Skyrta, who had made a mistake that resulted in his capture. He had been spending time with a widow he knew and had let his distinctive bay horse out to pasture nearby. Some lowlife had recognised it and before long the authorities had knocked at the door. Sensing something suspicious, the otaman had attempted to clamber out of the window that opened onto the garden at the back of the house. Unfortunately it was too narrow for him. Not for nothing was he known as Skyrta, meaning haystack. It took ten Muscovites to free him from the window.

As often happened, Mudei knew what to do. When Raven opened the door wider he approached the barn and stood at the threshold. Tina greeted him, 'Let's get acquainted. You're a handsome fellow,' she said, approaching the horse and embracing him, burying her face in the luxuriant mane that swathed his neck. Mudei, the scallywag, blinked sweetly and almost purred like a cat, instead of saying as he should have done, why do you need me, beautiful lady, when there is a man, precious as gold before, you. Embrace him, caress him, kiss him. Tina, as if she had heard that wordless wish, turned to face Raven, stood on her toes and kissed him softly and fully on the lips. He unfastened his coat and hugged her so desirously that she moaned softly, 'Do not suffer, take me,' she breathed. 'Enter me.'

It only took those words with which she made a gift of herself for him to fall to her. He threw his coat onto the straw, which no longer smelled rotten, but of young wheat ears. His hands wandered in her clothing and she gave herself passionately and freely to him, albeit briefly. He held back, like water is held back in a mill wheel, but when her body trembled and the mouth he kissed was rent with a cry she had held in for long enough, he felt the sharp benediction of flowing into one with her. At the last moment, he pulled back, but she again pressed against him with all her force, 'Do not be afraid, I am yours, yours, yours.'

They faced each other and spoke quietly. 'Is it OK to do it again now?' he asked.

'Do what?' She pretended not to understand him.

'Well, ... this ...'

'Are you really so bashful? Just say it straight out, make love with you.'

'This isn't straightforward. Making love is something that is very loving and tender,' he said. 'But I mean ... You weren't afraid. I have heard that women have certain days.'

'You know too much. No, I'm not having one of those kind of days that you talk about.'

'Do you want a child?'

'If I became pregnant I would keep the baby.'

'Why would you want a child without a father?'

'And what are you?'

'I wouldn't be with you.'

'Why wouldn't you be with me?'

'You know the answer.'

'Don't you love me?'

'I love you very much.'

'Say that again,' she beseeched him.

'I love you very, very much.'

'Then why wouldn't you be with us?'

'You know why,' he repeated.

'I know nothing.'

'Our battle is lost,' he said, 'and eventually …'

'It's never too late,' she interrupted. 'We could go somewhere, where no one would find you. Even over the border. I have heard that you can cross over the Zbruch.'

'What would we do there?'

'There are many of our people there. That's where our government is.'

'There is nothing of ours left here now.'

'We would be able to make a new life for ourselves,' she said.

'Perhaps … only not for me.'

'Why not?'

'Because my flag was not embroidered with the words, *A Free Ukraine or Flee Over the Border.*'

'They don't choose death,' she said.

'But she chooses us.'

'You don't value life,' Tina was reproachful. 'You are still young but are already saying farewell to your life.'

'That's not true, I love freedom and freedom can only be bought with blood.'

'And what if there is no hope of freedom? You said it yourself, our struggle is lost. Who needs one more death and yet another unmarked grave levelled with soil?'

'Our goal arises and grows on those graves.'

'You are just being stubborn,' she said, offended. 'You don't hear me.'

'I hear you like my own heartbeat.'

'No, you are deaf to me. I wanted so much to dream with you

today.'

'Futile dreams only bring sorrow my little sparrow.'

Tina suddenly turned her back towards him and he felt her body move as she cried.

'Don't cry,' he said, 'I didn't mean to hurt you.'

'I know that you don't love me,' she sobbed.

'You know nothing. I loved you even before I first met you. I always wanted to be with a woman like you.'

'No, you are disillusioned with me. And I know why.'

'You do! Why?'

'Because I was not a virgin.'

'That's the first time I've heard.'

'You are laughing.'

'Why would I laugh?'

'You make a joke out of everything and that's the last thing I need,' she said. 'Why didn't you ask how I became a woman?'

'Why would I?'

'I thought that was always interesting to a man.'

'Not to me.'

'I want you to know.'

'It isn't of interest to me.'

'I must tell you about it.'

'I know that it happened to you when you were thirteen.'

'Why thirteen?'

'It was so. You crawled into the cherry tree, the berries fell off the branches, heavy and ripe. You gathered them in your hand, threw them into your mouth and your lips, face and hands were stained with cherry juice. Then you saw the red rivulet running down your thighs. You thought you had squashed cherries there, it was not juice but the first time of the month and so you became a woman. Was it not so?'

Tina did not reply immediately. 'Where did you get that idea?' she asked finally, turning her face towards him. He felt such tenderness towards her that it pierced his heart. It was as if this young, untested girl had come to him from a mature cherry tree.

'Come to me.' He kissed her damp eyes and then, slowly, her pale breasts; he caressed her nipples, ripe as cherries, and her small

166

crucifix that was warm from her body.

'You are tickling me to death with your beard.'

'I can endure it no longer, give me more of yourself my darling.'

This time he stayed in her paradise much longer. The sweetness was protracted to the point at which they lost all reason.

'You are crucifying me,' she said and only then, when she had lost all strength, did he release himself.

She was exhausted and silent for so long that he pined to hear her voice. 'How did you find me?' he asked.

'Where?'

'In the church, the refinery and the hospital.'

'I never lost you. I have always followed in your wake. Don't you understand?'

'And in the staff headquarters in Uman?'

'No, that's where I saw you for the first time.'

'Well, why did you say farewell so quickly?'

'I am not a hen you can just grab.'

'You are my white-chested bird,' he said, 'but we may not meet any more.'

'No, that's not so,' disputed Tina.

'Why not?'

'I am a bird who flies here and there on this small world. I just pray every day for you not to perish.'

'I have felt this and lived more than once because of your prayers. When I was given the cap with the ribbon on which was embroidered, *Return With The Dawn*, I worked out whose gift it was. At first I thought it was a parting gift from my beloved, then I read those words and understood that it was my protection against evil. Tina, I have sinned and lost your cap.'

'Where?'

'In battle.'

'Better to lose that than your head.'

'That's what I thought - God took your cap rather than my head, but I regret its loss very much.'

'You are covered in scratches.'

'They don't hurt.'

'They are still frightful to me. Wherever I touch you there is a mark.'

'Did you plan everything that happened at the refinery?' he asked, changing the subject of the conversation.

'They requested that we entertained them with some *Khokhol* vaudeville. They had so much produce that they decided to organise a celebration. As the director of the theatre group all I had to do was convince them that the best place for this was the club at the Lebedyn refinery. I knew that you were nearby.'

'Everything is so easy for you,' he said in astonishment.

'I didn't give the role of *Shelmenko* to that comic with the fangs though. When he tore up to us behind the scenes my heart was in my mouth.'

'That's what he's like,' said Raven, smiling. 'I've known him for quite a while and I'm scared of him myself.'

'I'm a little cold,' she said, pressing against him.

'Cold?' Raven, who could have slept in the snow, had never thought that she might freeze on a coat covering the straw.

'I will warm you now, just once more, then you can dress. I have warm water in the flask there.'

'You have no conscience,' Tina cried out. 'You knew everything in advance.'

'But what did I know?'

'What the warm water would come in handy for.'

'Well, it's like this, water is always necessary.'

'No, you knew that you would lie with me. You are a Casanova.'

'This only means that I love you.'

'You are a Casanova,' repeated Tina. 'I heard long ago that Raven had a sweetheart in nearly every village.'

'Really?'

'I'll strangle you, you insatiable stallion,' said Tina, but in such a tone that it only inflamed his desire further. Even Mudei, who had found a quiet corner for himself and was nosing around for some sustenance, heard the word stallion, twitched his ears and ceased chewing.

This time Raven took her gently, with all the tenderness

168

that his toughened nature could offer. His lips roamed over her body, like a drunken bee roams over the flowers. He was astonished by the gully between her breasts, the smoothness of her stomach, the gentle hillock covered with grass as fine as silk, her rounded buttocks, her slender fingers and short hair, and how cold teeth can be in a thirsty, feminine mouth. For him, her body was a world complete with its forests, lakes, hills, gullies, valleys, warm springs, scents and that secret that he would never tell anyone.

'I'm not cold now,' said Tina, but he wrapped her tightly in his coat and bore her like a swaddled baby in his arms.

'Rest now, my little sparrow. We will have to move soon.'

Raven caught himself speaking to her like he spoke to the Cossacks before they ventured out with those last words, move soon.

Tina closed her eyes, grew calm and breathed so quietly and evenly that it seemed she was asleep. Raven was afraid of moving and waking her.

'Where did you take that girl?' she asked suddenly.

'What girl?'

'The one who plucked the ripe cherries.'

'Isn't that how it was with you?'

'That's how it seems to me now. The more I think about it the more I see that's how it was.'

'Of course.'

'But how could you know that?'

'Well, I saw it, that's all. When you want something very much it is possible.'

'What else can you see about me?'

'Nothing. That's enough for me.'

She fell silent and then, without opening her eyes, said, 'I must tell you about it.'

'What are you talking about?'

'That which doesn't interest you. I don't want to keep it to myself. I ...' Tina's mouth sealed shut as if her words were tied in her throat, 'I was raped by some of the rabble.'

He could only feel the blood banging in his temples.

'There were three of them in ...'

'Stop!'

'They came in the night to the house of Grandmother Maria, where I was staying. One of them knocked on the window and said he was from Raven's unit, Maria hesitated and I urged her to let them in. I grew foolish because your name was mentioned and didn't think about the need to be vigilant. I expected to hear something about you …'

'I adore you,' he said.

'The three of them entered the house and immediately I saw their flat muzzles I knew what they were, but it was too late. They locked Grandmother Maria in the granary and threw themselves at me.' She became silent and gathered her strength before continuing, 'Maybe you don't know this, but it's not easy to rape an adult woman like me. One man alone can't do it if she is strong and fully conscious and I was suddenly filled with such strength. I bit them, lashed out with my arms and legs and scratched them, leaving red welts on their bodies. They would have been unable to do anything to me if one of the *katsaps*, a sickly looking wretch with a red birthmark on his jaw, hadn't struck me and left me disoriented. On the table there was a mixing bowl and a rolling pin because the next day was the Feast Day of Saint Macarius. That slime-ball took the pin, "I'll stuff this thing into you," he said and then struck me on the back of the head.'

Raven listened with a feeling of estrangement. It was as if this had not happened to her but to someone else, a long time ago and in a distant place, but something at the edge of his consciousness whispered, 'On Macarius, the show at the refinery had been after that date ... Tina wished for revenge ... A red birthmark on his jaw …'

He placed her, still wrapped in his coat, on the straw, while blindly groping for his tobacco pouch. When he found it he spent a long time rolling a cigarette, pouring the tobacco into fingers that clumsily disobeyed his will. It was now completely dark in the barn.

'I had to tell you.'

The flame of the match illuminated his rigid, stone face, 'Do you feel better?' he asked.

'Yes.'

'Well, okay then.'

He inhaled the twisting, rich smoke greedily, and with each drag the glowing tip of the cigarette illuminated his knotted beard and stony face against the darkness. He finished smoking and, not knowing where to throw the stub in such a flammable place, snuffed it out with his fingers.

'Are you ashamed of me?' Tina asked.

'Don't you dare speak like that. I would never be. Do you hear me?'

'I don't want you to simply endure me with regret.'

'Stop there or I will …'

'Do what?'

'Take a stick and spank your behind.'

'Go on! Go on!'

He stripped the coat from her and spun her so her buttocks were in the air, but not having a stick to hand punished her in a different way.

'Sweet punishment,' said Tina, with barely restrained delight.

He sat to roll another cigarette as the horse snorted from the corner he had found for himself.

'What's that? Is he listening to us?' asked Tina.

'Who?' Raven asked, not understanding.

'Mudei.'

Raven was astonished by what she had said, 'How do you know my horse's name?'

'I know everything about you. Lord, it seems that's how it was. I always followed in your wake. Didn't you realise?'

'I understand my little sparrow.'

'But what does Mudei mean?' she asked.

'I don't know,' said Raven, shrugging his shoulders. 'Perhaps it means something in horse language, but he won't enlighten you. I like it though.' He lit the cigarette and now his face, illuminated momentarily by the flame, even seemed rather merry.

'I used to smoke once,' said Tina proudly. 'When I studied in Uman, me and the other girls even smoked that strong Makhorka tobacco to ward off hunger. You know that smoking wards off hunger?'

'And you know that it snows in winter?' Raven said ironically.

'Oh, what an idiot I am this evening, I forgot completely. I have brought you supper and you have turned my head so that everything is muddled in there.'

She groped in the darkness and found a jumper that she pulled over her head before going to the barn door and returning with a bag. She put a fried chicken, bread rolls and a flask of *horilka* in front of him, and remembered a little cup for the vodka and a cruet of salt. He filled the cup and gave it to Tina. 'Warm yourself a little so that they won't worry about you at home.'

She drank a slug of *horilka* and gulped mouthfuls of air for a while before she tore off a crust of bread and chewed on it.

'No, that's not how it's done, help yourself.' He tore off a chicken drumstick and presented her with it.

'I am fasting for Easter,' said Tina.

'Oh right, then excuse me, the regime we have in the forest doesn't make allowances for religious fasting.' Raven filled the cup to the brim and proposed a toast, 'For you my little sparrow,' he said, before draining it to the dregs.

Tearing off huge chunks of chicken, he lavished them with salt, making them so tasty that his ears tingled as he ate. Raven had missed having good hearty victuals, not to mention food prepared by a woman's hand. He relished the fact that it was his beloved sitting nearby who had made the food and who did not take her eyes off him. Tina did not bother him by talking while he ate; it was as if Raven were conducting a sacred ritual that demanded silence and utter concentration. Afterwards, when she gave him a towel, Raven moistened it with *horilka* and methodically wiped his mouth and hands.

'I thank you, my little sparrow.'

'I'm so drunk,' whispered Tina.

'You are playing with me.'

'Will you get a stick again?'

'I'll pick up a good sturdy board.'

Raven rose, went to Mudei in the corner, rifled in his saddle bag and returned to the cosy little nest they had made.

'I have brought you a present, ' he said. 'This is due for the cap you gave me.'

She took the dainty little box from his hand, feeling how pleasant it was to the touch, and opened it while Raven struck a match.

172

'Oh!'

A diamond shone with an ethereal blue light on a gold ring. Its substantial mass was surrounded by lesser stones that glittered like dew. The match had burned down to his fingers before Tina asked, 'Where did you get this marvellous thing?'

'Don't worry, I didn't steal it.'

About a year ago they had raided Fundukliivka Station and attacked the Rostov to Kyiv train. In one of the carriages there was a *Chekist* with a whole chest of looted gold and precious stones.

'When will I get to wear this beautiful ring?' Tina was still dazed and surprised by his gift.

'You deserve to have even more beautiful things. Measure it first.'

'But which finger?'

'On which finger do you wear a wedding ring?'

'I'll wear it now,' she said. The ring fitted her finger perfectly.

'Do you see that? I knew they had made it for you ...'

'Listen,' she said, her voice demanding a response. 'Perhaps this is your parting gift. If that's so then I won't take it.'

'What are you talking about? On the contrary ... at least ...' he almost said, for that ring will at least pay them to take you over the border my little sparrow.

'We will see each other more often now?' she asked.

'Of course.'

'It will be Easter soon, I will bring you supper as if I were bringing it to my godfather.'

'No, my little sparrow,' he said. 'I won't be here at Easter.'

'Why not?'

'Don't ask and don't get mad at me. That's just how it has to be.'

He did not want to admit it to himself that the following night he would be on the road. They were moving from their established base in Lebedyn Forest and nearer to Kholodnyi Yar, where the otamans Zaharodnii, Hupalo and Holyk-Zaliznyak awaited him.

'When will we meet again?' she asked.

'I will let you know when I am able to meet. I adore you my little sparrow,' he said.

He drew another breath from his cigarette. A tense silence had settled upon the barn, which was suddenly broken by a pervasive, protracted sound like the hoot of a bird, Pu ... hu. Perhaps an owl had flown to the barn and perched on the thatch, or perhaps Liashch's troubled spirit was crying into the night.

Chapter 2

1

One night Chort, Veremii's adjutant, appeared again at the home of his wife and mother. He approached the baby's cradle, touched him lightly and gazed at the baby in a way that made Hannusia feel uneasy. She wondered if he would put a curse on the child with his heavy, owlish brows. He took out his pouch, which contained some gold coins, waved it above the baby a couple of times and laid the money by his side.

'Boy or girl?' he asked.

'A boy.'

'What is he called?'

'His father will give him a name.'

'That's appropriate,' agreed Chort.

He told them he had come to see them so they would not lose hope and, while drinking a measure of *horilka* and taking supper with them, narrated such a strange, chimerical tale that Hannusia and her mother-in-law did not sleep that night.

He began, reproachfully enough, by informing them that Veremii had recently been shot at the Cherkasy interrogation unit, but added, 'Cheer up, sweetheart, don't get down, everything turned out fine. Do you remember that Veremii had a pocket watch on a chain?' They looked at each other fearfully, unsure where he was going with this story, and nodded.

'It was silver,' said Hannusia. 'Veremii brought it back from the war and treasured it. He said that watch had brought him success.'

'It brought, what it brought,' affirmed Chort. 'I'm coming to that now. The watch did have some hidden power.'

'It wasn't just a simple watch,' said Hannusia, 'there was an inscription on the lid. It had been given to him for his courage.'

'Yes, yes, for his courage,' said Chort, nodding. 'Veremii was never a show-off, but he told me, in his modest way, that he had been awarded that watch by Colonel Almazov when he served in the horse-artillery division. He said that the watch had been his protection from that time onwards. But that's not what I'm talking about, I am talking

175

about the power that it contained. When they captured Veremii and dispatched him to the unit, they threw him into a cell with petty criminals. One of the livelier footpads had the bright idea of stealing Veremii's watch. No, I tell a lie,' said Chort, correcting himself, 'Veremii saw he was doing it, but instead of ripping off his hand, which you know he could have done, he played dumb and kept quiet and do you know what?'

Hannusia and Veremii's mother stared at Chort, who was dragging out their veins from their bodies with his lengthy rendition of events.

'No, you don't know?' he asked, a little delightedly. 'Then I will continue. Perhaps an hour passed before one of the guards entered the cell where he was being held, asked Veremii to make himself known and demanded that he came to the cell door. The men in the cell held their tongues. The guards asked again and threatened to whip the answer out of them. Again, no one replied. Then Veremii approached the crook who had stolen his watch and said, "Leave now Veremii because we will all be punished if you don't." The guards grabbed the crook and dragged him off to be interrogated. Maybe the crook would have lied a little and tried to wriggle out of it but when they found Veremii's watch they didn't want to listen to his protestations any more and promptly shot him. Veremii escaped when he was being transported with some other prisoners. It was easy because they don't guard the crooks as closely as the political prisoners.'

'If he had escaped, he would have let us know,' said his mother quietly.

'How easy do you think it is to just take to your heels and let your family know your whereabouts?' Chort wrinkled his beak-like nose. 'It's not the right time now.'

'Why did they come to us if they knew that Veremii had been shot?' Hannusia asked.

'What? They came again?' he asked in surprise.

'They haven't given us time to take a breath,' said Hannusia. 'They have included me on the list of those who will be shot without a trial in reprisal for rebel activity.'

'Listen, we could hide you and the child,' said Chort, casting an owlish eye at the cradle.

'Where? In a dug-out in the forest with this screaming baby.'

'Why would we hide you in a dug-out? We have people loyal to our cause at the farms.'

'No,' said Hannusia, 'we will wait a little while longer. Perhaps they are just trying to scare us.'

'Perhaps,' agreed Chort. 'I think that while they still haven't found Veremii, they won't take you and the child. Where would they find a more enticing bait than you to lure him out of hiding? However, you must know that we have somewhere to hide you. You would be warm and well fed.'

'Until when?'

'Until everything changes for the better.'

'It seems to me that it will never change for the better.'

'Everything changes. This will change also.' He rose to say good bye.

All things change, the wheel turns and things lament perpetually and all turns back upon itself, thought the old raven in a dream. He had passed the night in the branches of a pear tree in Petrivka. A tree that was also ancient, like him, and had put forth barely any buds this spring.

The raven awoke when the door of the house squealed open and an ungainly man emerged. Even in the darkness it was easy to recognise that long nose, gnarled and knotted as an old oak. Chort mounted his horse and rode into the forest. The raven blinked again and let himself sink into his half dream, half nightmare, for how deep a sleep could be at his age. He had lived for almost three hundred years, which was an unheard of and fortunate instance of longevity among his kind because, although nature gives them the potential to live for centuries, only a few of them live to be older than one hundred years. Many perish from cold and hunger while they are still young, or from the diseases that always afflicted their tribe. Their legs are particularly affected by ailments. It may seem that if you are on the wing you do not really use your legs, but it had rained heavily during the previous winter and then the frost had struck suddenly, and ice fettered the wings of many. They were unable to fly and hopped along

177

on their weak legs until the foxes took them. Our raven saved himself by hiding in an empty foxhole. No one searches for something good right under their nose.

The raven remembered many occasions when incomers had crawled over the land and the locals had been forced to abandon their homes and go into the forest to defend their country. Clouds and clouds of incomers would swarm in on foot, on horses, or on wagons. They had even created some iron sleigh runners that could tow an entire house crammed with people. There was even smoke coming from the chimneys of the houses.

They were not in existence two hundred years ago, thought the raven, but the same thing happened here as happened elsewhere. New arrivals ruled and the native population, who were brave enough, bore their knives in the forest. They had appeared again, for history turns in a perpetual circle and there is nothing new under the sun. People are inclined to evil acts and the raven could remember so many times when evil had the ascendancy. People are a wondrous creation, they kill each other perpetually, but the raven had never torn at a living being with his talons, even during times of ferocious hunger. He suffered sparrows and the smallest mice to pass by unharmed. Yes, he ate corpses and carrion, even pecked out their eyes, because he knew they would not arise and live again. Death is death and mine will come upon me soon, in an unknown place, he thought.

2

At last, after we had watched and waited for so long, we did not hear a call to rise but its distant rumbling. Two emissaries, sent by Yurko Tiutiunnyk, came over the border to initiate preparations for a general uprising, just when, for the first time, we were hesitant and tormented by fatigue and poisonous feuds.

In the summer of 1922 we gave the commune such blows that sawdust poured off its well-hewn trunk. We scourged the requisition units, military emergency units, militia, special assignment units, struck at various Red institutions and carved up activists of all kinds. They were afraid of our spirit and when they travelled the tenth part of the road that ran through the forest, they thought they saw one of our avenging shapes in every tree and bush. It often seemed that the redoubtable passion, which burns in a rebellion's actions, had returned to us.

The villagers again looked to us because, after a long period of hunger, the harvest was due and the occupiers were already eager to get their insatiable talons on the grain. No one wanted to hand over the products of their hard labour and even the Jews of Zlatopol began to help Larion Zahorodnii. They asked for a letter sealed with the *tryzub* from the highest partisan commander to thank them, at which point Larion, with his unchanging smile asked them, 'What higher authority do you need than that with which I am endowed?'

'If you would be so kind, we would like the letter to be from the command based in Tarnov,' they said.

'That's fine,' agreed Zaharodnii, hiding the leather bag containing the coins in his coat pocket. 'I will pass on this to General Tiutiunnyk and you will receive a letter of thanks duly endorsed with the seal from Petliura himself.'

Although, as I say, not everything was going so wonderfully among the rank and file, everyone knew that the time immediately after the harvest would be the best for a general assault. But everyone had his own idea of how to go about this and the otamans hesitated, like everyone else, wondering what might be the best tactics. Hupalo and Zaharodnii locked horns in this dispute. Denys said that it was necessary to be restrained for a while and not engage in operations against the Reds so that we did not incite reprisals against the villagers. Larion, on the contrary, argued that now was the time to batter the requisition squads and all the Red butchery. Still, nothing would have happened if they had only argued about military tactics, but Hupalo button-holed Zaharodnii, 'You, Laryk, are outlining a brave and gallant course of action well enough for us,' he said, waving his Cossack forelock, 'but I have nine brothers and sisters and all of them are hostages.'

Hupalo suddenly fell silent and bit his tongue. It was not good to talk to Larion like that. One year ago, on his birthday, the occupiers had burned down his house and shot his father, Zakhar, on the spot. His pregnant wife and father-in-law had been tortured to death after they were taken to the Yelysavetgrad secret police base for interrogation.

'I am not Laryk to you,' said Zaharodnii cuttingly. 'Laryk sells whistles on the bazaar.' As always he smiled, but there was such sadness in that smile it would have been better if he had been angry.

'Forgive me, Sir Otaman,' said Hupalo, lowering his eyes. 'Forgive me. I didn't think. I am not going away from that. We do need to crush the Red Army scum, but we have to do it without bringing reprisals against the innocent.'

'And are we both guilty?' Zaharodnii asked sharply.

'We are soldiers, we know what we are getting into and now, until everything is resolved, I am calling on us all to have some forethought.'

'Until what is resolved?' Zaharodnii asked, yet more sharply.

'The situation over the border,' said Hupalo.

'Which border?'

'I'm talking about where our insurrection headquarters is based.'

'I want to shit on that particular place from a very high tree.' Zaharodnii seethed. 'Are you still so unaware of what we are to them? There is one thing I can't understand, if Petliura and Tiutiunnyk aren't planning to return to Ukraine then why don't they, being so smart, pass on their command to someone else? Can't they find someone there who could take command of the struggle here, rather than issuing directives from some foreign morass? I regard this as a crime. A crime for which they must answer.'

'Whoa-ah!' Hupalo interrupted. 'We've gone way off track here.'

'I've gone way off track with this,' said Zaharodnii, becoming more incensed. 'Was it me who called on you to disband or those who are driving bitches around in fashionable vehicles? Perhaps they are sitting down to dinner with them in restaurants abroad.'

'That's enough, both of you,' I said, joining the argument. 'First, let us bring ourselves to order. We must place ourselves under the authority of a single otaman so we quarrel less.'

'What for?' Hupalo asked in surprise. 'We are given to operating in small groups now.'

'All the same, we must have a single commander,' I said, 'for discipline and for the agreement of further operations. Regarding tactics, which the otamans were engaged in discussing, then, with all my soul, I am on Larion's side. Therefore, I say that while we are based in Kholodnyi Yar and Chornyi Forest, we should place ourselves under the authority of Otaman Zaharodnii.'

Hupalo wrinkled his nose and scratched the base of his forelock as if reluctant to endorse my proposal. However, he announce his agreement to placing himself under Zaharodnii's authority. Yes, he would follow Zaharodnii's orders even if he commanded them right now to pickle one hundred vats of red cabbages for the winter.

We did not know then that the commander of the Black Sea Insurrectionist Group, the captain of the U.N.R. Army, Hamalii, and his Chief of Staff, Zaviriukha, had already arrived in Yelysavetgrad to organise a general insurrection and were seeking the most direct route to us. They were conspiring in private apartments and, without undue haste or fuss, began the gradual establishment of relations with the underground in the town and with reliable, well-vetted people, who could guide them to the otamans of Kholodnyi Yar and Chornyi Forest.

It happened that the first otaman they approached was Hupalo. Denys had a good friend, Mykola Sylvestrov, the son of a forester, who had been useful to the rebels on more than one occasion and who told Hupalo that Colonel Hamalii and Sergeant Zaviriukha wanted to meet with him. Hupalo agreed, but stipulated the day, hour and location of the meeting himself. The situation demanded a cool head because he did not know why they came or with what purpose. Hupalo said that he would wait in Chornyi Forest among the birch foliage, near a strip of woodland known to them, at seven o'clock in the evening. Sylvestrov would lead them and show them the route. After listening to these words, Hupalo placed his hand on the hilt of his cavalier sabre and looked expressively at his friend to ensure that Sylvestrov understood that, if there was any provocation, his head would be the first to roll.

That evening Hupalo concealed twenty Cossacks near the meeting place, among them were his brothers, Ivan and Stepan, and two of his bodyguards. He rode to the rendezvous on his long-legged stallion, ready for the meeting. He had not reached the rendezvous when he saw three riders, Sylvestrov and two others, who looked like Red Army soldiers. Hupalo halted his horse and took his Austrian rifle from his shoulder. His guards, Martyn Doroshko and Fedir Momsa, had already done so. He recognised Mykola, but still bellowed angrily, 'Who goes there? Dismount and lay your arms on the ground quickly.'

'They are on our side,' replied Mykola, 'maybe you could order us to lie on the ground ourselves.'

'Lay down your weapons. Am I talking to you or not?'

When they had complied with his order, Hupalo rode to them and leaped from his horse. 'Tell me what you want?'

Before getting acquainted with them he took a silver watch, which hung from a simple chain, out of his pocket, looked at it and nodded to himself, 'Aha, you came punctually. If you had been late, only a fool would have waited here for you.'

He looked at the strangers, one of whom was dressed in a dirty, green uniform, like a member of a requisition squad. The stranger looked back at Hupalo with such sincere interest and enthusiasm that he confused the latter. This guest had a pale face, which was a little elongated, giving the impression that he was perpetually surprised, but also honourable and attentive. It was immediately apparent that he was not a forester.

'Sergeant Zaviriukha.' He introuced himself and squeezed Denys's hand in a powerful grasp.

Hupalo did not reply with his name, but just nodded his head and moved his gaze towards the other stranger, 'Aha, if that is Zaviriukha, then this must be Colonel Hamalii.'

His face seemed familiar to Hupalo and he suddenly recognised Yalysej Lyutyi, with whom he had served alongside in 1920, in Kost Blakytnyi's Steppe Division. Hupalo knew that Yalysej had his own squad now and that it roamed near Kryvyi Rih, but he had never expected to see him in the role of Colonel Hamalii.

'No, no Denys, I am not the commander of the Black Sea Group,' said Yalysej, seeing Hupalo's surprise, 'Colonel Hamalii couldn't make it today. I accompanied Sergeant Zaviriukha here so that you would not be suspicious.'

This explanation was not to Hupalo's liking. He knew Sylvestrov and Yalysej, but he did not trust anyone completely. People were now visibly bending under the pressure of the occupation and even if they were not yet in the net of the *Cheka*, they could still fall into it.

'Well, that's how it is again. We agreed on one thing but another happened, and instead of Hamalii, we got Zaviriukha.' This was not right as far as Denys was concerned.

'I see that you're not happy, Otaman,' said Lyutyi. 'Don't you trust us?'

'I am not an otaman,' said Hupalo, guardedly.

'What do you mean, you're not an otaman?'

'I am Hupalo-Harasko and only in temporary command of the squad.'

'Oh, right.' Lyutyi looked in surprise at Sylvestrov, as if to say, what kind of news is this? But Sylvestrov only shrugged his shoulders in reply.

'Well, that's an otaman's horse you have there.'

'I bought her from the Chief of the Znamianskyi garrison,' Hupalo softened a little as he recollected how he had 'bought' the stallion.

'And did you dispatched this same chief to the heavenly chancellery?' asked Lyutyi merrily.

'No, they would not accept him there. I gave him to the beasts for supper.'

'Good lad. And you are still fooling around pretending that you are not the otaman. We didn't come to you for empty chatter, Denys, the hour has come for which we can all wait no longer. Lead us to the squad, Sergeant Zaviriukha has some serious conversation for us.'

'That's true,' interjected Zaviriukha, who had maintained a polite silence for long enough. 'We are wasting time.'

'Don't fuss yourself,' Hupalo said, cooling him down, 'you are going nowhere in a hurry, we don't know yet if I will let you leave the forest.'

'Your caution is indeed praiseworthy,' said Zaviriukha.

'But how could I act otherwise? I don't know you and I don't trust you. So please excuse me.'

'Haven't your friends explained to you?'

'I have no friends,' Hupalo said sharply.

'Well, this is going too far,' said Zaviriukha darkly. 'Either we go to the squad or we go back.'

'No, we will sit and talk here,' said Hupalo firmly. 'I will listen to what you have to say. If not I will consider in which direction you are heading.'

Hupalo's bodyguards, Martyn Doroshko and Fedir Momsa, who were still on horseback with their rifles at the ready, looked at each other merrily. It seemed that this was how they liked it.

Hupalo nodded at them to stay in place and led the guests to one side and they sat on the ground. It seemed that Zaviriukha really did have something to say and, after a little while, the otaman thawed a little. The sergeant gained his trust more because he spoke as if he were using Hupalo's own words, about things that had long been boiling up inside everyone. He said that they had a last chance to raise a general insurrection against the Muscovite occupants across the whole of Ukraine. However, for that to happen, all the underground and rebel forces had to be united under a single command.

'Our armed forces, which are currently over the border, will come here in substantial numbers. There will be no less than thirty-thousand soldiers crossing the River Zbruch in three groups. General Bezruchko will lead a section of the military to Kyiv, General Udovenko to Odesa, and General Tiutiunnyk, at the head of the cavalry, will ride rapidly between the two armies towards Kholodnyi Yar, which will become the centre of the general uprising. We intend to engage in a massive rebellion with our own forces before then, but for that we need discipline and obedience. It is necessary to gather all the units into a single fist, to embed our own capacity for action, and we need, as soon as possible, to hold a meeting of all the otamans to agree on our operations and the date of the general uprising,' said Zaviriukha.

When he heard the proposal for a meeting of all the otamans, Hupalo became guarded again. The operation seemed good, but things were not that simple. Perhaps this was a *Chekist* ploy?

'Which otamans would you be able to organise a meeting

with?' asked Zaviriukha. 'Next time Colonel Hamalii will definitely be here.'

'And who among the otamans are of interest to you?'

'Zaharodnii, Raven, Holyk-Zaliznyak.'

'I will try to communicate with them,' said Hupalo guardedly. 'And when do you plan to hold the meeting?'

'It will be at least a week from now. I will let you know through Mykola.'

Hupalo had not noticed the dusk drawing in as they conversed and when Zaviriukha gave him a written order from the commander of the Black Sea Insurrectionist Group, handwritten on a piece of checked paper, he was unable to read it and said that he would look at it by the firelight after he had returned to the camp.

3

Bandit terror is raging once again in the areas adjoining Kholodnyi Yar and the Chornyi and Chutovskyi forests. The conditions are reminiscent of former times when the rebellion was in full bloom.

In addition, the rebel bands have potentially greater forces in the form of underground organisations, insurrectionists and the 'secret hundreds'. They are vigorously preparing for a mass uprising at the first sign, when they will join numbers of the operational groups.

Raven's gang has operated with particular distinction. On June 11 they struck against a peat extraction facility at the Ivanova dam, seven versts to the west of Smila. They plundered various institutions and scattered leaflets with a call to 'Kill the Communists and Katsaps!'

On August 6 a skirmish occurred between the bandits and a flying unit of the 73rd regiment, under the command of District Chief Zommer-Charryn, which resulted in his death. Three platoon commanders were also lost, along with one political manager and 12 Red Army soldiers. As a rule, the bandits feel free to travel around the villages and farms as if it were their own country. Peasants of the Sentovskaia district, from the Kulikovskyi farms, say that the forest rebels visit frequently and take produce and fodder, but pay for everything with interest. They are replete with many different currencies - Soviet, Tsarist, Polish, Petliurite.

In more recent times, Raven's gang often operates jointly with the gang of another well-known leader, Zaharodnii. Ataman Hupalo maintains a separate force and has concealed his men in Chornyi Forest, several versts from Horlivka Station. That is in a zone declared criminal by soviet power. Anyone who is discovered there may be shot on the spot. It follows that we should pay attention to this artful and skilful thief. He is about 35 years of age, has a Cossack's forelock and loves to recite Shevchenko's verses before his bandits.

It is not apt to speak about the serious conflicts between the atamans. We have information that Raven is wounded again and resting in the lair of his colleague, Hupalo.

Plenipotentiary of the Chief of Staff Glazunov
PP Chief of the Operative Division Semenov
Correct: Office Secretary Diakonov

From information collated by the Kremenchuk staff of the secret police department, 20 August 1922

Laying his 'leisure' coat on the grass, Raven stretched out in the cold air at the edge of a small clearing, waiting for the boys to bring their dear guest. He was trying to write on a crumpled piece of paper with his left hand, but did not produce anything legible. It would have been easier for him to wield his sabre in his left hand than the partially sharpened pencil, but his right arm was not yet obedient to his will. Not long ago, a bullet had wounded him near his right elbow. It had missed the bone and only torn a vein, but the loss of so much blood had weakened him.

He was wounded at night when his men had joined forces with those of Larion Zaharodnii and attacked a Red Army garrison in Fedvar. They had heard that the Reds had given arms to the town turncoats so they could battle with the bandits. There were about thirty of these 'brave lads' and they, the fuckwits, were firing chaotically into the woods in daylight. They had managed to get the silly devils to throw their useless weapons into their cart. Vovkulaka had confiscated one of their flags, embroidered with long, curving Russian letters that read, 'The Fifth All Ukrainian Gathering of Workers and Peasants, Soviets and Red Cossack Deputies'.

They flew to Dmytrivka with these valuable trophies, but unexpectedly stumbled onto the cavalry of the 75th Brigade and had to withdraw. The night saved most, but not all, of them. Matvii Momot, the oldest of the Momot brothers, perished. The two youngest brothers bore him in their arms for a long time 'so that it would not hurt so much' but he was already beyond any pain.

Raven was wounded in the elbow. He thought it was just the usual scratch and did not pay it any attention until he felt blood streaming from his sleeve, and the darkness in his eyes obscured the darkness of the night. It is shameful to say that he lost consciousness and did not see how they grabbed him and laid him on a cart, which took him to Hupalo's camp, or how they brought a blindfolded doctor from Znamyanka. A large man, who looked like a vet, sewed up Raven's vein and said, 'He needn't be afraid, the hand won't wither.'

The hand of the Cossack who guided him back to the village, like a blind mole, was certainly sturdy enough.

Raven was recuperating in Hupalo's camp. He had recovered his strength a little and was angry at Vovkulaka for coming to him with food that he said was good for those who had lost blood. He brought him cheese, butter and raw eggs, and pressed him to eat carrots. Raven could not endure it, 'Take away this vegetable patch. I am not a hare, nor do I have hare's blood. Give these delights to Khodya. He'll devour them without any problem.' He kept a morsel of bread and a mug of milk next to him in the shaded area under a bush.

Meanwhile, Hupalo, Zaharodnii and Holyk-Zaliznyak were going to meet Zaviriukha, to lead him back to the camp. Hamalii was also due to visit them in a few days, but for now he had another matter that required his attention; Yalysej Lyutyi had invited him to a council of the Kryvorizzhia otamans.

***

Again, there were thirty Cossacks concealed in the foliage, but this time three otamans were riding to the meeting place in the cleared area of the forest. They were a stone's throw away when Zaharodnii's horse stumbled.

'Denys,' he said, drawing on the reins, 'go ahead we are behind you.'

'Why so?' said Hupalo, not understanding.

'The horses aren't walking in step with each other,' replied Zaharodnii, and looked at Holyk-Zaliznyak. 'How are you feeling?'

'Like before the first meeting, a pinion up his arse,' confessed Mefodii.

'OK, let's go.' Hupalo spurred his horse.

As he approached the clearing, he noticed a rider who was already known to him. He was dressed like a member of a requisition squad. The rider, in his turn, recognised Hupalo's forelock and he rode to meet him. They shook hands and Zaviriukha asked why he was alone, then realised that the Cossacks were being vigilant for their security.

Zaharodnii and Holyk came to meet them, but did not hurry to shake hands, instead they cast suspicious glances at the stranger and deliberately did not halt their horses. They circled around Zaviriukha, who was looking enthusiastically at the otamans. His astonished face seemed to become more elongated. At last, he took a concealed message out of the lining of his coat and gave it to Zaharodnii. It was his credentials from the Head Insurrectionary Staff, signed by Tiutiunnyk, which affirmed that he, Sergeant Zaviriukha, was the Chief of Staff of the Black Sea Insurrectionist Group. Zahorodnii knew Yurko Tiutiunnyk and his swerving, hooked signature and did not omit to say this out loud as he passed the message to

Holyk-Zaliznyak, 'Look at it. This isn't anything dodgy.'

'What do you mean, that it's not fake?' Zaviriukha asked in a satisfied manner.

Zaharodnii replied in his own manner with a question to Zaviriukha, 'Isn't it dangerous and alarming to bring such a document into a zone that has been pronounced beyond the law?'

'There is no one more frightening than you here, Sir Otaman,' said Zaviriukha, and Larion at last smiled into his black beard.

'Then away to the camp. Let's talk as is fitting.'

Hupalo was a little annoyed that Zaharodnii, even if he was within his rights as the senior otaman, was behaving as if he were on his home territory by inviting the guest, when it was Hupalo's prerogative as the master here. However, he kept silent and was the first to direct his horse towards those paths that he knew better than anyone.

They travelled through the forest, which was a little dark, even on this glorious August day, through shrubbery and dense undergrowth. It seemed that these wild woods were alive; that human bodies moved around every tree, and watchful eyes stared from the smallest bushes. Soon Zaviriukha noticed people moving freely between the trees, staring from the bushes and looking curiously at the otamans who were guiding an unusual guest to the camp.

They came to a clearing at the edge of which they found Raven lying on his coat. His right arm was in a sling and within arm's reach of him were a rifle, revolver, notepaper and a mug of milk. Zaviriukha greeted him and Raven rose precariously, knocking over the mug and sending rivulets of milk running over his coat. When Zaviriukha jumped off his horse and stretched out his hand to Raven, instead of shaking it, he clumsily embraced the guest with his left arm.

'I heard about you long ago,' said Zaviriukha, 'and I'm glad to make your acquaintance. Are you badly wounded?' he added, indicating to the sling with his eyes.

'I can shoot with my left hand,' replied Raven. 'I am only unable to write.'

'Well, we have enough scribbling and chatting going on. The main thing is to be able to shoot.'

Zaviriukha could certainly talk. All the people who came from over the border spoke as smoothly as silk, as if they had graduated from an elite academy that specialised in the art of rhetoric. When Zaharodnii summoned the officers into the circle of his listeners, ten more men joined them. Zaviriukha gave a long speech, which did not fray anyone's nerves. It seemed to them, as it had seemed to Hupalo, that he spoke with their lips and their words. He spoke of their torn country, of the unconscious *Khokhols* who thrust their heads into the Muscovite yoke, of the pleading of Mother Ukraine, and how all should unite against the plague. He said that the time for a general uprising was coming and the date would not be decided abroad; it would be decided by the otamans' council. Therefore, he asked them to be aware of the huge responsibility that was on their shoulders.

'We are obliged to be ready for a rapid change in our working methods,' said Zaviriukha. 'We must regroup so that each one of us knows his area in detail, the place for which he is responsible, so that we can work with you gentlemen and not wander through the forest aimlessly occupied with who knows what.'

Words are words, but Zaviriukha moved to action. Each otaman was given a cipher with the code name 'Testament', to enable him to communicate secret information securely. He also provided them with some written orders from the Black Sea Insurrection Group and then waited to listen to what the otamans had to say. But what could they say? They could not have two opinions, they needed to go to work and meet with Colonel Hamalii as soon as possible, to agree on a date for the otamans' council.

'We will meet in the next few days,' promised Zaviriukha. 'You, Raven, I see are dissatisfied with something.'

'Err, how do I explain this to you?' said the otaman slowly. 'I will place myself under the authority of the group headquarters and implement these orders on one condition, that, unless it's clearly necessary, I will not undertake any regrouping or relocate anywhere distant. I will work on the line between Znamyanka, Kholodnyi Yar, Yelysavetgrad and Lebedyn. Here they know me like they know Zaharodnii, Zaliznyak and Hupalo, and I am always able to rely on the support of the people from the villages. We'll see what happens next.'

'Okay,' agreed Zaviriukha and turned to Zaharodnii. 'And if

there is an uprising, how many swords could you provide today?'

'It's hard to say,' replied Zaharodnii. 'It depends on what flame is burning. If it reaches to the heavens, then tens of thousands; if it's just on command, then we, Raven, Hupalo and Zaliznyak, could supply a good thousand. That's without otamans Pryjmak, Svyshch, Orel-Kurka and some other units.'

'That's not bad for a start,' said Zaviriukha. 'I see that you haven't been wasting your time here. I will tell Colonel Hamalii about our meeting and we will come together next time.'

'Come the day after tomorrow, that is the holiday of the Transfiguration of Jesus,' advised Hupalo. 'We will meet in the Cossack manner.'

'You don't forget holy days here?'

'If we forget about the Saviour, the Saviour will forget about us,' said Raven.

'That's glorious, only unfortunately we can't come the day after tomorrow.'

'Let's sit down before you set off home,' proposed Hupalo. 'The boys will bring melons and *horilka* fragranced with grass and we will throw a few drinks down our necks.'

'Maybe just one before I depart. You told me what kind of zone this is.'

They sat on the ground in a circle, where they had previously been standing, and a massive, green carafe appeared in Hupalo's hands. In the middle of the grass tablecloth rolled green-skinned, young melons, tomatoes and baked potatoes. After the carafe of *horilka* had travelled between them, Holyk-Zaliznyak, who had been silent for long enough, was drawn into the conversation and taking a photograph of a kind-faced, young man in a greatcoat of a Red Army commander out of his pocket, passed it to Zaviriukha. 'Can you work out who this is?'

'Your brother?' said the sergeant, shrugging his shoulders.

'No, a pinion up his arse,' purred Mefodii. 'The commander of a Red unit, still fresh. We only pickled him the day before yesterday.'

'Look,' said Zaviriukha, enthusiastically. 'You wouldn't say he was dead looking at him. Are you collecting these cards?'

'No,' said Mefodii, 'I make a gift of them to the girls.'

'What for?'

'It's like this you see. They write on the back of them, 'to Hania from Vania' and use them to scare off the poor peasant activists who are hassling them. It says, see what a cavalier my man is, if you dare so much as lay a finger on me, he'll cut off your balls.'

'That's glorious.' Zaviriukha smiled. 'They become a serious document. Did you think up this yourself or did the girls suggest it?'

'My sisters,' said Mefodii. 'They came to me and said, "If you are going to sit in the woods, then make some photo cards for us so the men won't bother us." So I did. I gave the older one, Sashunia, a photo of the garrison commander and Zinka, though she is still a maiden, the one of the commander.'

'Glorious. Is it true,' Zaviriukha said, turning to Zaharodnii, 'that not long ago, you fermented the head of the district *Cheka*?'

'What do you want? To look at his photo?'

'Are you also collecting them?'

'No, there aren't enough pockets for me to put them in. That head *Chekist* wasn't alone, he was with his comrades,' he added, saying the last word in Russian. 'Oh, it was a delight beyond words,' he recollected. 'Instead of photos, I found some papers in his bag in which I read that, in Haisyn, in a very interesting location, there is quite a bit of gold hidden.'

'Quite a bit? How much?' Zaviriukha asked.

'Five *poods*. It's necessary to go and look over that place in Haisyn, ha.' Zaharodnii looked at Raven, who in turn wrinkled his forehead so intensely that Larion did not know what he meant. Was Raven supporting him and implying they should have a look, or giving him a sign to talk less about the Haisyn gold. Larion fell silent and gripped a chunk of melon in his mouth.

'All this is great, even romantic,' said Zaviriukha, 'but we have to cease the shedding of blood. The greater business may be lost amid such trivial distractions. From now onwards, if you want to do serious work you are obligated not to undertake any independent operations without permission from the headquarters of the group. Have you forgotten that there is an order from the head insurrectionary staff to refrain from action, pending a new signal from the centre?'

'Stupid,' said Zaharodnii, dribbling a melon seed out over his lower lip, 'these leaders who would guide us are like a dimwitted priest offering inane prayers.'

'Why is it stupid?' Zaviriukha asked.

'Because no one sought our advice.'

'You are right there, Zaharodnii. Now everything will be different and no one will disregard your views. I say once more, everything has to be decided by the otamans who have taken the fundamental burden of struggle upon themselves, but there must be a single command centre. Leave the trifle of the Haisyn gold for now, let's first have the head otamans' council.'

Raven winked at Zaharodnii, but this time Larion understood him correctly. *Let the man say what he wants, we'll do things our way.* The otamans knew that Zaviriukha was not talking foolishly, but they wished to preserve their honour. In truth, they liked the sergeant. It was the first time one of their own kind of men had approached them from the government in exile. Having shaken their hands in farewell, he went to his horse and did not dance stupidly by it but thrust his foot into the stirrup and mounted so easily and agilely that there was no doubt. You could not sit a cavalier like him in the staff headquarters. This man, from everything they could see, had smelled gunpowder and clattered his sabre off enemy skulls.

Zaharodnii and Holyk-Zaliznyak went their own way and Raven stayed in Hupalo's camp, nursing his wound like a lame duck whose flock had left it behind. You should be glad, he thought, the ice is cracking. But somehow there was no delight in his heart, he knew he had to eat and gather his strength, but he could neither eat nor drink. A feeling of ennui and melancholy, which he could not dispel, settled on him. Ennui that he usually never allowed to draw so close to him because it was a poison worse than any pain or disease. The revolt for which he had waited was so close, but a feeling of emptiness oppressed him with mortal anguish. Raven stretched out, seeking some felicity in his recollection of the woman who had once been on this coat and left the fragrance of her body. It was a body over which his thoughts wandered sweetly.

He was suddenly torn out of his intoxicating reverie by a thought, and shouted at the nearest Cossack, 'Bring Vovkulaka to me.'

'Is he the one whose teeth are too big for his mouth?' asked

Hupalo's fraternal man, who still did not know all Raven's Cossacks well.

'What? Is there someone called Vovkulaka in your band too?'

'No, we have a Vovkodav, a Vovhura and a Vovchun, but they all have normal teeth, not fangs.'

'Find me the one with the fangs.'

After two minutes had passed, Vovkulaka was standing in front of Raven.

'I agreed with the boys that I would bring you some calf liver, it is good for the blood,' he said, singing his usual song.

Raven interrupted him, 'I have a special commission for you.'

Vovkulaka's nostrils flared eagerly. It was a long time since he had been given some quality work to do.

'Take two others and check out every place, every nook and cranny where Red deserters can hide. Ask in the villages and farms.'

'Why are you interested in that garbage?'

'Listen carefully. Shake down everything from Chutovskyi Forest and, if you have to, Lebedyn and Zvenyhorodka. I need the deserter with a red birthmark on his jowls. I think he will be unique. When you find him establish if he was in Lebedyn last summer.'

Vovkulaka focused his mind with all his strength. He did not want to lose the slightest detail of Raven's order. The otaman had never before presented him with such a surprising directive. It was tempting to enquire further, but Vovkulaka sensed this was not an occasion when he needed to know everything.

'If he is in our region, we will find him,' he said.

'Vovkulaka, I need him, no matter what it takes.'

'Alive.'

'No, dead. I don't want you bothering yourself too much with him. There are two other scum-bags slithering around with this monster, who should also be despatched into the other world.'

'You just want me to kill them, that's all?' asked Vovkulaka in disappointment.

'No,' said Raven. 'Do to them what we do with rapists.'

'Understood.'

'I am placing my hopes in you Vovkulaka. Dress in Red

Army gear, don't carry a banner and don't be foolish. Take Khodya, he resembles a Red more than you. Who else do you want?'

'If it's possible, let Bizhu come with us.'

'Okay, take the French guy with you,' Raven said as he smiled.

Bizhu was the youngest of the Momot family and was very fond of the name Bizhu, which means, I run. Whatever he was asked, wherever he was summoned, the word 'Bizhu', was always on the tip of his tongue. If he began to narrate something it was usually, Bizhu, I run up to the girl and she runs to meet me, then we run into the bush and then we run out into the night and into the sky. Well, lads, I must run for I have to run, then I'll run back and say where else we ran. That was Bizhu, a sincere, quick-spirited lad who would not hold back from anything required of him and was so light on his feet that he could run all day, as swiftly as a horse.

'If you don't find him, return when the week is up,' said Raven. 'I am ready to take the sabre in my hand and there will be much work to do.'

'We will find him,' Vovkulaka assured Raven. 'If he hasn't drawn back to his Russia, we will discover him, even in the bowels of the earth. Well, shall I run Bizhu now?' Vovkulaka said, showing his fangs, and Raven realised he was joking.

'With God.'

Chapter 3

1

Hotsman and his men had returned and they were taking Hannusia to be shot. It was a balmy summer day in August. The fields were brimming with flowers, there was brilliant sunshine and the sky was as soft and silken as a dove's plumage. Birds sang and grasshoppers chirruped as Hannusia was taken through fields and past gardens to the Kryve gully where she and Veremii had once dug clay for a house. And look at what was happening now. She would be forced to lie in the clay and there was no need to dig; a pit had been prepared for her.

Hotsman had kept his word and not visited their house for one month, and both women were beginning to think that maybe he had forgotten them, but after the Transfiguration of Jesus he flew on them with a squad of anti-banditry unit men.

Eight riders galloped into their yard and Hotsman asked Hannusia for the last time, 'Does this mean that his bandit life is dearer to you than your own or your bastard's? Well, I agree, let it be so. But in this case you are the one who will answer for all his criminal actions. The law is such that now you are answerable. Your name is on the list of those who can be executed for the bandit's crimes. I ask you again, bitch, where is your bandit?'

'He has perished,' said Hannusia.

'You are lying, bitch.' Hotsman twitched his blistery neck, grabbed the revolver and laid it on the cradle where the baby, frightened by the *Chekist's* shouting, was crying. 'I'll calm your bastard and then you.'

'Kill me, me.' Mother threw herself at him, but he struck her with his revolver so violently that she was thrown against the wall and crumpled quietly onto the bench.

'Speak animal.' He grabbed Hannusia by the hair coiled on the nape of her neck, her tresses dangled over her shoulders and breasts, and dragged her so violently that candle flames danced across her vision. When Hotsman fired into the cradle, lightening flashed painfully across her head and the sound deafened her. She did not realise that her child was still alive, even though he continued to cry.

Hotsman was only trying to frighten her and he had fired with the intention of missing the baby, but she did not think about the child or herself. It was as if she looked on everything like the turbulent images of a dream in which she was being carried along powerlessly. When he ordered her to take the child and leave the house she did so, lifting the baby in his bedding and pressing him to her breasts.

They led her from the village to the Kryve gully. Some distance behind them she heard the voice of her mother-in-law, who had recovered consciousness. The baby cried in her arms, but Hannusia did not hear, she only heard the birds singing and the chirruping of grasshoppers. She saw everything as if she were looking down from on high. She had bare feet and was dishevelled, but still pressed her child against her breasts with all her strength. She had become oblivious to him and it was as if she were holding a mere vessel. In her trance-like state she thought of the whole world, of all its birds and blue flowers, speaking to it so loudly and with such anguish that people in the village heard, and long after she had gone told each other of how, when she was being led out to be shot, she spoke yearningly, 'Farewell world of pure light. Farewell dear birds.'

Hotsman's horse trotted ahead of them as he looked into her face, over which a lock of hair had fallen, and screamed in a shrill voice, 'So, the angels stole him. Why don't they steal you right now, you witch, and we'll see how they do it?'

Hannusia had not noticed him for a while, he was not in that world to which she was saying farewell, and this angered him still more. He led her to the edge of the gully, which fell away so steeply that one felt terrified by just looking at it, and ordered his 'special troops' to dismount and prepare their rifles. They did this quickly, stood ten paces from Hannusia, and aimed their rifles at her. Hotsman waited before giving the command to fire because he wanted to toy with her for a while longer and to interrogate her further. He was getting ready to take the baby from her and hold him by his leg over the edge of the ravine. Maybe then her tongue would be untied.

He approached Hannusia. 'Give the baby to me,' he demanded and stretched out his hands, but Hotsman was no longer in her world, her unpeopled world where there were only flowers and the small voices of birds who sang to Hannusia. For the last time she said, 'Farewell, world of pure light. Farewell, dear birds.'

The body of her child flew through the air with her as they both hurtled into the ravine.

Hannusia, Hannusia, my pure spirit, you did not have a few minutes more that would have sufficed for your salvation, you threw yourself and your child over the edge. If only your mind had been clouded as you fell onto the clay, still holding your child. A thread of blood flew from your lips and it seemed the child had died too. Do you hear my darling, the baby was stunned but then cried again and that cry announced his life.

Suddenly, there was a hoarse shout of, 'As you were!'

Three Red Army troops galloped from a patch of forest not far from the gully, it was so scant it would barely have provided cover for a hare. There was an urgency in their sudden gallop out of nowhere, as if they were obeying some significant order. They went straight to Hotsman, 'As you were. It's an order.'

'Who are you? Which division?' Hotsman's eyes blinked at them in confusion. He still had not recovered from what had just happened and now these three riders galloped out of nowhere. 'I asked you which part of our forces are you from?'

'And you are what, blind? The anti-gang unit.'

Seeing a Chinese man among them Hotsman calmed down a little, but what was this about giving him orders and who could have issued them apart from Hotsman himself?

'We have to arrest you for this,' said their commander, who had such a terrifying fanged visage that Hotsman's stomach turned over. 'This is an order from Division Chief Kapsapinskii.'

'Who?' Hotsman's eyes glittered with fear.

'You will know later,' replied the fanged one, pressing his rifle against the crown of Hotsman's head. 'All of you, lay down your weapons now.'

The special troops were preparing to resist, but Hotsman, more balanced due to the cold touch of the gun on his crown, gave them a sign to comply. When their arms were lying on the ground, Vovkulaka, not having time to reflect, fired a shot. This was followed by Khodya and Bizhu, who also fired their rifles. Vovkulaka got a good shot that sent part of Hotsman's brain spattering from his skull and onto the other troops, who fell very shortly after him without having time to work out who, without a judge or prosecution, had cut them down on the spot.

Vovkulaka galloped to the edge of the ravine and led his horse down a path into its depths. Hannusia was lying on her back without breathing. She was not yet rigid, though the thread of blood by her mouth had stopped flowing and had hardened. She was still holding the baby to her breast. It writhed in her embrace but did not cry, instead it quietly gasped for air. Vovkulaka jumped from his horse, got down on his knees and touched Hannusia's neck. He crossed himself before freeing the baby from her embrace and taking him in his arms.

Without really knowing what to do next, he murmured, 'Choo choo,' as he tried the best he could to soothe the baby, but Vovkulaka's cooing resembled a wolf's prolonged howls. He pursed and smacked his lips, like one would do with a horse, and the baby fell silent and smiled at him. He did not know how to conduct himself, but noticed a terrified woman running towards him, with an old grandmother limping hurriedly in her wake. It was Veremii's mother and her neighbour, Tanasykha. She fell by Hannusia and did not utter a word, but wrung her hands on her breast, unable to move her gaze from the motionless body of her daughter-in-law. Tanasykha charged at Vovkulaka, 'Did you do this, you Antichrist?' she screamed.

'This isn't our work,' said Vovkulaka. 'We are your people.'

He smacked his lips at the baby again and Tanasykha declaimed over Hannusia, 'Open your eyes our bright star, part your cranberry-red lips and speak even one word to us.'

Vovkulaka could not listen to that kind of emotional talk. He moved to one side and turned away, but when he wanted to smack his lips at the child again he could not purse them properly and made only a faint sound. He blinked his scorched lashes, slightly nonplussed, as Veremii's mother spoke to him, 'Sonny, sweetheart, I bless you. Take this child and hide him with good people on a farm somewhere, for the Reds will return and kill him. You have your people, let them take him, but tell no one that this is Otaman Veremii's son, for they will find him.'

Vovkulaka was completely lost. He surely had other serious work to do. He, Khodya and Bizhu had been seeking the deserters for three days now and had heard nothing of a foreigner with a red birthmark on his jowl. They were simply passing through the village on their journey and had stumbled accidentally on the 'special troops'. They would simply have passed them by, not wanting to risk leaving the otaman's directive unfulfilled, had they not seen that the monsters were leading a woman and child to their deaths. Vovkulaka had not held back when he said that they should deal with the situation because there were not many of them.

They were a little too late to save the young woman, only the baby would live and they had to take it. How could they refuse? Vovkulaka was already thinking about where the boy could be left, even if it was only in a temporary place on the route they were taking to Telepyne and Pastyrske.

The boys liked the baby and Khodya took him in his arms and cooed in his own manner. The child became quiet, as if enchanted.

'What's his name? Vovkulaka asked.

'Yarko,' replied Veremii's mother.

'Don't fret Ma, we won't let misfortune come on Yarko.'

Before they threw the corpses of the special troops into the ravine, they went through their pockets and Vovkulaka found two gold coins in Hotsman's britches.

'What a skin flaying murderer,' he said in disgust as he wiped his hands on his trousers, spat over his lower lip, and was ready to heave the corpse over the edge when he thought again. He unfastened Hotsman's belt, took off his boots (not easy with a dead man) and, taking the britches from below, tipped Hotsman out of them and into the ravine. Only his trousers were left in Vovkulaka's hands. 'Why throw away good stuff like this?'

The old, black raven was sitting on his perch in the ash tree and observing everything. He saw how Tanasykha brought the cart and, together with Veremii's mother, took Hannusia home. After the men had thrown the corpses into the ravine and gone their own way, the raven regretted that he could not feast on the dead, for who, if not him, must follow the three men and see where they put the child?

Hamalii finally came to us. He arrived at the meeting place with Zaviriukha. We purposefully did not emerge from the trees to meet them, instead we looked from a distance to see how they behaved, whether anger would make them utter an unguarded word and give something away. We tried their patience for two hours. From where we were situated in the foliage, the guests appeared nervous and we could sense they were ready to leave when Larion Zaharodnii and his adjutant, Tymosh Kompaniyets, together with another Cossack, rode out to them.

'Please excuse us for the unpleasant delay,' Zaharodnii said, gliding his smiling eyes over the sturdy man, who was notably more severe than Sergeant Zaviriukha. He seemed wrathful, perhaps because they had compelled him to wait until it was almost evening.

Zaviriukha spoke in a tone design to placate them, 'Let's get acquainted, Sir - Colonel Hamalii, Otaman Zaharodnii.'

Larion, who did not converse with them for a long time, led them in the direction of the village of Vodiane. A Caucasian rug, woven from goats' hair, was spread out in one of the clearings.

'Please sit, the truth is not to be found standing on your legs.'

Only then did Holyk-Zaliznyak emerge from the branches where shadows moved; Hupalo appeared from the other side, but I remained in my position. For one thing, I felt ill, for another I did not want them to think that we were all dancing to the tune of their bugle now. It was necessary to look into things further.

Hamalii certainly felt our distrust and praised it. It would have been wrong to act otherwise. Nonchalantly he produced, from somewhere in his pouch, the journal, *Son of Ukraine*, and gave it to Zaharodnii.

'Cast an eye on this, Otaman. Don't take it as me being vainglorious, I show it to you so that we can become more closely acquainted.'

Zaharodnii opened the paper and at once saw Hamalii's smiling face, which seemed to be asking him, *Well, how's that?* The text beneath the photograph made it known that Colonel Hamalii had been commissioned as the commander of the insurrectionist military of southern Ukraine. Since the photograph had made an impression on the otaman, Hamalii added, 'Tiutiunnyk insisted that I wore the Iron Cross for the photograph, but I'm not fond of that kind of ostentation. Heroism isn't to be found in awards. Is that not so, Sir Otaman?'

'No, heroism isn't to be found in awards,' agreed Zaharodnii, handing the journal to Hupalo.

'Then in what is it to be found?' Hamalii looked with interest into the otaman's eyes. 'In what do we find heroism?'

'The highest example of heroism is to die in battle,' replied Zaharodnii.

'Bravo, Otaman. However, we are obliged to live and bring victory to our country with our sabres.' Hamalii cast an eye on Hupalo and Holyk-Zaliznyak. What would they make of the newspaper item in *Son of Ukraine*?

'Is Raven late?' he asked.

'No, he won't be coming,' said Zaharodnii.

'Why not?'

'Raven is wounded.'

'Is he wounded so badly that he can't come to our meeting?'

'He has lost a lot of blood.'

'Oh, is that so?' Hamalii said sombrely. 'I see, Sir Otaman, that you are not hurrying to implement the order from headquarters. You are continuing to wage war, and in Tsybuleve I hear that you arranged a real massacre.'

'How can I implement the orders of a person I have never seen face to face?' Zaharodnii asked in surprise.

'Don't you understand that these small, independent actions might cost us the larger business? This is the fifth year disorder and otaman brutality has ruled Ukraine and more than one good objective has fallen foul of them. Everyone agrees that we cannot continue to work like this, but people keep going back to their old ways. Understand who you are. Is it worth risking your life to kill another ten Bolsheviks? For now we need to lull them into a false sense of security.'

'Well, at least I wage war more honourably than them,' said Zaharodnii. 'Why do they call me a bandit when I struggle openly with them in war? Do you know what the *Chekists* thought up? They gave all the forest workers poisoned powder and on pain of death told them to sprinkle it in my food if they had the chance. If you don't believe me ask Mykola Sylvestrov. So which of us is a bandit?'

'That's understood.' Hamalii nodded, 'I'm not talking about that. In the very near future, in September, we will commence a significant project with you that will not permit any independent, uncoordinated acts. It is necessary to bring an end to the uncontrolled torrent of otamans and place them under a single centre. We have to do a stock-take of all our forces and of every forest rebel. The smaller units have to be united in squadrons and divisions, to strengthen the areas they influence. It's now time to drive away the criminals who have adhered to our movement and to destroy the uncouth ones among us. Look what it has come to. Some otamans even keep their sweethearts close to them.'

'You are exaggerating,' argued Zaharodnii. 'Yes, there are often women in the squads, but they do their work conscientiously. In Kholodnyi Yar, I met Cossack Dosia Apilat, she is worth three men.'

'I am categorically opposed to bringing women into our work,' said Hamalii, raising his voice. 'Five years worth of experience has convinced me, an old partisan, that most of our setbacks have occurred because of women.'

'So, perhaps you are going to forbid us that,' Denys Hupalo tugged the roots of his Cossack forelock.

'No, that about which you are talking is permitted and necessary, but in the appropriate place,' said Hamalii, smiling. 'We can only allow those women to work who have shown their worth over many years. For the most part, wives or sisters. But it isn't worth making even these women a sacred part of our plans, rather we should only use them for communication. So, read this order.' He gave Zaharodnii a paper written in a tiny hand.

Running his eyes over the introduction about the importance of this historic moment, Larion was pulled up by the severity of the warning:

All who act against the interest of the country, including the otamans for whom personal authority is dearer than our objective, will be destroyed by terror units appointed for that purpose.

Next there were directives for command and the disposition of forces that directly concerned the otamans who were present:

Ataman Zaharodnii is hereby appointed the commander of the First Cavalry Division of Kholodnyi Yar. The division covers the following areas: Yelysavetgrad, Novomyrhorod, Zlatopol, Shpola, as far as the Bobrynska Station, Medvedivka, to the Dnipro, Chyhyryn and Znamyanka.

Otaman Zaharodnii is to take all the individual chiefs and Cossacks, who are currently acting independently, under his command. If there is any difficulty in disarming them or any non-fulfilment of orders, they will be severely punished by means which can include execution.

Otaman Holyk-Zaliznyak is appointed the commander of the First Armoured Car Division of the Black Sea Group, which will be formed simultaneously with the First Squadron of the Cavalry Division.

Holyk-Zaliznyak is appointed commander of the first squad, Raven is appointed commander of the second squad, and Otaman Hupalo is appointed commander of the third squad. The names of the squads will be conceived and reported to the headquarters of the group.

Commander of the Black Sea Insurrectionist Group, Colonel Hamalii
Chief of Staff of the Group, Sergeant Zaviriukha
24 August 1922. Zapillia

Zaharodnii read the order and, if it was not for the permanent smile in his eyes, it would have been possible to say that his face had become serious. He wanted to hand the paper to Holyk-Zaliznyak immediately, but Hamalii stopped him. 'That isn't necessary. Everyone who is affected by this order will receive a personal copy. What is your impression, Mr Zaharodnii?'

'This is all good. However, I am interested in the date for the commencement of the uprising.'

'You will determine the date at the otamans' council,' Hamalii reminded him.

'When and where will the council be held?'

'Soon. We have planned for the location and conduct of the conspiratorial meeting to take place in Kyiv.'

'No,' Zaharodnii shook his head, 'I will not go to Kyiv. I think that most otamans will not agree to be pushed there. Let us hold it somewhere nearer.'

'Then propose somewhere yourself, Cherkasy, Zvenyhorodka, Smila …'

'That is more like it. Maybe Zvenyhorodka?' Zaharodnii suggested. 'That wouldn't be a bad place. It's nearer for Honta-Lyutyi, whom I haven't seen for a long time.'

'Think about it,' said Hamalii. 'Everything is in your hands. Tiutiunnyk, Hulyi-Hulenko and the representatives of our government will travel from abroad to attend the council.'

When Zaharodnii narrated this conversation to me later, there was something I did not like about it, but I could not understand what it was. Something scampered around in my head, waving its tail and making me restless. Something I could not apprehend. Everything in the conversation and in the orders issued by Hamalii was logical and I thought that maybe it was this same iron logic that was putting me on my guard when everything was so rigorously correct, so perfect it called forth doubt. I said as much to Zaharodnii, but he only smiled.

'It seems that the truth is on Hamalii's side, we're not accustomed to intelligent orders from beyond the border, or to placing ourselves under someone's authority.'

'And what if he orders me to be destroyed for disobedience?' I asked. 'Would you then also comply with his order?'

'Is it possible for that to happen?' Larion looked at me in confusion and I saw that the smile had departed from his narrowed eyes for the first time.

The gangs of Zaharodnii, Raven and Zaliznyak have united and become more persistent on the section of railway between Znamyanka and Bobrynska. The bandits held up a freight train between the Trepovka and Khirovka stations and seized 25 poods of smoked fish, which they hid in the Nerubaevskyi woods. Later they returned to the railway and stopped a passenger train. They inspected the documents of the passengers and shot five secret police staff, taking valuable documents and baggage from them. When they returned to the Nerubaevskyi woods, they discovered that the fish had disappeared, having been taken by militiamen from Mykhailivka, who had tracked the partisans. Someone informed the bandits where the fish had gone and this so angered them that they hurried to Mykhailivka and the militia ran off in all directions. The gang not only took fish, but also four horses with two carts, five bags of flour, three bags of buckwheat, groats, two kegs of oil and one keg of honey.

It has been noticed recently that there is a general movement for the bandits to form larger groups. The gangs of Zaharodnii, according to our information, currently comprise 150 sabres and up to 100 bayonets; the gangs of Raven, in the region of 100 sabres, and all its fighters, as if by selection, are very well dressed and have good horses. They have even succeeded in converting some Chinese onto their side; at least our agent saw one bandit of Mongolian extraction who appeared to be endowed with the secret art of hand-to-hand combat.

Raven is a crack shot and, rumour has it, on one occasion he fired a bullet effortlessly from his revolver and knocked a sunflower from the hand of one of his men who was eating its seeds during a serious conversation.

At present, resting up in Ataman Hupalo's

lair, Raven writes constantly in his note
book, possibly verses or his impressions.

Informer Reut.
Correct: Office Secretary Khlopushyn

From information collated by the Kremenchuk division of the secret
police department, 30 August 1922

After five days Vovkulaka, Khodya and Bizhu returned to Chornyi
Forest and found Raven in a different place than previously, though it
was also a clearing. He was lying on a coat, as before, and writing in
a note book with his right hand. On seeing the Cossacks Raven rose,
and Vovkulaka noted that he no longer had a sling. His right arm had
recovered and even his face showed that he had rejoined humanity.
Raven saw that they were in a happy mood and had clearly done
something worthwhile. They had driven the horses until they were
foaming at the mouth, but they looked good. The glittering points of
the Cossacks' eyes shone on him from faces burned almost black and
ceramic with the sun.

Vovkulaka held something that looked like a reasonably sized
melon and Raven waited to be bothered with the usual proposition.
Vovkulaka thought that anything red enriched the blood. If he waited
until he had eaten it before telling him about their wanderings then
Raven would smash the melon over his head. However, Vovkulaka had
enough sense to begin to tell of their adventures immediately, but he
went so far away from the point, about how they had travelled, where
they had slept and who they had met, that Raven interrupted, 'Did
you find the deserters or not?'

'As always Otaman, first listen to everything in order, for I
forgot to tell you the main thing.'

Vovkulaka blinked guiltily and again talked about how they
had interrogated people everywhere and how no one had seen or heard
of them until they had almost reached Veremii's village, when the
incident with Hannusia happened. Raven, hearing this terrible news,
did not interrupt Vovkulaka, who then narrated events as he wished,
to the point where it was, in a way, young Yarko who had led them to
the deserters.

'That's how it often is in life,' said Vovkulaka in amazement. 'There is a necessity to the way it flows.'

He philosophised and talked for so long about the power of providence that even Bizhu could endure it no longer and poked up his head, 'Then we ran to Dementsi and then came to a forest where we sniffed something. Vovkulaka went to a house to make arrangements for the baby and I ran …'

'Cease,' thundered Vovkulaka, so severely that Bizhu's head drew back into his shoulders in surprise. 'Be silent until you are asked something. This isn't Grance to you.' Vovkulaka snarlingly mangled the word France because Bizhu was known as the French guy, perhaps because his nickname had a Gallic ring.

Vovkulaka continued to talk about how they had gone from one side of Kholodnyi Yar to Lubenetskyi Farm, near the village of Dementsi, where Prokipko Kvochka's family originated and where his older sister and her husband still lived with their heap of children. Vovkulaka had once been a guest there with Kvochka. He had seen all the trivia for which Kvochka's brother-in-law had forsworn joining the forest rebels and thought that he would have been better off in the forest than at home. Vovkulaka also thought that another baby in this camp full of children would pass unnoticed, so left the little sparrow to be looked after by Kvochka's sister.

He had stashed the men and the baby at the edge of the wood and gone to Kvochka's house to check what was going on there and to make sure that no one had led any foreign devil to the place. He saw Kvochka's brother-in-law working near the barn. Seeing Vovkulaka, he dropped his pitchfork and led him into the house that was awash with children, who, seeing such a fearsome 'uncle', hid behind their mother's skirt. Prokipko's sister was sitting on the bed and breastfeeding a baby. She was glad to see Vovkulaka and did not consider hiding her breasts, which were dove white and swollen with milk. She was pleased at the chance to ask about her brother, whom she had not seen for a year and did not know if he was alive.

Vovkulaka knew nothing about him because he had not seen him since they had joined with Otaman Derkach last autumn and crushed one hundred of the enemy; after which, Vovkulaka had befriended Kvochka and together they had gone to his sister's farm.

Vovkulaka knew that last summer Derkach and many other Cossacks had handed themselves in to be amnestied, maybe Prokipko was among them. Who knew or could even think of that now? Vovkulaka told Kvochka's sister and her husband why he had come and asked if they would take the baby for at least a week or two until they found a safe place for him.

The sister, wiping away tears for Hannusia, said, 'Bring him quickly, the poor, hungry thing.'

Her husband bowed his head, 'They might seek this child. Someone might lead them to us and if they come here they will not waste time finding out who is and isn't Veremii's son. They will kill us all.'

'But I doubt that they will come immediately,' Prokipko's sister calmed him. 'Did you hear? The partisans are going to take the baby and shelter him elsewhere before too long. Bring him here quickly before I fasten my blouse.'

Vovkulaka ran to get the baby. He wanted to leave before they changed their minds because he had his own urgent work to do. When he saw how young Veremii fastened himself to her breast, he asked her if the Reds ever came to the farm.

'So, how did the baby lead you to the deserters?' Raven's patience was beginning to ebb away. 'What were you talking about?'

'Don't interrupt, Sir Otaman,' Vovkulaka took a breath. 'Listen how time flowed fortuitously, thanks to the providence of God and destiny.'

He began again with how he had asked if the Reds ever came to the farm, and Prokipko's sister had told him that they had not been for a long time, until the previous night when some had come to gather what they could. They had stolen chickens, a rooster and even pumpkin seeds that we were drying out.

'I heard them,' said her husband. 'I heard the way the chickens were clucking on their perches, but I did not go out to them. I knew that it was thieves and if I went out, I might end up dead. I looked through the window and saw three of them heading back to the forest.'

Vovkulaka listened, his brain worked quickly and then, looking at Yarko, who had finished sucking on the woman's, now empty, breast, took the gold coins he had obtained from Hotsman and put them on the table, 'This is so that mother's milk doesn't dry up,' he said, ashamedly. 'And you,' he turned to the master of the house, 'come with me.'

At the edge of the forest, where his mare, Tasia, was standing (she had replaced Vovkulaka's slain mare), he took out Hotsman's britches from the saddle bag and gave them to him. 'Don't worry. I will return,' Vovkulaka assured him and said farewell.

They were travelling across the forest towards Telepyne and Pastyrske when Vovkulaka noticed the husks of pumpkin seeds on the grass. It was clear that the foreigners, being famished and on foot, and pausing as they stripped the seeds, could not have been more than one *verst* away. They could not walk a step along the path without coming across the husk of a pumpkin seed. Vovkulaka, Khodya and Bizhu followed the trail for one and a half *versts* before they smelled the smoke from a camp fire. They hurried stealthily, but rapidly, nearer to it and saw, by the spring, three ragged, round-faced men cooking something in a cauldron, probably a hen or a rooster. They did not know they would not have the chance to eat it.

The Cossacks approached them calmly and greeted them as if they were their own. They did not reach for their weapons and, although the deserters were not pleased by this meeting, they looked silently, even cautiously, at the three gallant soldiers. The fanged Illia Muromets, the round-faced Aliosha Popovych, and the slant-eyed Dobrynia Mykytovych. What was their worth when weighed against these three, Tiukha, Matiukha and Vanka Dolubaj? On another occasion Illia Muromets would not have looked in their direction but now his heart pounded when he saw one of them had a beetroot-coloured birthmark on his jaw. He turned to him and said, jauntily, 'Good health, we saw you in Lebedyn, do you remember?'

Tiukha, or perhaps Matiukha, or was it Vanka Dolubaj, smiled at Muromets and said, 'Yes, yes it may be so. Last summer the three of us were hanging around there.'

Vovkulaka wrinkled his brow at Khodya and Bizhu, who disarmed the men in a second, knocked them to the ground and 'tickled' them so that the three good friends kept blaming each other and in doing so revealed every last detail. Their reward for which was castration. Vovkulaka purified them with his own hands like with

210

boars, only boars have a use afterwards and provide good *salo*, but these three had breathed their last breath now.

'And at this moment I was running,' said Bizhu, sticking in his nose again.

Vovkulaka thundered, 'Cease! Let me continue or I will run after you so you won't know which end of the earth to flee to.'

I will illuminate what happened next. While they were dealing with the bodies and the chicken was boiling in the cauldron, Vovkulaka, Khodya and Bizhu had a pleasant wash in the nearby spring and then tucked into that tasty chicken. 'Tasty Cock-a-doodle-doo,' Khodya praised it, grinding the bones in his teeth and eating the pumpkin seeds they had taken from the thieves. Vovkulaka had forbidden him from shelling them on the road because he did not want them to leave a trail, having used one themselves to find and slay the men.

'Tasty pumpkin,' Khodya smacked his lips. But he obeyed Vovkulaka and only ate wild pears on the road, wild roses, not yet in full bloom, young birch nuts, horse sorrel and wolf berries, which gave him strength enough, if needs be, to hew down an oak.

Vovkulaka assured Raven that everything he had said was the truth, Khodya and Bizhu would not let him lie, and if someone had doubts there was a document with a seal. At which point he produced a human head. The face had turned bluish, but the birthmark on its jowl was still visible.

'Good lads,' Raven praised them. 'Great work, only take this carrion further away so that it doesn't stink up the place.'

'I'll run with it.' Bizhu leaped forward, grabbed a spade and rolled the head back into the bag.

'Run and come back quickly, then we will have lunch,' said Raven. 'On the railway we bought pickled fish to go with the potatoes.'

Khodya's Adam's apple bobbed up and down, 'The fish is great,' he said in his thick accent, swallowing back his saliva.

'Go, go,' Raven smiled at him, 'your fish can't wait for you.'

When he was left alone with Vovkulaka, the otaman asked in a quiet voice, 'You heard nothing about Veremii there?'

'I heard nothing about him anywhere,' Vovkulaka bowed his head.

'Okay,' said Raven, 'don't worry about the child, I know where to hide him.'

***

After two weeks had passed and September had arrived, Raven met with Larion Zaharodnii in Chuta Forest. His spirits had revived a little. Larion had previously been worried that Hamalii was drawing away from organising the otamans' conference. Well, perhaps not Hamalii, but someone higher up who was waiting for what they considered to be a more appropriate time; when the ranks of the partisans and the Ukrainian military, who, with the permission of the Polish, were gathering near the border, were ready to go. He was encouraged now when he told Raven that Hamalii was not casting empty words into the wind.

'Here, read these orders.'

Before Zaharodnii opened his field bag he looked at Vovkulaka and his adjutant, Tymosh Kompaniyets, 'Lads, go and seek the wild goat.'

When they had gone and left them alone, Larion showed Raven Hamalii's order:

Top Secret - Only to be handed personally to the commanders of divisions, squadron leaders and chiefs of staff. Burn after reading.

Operative Order No. 6 - To provide the staff groups with the information required for planning a general uprising rapidly.
1) 1109, 01249 7055 0199 have on their terrain 63 09 4018, 7402 9953 ...
2) 7042, 8610 9738 7218 each and all together are 6032, 0946 ...

This was an order written in the *Zapovit* or testament code and demanded an overall report regarding the quantity of partisan squadrons and their arms.

'Until there is a real signal,' said Raven, 'and while I don't see for myself that everything is as he says it is, I won't be making any reports to anyone and I wouldn't advise you to either.'

'Now read this one,' said Zaharodnii calmly.

The other order from Hamalii was written on a piece of lined paper. It was first and foremost a declaration:

Top Secret - Order No. 8 from the Black Sea Insurrectionist Group

During the hard years of struggle not many warrior leaders, who understand the significance of the present moment and do everything for our victory, have arisen out of the general masses. We have many otamans, officers and Cossacks who are aware of what is needed, but who do not implement the orders of the staff group and continue to operate according to their own judgement. Every week we are compelled to destroy the traitors who have arisen in our ranks. However, in spite of the difficulty of the work, the morale in the Black Sea Group is good and our business progresses successfully. All this is thanks to the iron will and arduous work of otamans Zaharodnii, Raven, Holyk-Zaliznyak, Hupalo, Lyutyi, and their officers and Cossacks, who are conscious of their responsibility for the fate of the country.

Received from Otaman Hupalo 200,000,000 roubles to address the organisational questions of the group.

From the government of the U.N.R. and the High Council of Otamans, we pass our sincere thanks to these warriors.

To be read to all the divisions and squadrons.

Commander of the Black Sea Insurrectionist Group, Colonel Hamalii
Chief of Staff of the Group, Sergeant Zaviriukha

Zapillia, 10 September 1922

Again, something about this order made Raven wary, but this time he caught the beast by the tail and asked, 'Don't you see anything strange about this Laryk?'

'What could be strange about this order?'

'That they kill some for disobedience, but Hamalii thanks me, you, Denys and Mefodii.'

'But what good is he without us?' Zaharodnii turned up his nose. 'Who else would he embark on a rebellion with?'

'I don't know, there is something not to my liking here.'

'In this next letter there is a greeting for you.'

Larion took out another paper from his field bag, at the top of which was written in pencil:

To Zaharodnii

Sir Otaman, let us have patience, do not fall into disbelief, be encouraged, bear up bravely and do not let the spirits of the boys fall. I have done and will do everything that is necessary, we are closer to our goal. Let us be noble in our work and in our calling. My greeting to all the otamans and Cossacks!

Colonel Hamalii

'Thank you for the greeting,' said Raven, not without irony, as he returned the letter. 'Our spirits won't fall. They should worry more about their own spirits.'

'Then read this,' Larion was almost trembling from excitement as he took out a scrap of paper from his bag. Raven had not seen him like that for a long time. This was also a note personally addressed to him, Otaman Zaharodnii, the Commander of the First Kholodnyi Yar Cavalry Division. However, the letter was written in a different style:

Larion Zahorodnii. It began by using his patronymic, in a formal tone.

The day after tomorrow, I will go to Zvenyhorodka to finalise the location of the otamans' meeting. It is extremely regrettable that I was not able to see you in person, but all your requirements have been taken into account. Be strong, there is little left to do.
Sergeant Zaviriukha

214

'So we have started work now,' said Larion.

Something about this summons crawled off the page and stung Raven sharply, but he could not comprehend what it was.

'So, what do you think?' Zahorodnii asked sharply.

'What indeed?' said Raven as he pondered what it was that troubled him.

'Don't you understand? The ice is cracking. Get ready for a trip to Zvenyhorodka.'

'Well Laryk, I am always ready.'

He re-read the letter, searching for the source of the unease that pierced him, but everything seemed correct and encouraging. Commissar Dybenko and Brigade Commander Kuziakin, with whom Raven had held talks in Zvenyhorodka, had left long ago. The town was situated centrally between Chyhyryn and Uman and would be the most convenient place to travel from Horodyshche, Korsun and Lysyanka. Everything seemed logical and this would usually have seized him with enthusiasm.

Zahorodnii suddenly also grew sombre, 'If nothing comes of this scheme, I will ask that Hamalii helps me leave the country,' he said. 'I have no house or family here now,' he added in explanation.

Raven looked through him with a fish's dead, unthinking gaze.

'How is your hand?' asked Zahorodnii, with sudden curiosity.

'Like this.' Raven took a young alder by the trunk and tore it from its roots.

'Well, Vasyl Chuchupaka won't be on your case now.' Larion smiled. 'He would have given you twenty lashes for destroying the tree.'

'Vasyl is no longer with us, unfortunately,' said Raven. 'I have a request for you Laryk. I want three days leave.'

'Is it an affair of the heart?' asked Zahorodnii, blinking.

'No, I have work over the other side of Kholodnyi Yar.'

'Go. Just don't be any longer.'

Chapter 4

1

Prokipko's older sister did not want to part with the child. She already thought of him as her own and had grown used to breastfeeding him. She told Vovkulaka how much she would miss him and begged him to let the child stay. Vovkulaka bowed his head regretfully and thanked her for her kindness and just spirit, but he had been sent to take Yarko. Her husband said that he was also used to having the baby and was ready to take him into the family, but accepted that it was not up to them to decide.

Prokipko's sister wept as she sent Vovkulaka on his way with the baby. She wrapped Yarko in a clean blanket and tied a woollen kerchief around him to enable Vovkulaka to tie the ends around his neck and carry the baby safely, as if he were in a cradle. She also gave him a bottle of her breast milk, and the whole family walked with them as far as the gate.

The old raven followed the tearful proceedings from the vantage point of a tall poplar and, though his wings were not as sturdy as they had been in his youth, he followed Vovkulaka as far as the edge of the Irdyn Marsh, where the wolf-like partisan handed the baby to his otaman.

The otaman travelled on an imperceptible track through the stagnant quagmire, which only Mudei's sensitive hooves could discern, until he came to blind Yevdosia's house. When she opened the door, Raven pleaded, 'Take this child for a time. Only you can watch over him and guard him from evil people, sickness and misfortune.'

The night had already drawn in but Yevdosia did not light a candle, instead a lamp flickered from its place on a shelf. Raven saw by its light how she smiled to herself as she listened to him, but then the baby moved quietly and reluctantly, as if he was too idle to cry but wanted to remind them of his presence.

'Let me see him now,' she said, taking the baby from Raven, laying him gently on the bed and carefully feeling his small body from head to foot. 'He's a strong lad.'

'Strong or not, he's still a little baby,' Raven said, surprised at how the child quietened when Yevdosia was near. 'Do you still have the goat that gave you milk?'

'Would you like some buttermilk?' she asked, remembering how he liked it.

'I would. But I'm wondering if you have some milk for the child.'

'Don't worry about the child. If you want some buttermilk stay overnight with me. I will make you such good buttermilk that later you won't recognise yourself.'

'Can you really churn butter from goat's milk?'

'With the help of a Cossack like you. You could beat it, even from a billy goat's milk.' Yevdosia smiled. 'Get ready, I will bathe you my hard-headed vagabond. Did you like how I bathed you before?'

From somewhere in the remote past the aroma of wild orchids, Pontian azaleas and incense wafted around him. Raven had sensed this bitter-sweet essence as soon as he had stepped on the marshy ground that stretched alongside the River Irdyn, but he had been unable to understand for a long time what the cloud of wondrous fragrance was. Now he realised. The orchid, incense and azalea blossomed in the wet ground that had remained unfrozen here during the last ice age.

'I do love it,' he agreed. 'However, in this season it is still possible to bathe in the Tiasmyn.'

'Perhaps it is possible for your horse, but only if he is sweating and foaming at the mouth,' said Yevdosia.

'Has Dosia been here recently?' he asked, not paying any attention to Yevdosia's taunts.

'It's a long time since she was here. She said that when she had ceased battling against the occupier she would cut her hair and become a nun.'

'Why?'

'Because of you, thick-head.'

'Well, Dosia's hair is too good to cut,' said Raven.

'She is so familiar with the Motryn Monastery that she could become a novice there. I heard that since it was ravaged by the soviets it is coming to life again and taking people into its service.'

'But old Motryn will never be the way it was again.'

'It won't be, but I am talking about Dosia. She might have

already stopped fighting and exchanged her sabre for a prayer book. She hasn't shown up here in a long time. Why are you asking about her?'

'No reason. Something has come back to me. Please forgive me.'

'Why do I need to forgive you?'

'For everything. For the trouble, the child I have handed over to you, and my haste. I have to rush off now.'

'OK. Whenever I read your cards the queen of hearts appears next to you.'

'No dame is needed now,' said Raven, 'I have work to do.'

'Your hands don't ache from that work?'

'They ache, but only at night.'

'I can't help you with that. But there is one thing I am able to do for you.'

'What is that, Yevdosia?'

'Pray for you.'

She took a large cooking knife from the shelf under the icon and placed it against both his palms and then his forehead.

'Be healthy and strong for me.'

'And if something happens to me, take this boy ...' Raven began, but she spoke over him. 'Get on with your task. You will come back quickly to me.'

2

I returned to Chornyi Forest on time. Zahorodnii had just pleaded for permission from Hamalii to be allowed to hold up a train so that we could re-clothe and re-shoe ourselves. I say pleaded and not asked because that is how it was now. Hamalii wavered for a long time because he said this would hinder more than help us. It would draw the attention of the Bolsheviks to the railway and Chornyi Forest and that was not needed before our campaign had even begun.

'Who knows, perhaps we could go through the station to Zvenyhorodka,' said Hamalii.

'No, the otamans won't go by train because many people know our faces. We might be recognised. Anyway, we travel on horseback. Let us hold up just one train,' Zahorodnii replied.

Hamalii still blustered for a while, wrinkled his nose, and then gave way a little. 'Okay, hold up one, but don't spill any blood. Get hold of some Red Army uniforms, arms and food, but don't harass anyone. If you come across any *Chekists*, despatch them to the heavenly chancellery to make their report there,' Hamalii said finally, his face relaxing.

The regular railwayman, Holyk-Zaliznyak, and his Cossacks disassembled part of the railway quickly. The passenger train from Rostov to Kyiv had come to a halt a couple of *versts* before Tsybuleve.

'It's us. Hello,' we said in Ukrainian. Then added in Russian, 'Dear Comrades, accept our bread and salt.'

There weren't many of us, maybe fifteen riders, and some of Holyk-Zaliznyak's infantry, about ten, but there were only about fifty military *katsaps* in one of the wagons and a mixed crowd of people in the others. The boys gathered their watches, boots, belts and, in particular, stuff to smoke. The troops had been gasping for a cigarette for three days and there was an abundance of Makhorka tobacco and Ada cigarettes here.

When we captured the *katsaps* they hurriedly handed over their weapons and undressed so quickly that you would have thought a hot sauna was waiting for them. The operation was completely dull until one fat Steppe marmot, who had obviously slept for the entire journey, helped us out a little.

Surprised that we were dressed like him, he asked in Russian, with some confusion, 'I don't understand. Are these bandits?'

'You are the bandits,' disputed Zahorodnii, adding in a mixture of Ukrainian and Russian, 'and we are the warriors of the forest. Can't you see that we don't even kill rodents like you?'

'Right. Warriors,' blustered the marmot under his breath, but we heard him.

Tymosh Kompaniyets, Larion's loyal adjutant, flicked his whip into the air, hitting the marmot's back so sharply that he whimpered like a dog.

'How dare you speak to the otaman like that with your unwashed muzzle?'

Tymosh grabbed him by the scruff of the neck, hoisted

him into the air, and was about to throw him off the train when Zahorodnii stopped him.

'See what he's like,' screamed a *katsap*, like a town crier. He was wearing dirty underpants with their cords untied, but behaved as though he were in control of the situation. 'Hit him again. He has been secretly drinking vodka from under his coat all the way here and now he is trying to get us into trouble with his drunken remarks. What scum.'

Tymosh Kompaniyets was unable to follow things very well in the Muscovite tongue, but he thought that the town crier was being offensive to him and, without hesitation, flicked his whip again. Its metal end hit the town crier in the centre of his head and he slumped into unconsciousness, without making a sound. Blood streamed onto his shirt.

'Well, you are like children really. God help us,' said Zahorodnii, shrugging his shoulders. 'It was agreed that we would do this without bloodshed.'

'But why did he get on my back?' asked Tymosh angrily. 'Calling me a bitch, insulting me, referring to me as scum.'

'Hey, you didn't hear that he also called you a hopeless drunkard,' smiled Zahorodnii. 'Well, let's grab everything we need and go.'

Along with clothing and shoes, we also took ten revolvers and a rifle, which we hid in Chut because we had enough of our own. We failed to find any good food, but on the way back to the camp I noticed Khodya was chewing something continuously; a bit of skin or a dried pig's ear.

***

Hamalii's final order was ready at the time we were holding up the train:

Top Secret - To be handed over in person

Order No. 10

Sir Otamans, Officers, Cossacks,

The time has come upon us when you are required to place all your heart into the struggle for Ukraine. Remember what a heavy responsibility now rests on your shoulders. A general uprising will begin shortly. Poland and Romania have signed a treaty agreeing to support the revolt. Our own and foreign forces are gathered on the border.

Our army will cross into Ukraine on the night of 1 October. We need to decide whether our operation will begin here overnight on 29/30 September or whether we move to support our forces on the strip of land by the border where fateful events are about to unfold. We will adopt all the main resolutions at the High Council of Otamans that is ordained to take place on 28 September in Zvenyhorodka. Well-known Ukrainian leaders will cross the border to attend the council, including Lieutenant General Hulyi-Hulenko and the representative of the revolutionary staff headquarters, Captain Stupnytskyi. Tiutiunnyk himself is unable to attend, as was previously planned, because he is occupied with organisational questions pertaining to the forces gathered near the border.

Commander of the Black Sea Insurrectionist Group, Colonel Hamalii
Chief of Staff of the Group, Sergeant Zaviriukha

22 September 1922, Zapillia

One week later Zaviriukha came to Chornyi Forest and told us it was time to travel to Zvenyhorodka for the council.

3

During September the banditry in the Chyhyryn, Yelysavetgrad and Zvenyhorodka districts, which are the central hot-bed of political resistance, have perceptibly quietened. The state organs in these places ascribe this improvement to their own merit. However, it is suspected that the calmness is due to the gangs radically changing the character of their actions. Thus, for example, the band of Zahorodnii, Raven and Zaliznyak held up the Rostov to Kiev passenger train and disarmed 47 of the Red Army men who were to be demobilised. The bandits did not shoot anyone, but they did beat to death two Red Army men who resisted them. Such conduct from the 'warriors of the forest' is regarded as a devious, tactical measure prior to a revival of their banditry.

Duly Authorised Officer of the Secret Operations Section, Lifshyts
Correct: Office Secretary Khobotov

From the operative report information collated by the Kremenchuk division of the secret police department, 28 September 1922

Zaviriukha arrived. He had been guided by Sergeant Gordienko and Cossack Sereda, who had been borrowed from Otaman Lyutyi to provide his guide with a guard. We were told that it was time to go to the higher council. Lieutenant General Hulyi-Hulenko, the representative of Tiutiunnyk, Captain Stupnytskyi, and the commander of our group, Hamalii, had already travelled to the venue. Zaviriukha said that we had hung around a little too long and now we needed to get a move on.

Zahorodnii, Hupalo and Holyk-Zaliznyak had waited for him from the previous evening and through the night, but he arrived just before morning; a fact that was not much to their liking. Denys Hupalo, who had hidden his long forelock beneath a Red Army hat, began to assure Zahorodnii that something was not right and that Zaviriukha was leading them into folly, but Zahorodnii dismissed his suspicions and asked him to explain himself and then he would listen.

'Well, he was late for one thing.'

'Who hasn't been late, especially when business in which

222

many people are involved is under way? Hamalii and Zaviriukha have done everything to ensure us that they're not guiding us and that we are leading them. Don't you understand?' said Zahorodnii, firing himself up. 'Everything is being done in the way we like it. In spite of their order, we didn't stop fighting the Reds and Hamalii thanked us for it. They wanted to have this meeting in Kyiv and we said no, let's have it in Zvenyhorodka. They tried to insist that we would travel by train because we are near Khirovka Station. "Sit and travel in comfort" they said and we said, "No, we are going on horseback." So who is leading who? Explain it to me please.' Zahorodnii was unable to restrain himself.

Raven, thanks to Larion's heated speech, suddenly understood what had bothered him about the plan and the conversation they had with Hamalii. The concerns that had been moving in his subconscious suddenly became illuminated, like a flare gun fired into the sky. 'He suggested Kyiv on purpose because he knew we would never go there. He manipulated us into going to Zvenyhorodka, which is what he wanted. Larion, think, use your head and you'll see it.'

'No,' Larion disagreed, 'I remember quite clearly that we were also talking about Smila and Cherkasy.'

'He gave us three places to choose from and it seemed to me that he emphasised Zvenyhorodka. He wanted you to think that you had chosen it.'

'Don't beat me around the head with your nonsense,' said Zahorodnii, but his expression had changed.

'They also deliberately suggested going by train, knowing that we would refuse and immediately agreed to our suggestion that we travel on horseback. All this was so it would look, like you say, as if they were dancing to our tune. Do you understand now? What a diabolical piece of work this is.'

Zahorodnii's expression had changed yet more. 'You're exaggerating,' he argued. 'I determined how we would travel. You do as you please. No one will be forced to agree with the plan. For the past month we've had an understanding with the group headquarters and I don't know what's got into your head.'

Zaviriukha, Hordienko and Sereda arrived and suggested they hurried because they still had one hundred *versts* ahead of them and were travelling by horseback.

Zahorodnii said farewell to the Cossacks. He approached each of them and shook their hand. His eyes still smiled, but it was a smile that was forced and confused. The sign of some destiny seemed to be imprinted on his darkened face and it looked as though he was limping more heavily.

'Are you coming?' he asked Raven.

'No.'

'Then let's say goodbye.'

'Forever?' asked Raven.

'Do you want to bury me alive?' Zahorodnii blew up at him.

'Only because you are thrusting your head into the devil's maw.'

'Have you become a soothsayer? You really shouldn't visit witches so often,' Zahorodnii snarled.

'So it's like this now?' Raven felt a pain in his heart.

Larion suddenly became quiet and his shoulders sagged. 'I have to see Hulyi now,' he said, placating him. 'I have to decide what we do next.'

Zahorodnii instinctively went to Raven and clumsily embraced him. Then he looked around and was going to leap onto his horse, but his leg slipped out of the stirrup before he managed to swing himself into the saddle on the second attempt. Holyk-Zaliznyak, Hupalo and their bodyguards were already on horseback.

'What about you?' Zaviriukha looked at Raven.

'I'll follow you.'

'I don't understand.'

'I'll follow you, Sergeant,' Raven repeated.

'Where and when?'

'You will see. Get a move on, you're already late.'

Zahorodnii looked at everyone again, waved his hand and tugged at the reins. Tymosh Kompaniyets wheeled after him, followed by seven other riders, Zaviriukha, Hordienko, Sereda, Mefodii Holyk-Zaliznyak, and his adjutant Oleksa Dobrovolskyi, Denys Hupalo and Vasyl Tkachenko. There were nine of them altogether and in their Red Army uniforms they looked like a security patrol. They reached the station without incident and the anxiety that had troubled them as they said farewell to the other men was laid to rest.

'Zahorodnii,' interjected Zaviriukha, who had maintained silence for long enough, 'now you lead us as far as Skalivatka.'

He knew how their path would go; through the territory in possession of Zahorodnii, around Novomyrhorod, Zlatopol and then to Kapitanivka, Lebedyn and Shpola. Maybe Raven, who had been bitten by a stupid anxiety bug, would catch up with them there. About two *versts* from Skalivatka, before they got to Zvenyhorodka, they had been told to go to the railway guard's lodge and enter using the password, *Who is there in the night?* to which the correct answer was, *Chornomorets*.

Before they reached Kapitanivka, Larion suggested they caught their breath in the forest and let their horses rest for a while, but Zaviriukha did not agree. 'We have wasted enough time for me. If we want to get to General Hulyi, we can't hang around for a minute longer.'

It was a pity they ignored Zahorodnii because then they might have avoided the Kotovsky Red Army cavalry, who the devil had sent to meet them, near Zhuravka, immediately after they had passed through Kapitanivka. It was fortunate that saw each other about two hundred paces away and did not meet face to face. They halted and stared at the Red patrol, which had come out of nowhere. Zahorodnii waved his hand at them in a friendly way and tugged at the reins, steering his horse to the left. To throw off suspicion, the rest of the riders followed him without hurrying. They turned calmly to the side and continued in a gentle canter to give the impression they were continuing to travel on their road and allowing them to travel on theirs. However their 'brothers', seeing something suspicious in this 'wish to avoid a meeting', followed them. The Red Army men quickened their pace.

The Cossacks knew it would have been stupid to get caught up in a dispute here, even though Denys's forelock was concealed by his helmet. The nostrils of Zahorodnii's steed flared, and Mefodii Holyk-Zaliznyak took his rifle from his back. 'They won't leave us alone,' he said. 'But what can we do?'

Even if the Reds had been fewer, a skirmish now would put the main goal of their expedition at risk.

'We'll try to get away from them,' Zahorodnii decided. 'Only shoot if they are breathing down our necks.' He spurred his horse into a gallop and they all followed in his wake, but the quicker they galloped, the more rapidly the Reds pursued them.

'Forward,' cried Zaviriukha nervously, but his command was not needed. The other Cossacks, leaning over the necks of their horses, fell into a single rhythm with their steeds, rising and falling, guided by an unseen power, flying over the fields and out of sight of the enemy. Shots rang out behind them and bullets buzzed overhead, but it was no more than the droning of insects to them until their fatigued horses began to flag and the Reds drew closer. When the distance had decreased to about fifty paces, Zahorodnii half turned in his saddle, aimed his rifle and fired. The man hurrying towards a bullet is always struck more powerfully than the man running away from it and the lead Kotovsky soldier was blown clean off his horse. The man running away has another advantage over his pursuer, the opportunity to lob a grenade in his wake. There is no need to throw it forcefully, the man in pursuit almost runs onto it as it explodes. So, Tymosh Kompaniyets, who responded to the otaman's shot like a signal, threw a grenade gently so that the Reds heading the pursuit could not evade the blast. The enemy's horses reared with a wild neighing as the grenade exploded, casting their riders out of their saddles, and they were able to widen the gap between them and their pursuers.

The Reds paused for a moment, losing the urge to pursue them, but then resumed their chase, albeit without the same ardour and savage bellowing with which they had begun. They followed the forest rebels as far as Tovmach and might have caught them were it not for the twilight darkening the same forest where Raven had been born under a walnut tree. The fugitives could at last pull up and take a breather. They would have rested longer if Zaviriukha had not urged them on, 'It's time to go. Glory to God who helps us to achieve our plans. Let's go.'

By nightfall they had passed Kapustyne, then Stetsivka, and two *versts* from Skalivatka they went to the railway guard's lodge where a yellow light radiated from a small window. The other riders remained in a slender strip of forested ground that stretched alongside the guard's lodge, while Larion and Zaviriukha approached the window cautiously. The moonless September night was as black as pitch, but overhead a few stars shone. Zaviriukha tapped gently on the glass. There was a bustling inside, someone coughed and then a man's voice said, 'Who is there in the night?' It was the password.

Zaviriukha was silent for a moment before replying, 'Chornomorets.'

'Enter.'

They entered the building where it seemed there was not enough space for Zahorodnii because it was so confined, but no one was planning to sit down. A drowsy man, dressed as a railway worker who only lacked a cap, said that everything was going to plan. He did not know Zaviriukha or Zahorodnii by sight and therefore cast his eyes from one to the other, trying to work out who was in charge. Finally, he explained that Hulyi had ordered them to go to Cherniachka Farm. They were waiting for them in the end house with a spacious verandah and three windows looking onto the street. The same password should be used. Having said all that was required of him, the railwayman looked at the door without hiding his wish to say goodbye to his guests as quickly as possible.

They went into the night and before long reached Cherniachka Farm and Zaviriukha and Zahorodnii went to the house that had been described. A dog barked so loudly in the yard that it was almost impossible to hear anything over the sound it made. Even when the master of the house emerged and put it in the kennel, it continued barking incessantly.

'Who is there in the night?' the farmer cried over him.

'Chornomorets.'

'Oh, thank God,' the man, whose massive, bald head gleamed in the dusk like a full moon through the clouds, approached them. 'I was afraid that you weren't coming. Hamalii ordered Sergeant Zaviriukha to go to town, but I don't know which one of you he is. The rest of you can stay overnight at my place. How many of you are there?'

'Nine,' said Zaviriukha, 'with horses.'

'We will go to the barn, it's very cramped in the house.'

When they had settled in their temporary lodgings, Zaviriukha cheered them by saying, 'You can catch up on your sleep here. I'll be back in an hour.' He leaped on his horse and hurtled towards town.

'If we catch up on our sleep here, we'll find ourselves tied up when we wake,' said Hupalo.

'I don't think so,' Zahorodnii disputed. 'Everything has gone to plan until now.'

'Well, that's what I think,' Hupalo took off his helmet and let his forelock swing at liberty. 'I've been thinking all the way here.'

'What about?'

'About this. That Zaviriukha will bring the *Chekists* here and hand us over like lambs to the slaughterhouse.'

'If he had wanted to turn us in, he would have done so ages ago,' Captain Hordienko interrupted. 'And if anyone doubts him, let's put someone on sentry duty.'

'So we can annoy that dog again,' said Hupalo, becoming yet more angry.

However, their fears were groundless and soon Zaviriukha returned, accompanied by the Commander of the Black Sea Group.

'How was your journey?' Hamalii shook Zahorodnii's hand warmly before greeting Hupalo and Holyk–Zaliznyak. 'The sergeant says that you could not get here without having an adventure and General Hulyi was certain that something exciting must have happened. He said that the boys are late because it's mushroom season and Larion is pickling the enemies' heads for winter. It seems that he knows you well.'

'We've worked together before,' Zahorodnii said as he nodded.

'He gave me a note to pass to you.' Hamalii handed him a piece of paper.

Zahorodnii took it but could not read in the darkness of the barn. A match flared and while it burned the otaman read the note twice because it was so compact. Does even a man with his authority have time to compose a petition? Thankfully he had scrawled a few words in pencil, which, though they were restrained and severe, were comprehensible:

Zahorodnii,
    It's either work or personal life.
    Hulyi-Hulenko

'That's clear.' Larion hid the note in his field bag. He understood everything in the note. Work meant the struggle and personal life meant a private interest, that which was convenient to you. However, it was pointless of Hulyi to remind him of this. If he had chosen the personal life he would have been far from here now. Hulyi had arranged for him to be passed the note, not as guidance, but as a signal that he had arrived and was waiting in Zvenyhorodka. He often repeated the phrase that was in the note and for those who knew him it was like a password.

'It's getting light,' said Zahorodnii, looking through the doorway as the few stars left in the sky were fading into the dawn.

'That's fine,' said Hamalii. 'It's quiet in the town and everything is under our control.'

'Well, let's go then.'

'Not all at once. We will go with you first Zahorodnii and one other; either Hupalo or Zaliznyak. The rest will come later with Zaviriukha. Vigilance and foresight are paramount. We have to go to another of our men first so we can have breakfast before the meeting. It's also time to feed your horses, is it not?'

'Well, let's get on with it,' grumbled Hupalo, hearing that there was yet another assignation to pass through.

Hamalii did not like his tone, but said, in a respectful manner, 'You are right there Otaman, let's begin. Are you coming with us?'

'No, I will come with my adjutant,' Hupalo replied.

'Then we will meet at the council.'

Hamalii looked at Holyk-Zaliznyak, who nodded, and the two of them and Zahorodnii left first.

When they crossed the little bridge across Hnylyi Tikych, it was already growing light and the town was calm under a dense blanket of morning silence. A cow lowed somewhere and a lark sang overhead. If someone had seen these riders in Red Army uniform, they would not have paid them any attention.

***

The miller, Okhtanas, let them into his house, which was near the watermill by Hnylyi Tikych, and here they had breakfast. It was obvious they were at a miller's house because everything was made with flour. *Varenyky, halushky, hrechanyky* and *potaptsi*. He fed the horses generously and placed a carafe of *horilka* on the table for his guests.

'What's this? Are we going to a wedding?' Zahorodnii looked at Hamalii.

'It's just to whet your appetite.' Okhtanas smiled guiltily. 'We never lack this stuff.'

Hamalii nodded approvingly at Larion, but also refused to drink. Mefodii hesitated briefly before taking the glass that was offered to him so he did not offend the master of the house. He drank, crowed and wolfed down the *hrechanyky* so rapidly that he amazed Zahorodnii by the way he was cramming everything into his torso, which was as skinny as the rungs of a ladder. Larion only ate a little, having become anxious during the journey, and because the nearer the time came for the otamans' council, the more a strange foreboding settled on him.

Hamalii saw this and when the miller had left the room he tried to calm him, 'You are worrying pointlessly, all our plans have been thought out to the last detail. We have a district military commission here and some of our people are in the *Cheka*. We wouldn't do this blindly.'

'I know,' said Zahorodnii coldly.

'We're not going to a wedding, you were right to reprimand us for that,' continued Hamalii. 'Don't forget that we are going to a meeting of the district military commissioners. You have an ID card from the Telepyne district military commission and they are all obliged to assist you.'

'I know,' repeated Zahorodnii. 'No one should get agitated. I just didn't want to let down Hulyi, and Sergeant Zaviriukha was hurrying us along the entire journey and now we're sitting here as though we are at a festival.' His wrath changed direction. 'What are you doing, haven't you seen *halushky* before?' he suddenly snarled at

230

Holyk-Zaliznyak, who, having finished the *hrechanyky*, was throwing himself into the bowls of *halushky*.

'I've seen them,' said Mefodii, 'but let me eat like a human being for what may be the last time.'

'Well, if that's the mood you are in we might as well pack up and go home,' said Hamalii angrily. 'No one forced you to come here, either work or ...'

'Forget the political activism,' Zahorodnii interrupted. 'Are we going or drinking? For if I do drink, this little flask will not be enough.'

'Let's drink now then,' said Holyk-Zaliznyak enthusiastically, but Hamalii stopped him.

'Later.'

He drew out a pile of tightly folded maps from his field bag, divided them into two packages and handed them to the otamans.

'So we do not waste time I am passing you the military maps of your districts.'

'This is real work,' said Zahorodnii.

Hamalii took out a military watch from his pocket. It had a compass on its open cover.

'Well, let's go with God.'

They thanked the miller for the food and went to the centre of the town. They passed the Borukh barbers, the Likhter grocers, where the cooperative had been, and the grammar school were Raven had held negotiations with Dybenko and Kuziakin. At last they reached the Vynokur Inn where the gathering of district military commissioners was due to be held and where the otamans' council would take place.

By the hitching post, to which ten different kinds of horse were tethered and where they hitched their own, a few military types, who looked like disguised Cossacks, were smoking on the verandah. Some of them looked with interest at the newcomers, trying to see if there was anyone they knew among them. Zahorodnii and Holyk-Zaliznyak returned their stares, trying to see if the Zvenyhorodka otaman, Honta-Lyutyi, was among the smokers; if Antin Hroznyi from Horodyshche Forest, who had replaced the slain Trokhym Holyi, was here; or possibly if Raven, who had been bitten by some foolish anxiety, might have popped out from the earth.

They did not see anyone they knew, but the boys on the balcony welcomed them warmly and cast conspiratorial glances at the otamans. Larion and Mefodii would have loved to smoke with them if Hamalii had not told them they first had to enter the building and make their arrival known.

'Then you can meet whoever you like.'

Zahorodnii was almost frighteningly eager to see Hulyi, on whom he placed the greatest hope for the success of their venture.

Hamalii opened the door politely, allowing the otamans to enter ahead of him. Zahorodnii was the first to step over the threshold and in the straw-scented darkness he barely had time to blink before his hands and legs were seized in a vice-like grip and his neck was immobilised. Holyk-Zaliznyak, who followed next, did not have a moment to turn, but managed to fire his revolver, intending to put a bullet in his head. Someone grabbed his hand and the bullet hit the ceiling. Then such a coldness descended on his meagre body that he could not move.

'Hamalii, are you are with them too?' cried Zahorodnii. His voice choked but he did not hear a reply.

***

From the cryptogram of the appointed representative of the G.P.U. on the right bank of Ukraine, Yefim Yevdokimov, 29 June 1922

No. 3/479:

Top Secret

To the Head of State Political Administrator of Ukraine, Comrade Mantsev

We hereby forward a report on the operations of the Petliurite partisan groups, whose activities cover extensive areas of the Kremenchuk and Kiev provinces, and in particular the Kholodnyi Yar and Znamianskyi forests.

The centre of our own work is at present in Yelysavetgrad, where a special group of the police representative operates. It is clear from the material below that we have the real possibility of profoundly influencing the development of these gangs; thereby revealing who they are and uniting many bandit groups under our management, to ultimately annihilate them. There are favourable circumstances for this, which include the fact that all Petliurite atamans are waiting impatiently for a signal to revolt from their leaders over the border. They are yearning to unite under the direction of a single command centre, but their leaders over the border are silent and they have no serious communication with them. The well-known Petliurite, Trokhymenko, (the former officer of the main insurgent headquarters of Tiutiunnyk in Tarnov) whom we captured after he crossed the Polish border to undertake subversive activities, has come over to our side after appropriate processing. In April he proposed the plan to remove the leaders of nationalist gangs. He will be helped by another Petliurite, Tereshchenko, seized and enlisted into our ranks, who has been examined by our agent.

For our operation we have established a group of workers under our representative in the town, who will implement the following plan at the most suitable time:

1. Accelerate the violent activities of the insurgence centre to provide it with the appropriate authority among the rebel groups.
2. Intensive work on structuring robust means of communication with leaders/atamans.
3. Acquire a list and the structure of the gang participants.
4. Relocate the centre of development from Yelysavetgrad to another area that would be more convenient for us to maintain fast and regular communication, but at the same time not too distant from the main insurgence centres. A convenient location would be Zvenyhorodka, in the Kiev government district.

5. The main goal of our work is to organise a meeting of rebel leaders that will allow for their final liquidation.

The information we have, and the unconditional authority enjoyed by our confidential employee among the Petliurite atamans, gives us every chance for the successful execution of the plan.

Plenipotentiary of the group, Yevdokimov
29 June 1922

From the cryptogram of the appointed representative of the G.P.U. on the right bank of Ukraine, Yefim Yevdokimov, 25 September 1922:

We are close to the time when the development of our plan will be realised. As a fundamental element of the plan for the liquidation of the leaders, the following is necessary:

1. All heads/atamans who arrive in Zvenyhorodka will be seized by us when they present themselves.
2. The appropriate divisions of the G.P.U. will be involved in the liquidation of the leaders and, for the more successful undertaking of the operation in different towns, our skilled representatives under the direction of whom this work will be undertaken are available.
3. To prepare for the meeting we have sent a group to search for secret apartments and facilities. The group has prepared two railway buildings and three apartments.

The plan for capturing the heads who attend the meeting is as follows:

1. When they arrive, the atamans, accompanied by our representatives, will go to the specified railway guard's lodge and then to the apartments, where they will be seized, one at a time.

2. Given that the atamans will arrive accompanied by select Cossacks/bandits, we are, along with the military command, taking appropriate measures to ensure the successful undertaking of the operation in the town. The assistant to the plenipotentiary, Comrade Frinovskyi, and the divisional chief, Comrade Nikolaev, have gone there, accompanied by a group of 20 people, including officers and a reinforced group of Red Army soldiers.

There are all the grounds to hope for a successful outcome of the operation that we have unambiguously named 'Testament'.

From the cryptogram of the appointed representative of the G.P.U. on the right bank of Ukraine Yefim Yevdokimov, 29 September 1922:

Yesterday, according to our group, Operation Testament was undertaken successfully, with the capture of the leaders of the Petliurite gangs who had arrived in Zvenyhorodka for the so called 'Supreme Atamans' Council'. Initially we seized the most prominent atamans heading the Kholodnyi Yar insurgence committee, Zahorodnii and Zaliznyak. The well-known ataman of Chornyi Forest, Hupalo, has been captured, together with the closest assistants/adjutants of all three leaders, namely Kompaniyets, Dobrovolskyi and Tkachenko.

Operation Testament was carried out in extremely intensive and complicated conditions, and it was only owing to the experience, endurance and courage of its leaders that we succeeded. We must simultaneously note that some atamans, whether due to extreme caution or for any other reasons, were not at this council. In particular, leaders with enormous influence over other bandits, such as Honta-Lyutyi, Savchenko-Nahornii and Raven, avoided arrest. However, the capture of their accomplices, and subsequently a significant easing of insurgent resistance, increases the chances of the rapid capture of these enemies and the destruction of their diminished groups.

In the very near future a special group will be sent into Yelysavetgrad and its periphery, with the specific orders to liquidate the atamans who did not attend the meeting. This operation will have the objective of the elimination of insurgent leaders and all nationalist-underground workers, and is given the name 'Sincere'.

Regarding the bandits seized by us; all have been sent under a reinforced escort to the Lukianivska prison in Kiev.

In order not to expose our valuable agents, Trokhymenko-Hamalii and Tereshchenko-Zaviriukha, we have also temporarily arrested them (as agreed upon with the latter), together with two more informers who accompanied the atamans to the meeting. Their incarceration in the cells with the bandits will allow them to acquire further information that will be extremely valuable to us.

Part Three

Chapter 1

1

In the evening Yevdosia bathed the child and dressed him in a clean Ukrainian shirt of the kind babies wore, which she had made herself with manufactured flannelette. She fed him with goat's milk mixed with an infusion and placed him on the hard wooden bed on which she herself slept. She was fearfully fond of the little boy, who was growing as rapidly as a cucumber by the hour. He moaned or called softly and did not cry or scream, even when his first tooth came through. Once he grabbed Yevdosia's finger and drew it to his mouth and she realised that the baby's gums were irritated. She thought about letting him suck on her nipple, but was a little uncomfortable in doing so. However, she could not forswear soothing the child and, a little ashamed, she unfastened her blouse, exposed the nipple, which had never been touched by an infant's lips, and smeared the tip with honey. When she held the child to her chest he sucked greedily and bit in a way that made her feel a pleasant warmth. She slept with Yarko like that all night, soothing the pain in his gums and awakening in herself the yearning for motherhood unknown until now. She gently touched his soft body and carefully examined his face, his small ears and his silken hair, which was already quite long, with the tips of her fingers. She saw all that she wished to see because she was not as blind as she appeared.

Yevdosia was able to see when she was born and her baby-eyes had gathered and recollected the way the world appeared before misfortune struck. Her mother, the sorceress Perchytsia, had laid her to sleep in the shade of a lime tree that was in bloom so she would gather strength and health from the tree, but the opposite happened. Although Perchytsia was a wise woman, she had left the baby unattended in the midday sun and it had burned out her sight. Now Yevdosia remembered the world with the eyes of a baby, and perhaps a little boy like Yarko could have become her eyes, her miracle, her happiness. If only the cards would fall how she wanted, she would

239

begin a new life with his young soul, with a renewed heart, and with the eyes of the child whom she loved so much. If only they would leave him with her forever. However often she cast the cards, which had passed through her hands over and over and which she read with the tips of her fingers, their immutable colours and patterns told her that the child would travel on a distant road. He had only just learned how to hold his head upright on his fragile neck, how to sit up a little, and had begun to burble, 'Ma', but she knew he would have to walk on a distant thoroughfare that stretched beyond her vision.

After she had lulled the baby to sleep, she picked up the rough, worn pack and cast the cards again. They were so worn and tattered that a sighted person would not have seen images on them, but again, through her finger tips, she saw the road and heard the thud of a horse's hooves coming to the Irdyn Marsh. When she had read the cards for Raven, a darkness as deep as sorrow had touched her lightly and entered her heart.

Yevdosia went to the icon in the corner of her room, knelt down and prayed. 'Protect and guide him from evil, Lord.'

2

No one knows when fate will make a gift to him of the happiest days of his life, but I knew that they were ahead of me in almost two weeks when I would be with my beloved. Lord, this was a gift of such riches; day after day we would be near each other. We would pass the nights together. I would watch her as she slept, breathed, smiled and spoke, and would wrap her in her bedding like a child.

I would take Veremii's son and her from this hell and leave them somewhere safe, then return to the forest and continue to battle while there was still a single Cossack with me. If fate preserved me, and wondrous things do happen in this world, I would find them, however long it took, I swear to God, and we would begin a new life together. I would not go there with a foreign name and the shame of defeat and exile, but with a legend.

After the otamans failed to returned from Zvenyhorodka, a wave of arrests of members of the underground and people suspected of

240

nationalist sympathies rolled over our country. They were arrested in Chyhyryn, Yelysavetgrad, Shpola, Cherkasy, Smila, Zvenyhorodka and many other places. I did not think for a moment that Zahorodnii, Hupalo or Zaliznyak could have sold a single one of them down the river. It was obvious that this was the result of Hamalii and Zaviriukha, who had betrayed us, like Cain had betrayed his brother, after gaining the trust of the underground movement. Their deceit had succeeded, not because of our gullibility or lack of foresight, but because of the criminal passivity of the government in exile.

Hamalii, Zaviriukha ... only our own kind could twist and betray us. Turncoats. Even when I sent a message to Zvenyhorodka (we still had informers in soviet institutions) and learned that these two monsters had been caught and taken to Kyiv with the others, I had not the slightest doubt that this was initiated by our former soldiers and renegades. It was such a secret conspiracy that even the guards would not know who was the 'bandit' and who the *Chekist*. It was certain that General Hulyi was not in Zvenyhorodka. How would he have got there? No one had heard about Lieutenant Stupnytskyi. It was certain that the provocateurs used these names as a tool for their deception.

I now berated myself for not having shot 'Sergeant Zaviriukha' when he came to us on that last day, with Hordienko and Sereda, before they travelled to Zvenyhorodka. Yes, I had not been entirely certain of their treachery. I had hesitated. I know how hard it is to struggle with deception when it warms your last hopes with life. Only by shooting the hireling could I have prevented the otamans from taking that fateful step. Let me have been judged and pronounced the outlaw because in a day or two the truth would have been revealed. We would have saved many and returned to our own ways. Now everything had been turned on its head. It is no wonder that anyone who had the chance was taking the path to salvation and away from the forest. I looked on this with understanding and helped the lads who wanted to leave with money and documents, but I did not announce that the unit was disbanding. The struggle was having the life choked out of it but, come what may, we must continue with our very last strength, with our last defiant grimace at the enemy. No catastrophe would ever place the memorial cross on the grave of our goal of having our own country.

As for me, I could grit my teeth and hold off despair and the reproach of sorrow if it were not that I had a mountain of potentially calamitous threats poised to tip over me. On leaving Chornyi Forest, for who knows what our enemies might conceive having sniffed out all our lairs there, I considered how to avenge the otamans' council. Even if there was no hope of victory the desire for vengeance burned within me; a desire that burned in all Cossacks and had led most of them to the forest in the first place. Also, we needed to settle the matter with the foe, to remind them of our presence and to show the boys that it was still too soon to lower our hands and lay aside our weapons.

Furthermore, it was time to take care of Tina. My contact in Zvenyhorodka had informed me that her name was on the local list of 'people suspected of nationalist sympathies'. Almost every teacher and every member of the *Prosvita* cultural movement was on the Bolsheviks' list of suspects, and her performance at the Lebedyn sugar refinery was enough to add her to their blacklist. It was clear that they would take her in before long. Perhaps she had not been arrested because of a special consideration or because I had been at liberty for long enough and they knew that our group was in the vicinity.

I now acted as if, in my most sincere desire to help Tina cross the border, there was an ulterior motive. By enabling Tina to 'leap over the Zbruch', (do you remember that this is what she herself wanted) I could also send young Yarko to safety with her. The baby would have a mother and I felt that the long and difficult road to the border would be easier to traverse if we had a baby.

'What about you?' asked Tina.

We were conversing in the house of Father Oleksii, who had taken a request that we meet from me to her and who, the worthy soul that he was, had proposed we meet at his place. The autumn nights were already cold so I had agreed to his suggestion, though I knew it was risky because his premises might be under surveillance. I placed my hope in the night, as if it were an old friendly aunt who would hide me from the vigilant eyes of the enemy. Even bullets are less dangerous in the dark. The main reason for accepting his suggestion was that I had complete faith in him and knew that, indisputably, he would be on the *Chekists'* list of nationalist sympathisers.

It is hard to credit that after so many rebels had taken amnesty and told all, and that after so many betrayals, the Bolsheviks still did not know about the service to sanctify the weapons that he had conducted in Lebedyn Forest during the spring of 1920. I can still feel the cold drops of holy water from the service on my face. We had laid our rifles, handguns, pistols and grenades before us and had descended to our right knees. While Father Olesksii blessed us we each held a bare sword across our left thighs because we swore to use our arms only against the foe. He seemed inspired and full of power as he waved the straw brush, dipped in holy water, and declaimed, 'Our enemies perish like dew in the dawn.' The cold, stringent drops struck our faces as we raised our eyes upwards to look at the sun, believing that it would be so.

Even without taking into account the sanctification of the weapons, the unrestrained supporter of the so recently permitted Ukrainian Autocephalous Orthodox Church had committed enough 'sins' in the eyes of the enemy for three hundred arrests. Even his earthly life so bedevilled the Bolsheviks, poor peasants and ardent young communists that they stuck their noses into the Cherkasy district church council and demanded that the '*Petliurite* Priest' be defrocked and deprived of his position in society for his wayward conduct in the eyes of the citizenry.

It needs to be said that Father Oleksii lived with his villagers in the same spirit they lived. He would smoke a pipe with them or knock back a glass of *horilka*. They would go to him for advice, ask him to be a godfather or to attend wedding receptions, and he had such parties that the singing did not stop until the third cockerel had crowed. Everyone grew quiet when he approached the piano and, in his dense, velvety baritone, began a song about two doves in love. When the delicate Lady Olenka (so he called his wife) joined him with such an angelic voice some people could not hold back their tears.

However, the godless village rabble bayed so loudly that the authorities decided to remove him and the community was filled with woe at the possibility. A parochial gathering gave the thumbs down to the district church council and they not only re-elected Priest Stavinskyi for a further term but adopted a resolution to expose and punish the Antichrists who had slandered him. So Father Oleksii was further strengthened in his authority. His Cossack pipe continued to fume in masculine company, and he was always the first to raise a toast to the health of the baby or the young couple at christenings and weddings.

On summer evenings chords of piano music regularly echoed from his open window, until that dusk when a grenade was thrown through it. Father Oleksii, who played Schubert in a double-handed duet with his wife, heard the window rattle and saw a cylindrical object, with a long, stick-like handle, fall to the floor. He squinted at it for a moment, then, without hesitation, threw himself over the grenade, covering it and saving his wife. Olenka, who did not know what was happening, almost fell on top of him as she approached to see what a terrible misfortune had come on them. It was clear that God was watching because the grenade did not explode. Father Oleksii rose slowly and looked at the failed bomb. He took it by the handle and threw it back whence it had come, before sitting down again to play Schubert.

The piano was in the reception room where Father Oleksii had led Tina and I for our nocturnal meeting, but now the window was sealed firmly shut from the outside and there was a green drape over it. He had lit a lamp by which to see. We arranged ourselves on the broad Ottoman, which was covered with a green fabric matching that which hung over the window. We looked at each other more than we touched. We looked long and yearningly, casting off our clothes for the heat from the ceramic tiled stove was making our heads swim. It was a long time since I had been in such a quiet, warm place, and Father Oleksii, who knew this, had, in his good-spirited way, loaded the stove well and done everything possible to ensure that we would have peace and quite. On the table, which was covered with a white cloth, he had placed a carafe of *horilka,* flavoured with wild grass, and a bottle of red wine, together with bread, a slice of salted meat and a pot of stew - How did he know what I liked to eat? There was also a pot of buttermilk covered with an appetising brown skin, but Tina and I were not going to sit down to supper. We caressed each other longingly and were unrestrained with our touches and our kisses. Lord, who conceived the miracle of such a wondrous touch and the brushing of lips that unites two bodies in a single life, mingling their blood and their pure spirits. I speak truthfully when I say that after our first lovemaking I never thought of another woman. Our previous sojourn in paradise had been such a long time ago that I now took her as if for the first time and I had never seen her naked. This woman, barely ripened from the cherry-bright girl she had been, became the revelation of another enchanted world, with its hills, forests, valleys, rivers and lakes, in my embrace. This was such ecstasy. I knelt on the floor, Tina was on the Ottoman and she turned her face towards me as I took her by her buttocks so her body was open to me in all its wanton abundance. We met each other in another place and surrendered utterly to delight. Someone unseen touched the keyboard lightly, or maybe the strings resonated with the cries of my sweet, fragile sparrow.

***

'What about you?' Tina asked.

'I will lead you over the border and return. I will come and find you later,' I said, avoiding her gaze.

'Later? When?'

'Shall we have supper?' I embraced her, touching her hair gently with my lips; it smelled of dried grass and was rich with fresh milk.

'Later? When?' she repeated, pressuring me to answer.

I am a bit thick, Yevdosia spoke truthfully about me when she said that, and for a long while I did not know how to answer. I eventually said, sincerely, 'When I can.'

'If you are bothered about the child I could care for him here,' said Tina. 'He will be our child.'

'And when they ask where you got him will you say that the stork brought him to you?'

'I will say that the raven bore him to me in his beak,' she smiled sadly. 'Don't worry, I'll dream up something.'

'Tina, I'm thinking about both of you.'

'Maybe you are worrying pointlessly and ... things will yet change.'

'What will change?'

'I don't know.'

Tina gently pulled herself from my embrace and began to dress. I watched her movements with wonder, for when a woman dresses it holds more fascination for me than when she removes her clothes, especially when her buttons do not slot into their holes. How could she talk about anything serious while she was doing this? It was so moving when Tina, as she fastened her blouse over her breast, reflected aloud, 'Maybe everything isn't as hopeless as it seems to us. They are allowing Ukrainian schools. They have agreed to the independence of our church. Ukrainian books and papers are being produced.'

I waited until she had finished fastening those troublesome buttons and said, 'There is no greater deceit than offerings from the hand of the enemy. Only a naive ignoramus would rely on their good nature.'

'But it's not just promises, there's a lot being done that you simply don't know about.'

'The greater the devil's kindness, the more cunning the trap he prepares. Don't you understand?'

She bit her lower lip and it was painful for me to see her as she was now. 'Maybe it is so. But ...'

'What is this 'but' you still have? Is it big or small?' I tried to take a more light-hearted tone, but furrows of sadness gathered between her slender eyebrows.

'I don't want to be there without you.'

'But you've been without me here most of the time. Believe me, there simply isn't another way out of this.'

'I'll wait here for you,' she said.

'No, it's not safe. I don't know what will happen tomorrow.'

'To you?'

'No, my little sparrow, to you.'

'Then take me to the forest,' she implored.

'It's not possible.'

'Why not?'

'How could I be an otaman if I brought a woman to the unit? Well, think about it yourself. I thought it all through long ago. There is no other way, believe me, we have to go as soon as possible.'

'Into the wider world?'

'It isn't as distant as it seems to us. Our people live just the other side of the Zbruch. Ukrainians, like us, but free. They will help us.'

'If you think there is no other way, let it be so,' she said in a somewhat absent voice.

'Let it be so, but give me time to go to Shpola, I have to prepare my people because I will be disappearing for a while.'

'For a long while,' repeated Tina, not hearing me. 'And what ... what if it's forever?'

I no longer knew what to say, there are many things one can ponder for an eternity and still come to a dead end. Tina felt this too and led me out of my impasse.

'Pour me another one,' she said. 'No, not wine, that grass-fragranced *horilka*.'

3

Following a number of successful operations undertaken in October by sections of the military and our agents, the bandit movement in Kholodnyi Yar is almost crushed. As early as September we knew the location of the valleys in Chornyi Forest used by the bandits. During the first days of October a group, headed by Comrade Linde, and strengthened by cadets from the Yelysavetgrad School of Red Commanders, was directed and stayed there to ensure the utter destruction of the Petliurite gangs. With no regard for the density of the large, forested area, it bogginess and the impassibility of much of the terrain (the cadets were up to their belts in water and marsh as they traversed some routes), each section of woodland was surveyed without revealing any bandits. It seems that their much diminished groups are finally decaying or, at worst, splintering into smaller gangs and avoiding clashes with our forces.

Notwithstanding this, on 12 October, in

villages near Moskalenky and 25 versts from Smila, Raven's gang (it's not possible to determine how many they were) attacked a supply squadron which they had followed to Bobrynska Station, together with 12 wagons loaded with supplies. By a fortuitous coincidence a group of ChON (the special purpose detachment) appeared at the right moment, as well as the local militia and self-defence group from the village of Rotmistrivka. As a result of the skirmish and the subsequent pursuit of the gang as they escaped, the platoon commander, Rastorhuev, died courageously, along with five ChON fighters, three militiamen and two supply squad members. There were also some wounded.

It is hard to estimate the losses of the opposing forces because they carried away their dead and wounded as they retreated. Finally, it was possible to track down and destroy yet one more bandit who went to Buda Farm at night. Yet again, the result has surpassed all expectations, for it appears the man is no other than Ataman Raven, according to the testimony of local residents. The corpse was taken to Cherkassy where it has been photographed.

Therefore, the information about Raven's capture in Zvenyhorodka, supplied previously, has now been revealed as incorrect.

Appointed Representative (signature)

From operative information collated by the Kremenchuk division of the secret police department in the Chyhyryn district, 21 October 1922

If only he had known how the fire storm at Moskalenky would end. When he thought about it, Raven resolved that he would not get involved in any similar musical performances, with two choirs swapping bullets, until he had stashed Tina safely over the other side of the Zbruch. That was if he got her to agree to this excursion. He did not have the right to expose himself to danger, but he could not resist the temptation.

They were staying in Hrafskyi Forest, nearer to Lebedyn, where they had a rest and some much needed calm. The perpetually agitated Bizhu, who had been on guard at the side of the camp that faced Moskalenky, flew up to them and reported that a convoy was moving along the Smilianskyi path.

'Twelve wagons,' he clarified. 'And two of those 'smoky' requisitioners on each of them. Pah! If we run to them now, we'll catch them. Do you hear me? If we run now it'll only be a second before we deal with them and we can run back.' Bizhu primed himself for another sprint, even though he knew they always travelled to these assignations on horseback.

Raven thought about how many and which of his Cossacks to throw at the enemy. He saw that a delighted wantonness for battle was glittering in Bizhu's eyes and realised that he also felt a familiar itch inside. He was almost ashamed of his caution and hurried to saddle his horse. Within a minute, ten of them were hurrying in the direction of Moskalenky and only the density of the forest prevented them from spurring the horses into a gallop.

Raven, Koliada, Vovkulaka, Khodya, Bizhu and his middle brother Zakharko, Diadiura, Viun, Kozub and Sutiaha. Ten happy warriors revelling in the fact that after an enforced break they had the chance to loosen up with a battle and replenish their stock of victuals. Koliada tore ahead. He was from the nearby village of Makiivka and those wagons creaking on the Smilianskyi path might bear his blood family's goods and chattels. It was he who proposed they bear sharply to the right, leap onwards into the field ahead of them, and sit in the Budianskii fir tree forest near to the well-beaten path that the requisitioners would take.

It was a serviceable thought and soon they hurtled out of Hrafskyi Forest, flew over the field and hid in the firs, which were so dense the horses could barely turn around. The branches, laden with needles, whipped their faces as they rode.

They had waited for half an hour or more, observing the road, but there was no sign of the convoy. Raven looked at Bizhu, who had brought the news, and at the confused Koliada, who had persuaded them to go far ahead of the convoy to the forest. Waiting for a battle always made them nervous and they yearned to smoke. Kozub took out his cigarette case but caught the otaman's glare and hid it hurriedly.

'What, you smell tobacco?' Vovkulaka flashed his toothy smile.

The first wagons glimmered in the distance. It seemed as if they were not moving and unless you knew in which way they were travelling it was impossible to guess by looking at the tiny, apparently static, specks. An unpleasant thought passed through Raven's mind that someone could have noticed the riders heading towards the firs and the requisition squad had halted to consider what to do next. Perhaps they had sent for help. But no, Koliada had calculated correctly, the wagons were heading in their direction, albeit slowly.

'They are bringing a tasty bite for us,' said Khodya, his mouth watering.

It was a cloudy but warm autumn day. The possibility of rain hovered in the air, together with the stringent fragrance of the firs. Koliada looked tensely in the direction of the convoy and his forehead wrinkled. It was the first time Raven had seen him like that. His sharp, ascetic face usually seemed estranged and remote, but now a shadow of evil foretold passed over his features. Raven had long ago learned how to recognise the sign of a man who would be overtaken by misfortune and knew this was its shadow; perhaps the shadow of death.

'Get the Lewis ready.' He nodded to Diadiura, one of the vigorous village men; he was about twenty, but had a more profuse beard than his chief. Diadiura tried to emulate the otaman in many ways, often even adopting his lack of enmity. The lads smiled in a good-natured way when he gestured slowly with his hands as he said, 'Well, that's the hand of cards that fate has dealt.'

'Well, they've loaded a lot on those wagons,' said Bizhu. 'They are crawling like terrapins.'

'Well, run and tell them to get a move on and then run back,' Vovkulaka said bitingly. He was also nervous. The thought that their presence had been noted had also crossed his mind. Perhaps the requisitioners were preparing to resist or, worse still, had sent for help. Why else would they be almost motionless?

Their forebodings eventually came true when thirty armed riders appeared from the direction of Hrafskyi Forest, where the rebels might have retreated to. It was clear, even from a distance, that they were looking towards the firs, so someone must have seen the rebels heading there. They were not hurrying anywhere, indeed they had halted their horses as if they too were waiting for the convoy.

Raven sent Bizhu and Viun to the other side of the firs to determine if it was easier to exit through the fields there, but an unpleasant surprise awaited them. An armed group, a Jewish self-defence squad, was drawing towards them from the village. As the boys brought this news, twenty of the requisitioners left their wagons on the road and headed towards the firs from the right. The rebels were totally encircled.

'It's a pity that we only have one Lewis,' said Vovkulaka, scratching the back of his neck.

'And not many grenades,' added Viun. 'If we had known.'

'I am to blame,' said Koliada, quietly. He was pale, as if already stale and dead.

'What are you talking about now? Pack it in.' Raven looked piercingly at him.

'I'm the one who led you here.'

'Nonsense! That's how the cards fell. But we don't know how they have fallen yet.'

'Or what they tell us,' Diadiura threw in, but no one smiled this time.

'Correct,' Raven said. 'We still don't know who has the strongest hand. Listen, we won't try to break out at once, they'll expect that. We will wait. I don't think they will crawl into this forest, it's very dense and overgrown. The self-defence squad won't crawl into here, that's the truth, and if someone does dare to they will regret it. If they are dead they will be unable to regret anything. Diadiura what's your stock of machine-gun belts?'

'One,' said Diadiura guiltily.

'One hundred bullets … Shoot only if you have a clear shot. Now, all of you need to hurry and take up defensive positions on both sides of this ditch. Tie your horses so that you can release them quickly. Sutiaha, Bizhu and Viun, go to the rear and cover our backs.

Are there any questions?'

'If we run, where shall we regroup?' asked Bizhu.

'There, where we ran from, here.' Raven smiled.

The unit that blocked their retreat to Hrafskyi Forest was not in any hurry to advance. The requisitioners, who were also on foot, waited about one thousand metres away, afraid to aim their fire. The Cossacks, seven in number without their rearguard, lie in the ditch, ten steps apart from each other. They waited for the attack, while their enemies waited for them to attempt to escape. They were measuring their endurance against each other rather than their strength.

Drops of lazy autumn rain began to fall, so few at first that they only saw damp splotches on the barrels of their rifles and the cover of the Lewis, which Diadiura had positioned on its tripod in front of him. The Cossacks had a special regard for the Lewis; the gun sometimes malfunctioned but it could be fired easily from horseback. They only lacked the ammunition for it and it was becoming increasingly difficult to obtain.

The days are short in October and it grows dark quicker under the boughs of the forest. When the heavens cloud over and rain falls, daylight becomes almost absent, but the darkness was handy for the Cossacks. What were the Muscovites waiting for? Would someone still come to their aid?

'Oh, come on, come on,' Kozub harangued them, holding his nicotine stained finger on the partially squeezed trigger. It was so brown that it looked like he had been shelling walnuts. He wanted everything over quickly so that he could have a smoke. How long would they draw out this?

Even Khodya stopped chewing his grass stalk and looked askance at the wagons abandoned by the requisitioners. The wagons carried sackfuls of flour, cereals and other goodies yet unseen. Khodya did not want to believe that none of this would fall into their hands now. He reflected that if the enemy began to penetrate the forest it might not be a bad idea to retreat around the wagons. Perhaps he could grab something as he fled.

Koliada's face was pale and almost sleepy as he prayed. He beseeched the Mother of God to lead evil away from them, to act for his friends and, if it were needed, he would pay for her aid with the price of his life. He would not take offence if she gathered him from this world; he had long been prepared to go to the other side, either to heaven or to an unknown place. He was ready to go now, if only the Mother of God would protect the boys. At first he whispered his prayer but then, in the strength of his passion and inflamed by prayer, he forgot himself and began to beseech their protector, the Virgin Mary, louder and louder. Vovkulaka, who was to the right of Koliada, began to listen.

'Who are you singing carols to?' he asked, but Koliada heard and saw nothing; he was already far away. He pressed his face against his rifle as if it were an icon.

Vovkulaka saw and heard everything and, like always before a battle, his eyes glittered with a quiet delight. Such rapture also came to Zakharko Momot at moments like these, but now his round, duck-nosed face was masked with a cold rapture. Only his gaze drifted slowly over the enemy ranks. His lips moved as he counted the riders.

Raven believed this was a ChON flying squadron and it was from there that the most skilled and dangerous strike would come. Although the special troops remained in one place, occasionally one or another of them would approach the rider of a white horse, who was clearly their leader and was holding back for some reason. Perhaps he was waiting for someone or he still expected the bandits to try to break through the ring of weapons around them. After a short time Bizhu appeared, he was out of breath and broke the news that five militiamen were approaching from the left flank of the forest.

'Five in all?' Raven asked. 'Continue to watch them.'

He thought that if the white horse was not fitted for battle it was meant to be on parade, and at that moment the big parade-ground military chief, who was sitting on the white horse, raised his right hand on high. The rifles fired randomly and the Muscovites laughed stupidly as if they were in pursuit of a hare. Then shots crackled from all sides of the fir trees. The requisitioners also began to advance, but the heaviest fire came from the self-defence squad. This tough tribe had never made war on anyone. They fired away with gusto, not regretting their bullets wailing. They raised a commotion to create the impression that the strongest force was gathered there, for that might be where the bandits would try to break out.

It seemed that the gang was not going anywhere. The forest rebels stayed quietly in the ditch without giving any sign of their presence. The firestorm continued, branches flew into the air, needles rained down, and the air filled with the stringent fragrance of the firs rocked by the bullets.

Then something went amiss in the head of the commander on the white horse. Either he persuaded himself that there was nothing in the forest or he was fearfully desirous of flaunting the 'Order of the Red Flag' on his breast. Either way, his milk-white horse reared as he bellowed in Russian, 'With me! Attack! Forward!'

He galloped towards the trees and the special troops followed him, but they were not as capable as their commander. He held himself evenly in the saddle, rising and falling in rhythm with the horse. Raven, kindly disposed towards such a cavalier, let him come closer than was necessary before planting a bullet in his breast where the 'Order of the Red Flag' would have swung.

After five more shots and a short burst from the Lewis, two riders were struck off their steeds. A third flew head over heels with his horse, and the rest turned back. Raven gave the signal to his men to stop firing. The rebels were encouraged, they had not expected that beating off the first attack would be child's play. In reality, the Muscovites, after retreating, gathered to discuss how to smoke them out of the trees. They must have decided something quickly because after a short time they again took up their position in the field. Two of their emissaries went in different directions; one to the militiamen and one to the self-defence squad, who had squandered bullets by recklessly firing into the firs.

Evening drew in and the shadows, which were already dense with the grey murk of an autumnal rain, thickened. The one object that could be seen clearly was the white horse that was wandering around the field in confusion.

'We'll wait a little longer ,then we'll break out,' said Raven. 'At the moment it's impossible for even an insect to slip through.'

The enemy turned around and started moving towards them from all directions. It was clear that an order had come to stop this game of 'grandmother's footsteps' and destroy the gang in the firs. They were waiting for a renewed onslaught by the ChON special troops when the sound of shots, which had been swallowed up by the deafening stillness of the forest, began to ring out sharply and clearly. Raven understood that the enemy had already entered the trees and it seemed to him that he was able to distinguish the shots of his boys who were guarding their rear. He heard the shots with the roots of his hair and had not managed to give an order before Bizhu flew in and said that the militia, requisitioners and the Jewish force had entered the trees. Sutiaha and Viun were returning fire but could not stop the rabble.

'We've shot about five of them, but still they crawled and crawled.' He dabbed his forehead which was pouring rain and sweat. 'Well, shall I run?'

'Call the boys here,' Raven ordered. 'Kozub go with him and return quickly. We will break out.'

They still had a little time. The enemy forces were approaching very slowly because the young firs had very dense, interwoven branches and because no one wants to hurry to meet a forest filled with bullets. By now the Cossacks had gathered and Raven gave the order, 'To your horses!'

The dusk was becoming so thick that it was impossible for them to take aim and fire. Perhaps this gave hope to the ChON special forces because they threw themselves into storming the fir forest again, and stumbled on something so unexpected that they became totally confused. Instead of firing, the rebels rode to meet them and, in the murk where bullets are blind, the sabre revealed that it could see flesh. The stunned Muscovites took to their heels and dispersed so quickly that Raven only managed to sever one skull.

The path to Hrafskyi Forest was now clear. Only behind, where they had just been standing, the ragged enemy band emerged and raised such a storm of gunfire that the flames from their gun barrels illuminated the darkness under the trees.

'Time to go home lads,' cried Raven with all his might, as joy resounded in his throat. 'Home, devilish children.'

His familiar cry pierced even Mudei's awareness and he flared his nostrils, picking up on the mood of the rider. His body was pouring with dark rainwater and he turned his head to the side, where he could see most clearly what was ahead and at the same time what was behind. Raven pressed his breast against the horse's mane and noted how the boys, each in his own style, drove towards home with all their might. One headed sharply to the right where the wagons abandoned by the convoy stood and, even in the darkness, Raven recognised the squat but extraordinarily swift steed that had borne Khodya away from danger hundreds of times. Vovkulaka rode on Raven's right. He always stayed close to the otaman. His brown mare, Tasia, was an impetuous young horse and could pick up Mudei's scent and follow it obediently from one *verst* away. On his left, but a little to the rear, Koliada urged his bay horse that was already lagging behind as if it had lost a shoe. Raven looked at him from time to time. The Cossack was not to his liking today after he had blamed himself for bringing misfortune on their heads. There is a kind of volition in us that waits for a man so that in a moment of weakness it can seize him.

The otaman cast his gaze over his Cossacks to ascertain which of them was where, but saw no one now the autumn night had fallen swiftly and hidden Zakharko Momot, Sutiaha, Diadiura, Viun, Bizhu and Kozub. In the distance, to their rear, the rifles of the amicable military foe flared and rang as they continued in pursuit. Koliada lagged still further behind.

It might have seemed that the danger had passed, that at last they could relax, but that evil volition, which stuck to them like bindweed, seizes a man in his weakness. Raven, sensing this, kept Koliada within his field of vision and reined in Mudei to let his Cossack ride ahead, but Koliada slumped suddenly, leaned to the side and rolled onto the earth. Within seconds Raven leaped from his horse and was by his side.

'What has happened to you?'

'Shot in the belly,' groaned Koliada.

Raven realised the bullet must have struck Koliada some time ago when they broke out of the encirclement and he had held himself in the saddle with his last strength. Raven wanted to take his hand, but seeing Vovkulaka above him he leaped onto his horse and said, 'Give him to me.'

Vovkulaka lifted Koliada carefully and placed him in the saddle in front of Raven. The shots of their pursuers still rang out, but were harmless in the distance, like a breeze snagging at their clothes. Raven, holding Koliada upright, headed for Hrafskyi Forest with Vovkulaka. A third rider appeared from nowhere and dumbly headed towards them. Vovkulaka was almost ready to fire at him when he heard a familiar voice, 'Open your eyes. We are yours.' It was Diadiura. His tall hat and long beard made his head seem larger than his horse's.

'Who did I order to go home?' asked Raven.

'Well, you need a gun to back you up,' he thundered. 'Is he badly wounded?'

'Lay me ... groaned Koliada, 'lay me on the earth, I'm burning up ...'

Vovkulaka and Diadiura rapidly, but gently, laid him on the earth and covered him with fallen leaves. Raven also jumped from his horse and knelt on one knee by the wounded man.

'Bear up, I see no devil near you. Light a match.' He began to unfasten Koliada's jacket, but the dying man asked him to stop. 'That isn't necessary. Leave me here and you ... Raven, you know the farm where my brother lives. Let someone tell him where I am and he will take me.'

Raven felt Koliada's blood running over his fingers.

'We will carry you to your brother,' he said.

'No. Cover me with branches and go. My brother will take me away before the morning comes.'

'I will take you to the farm myself.'

'That's not necessary. It hurts ... Let Ilko know.'

Koliada's head slumped to the side and Raven was at a loss what to do. He waited, hoping that perhaps one of the boys would suggest something, but they were silent. What advice could they give now? Taking Koliada on horseback would squeeze out the last drops of life from him. They could tell his brother ... But how could Ilko help? They needed a doctor, or to bury Koliada in the morning.

Raven embarked on a desperate course of action. He ordered Diadiura to go to Lebedyn to get the doctor to come to Ilko's farm, and the others, including Vovkulaka, to make a stretcher from branches so they could carry Koliada to his brother's. The farm was two *versts* away and as they were making preparations night came to their aid by concealing them.

They sliced two thick pieces of wood from the trees with their sabres, laid a thick branch at the front, took ropes, which they always carried in their saddle bags, and assembled a stretcher. They laid the unconscious Koliada on their contraption and hurried through the forest towards Buda Farm, with Mudei and Tasia following. Behind them, in the trees, shots rang out from various armed groups, perhaps some still wandered the field seeking slain and wounded rebels.

'Leave me ...' groaned Koliada again.

'You don't give me commands now,' said Raven, encouraged that Koliada had spoken. 'Not while I'm in charge.'

'Leave me ... I am dying.'

'I forbid you to die. That's the easiest thing of all to do. What the devil use to us are you dead? Have you asked us if you can die?'

'Hey, have you asked us?' Vovkulaka joined in.

'Be silent you, for this also is your concern. He is going to give me a sign from the other world, something that will make me understand.'

'Well, you will see,' said Vovkulaka menacingly.

***

Koliada's older brother met them amicably. He had caught the whiff of gunpowder when he was in Otaman Yablunka's squad. After the otaman's death he had settled quietly on Buda Farm, concealing the sins of his past from the new government. The N.E.P. let him take charge of everything on his land - the barn, the pen for the animals, even a pond filled with carp. Ilko told his brother more than once that he would spit on all his goods and chattels and take to the forest if there was even a crumb of hope for a free Ukraine, but all he saw was a confused melee in the darkness. If it were not for the children, Ilko would say, as he scratched his neck, if it were not for his little fledglings, he would still stick up his head and take more than just a shotgun from its hiding place.

They tapped on his window and Ilko opened it at once, though no one was glad to see these nocturnal guests now. Hearing what had happened, he groaned and bustled as he hurried to throw the door wide open. He told them to bring his brother into the house.

While he lit a gas lamp, his terrified wife, Melania, appeared from somewhere near the oven.

'Oh, my God,' she exclaimed.

They lay Koliada on a bed, Raven unfastened his jacket and tore open the bloody shirt. There was a dark bullet hole in the left side of Koliada's stomach.

'I knew that everything would finish like this,' said Ilko.

'What? Everything?' Raven asked sharply.

'Everything,' repeated Ilko, and his lean, angular face, as sharp as his brother's, crumpled.

'Instead of weeping fetch a glass of *horilka* and a strip of linen.'

Ilko nodded at Melania and she stretched up to the cupboard to get some *horilka* and then took a towel, embroidered with a cross, from the chest. Raven washed the wound with *horilka* and Koliada groaned loudly. He was pale and the colour had drained from his lips. Ilko gently raised his brother upright and helped Raven to bind the wound.

'Water,' pleaded Koliada.

'We can't let you drink,' said Raven. 'Bear up, the doctor will be here soon.'

It only occurred to him now that the doctor might not come. Old Avrum Vitkup had aided them more than once, not because he sympathised with the forest rebels but out of respect for the Hippocratic oath. He did not care if he bandaged a Bolshevik or a partisan. For a gold coin of Tsar Nicholas, Avrum, without regard to his biblical age, would leave his bed in the depth of the night, don his *lapserdak*, pick up a medical bag, which was as old as he was and smelled of antiseptic, and hurry; even to the ends of the earth. It was good that he was as light and airy as a feather because he could sit easily behind a rider, fastened to them like bindweed, and be transported wherever he was needed. But that was in the early days of the occupation and now, as people changed, he might have changed also. Diadiura might have to bind him and bring him like a sheaf of wheat.

Raven and Vovkulaka had thrown off their sodden clothes so that Melania could dry them by the oven.

'I heard the shooting by the Budianskii fir tree,' said Ilko. 'I thought then that ...'

'What about?' Raven asked.

'About him.' Ilko nodded towards his brother.

'It would be better if you told Melania to heat some water and looked for a bigger lamp so everything is ready for when the doctor comes.'

Time passed slowly. Very slowly. The clock ticked on the wall. Its pendulum swung back and forth and the hands counted the time. Koliada's face was so calm it seemed as though it was moulded from wax, while his sinewy nose seemed yet more sharp and angular. His lips were compressed tightly, but his breathing was still visible. Two hours passed before Diadiura arrived with Avrum Vitkup.

'Oh, lads, lads, you are making yourselves wretched and not leaving good people in peace,' Avrum complained from the threshold. 'How long will things be like this?'

He approached Koliada, looked, nodded his head and then felt the wounded man's pulse. 'Take off this dressing,' he said, as if he did not have the strength to remove the improvised bandage himself.

Raven unfastened the crude bandage and the old doctor looked at the wound and pursed his lips.

'Peritonitis,' he said. 'Acute peritonitis.'

'What?' Ilko asked.

'An inflammation of the abdominal cavity. Neither I nor Jehovah himself can help.'

'I don't know who could help or how,' said Ilko, wrinkling his nose, 'but you, Avrum, can do anything. I know this, we all know the skill of your healing hands, you will save him and I will give you something of great worth. Take out that bullet.'

'I can take out the bullet,' sighed Vitkup, 'but that will not help, even if we were in a clinic.'

'Why won't it help?' Ilko asked weakly. 'Why did you come then?'

'I came because they fetched me,' said Vitkup.

'You are a doctor … Do something. Anything.'

'He no longer needs anything,' said Vitkup, quietly nodding his head a little.

'Why doesn't he need anything?' Ilko cried. 'Why? He asked

for water and we didn't give him any because we were waiting for you. My brother asked for water and, like a pig, I didn't give him any. Now, Vasylko,' he said to Koliada. 'Now I will let you drink.'

'It's unnecessary,' said Avrum. 'He is dead.'

Ilko drew his head into his shoulders and grew silent for a moment. Then he approached his brother warily and looked into his calm face for a long time, stroking Koliada's hair and crying bitterly. His wife cried with him.

'Take me home,' said Vitkup, who had not had time to remove his ancient *lapserdak*.

'Take him home and return here,' Raven said to Diadiura.

Diadiura and Vitkup left and Ilko said that he would bury his brother in the garden. If they could not bury him like a Christian in the cemetery, then they would at least bury him respectfully like a human being. He had a coffin ready in the attic.

'A coffin?' Raven asked in surprise.

'Now every good farmer has a coffin in stock,' said Ilko.

He went outside with Raven and Vovkulaka, gave them a spade and showed them where to dig the grave at the end of the garden. Then he went to dispatch his brother into that last dark place. He told Melania to prepare clean clothing, take an embroidered shirt from the chest and wash the corpse.

'I have never done this before,' said Melania warily.

'It's necessary,' said Ilko. 'It is woman's work.'

They heated the water because they needed to wash the corpse.

They both prepared Vasylko and Melania helped Ilko bring the coffin from the attic. When Raven and Vovkulaka returned, Koliada had already been placed in the pine coffin, with his hands crossed on his chest. Raven thought that the coffin was just the right size for the dead man's height.

'We will say farewell here,' he said, standing by the head of the coffin. He was silent for a moment before saying, 'You were a brave Cossack and a true defender of your country. You never hid from a bullet behind a stranger's back. You knew what you were risking for Mother Ukraine. The one thing that your stepmother, fate, could award you with was death in battle. We thank her for that.' Raven bowed and kissed the dead man, first on his crossed hands, then on his forehead. 'Forgive us, and farewell, we will meet on the other side.'

Vovkulaka, while kissing Koliada, was not as restrained and whispered something into the dead man's ear, which no one apart from Koliada's spirit might hear. 'If you can, give us a message from the other side. Do you hear me? Anything ... Just so that we know.'

'I didn't give you water before you died,' said Ilko. His face crumpled as he pressed it into his fallen brother's chest.

'Now we will never let you go away from us, Vasylko,' Melania wept. 'You will always be with us. We will bring you water and tend to your grave.'

Raven took a red, silk cloth from his bag and covered Koliada's eyes. When they had nailed down the lid they placed the coffin on a ladder so it was easier to carry, just as Diadiura returned.

'What happened?' asked Raven. 'Have you taken the doctor home?'

'Yes, but Vitkup has changed now. He asked that we stop waking him at night. He said that he is too old.'

'He's an old fox. He knows that no one will go to him in daylight. Did you see anyone on the road?'

'It was quiet everywhere.'

They lifted the coffin with the ladder. Raven and Diadiura were almost the same height and lifted it from the front, while Ilko and Vovkulaka were at the back as they proceeded to the end of the garden. Melania stepped ahead with a gas lamp in her hand. The grave was about two metres deep. They lowered the coffin on ropes and threw in handfuls of soil, then Vovkulaka and Diadiura, working in turns with the spade, filled in the grave.

'Well, that's all,' murmured Ilko. 'No cross, no burial mound.'

'Plant a cranberry bush instead of a cross,' suggested Raven.

They drank two measures of *horilka*, as is fitting at a wake, and had a bite to eat, *salo*, eggs and pickles.

Ilko persuaded the tired rebels to rest for a while until their clothes were dry. He placed straw on a bench in the side room and they put down their heads and slept. Dawn was just breaking when

262

they were woken by cries and bustle outside.

'Come out. You are surrounded.'

Raven ran to the window, squinted through the narrow gap between the blinds, and saw rifle barrels pointing at them through the fence. So, that is how it was. They had jumped out of the peril among the fir trees into an even worse, unexpected predicament because now they had a woman and two small children with them.

Who knew whether they were tracked by the ChON squad, whether Avrum Vitkup had sold them out, or perhaps a neighbouring farmer had seen them and hurried to perform a service to the commune. It was not the time to think about that now.

Raven had barely pulled away from the window when the glass was blown out of the frame and plaster exploded off the wall opposite. Three bullets had miraculously missed blowing apart his careless and, as Yevdosia would have said, thick head. The door opened and a pallid apparition stood before them. Ilko was standing there in linen underpants and a nightshirt. His face was as white as the linen he wore.

'Lads, my kin, be merciful … Have pity on the children.'

'How many are there?' asked Raven.

'Two.'

'Not your kids, the Muscovites.'

'How should I know? I just heard them walking on all sides of the house, from the street and from the garden. If you don't go out they will burn all of us alive.'

'We will go,' said Raven, 'don't sigh. Let us figure out what to do and you, crawl into the oven.'

'What good is an oven when they burn down the house? And there are children.'

Ilko knew what he was talking about. The vague shadows of dawn already moved with the light cast by the flames of the burning barn, which was nearer to the pathway than the house. The terrified pigs screamed, the hens clucked, the cows bellowed long and loudly, and among all that clamour, the neighing of the horses, which had been locked in the barn for the night, was heard.

'Give it up, bandits. We guarantee your lives.' These words were repeated a couple of times from the direction of the fence.

There was no more time for reflection. Raven exchanged a few hasty words with the boys before they threw their rifles on the bench and stuffed their revolvers in their pockets, so that they could grab them in a hurry. Each carried a grenade. Diadiura inspected the Lewis, lengthened the strap, and hung it over his shoulder in such a fashion that it was concealed by his broad back. Raising their hands in the air, they went outside compliantly, though looking at their progress from the outside, one would have said there was more pride than passivity in their ponderous steps. Raven went ahead, then Vovkulaka, then another profusely bearded chap, Diadiura.

'Closer. Come closer.' Someone bellowed over the noise of the livestock and the neighing of horses.

'Don't shoot.'

The thatch on the barn crackled with flames as the straw, drenched with the rain, sent pillars of sparks upwards and thick, yellow smoke engulfed the yard. The rebels approached the pathway unhurriedly, walking so that all three would be visible; swallowing their dissatisfaction together with the toxic, yellow smoke, which could be handy to either of the fighting parties, but at that moment it was unclear which.

Some idiot had hastily torched the barn to terrorise them, but another surprising thing happened that would have made Raven shake Ilko's hand if he had been given the chance. Ilko had been truthful when he said that he had a secret stash of arms, but who would have thought his hidden guns would fire themselves. There was such a thundering from under the eaves of the barn that jets of fire flew in all directions, as if cannons were being fired from its roof. The Muscovites threw themselves to the ground. None of them had the chance to recover before there was a further explosion, then more blasts of thunder. Shrapnel and bullets blasted out from the barn and it became clear that a substantial stock of grenades and ammunition was stashed under the roof and they were exploding with the heat of the fire. When the Muscovites finally poked up their heads, Diadiura swept his gun, firing into their ranks.

'To your horses,' he cried. Although he saw how Raven and Vovkulaka rushed to the barn, he continued to stand tall before the enemy line, sweeping it with the gun he held at waist height.

'To your horses,' he bellowed once more. He saw clearly enough that Raven and Vovkulaka had leaped on their steeds and heard how the otaman called, 'Come with me.' But a merry demon had settled in Diadiura; a devil that kept his finger squeezed on the trigger, which he did not release, even when a bullet thudded into his chest. He was rocked by the impact and backed towards the house where, when his shoulders touched the wall, he slid downwards slowly. Diadiura did not fall but instead sat against the wall, as if that were a more comfortable position from which to fire as he still aimed the gun in front of him.

Du ... du ...du. His heart was beating ever more faintly and it seemed to Diadiura as if he were hearing the hoof beats of Mudei and Tasia. He would not follow their riders on the road home now; he was going elsewhere.

***

The Muscovites kept firing at Diadiura for a long time. They must have thought the bearded rebel was sitting by the house to reload his gun. They maimed the dead man so badly that, when they approached him, his face was barely discernible.

'Yeah lads, you've dressed him up all right.'

'But he could have killed us all. He was sitting. He didn't fall down.'

One of the ChON men went to pick up the gun, but suddenly he jumped back when he thought the *Haidamak* rebel was still alive. Diadiura would not release the gun from his grasp, even in death, and his fingers had to be peeled from it one by one.

'I feel that this is the leader. Bring the farmer here.'

They brought Ilko to look at the corpse. He was still wearing his nightshirt and was as pale as a phantom. Even his eyes were blank and empty.

'Who is this bandit?'

Ilko stared with unseeing eyes and was silent.

'Are you dumb? Who is it? Don't pretend, you *Petliurite* muzzle. You won't avoid the punishment. Speak.'

Ilko moved his colourless lips.

'Well, who is it?'

'Raven.'

Chapter 2

1

When someone knocked on her door in the middle of the night Yevdosia opened it without asking who was there and allowed Raven to enter.

'Already?' she asked.

Raven sat on the bench nearest the icons, where a small lamp shone weakly, and looked at the bed where he had been recovering for an entire month last autumn and where Yarko now slept. He was no longer in his swaddling, he was like a small adult in a woollen blanket.

'How is he?'

'He's growing quickly.'

'I knew that your house would be the best place for him,' said Raven, 'but I have to take him further away now.'

'What for?' She waited for what Raven had to say, but did not expect him to reply so quickly.

'Because it's necessary, Yevdosia. It's that kind of time.'

'That kind of time. It's time you thought about yourself.'

'And what is there to think about?'

'Shave your beard and hide yourself among strangers. I told you long ago that no good would come of your soldiery.'

'You know what has come of it, misfortune, Yevdosia, huge misfortune.'

'Misfortune has no weight and no significance. You have to save yourself. You must think about yourself.'

'Tomorrow,' he said. 'Tomorrow, I will shave my beard.'

'Really?' Yevdosia seemed glad at first, but then a feeling of even greater regret entered her heart. 'Then this means I won't see you again?'

'Why not?' Raven spoke a little uncertainly.

'Will you stay overnight with me?'

'No. I will sit while you get the child.'

'At least have supper.'

Yevdosia lit a little lamp on the table and poured him a bowl of warm gruel. She sat on the bench with him and watched him while he ate.

'You heard nothing more about Veremii?' she asked.

'Nothing. Only fairy tales. Triumph gives birth to legends, but despair engenders lies.'

'That is always the way of the world.'

'Yes it is. There was once a quiet lad in my unit. He was a lone warrior, not one of the locals, and was called Ivas. When we were in battle he was fine, but in the silence afterwards he was transformed and fell into such a state of apathy and anxiety that it was tempting to throw him out to stop his mood infecting the others. He was silent and when he began to talk it was only about one thing, the Order of the Hand of John the Baptist. He said that he belonged to this secret order.'

'What is it?' asked Yevdosia, uncomprehendingly.

'Well, it's a secret brotherhood with a common goal that is hidden from the rest of humanity. The brothers believe that when John the Baptist was in jail, not only his head but his right hand was severed. Their most interesting belief is that after many years this hand fell into the clutches of the Muscovites and they preserve it somewhere near Pskov or Novgorod. That's why the *katsaps* have managed to build such a powerful state.'

'It's as crazy as a dappled mare's dream,' said Yevdosia.

'But the warriors of the order have taken it upon themselves to seek out the hand of John the Baptist.'

'Why?'

'Haven't you guessed? To take it and bring it back to Ukraine. He said that only then would the struggle for our state be successful. Poor Ivas, he tried to persuade me to join the order and search for the hand.'

'What about you?'

Raven put down the spoon, rummaged in his pocket and produced a tobacco pouch.

'Smoke here,' said Yevdosia. 'I want you to because then the house will smell of your presence for longer.'

'As for me,' he curled the cigarette paper and stuffed it with tobacco, 'I didn't argue with Ivas. Let everyone enjoy those things that enhance their faith. I didn't want to argue that it was nonsense, so I found other excuses for not joining the order. I would be ashamed to repeat them.'

'Tell me, my shamefaced one,' she said, tapping him gently and smiling.

'Well, you see, Yevdosia, the brothers of the order subject themselves to such a strict discipline. They refuse to sleep in Jewish houses, don't make love to women, and don't smoke or drink alcohol. The first, well okay, perhaps you could manage that, but how could a living man forswear all the other things?'

'Well, certainly not one like you,' said Yevdosia, teasing him again.

'And what am I? Am I not just like everyone else?'

'No, you are the best of us,' she said. 'It's not a sin to sleep in a Jew's house. You said it yourself, you could manage the first.'

'You won't trip me up with words.' Raven exhaled such a stream of smoke that the flame in the lamp jumped and was almost extinguished.

'I'm not tripping you up. I just know it will happen soon.'

'Where?'

'I don't know. But you didn't finish your story about Ivas. What happened? Did he throw everything away and head for Moscow?'

'He didn't go anywhere. When we seized Cherkasy a cannon blew his head and right hand clean off.'

'Mother of God,' said Yevdosia, crossing herself.

'That is such a sign. Tell me after that there is not a higher power over humanity.'

'Well, it's not a sign from God.'

'But why the head and right hand? Why not the left?'

'That's not for us to judge,' said Yevdosia.

'Maybe it is so. As for Veremii, I wanted to ask you something. Have you tried to use your power to divine what happened to him?'

'I tried but nothing came of it. I can't see everywhere. The cards fell to show he was alive once and then something confused them. I cast the grains and they were confused also. Some huge secret covers what happened to him.'

'That's a pity because I have planned something and I need to know whether he is alive or not.'

'Maybe you will tell me?'

'Not now.'

'Then do as you know best. Only let me see you once more to say farewell.' She drew close to Raven and ran her fingers through his hair, over his forehead and eyebrows, and around his eyes, touching his lips with her fingertips. 'Handsome. If you shave and cut your hair, even your beloved won't recognise you. It's now time to do like I have counselled you. Though I am sorry that I must say farewell to you forever.'

He kissed her hand, 'Thank you for everything Yevdosia.'

The old raven, who was sitting in the branches of an elm that had been struck by lightning, heard the door creak open and saw a man well known to him, who had a wondrous saddle bag that dangled from a strap around his neck. The bird soon realised that it was a sling in which a baby slept as snugly as if in a cradle. An old, blind woman followed and raised her hands to heaven when the man mounted his horse. The raven longed to follow and see where the child was taken but he no longer had the strength to roam far and wide. It was a moonless night and he was not a nocturnal bird who could fly anywhere in such darkness. He barely saw what the people by the house did, and when the rider rode into the night and the old woman sank to her knees, he could not see whether she was praying and bowing her head to the ground over and over, or kissing the horse's hoof prints.

2

The well-ordered soviet commissar, using his leave for the purpose to which he was entitled, was travelling with his young wife and seven-month old baby to be the guest of his beloved mother-in-law at her home in the small border town of Dunaivtsi. After a period of taxing work, and having been wounded in a skirmish with bandits, the commissar was entitled to rest and to show the grandmother her darling grandson.

Of course, I had no relatives in that distant town, but the documentation from the Matusiv district that I carried affirmed otherwise. In addition to this paper, I had some other documents, one of which affirmed the following:

This certificate is provided to Comrade Semenov Stepan Ivanovych and affirms that he is the head of a district military unit in the Matusiv district. He is on service and is entitled to carry weapons and firearms. All military and civilian institutions are requested to assist him with his duties as necessary.

In accord with this certification, Semenov Stepan Ivanovych had authorisation to carry revolver No. 44956, and a mandate that empowered him to conduct political activity in the district. It also gave him the right to use village vehicles for his convenience. In addition, I wore a military coat with a commissar's insignia and a hat with the infernal red pentagram over my brow, which made my newly shorn head a little warm and sticky. Well, there was nowhere to flee looking as I had, and now, with my new haircut and cleanly shaven features, even I would not have recognised myself. My face, unaccustomed to being exposed, felt the cold air roam over it. The skin on my jaw and chin was whiter than that on my weathered forehead and wind-beaten jowls, and in my fiery eyes there was such a lack of any depth that I did not want to look in a mirror. When Tina saw me she took a long time to recover from the surprise.

'Good Lord. This is a completely different man,' she said, guiding her cold fingers over my face.

'Do you love this other man?' I held Tina's hand against my face and kissed her palm.

'Obviously. I was once in love with a gallant staff captain, not a hairy *Haidamak* rebel.'

'Could a Red commissar suit you?'

'No,' she said. 'I like swarthy lads. That's why I'll put a fake tan on your face with the help of soot. I'm worried that someone will know what kind of bird you are in spite of your plumage.'

'Nonsense,' I calmed Tina. 'A commissar might have a beard and then shave. Are they going to check with the barbershop?' I kissed her eyelids.

At dawn, when it was still quite dark and good farmers were

going to market, we travelled by cart in the direction of Uman. I saw it as a good sign that our route took us through the town where we had first met. We went from Talianky, forty *versts* from Lebedyn, so we did not encounter any worthy, inquisitive people who might recognise us. I had a loyal contact in Talianky, from whom I had bought two horses and a cart in advance, and we stayed with him while Tina grew accustomed to the baby and our journey.

Using the map, I calculated that it would be almost a week before we reached the border, if we did not have any misadventures. Our wagon was littered with straw. It had a cloth roof and was so full of sacks and ropes that from the side it might have looked like we were really going to the market. We had a stock of food, oats for the horses, clothes and money, including soviet and Tsarist Nicholas era cash and Polish Marks. I kept some valuables in the leather pouch where I had hidden Tina's diamond ring. Our most precious treasure was Yarko, this golden child wrapped in a warm, woollen blanket in his cradle, with only his nose poking out. He was as quiet as a doll, not knowing whether misfortune or something else awaited him.

But what now? Very early in the morning we passed the large village of Dobrovody and before lunch went past Uman without any adventures. A few Red Army soldiers were roaming around before the bridge over the River Umanka, but no one stopped us or spoiled our pleasant recollections of this town. Five years ago I had met the most beautiful woman in the world here. The woman with whom I was now embarking on a dangerous journey and who was bearing herself with such aplomb that I was immensely proud of her. She wore a long, grey overcoat with a collar of lamb's fleece, a lambswool cap and fashionable shoes, with black stockings. She only lacked the diamond on her finger, but on this road we might encounter not only the Bolshevik rabble, but even more amusingly, our own Cossacks. What would happen if some riders did come out of the forest and told the commissar to get down and come here? They would have acted properly and in their place I would have done the same, but how does one prove that one is not a monstrous turncoat but Otaman Raven, who is not in his own territory due to a strange miracle?

So, let us hold our noses to the wind my sweet lady because we do not know yet what will come to meet us around the next corner, over the next hill, or past the next forest. Not long ago, here in the Uman region, the commune was shaken down like a pear tree by Otaman Dereshchuk. He was a former teacher who had taken up educating Red adults rather than children. Although I had not heard of him for a long time and did not know where he was or what fate had befallen him, I did not believe the forests here were bereft of any living soul, particularly because the leaves had not yet fallen. They were yellow, some were even turning red, but they could still hide the partisans' dwellings from the eyes of the enemy and the bad weather.

By evening we had travelled fifty *versts* and when twilight began to draw in we stayed in the quiet village of Tyshkivka. We asked to stay over-night at one house and I now became convinced that Yarko was more of an aid than a hindrance to us on our journey. 'Oh, he's so small, he has to be bathed.' A kind-hearted young girl bustled around us while her husband opened the gate and showed us where to hitch the wagon for the night.

During this journey, an interesting aspect of our villagers was revealed to me, one which evoked sympathy, but on the other hand seemed questionable. They bustled around their guests, even chance guests who had come with an unknown purpose, with an excess of kindness and without contrivance or forethought. For me, the thick-head, it was unpleasant to note how these kind, orderly people, so considerately accepted the family of a Red Army military commissar. They prepared supper, heated bath water, and provided the best room in the house in which to sleep. They refused when I tried to give them money, and at dawn, as they followed us out, the lady of the house gave us some milk for the boy.

'Did you ever see such kindness?' I said as we left the village. 'They were ready to turn their house over to nourish the representatives of the occupying power.'

'What does power have to do with it?' Tina questioned me. 'These people live according to Christian traditions. What do you want from them?'

'This goodness and trust will make us lose our country, also, for me, the Christian tradition …'

'And you are what, a pagan?'

'There is only one God, but I don't know any book more blood-soaked than the bible.'

'So, in other words, you are saying what?' The lamb's fleece cap turned to me almost reproachfully.

'Well, every page in it is dripping blood that Jehovah gulps down without ever being sated. Their God even turned the River Nile into blood. David was responsible for Uriah's death, and Solomon ordered Joab to be killed. Were praises ever sung to Moloch in this fashion?'

'That's the Old Testament,' Tina, the aristocrat and teacher, explained to me.

'A testament to bloodthirsty instincts.'

'Well, let's say it's so. What does Christianity have to do with your argument?'

'This.' I tugged the rein angrily and smacked my lips at the horses.

'Don't get angry. Would it be better if they hadn't let us into their house?'

'Yes.'

'But it was so sweet for me to sleep by you.'

'Forgive me. I'm not talking about that my little sparrow.'

Last night Tina had slept while laying her head on my shoulder. I had listened to her breathing, caressed her hair and longed for the night to never end. Really there was nothing to be mad about.

3

Having reached Haisyn by evening, I decided to go straight to the local military commissar's office so they could provide us with lodgings for the night. It is often safer to ignore the risks involved and demand official support, rather than try to find lodgings yourself and draw unwanted attention. So, having made enquiries among the populace as to the location of the military commissar, I headed for a brick building painted a rusty-red colour.

'Is everyone here?' I spoke in Russian to the guard on the door.

'Who do you need?'

274

'The commissar, isn't it clear?'

'The third office.'

I passed along the corridor, opened the third door and, ignoring the official in the antechamber, went through the next door without explanation and greeted my colleague.

Now, truth to tell, I was at a loss. The commissar sat at the desk and looked at me. I stood by the door and looked at him. We recognised each other immediately, but we were both quietly astonished by this unexpected meeting and each waited to see who would speak first.

'You.' He rose from behind the desk.

'Yes, Comrade Kalyuzhnyi,' I said in Russian. 'I am glad that we meet again.'

'Me also ... but you are ...'

The former Staff Captain Afanasii Karpovych Kalyuzhnyi, or Fania, Panas, was no less confused than I was. Apart from our meeting in Uman, he must have also recollected how he had jumped back from me in my father's house, thereby aiding my escape. Thanks to him for that. Now he was standing, panic stricken and trying to work out if it was really a commissar who was standing before him or a *Haidamak* rebel in disguise, who had come to separate his soul from his body.

'Who am I? Life changes. I owe you one by the way.'

We talked for a while and when Kalyuzhnyi realised the reason for me approaching him he regained his spirits.

'I won't let you go anywhere,' he said in Russian. 'You will stay the night with me.'

He did not request any documents from me, probably because he realised what was taking place. Indeed Kalyuzhnyi was not the first among soviet civil servants who sympathised with us. He was struck again by the unusual circumstance of this visit when I told him my wife, who was on the wagon with a child, was his old acquaintance Tina, who had worked in the Uman division headquarters.

'Is it really Tina?' In his agitation he spoke Ukrainian.

'Who else?'

'That's true ... There was Manyunia, but she is with me.'

'You married Manyunia?'

'Haisyn isn't far from Uman,' he said, smiling sadly. 'I went and fetched her. So today we will have a great time.'

Is it necessary to say how glad Manyunia was to see us? She did not know what had hit her. She was a good woman and had made her supposed speaker of the Shulyavskyi dialect, basically Russian, Fania, adopt his Ukrainian name, Panas, and at home they talked our native language. His Ukrainian had greatly improved from the time of our first meeting in Uman. However, it was not only Manyunia's teaching that had served to improve his spoken Ukrainian, for soon I would learn something about the Haisyn military commissar that would raise his standing significantly in my eyes. Realising that I was not the soviet official I pretended to be, Kalyuzhnyi let his tongue wag after a glass of *horilka*.

When Manyunia and Tina had lulled young Yarko to sleep and gone into the other room, he proposed drink after drink, as if gathering his courage. The home-brewed *horilka* was strong, but he did not gulp it down for too long. Finally, Kalyuzhnyi looked at me from under his lowered forehead, as if wary, 'So, you regard me as a turncoat because I went to serve the Bolsheviks, hold me in contempt, judge me.'

I assumed a surprised face, but he only said, 'Hmmm', as if to say, don't argue, I know what I'm talking about. Then he asked, 'And do you know how many of our men went over to the Bolsheviks after Petliura shot Captain Bolbochan? No? Also, you will not be aware that after Uman, I ended up in the First Zaporizhia Division of Petro Bolbochan. He was a true soldier and always in the forefront of his troops in battle. So, he isn't Petliura for you, who never killed an enemy in his life or even fired in their direction.'

'The chief otaman has other work to do,' I said.

'Of course.'

Kalyuzhnyi poured more into his glass, without offering me any, and drained it to the dregs. 'In the government, in the military staff bases, all of them have their own work because they gather in impoverished Polish lodgings. Austrian reservist ensigns, careerists and adventurers, without a profession or a Tsar in their heads. They only watch out in case someone else sits in their place. Then Bolbochan appeared. He had cleared Southern Ukraine and Crimea from the Muscovite troops without help and enjoyed the admiration and affection of his soldiers. In 1918 no one had the same authority as Bolbochan, so, in January 1919, Petliura ordered his arrest. He was held under guard for months and driven mad.'

Kalyuzhnyi poured himself more *horilka* and looked at me through clouded eyes.

'They released him and at the beginning of summer he took up military activity again. All who knew the captain tried to get closer to him. All wanted to be under the wing of his command. So now it began. His popularity made Petliura seethe with envy and anger ... Remember?' Kalyuzhnyi raised his voice and I saw his pupils harden in his clouded eyes, 'An order to destroy Bolbochan came immediately because he had disobeyed the high command. Who's order? Don't you know?'

I shrugged my shoulders to indicate that I did not know.

'It was issued by he who envied Bolbochan and sought to destroy any possible future rivals.'

'Without a court?' I asked.

'Well, there was a court,' smiled Kalyuzhnyi crookedly, 'of Galician soldiers. But what does that change? Listen now. It happened on Balyn Station near Kamianets. Bolbochan was being held in a wagon. They woke him in the night and led him to an empty place where a pit had already been dug. The squad that was ordered to shoot him was commanded by the chief of counter-espionage, Chebatorov. Have you heard about him? He was the chief *Petliurite Chekist*. I was in that squad.

It was June, but such cold ran through my body that my teeth chattered. We soldiers hid our eyes from one another and on Chebatorov's command we aimed our rifles. I felt my finger weaken on the trigger. Bolbochan was standing barefoot, wearing only his pants and a white shirt. He smiled at us with a smile that was not of this earth. Chebatorov gave the command to fire, but none of us did. "Thanks lads," said the captain quietly. He still did not believe they would shoot him. Chebatorov repeated the command. We again aimed our rifles and this time they fired, but Bolbochan didn't fall. All the bullets missed because we had wanted to fool one another. No one wanted to shoot Bolbochan. He stood and smiled. The furious Chebatorov called up another squad and said to us, "Look, cowards, this is how you should follow orders." The rifles thundered again, but the captain didn't twitch, he just smiled. Chebatorov could endure no more, he ran to the captain and shot him with his Browning. Bolbochan fell and a sigh emerged from his breast. Chebatorov jumped to the half-dead captain and began to trample him, shot him again, then kicked him repeatedly before shoving his body in the pit.'

Kalyuzhnyi, seizing his head with his hands, gritted his teeth and was silent for a while, then said, 'The very next day I enlisted with the Bolsheviks. I didn't want to wait until they asked me why I had refused to obey an order. I enlisted with the first, most convenient, Red Army squad. In 1919 it was easy to do that, no one asked what you had been up to earlier.'

He raised his glass without taking his eyes off me and drank again.

'And do you know what the worst thing is?' He shook his head. 'That I don't regret joining the Reds. It was already apparent that with such leaders, we would not see victory. After Bolbochan's arrest, Otaman Hryhorev went over to the Bolsheviks. I understood then that it was the end of this state.'

'Never say this state,' I butted in, 'that's what people who are foreigners say. Say our state.'

'Our?' Kalyuzhnyi's eyes glittered at me. 'And where is she, our state? She does not exist.'

'She is there,' I said.

'Where? Show me.'

'In the forest. Soviet power does not exist there. The laws of the U.N.R. govern us.'

'Well, even if it's so, I don't want to sit in the forest,' said Kalyuzhnyi. 'I don't want to sit and wait for them to smoke me out. It's better that I sit in the warmth and flay the skin off the scum that doesn't join us when I need to. I advise you to do the same. Do you hear me? To flay the skin off those villagers, fat on the N.E.P., who are ready to sell you out today.'

'That's the same as punishing children who don't know what they do.'

'They know. They only fool you into thinking they know nothing. And when there is a price on your head, these simpletons

278

will work out what they have to do. They'll be running ahead of each other.'

'Are you seeking to justify yourself?' I asked.

'In who's eyes?' responded Kalyuzhnyi warily.

'In your own eyes.'

'I don't need to justify myself. I would sit in the forest today if we were all together with the mendacious villagers and those leaders who direct things from Tarnov. They entertain girls in foreign hotels while you are a source of nourishment for lice, and you look death in the face every day while they produce another useless decree. No, I've had enough of their decrees. I'm better sleeping by a warm pair of tits, and time will show who has done most for Mother Ukraine. Then it will be clear.'

Kalyuzhnyi reached for his glass, thought again, and rose heavily from the table.

'It's time to sleep. I've rambled at you while you were silent.' He looked at me appraisingly. 'You were right to be so.'

4

At last, my dear colleagues came out to meet me. After I had started to worry that the forests here really were unpopulated. It happened on the fourth day of our journey as we travelled towards Kopayhorod. Shortly before, we had passed a village that had been burned to the ground; only black chimneys remained on the houses and carbonised beds were all around. The nightmarish spectre of what it had been. This was the mark of the barbarian horde; a typical sign of their vengeance on any who resisted. The local Bolshevik buffoons might engage in terror, but they did not burn villages. All around there was a cadaverous silence where not even dogs were heard, but by one dwelling we came across a grandfather with a little boy.

'Good health to you, old timer.' I tugged the reins, halting the horses. 'What has caused the terrible fire that has passed through your village?'

He looked at me with reproach and disbelief.

'Haven't you heard? The kids, our orphans, after their parents were shot, they were starving and tried to bake potatoes but burned the village.' He embraced the boy and pulled him closer. 'Children boss.'

So, his sorrow made the old man make a feeble joke because he dared not name the cause of this tragedy before what he thought was a Red Army officer and his wife. Tina took out some bread and a slice of *salo* from her bag and held it out to the boy. He hid behind the old man.

'Take it, don't be afraid.'

'It will be better if I take it,' said the old man. 'We shouldn't get him used to hand outs.'

We went onwards with a heavy heart. The old man stood on the road for a long time and looked at us. With one hand he held the boy against himself and with the other he clutched the food to his chest.

As we were leaving the village the forest caught our eye with its fiery autumnal hues. Here and there oaks flashed their greenery, and all glittered yellow gold. The aspen burned red and mingled among pale clouds of wild barley. At the edge of the road the undergrowth turned blue with ripe blackthorn.

We barely had time to enjoy this abundance of colour before … 'Hop … a!' Three riders appeared before us and bellowed. Three brother partisans and you, strange man, had wondered if such as they had vanished from these woods. Now you have work to do to convince them that you are not a horned serpent.

The boys rode towards us in the fashion of Larion Zahorodnii's men, who often divided his squad into units of three men because that was the most suitable disposition to manoeuvre and attack activists and other Bolshevik dregs; particularly those who might turn their shameful noses to the forest and flee like Military Commissar Semenov Stepan Ivanovych. They approached us.

'Oh, lads.'

One of them drew up before our horses. If we tried to move then the others would be at either side of the wagon in a flash. They were so sure of themselves that they did not aim their weapons because they could see I was not reaching for my holster. The one who was to my right was a real Viking. He had a blond beard and a complexion as ruddy as fire, almost the same burning colours as the autumn that surrounded us. He wore a black beret and a military tunic, which fell to above his knees so it did not to catch in the grass if he was in the fields. On his right sleeve I saw the senior officer's insignia of our army; a quadrant of fine, blue wool, with a yellow arrow across, and in the centre a *tryzub*, embroidered with metallic thread, and the letters U.N.R. glittered. What impressed me most were the eyes of this *Volhyniaka-Viking*. I had never before seen such deep-blue eyes. But instead of smiling in a friendly fashion they looked at me with malice (bravo, otaman, bravo) and even mockery (let me give you a hug, brother).

'Where are you going? What are you carrying and why?' asked the *Volhyniaka*. 'Didn't you read my pronouncement that Otaman Zirvyholova had returned from vacation and picked up his duties?'

'No, I didn't read it. I have come from far away.'

'Did you see?' He pointed with his riding crop in the direction of the destroyed village.

'I saw.'

'And what would you do with a Red Army commissar after that if you were in my place?'

'I would kill him, but I am not a Red Army commissar, I am the same as you Mr Otaman. Have you never been compelled to wear their rags?'

The malice in his eyes faded, but he looked at me with suspicion.

'I see that you are not a Muscovite, but I do not know who you serve. How will you show that you are one of ours and not theirs?'

'Only thus, if you kill me I will understand why. If it comes to that you won't be the first one led to kill his own side.'

'Take a good look at him?' said Tina jumping into our conversation. 'Isn't it clear that he has only recently shaved his beard? It was even longer than yours. I have shaded his jaws a little in truth, but you can still tell.'

Zirvyholova arrested his gaze on Tina and the blue in his eyes warmed in a moment, but the smile was crooked.

'I noted this a while ago,' he said, 'but commissars also have beards. I need some serious proofs that he is not a Red.'

'He is our most serious proof.' I pointed at the cradle where

Yarko was sleeping. 'He is the son of the late Otaman Veremii and I have to transport him across the Zbruch. If you kill me you will have to take on that obligation yourself.'

'Which otaman?' asked the rider on the other side of the wagon.

'Veremii,' I said, turning to him.

The sombre *Haidamak* rebel with a pock-marked face looked at me rather more welcoming than Zirvyholova.

'Is that the Veremii who served as a bombardier with Captain Almazov?'

'It may be him.' I shrugged my shoulders. 'Does that have any meaning now?'

'Yes, it does,' said the *Haidamak*. 'How could it not when we were on military service with Veremii in Captain Almazov's unit? He, Veremii, could move that cannon around like it was a toy. He was a strongman.'

'Yes, that's him. Our Veremii could lift up bullocks, lift rails from railway sleepers single-handedly, and tear off anyone's head.' I looked at Zirvyholova or 'head chopper' as his name meant.

'You said that he has perished?' asked the pock-marked man.

'Whether he has perished or not, he has disappeared without a trace and nothing has been heard of him for a year. They shot his wife, but his son came into this world and the otaman has not seen him,' I said, casting my eyes towards the cradle.

The pock-marked one carefully approached the wagon, bowed over the cot where Yarko was lying, and pulled back the blanket covering the baby's face. Such a warm and astonished smile appeared on his face that it was as if our straw-strewn wagon were the manger at Bethlehem. A sincere feeling of wonder tremored across his withered lips, which were tremulous with emotion and no longer obedient to his will, and they formed themselves into a pipe as he made smacking sounds at the child as if he were a horse.

Wonder of wonders, instead of being terrified of this disease-ravaged physiognomy, Yarko smiled back, showing his two milk teeth. When he saw them, a joyous bellow tore from the man's throat, 'The spitting image of Veremii. Good Lord! Even the bridge of his nose and the dimple on his chin.'

Otaman Zirvyholova drew closer to the cart and let his eyes, dripping with blue, cast their gaze on the boy, as if he also knew Veremii and wanted to assure himself that he was not being lied to.

'You are certain?'

'Beat me with a coal scuttle if I am mistaken,' the rebel said, crossing himself and covering the baby's face with the blanket. 'Can't you see it? So little, but he would cry out to you. What a Cossack.'

'Good,' said Zirvyholova. 'Happy journey, but be vigilant as you travel, not all of us served with Captain Almazov.'

The rider who stood before us moved aside and I flicked the reins ... 'Goooo!'

'I will return quickly,' I bellowed at the Cossacks. 'There is still much work to do.'

'Maybe if you hear something about our army you can whistle,' cried Zirvyholova. 'And if not ... don't hang your nose.'

My heart lightened, for I saw that not all was lost in this area. Let us concede that it was only in the forests, but there were islands of our underground state where lads roamed with *tryzubs* on their sleeves. There were only a few of us now, very few, but even on his first journey this baby had not evaded one of his father's comrades. So we must endure, we must stand firm to the last. He who is able, he who is given to, while our strength sufficed.

I looked back, but there was no one on the road now. It seemed to me that I had failed to say something very important to these lads. But what? I did not know myself but I knew that I must tell them about it.

5

The closer we came to the border, the more the Red Army soldiers thronged in the 'liberated' villages. They became more impudent and looked more closely at the Red Army commissar, who rode so freely next to his beautiful lady with such an unproletarian exterior. In one village, just before Dunaivtsi, we suddenly found ourselves among an entire rabble of angry Bolsheviks, who bustled from house to house clearly seeking someone they could not find. This band surrounded our wagon and a Judas in a leather coat, foaming with wrath, snarled at me with criminal arrogance, 'What are you carrying speculator?' said the Russian voice. 'There are so many counter-revolutionaries around and you are just taking a ride with your woman.'

Oh, with what deep satisfaction I would have blown a hole in him with my perfectly legal revolver, but I could not permit myself that delight. I turned to him, drew myself up to my full stature and, looking hard into his ugly eyes, slowly, very slowly, took out my credentials from my inside pocket.

He was a little confused because he had not asked for any documents, but he was compelled to take the papers and submit to my wishes. The loud-mouth wrinkled his forehead under his leather cap and baffled himself with the credentials of Matusiv Military Commissar Semenov. He moved his lips and knitted his brows tightly. It seemed to me that the wretch was unable to read and was just looking at the seals and insignia on the paper. In this Herod-like army it was often the case that illiterate but persistent people battled their way to the top with their big mouths rather than with their abilities.

After he had read a little, he asked suddenly, 'Where is your baby?'

'He's wrapped up there,' I flicked my eyes towards Yarko's cot.

He could not hold back from taking the strip of blanket that was covering the baby's face and we heard our quiet, golden baby cry for the first time on the journey.

The flunky covered Yarko's face with the blanket, but the baby cried even louder.

'You behave as though you are not a Russian man,' said Tina angrily. She waved her legs in the air, which were covered with black stockings, and swung herself into the back of the wagon with the cradle.

Taking Yarko in her arms she cradled him with such tenderness that my heart ached. 'Shhhh …'

'Go on your way, everything seems to be in order,' said the Herod-like lackey, handing back the document to me.

I had foreseen clearly that, although a baby would cause problems on this long and dangerous journey, he would help us more than hinder us. Now, when Yarko had helped us yet again, I felt a reproach of conscience. It was as if I had deliberately taken him for my own ends, using the defenceless isolation of an orphan to gain for myself a crumb of a truer life; even if it was not my life but one borrowed, albeit in love and truth. What if Veremii were alive and he suddenly embarked on a search for his son? This unasked for thought stole upon me at times. Grant, Lord, I thought to myself, that he lives and searches for his son, for there is a greater hope of salvation, and that they will meet where I am taking him. On the other hand, I was pierced with doubt over what I had done to Tina by foisting a child on her, which she had to take out of her personal morality. I had taken away her choice. Even if I had done so out of a profound belief in good and salvation. Such was our history with this golden child that we could not allow the Herod-like army to capture him. I had to take him to a foreign land.

'I know what you are thinking,' said Tina as we left the village. She put Yarko in the back of the wagon and again sat next to me as I drove.

'What, my little sparrow?'

'That you and I are like Joseph and Mary with a child, fleeing from Herod.'

'You are my delight,' I said, leaning over and kissing her bright eyes. 'I adore you.'

'How? Say how you adore me?'

'If you read my thoughts, you would know.'

'No, I want to hear from you. Please. Say how you adore me?'

'Fatally.'

'How is that?'

'I might stop breathing from sheer happiness.'

'Don't lie.'

'Would I lie to you?'

She was silent for a moment before saying, 'Don't torture yourself. You have done everything correctly.'

I looked at her, stunned with astonishment. Tina had read my thoughts.

'You can't even imagine how wise this is or how grateful I am to you,' she said.

'Really? You don't regret anything?'

'Not a jot,' she said. 'If everything works out as you thought it will be extraordinarily wonderful. Everything will work out for us. Surely?'

'Certainly,' I said. 'We have already done a lot.'

'There is one thing I would like to ask you.'

'What is it?'

'When you find us ... No, later, when you return, after everything, and find us in a foreign country, don't leave me again for a single day, OK?'

'Obviously. Why would I leave you?'

'Well, there are all sorts of reasons. But don't leave me for so long, for I can't endure any more. I will die without you.'

'Daft thing. Don't daydream about bad things.'

'Then let us dream about something wonderful. Tell me how we will live together.'

'I haven't dreamed about anything wonderful for a long time,' I said. 'Fate has been cruel to us. Though I have not lost that which I have.'

'What do you have?'

'You, my little sparrow.'

'Not only me. Do you know that there is a feeling that lives in me constantly, of which I am afraid to speak to you about.'

'Pointlessly. What shame can there be between us?'

'It seems to me that I gave birth to this child.'

'That's good,' I said, 'you will be a true mother.'

'No, it's not that. I tell you, this feeling lives in me. That I gave birth to this child from you. That God did not send this child to us by chance. There is some meaning here.'

'Certainly,' I said. 'Nothing in this world happens by accident.'

***

No, I know that nothing happens by accident. Each card shows its colour, not just according to the mind of God, otherwise how could blind Yevdosia, beneath whose roof I had passed the night, know all

286

the rules and principles that governed the Order of the Hand of John the Baptist?

However, let me tell everything in order. We arrived at the town of Dunaivtsi in the evening and swiftly found the priest's house by the church, where we had to present the letter from Father Oleksii. The Orthodox Priest Tymofii, who had a sparse beard and watery eyes, read the missive carefully. It contained as much talk of the Divine as Saint Paul's epistles to the Ephesians. However, having read the letter, he scanned us with his colourless eyes in an unfriendly fashion and said that now was not a time when he could safely accept unknown people into his house. He had already had it up to his neck as a result of his good nature and hospitable ways. It was because of them that he had been robbed, burned and whipped, 'So sorry sir, but seek another place to sleep,' he said.

We agreed and Tina said in response, 'As you wish, so we will do, but please let us first tend to the child at your house, for the poor thing is wet and, as you can see, it is cold outdoors.'

Father Tymofii softened a little, let us into the house and ordered his wife to prepare supper. She was a quiet and timid woman who wore a black kerchief that muffled her face up to her eyes. She was wondrously swift as she heated the water in which to bathe the child, 'What God has sent,' and lit a gas lamp beneath a green shade.

When Tina bathed and redressed Yarko, Father Tymofii softened still more and, looking at the child tenderly, said that he would not let us sleep anywhere else. That is what often happens with people. One flashes his eyes at you, whistles and licks like a puppy, but when it comes to a real job does nothing good. Another grumbles, argues and moans, then gives their last shirt to you. That was the kind of person Father Tymofii was.

While we had supper in his house and drank glasses of blackcurrant juice, we arranged everything in line with my plan.

It was dangerous for Military Commissar Semenov, Stepan Ivanovych to travel further by wagon and the border was a stone's throw away. He must go there on foot, like a typical civil servant from that area, Petro Mynovych Horovyi (I had obtained a document for this alias from Podil when we were in Chyhyryn) with a wife and ailing child, who we were taking to a doctor near the border. I had a stock of documents and civilian clothes and it would be useful to swap our coach-horses for a tall stallion on which I would return. Father Tymofii took this trouble on himself.

'I know a Gypsy who secretly trades horses,' he told us. 'He'll sort this out and, dear ones, in the morning you will need to head straight towards Balakyry and then travel through the fields for three *versts*, then you will get to Shydlivtsi, the border town. The main thing is don't be afraid of anything. Go without looking around, as if you had been there a hundred times, and don't worry about the Red Army soldiers, they don't bother townsfolk. When you come to Shydlivtsi, you will see a house with a red roof on the edge of the village. Go straight there and don't be afraid of anything, even if there are soldiers on the gate.'

'And straight to the *Cheka*,' I said, smiling, but in such a tone that he would know with whom he was dealing and, at the same time, indicating that if one is playing with fire then it is better to be aware of it before it is too late. From the beginning I had allowed myself to conjecture that a priest in a small border town may long since have fallen into the *Chekists'* field of vision, and a weak-willed one might have become one of their agents. I had lost faith in so many people recently that, although this spiritual man had a former friendship with Father Oleksii, he did not allay my suspicions. Apart from that, I remembered the warnings of Larion Zahorodnii about a secret and regularly inspected bridge across the Dnister to Romania that led straight into a Bolshevik trap.

'Well, why would it lead to the *Cheka*?' Father Tymofii took a handful of his sparse beard and looked at me sourly, as if to say I have deduced what you are talking about but bear up, then he said aloud, 'If I serve the devil, why would I send you to Shydlivtsi, couldn't the *Cheka* pick you up here in Dunaivtsi?'

That's possible of course, I thought to myself, but first you or your wife would have to leave the house and I will not permit that. Furthermore, why would the *Cheka* raise a commotion in the house of an informer and thereby expose his secret? Aloud I said, trustingly, 'We weren't talking about you, Father, but about the house with the red roof. Is it safe there?'

'It always has been. If something has changed they would

have let me know. If you are thinking of the risk, it's all around. You can't chop a log without risk and you want to jump the Zbruch without getting your feet wet. Am I not taking a risk with you? Look, you came to me disguised as a Red and with a letter of introduction from Father Oleksii. Can I be entirely sure that he, my trusted friend, is still alive? No, I can't. So, if you don't trust anyone then I don't know what the point of living on this earth is.' Father Tymofii spread his hands. 'Let's move on. In that house you will ask for Nychypir Petrychenko. He is a weak man and doesn't go outdoors, but his wife, Marusia, a great woman, will help you. She will be your guide and knows how you can cross the water without wetting your feet. Tell her from me that you are going to the other side.'

'We will say that we are going to the doctor with the child.'

'With the child?' Father Tymofii looked at me so expressively that the irises of his eyes enlarged around his pupils and became as sharp as the tips of grass stalks. 'No, no, not like that, we'll come to that. Listen, pay attention and everything will be okay. You are fleeing this Sodom and Gomorrah. As I say, go, don't be afraid of anything, and don't look back. It is written in the Old Testament that Lot's wife looked back and became a pillar of salt. So, be attentive and listen to my advice.'

Father Tymofii was surprising and became yet more so. He was such an orderly and good-natured man. He said that we would sleep in their room and that he and his wife would sleep by the stove because the other room was not heated.

I unyoked the horses and led them to the barn, drawing the wagon with them. In the anteroom, Father Tymofii led me to a table and, without explanation, climbed a ladder into the attic. Perhaps he would yet bring something to drink, I thought as I was sitting at the table and becoming drunk just from looking at Tina. She was half leaning, half lying over the bed, quietly singing above Yarko's cot. She sang about a cat who stole a ball of thread from a granny and carried it to the forest. In the dark green radiance cast through the light-shade she seemed unreal, a deception, like in a fragment of a dream that might disperse at any moment.

So Raven, this is your delight, as brief as a dream. A childhood tale sung by the woman who appeared to you in a moment taken from a story. A cloud of delirium enfolded within me, green and warm, and I saw in this light and in this world, this enchanting woman and this unusual child, and the story book, *The Cat in Shoes of Pig Weed Leaf*. Even the priest, who was suddenly standing in the doorway with a cradle in his hands, appeared like a magician greeting us with gifts.

Father Tymofii, smiling guiltily, showed me the cradle that was woven from wicker. It had ropes on which it could be hung. He directed his gaze to the ceiling where there was a hook in a timber beam. He stood beneath it and reached upwards. He held the cradle over his head, stood on his toes, and stretched his arms and himself towards the ceiling until I took the cradle from him and hung it easily.

'Never take good fortune for granted in advance,' said Father Tymofii, with almost the same words I would have used. 'I, like a fool, when I got together with my wife, acquired the cradle too soon. I was fooling myself. We're pushing forty now and still don't have a child, but we need this cradle now. Yefrosyniya, bring the child some nice bedding.'

His wife seemed to have been waiting for his word because barely a minute had passed before she returned with a handful of fragrant straw and a new, soft blanket and pillow. Soon Yarko was lying in the wicker eagle's nest and listening to a new nursery rhyme sung by the Dunaivtsi matron:

From far, far away
They brought us a lily-white one,
A child not easy,
A golden child,
Sleep baby sleep,
Aaa bye, bye …

The matronly lady, with her small face hidden up to the eyes by her kerchief, resembled a lizard in the green light. This timorous lizard swung the cradle to the rhythm of a song, which she seemed to make up as she was singing:

Swing in your cradle,

Stay with us forever.
Mother and father are near,
Sleep my little dove …

I do not know why, but this ditty awoke a strange, incomprehensible and causeless anguish in me. It awakened the doubts that had been lulled to sleep. Why had the priest suddenly changed his demeanour and warmed to us? What had made him change? No, I won't sleep tonight, I thought, I will have to be vigilant and we need four eyes to keep watch.

The priest poured more blackcurrant juice and, taking his scant beard in his hand, said, 'It will be really hard for her with a child in a foreign country.'

'Perhaps, but there is freedom there.'

'Freedom! Don't you know that everyone who crosses the border is placed in an internment camp by the Polish? They are interned behind barbed wire and subjected to starvation and typhus. No, it's not the place you would wish for her, but fresh disillusionment and misfortune.'

'We don't need scaring now. We need your blessing,' I said. 'We know it's not an ideal place to go, but at least they won't turn water into blood there.'

'I am not scaring you, I'm warning you.' Father Tymofii again looked at me so expressively that the pupils, which had been as sharp as the tips of grass stalks, were now wide and glossy, like berries. 'If you fulfilled my request and left the child with us it would be easier.'

Oh, that's what it was. I, thick-head, had only just realised why he had suddenly been so kind to us and why Mother Yefrosyniya had bustled around the table and then the child. Silence fell on us all. I looked at Tina, who was sitting on the bed, and saw how her hand was motionless on the cradle.

'How could we leave the child with you?' she asked quietly.

'Just so,' said Father Tymofii. 'As if he were our child.'

'How could you think like that about us?' Tina looked at me with tears trembling in her eyes. 'Why are you silent?'

'I don't think he wanted to offend us,' I said. 'He only gave voice to his honest wishes. However, he will respect us still more if we do not forsake the child. That's certainly the case, is it not?'

'Yes, but I ask you for the second time, is it not better to leave the child in peace and comfort than cast it into this dangerous migration?'

'The Lord will be kind to this child,' I replied. 'The trials ahead will strengthen his spirit and guide him through life.'

'But I ask you for the third time, won't it be better to place the infant on his native soil instead of sending him abroad as a fugitive before he can judge, while he is yet a weak babe without his own volition?'

'No,' I said. 'The truth is that fugitives are blessed, for theirs is the Kingdom of Heaven.'

Father Tymofii lowered his head. 'Then I take back my request. Mother, prepare them five loaves and two fish for the morning.'

'We don't have that much bread,' replied Mother Yefrosyniya, who was offended. 'There are two herring and one loaf.'

'Then bake them four round loaves for the road.'

'We thank you, Father,' I said, laying my palm on my breast, 'but we have our own stock of victuals.'

'Give the child warm milk, and the five loaves and two fish will be a nice find for you. So, you will see. Now it's time to sleep.'

I went outside and lit my cigarette by the side of the house, hiding the flame with my arm. The little town had gone to sleep ages ago and it was quiet everywhere. I thought that we would be able to sleep a little in this house as I returned to it and climbed into bed. I put the revolver under my pillow so I could hide it further away from this house as soon as it was light. Like it or not, the Podil surveyor, Petro Horovyi, must go to the border unarmed.

We left at dawn. I was wearing a long, black coat, with a civilian waistcoat underneath, and grey trousers, tucked into military boots, which any man of means could now buy or exchange at the market. We travelled like the father had advised us, simply and, if I can put it like this, without looking back. I carried Yarko on my chest in a sling tied around my neck, and with a bag on my back. Tina carried a bag containing her things and the food, including the five loaves, two herring and a flask of warmed milk. We went calmly to Balakyry. No one paid attention to us. Even if we did meet someone, we would greet them politely and go on our way.

Out of a yard, where many Reds were gathered, a dishevelled *katsap* ran and said straight out to me in Russian, 'What are you carrying in that package?'

'I am taking the baby to the doctor's,' I replied in his language.

'Don't you have a piglet there?' He laughed raucously and looked at what was in the sling in such a way that my right hand itched for my sabre. 'Who's that? His mother?' The *katsap's* eyes glittered at Tina with such hunger that I prepared for the worst.

'Conduct yourself carefully, Comrade,' Tina suddenly hurled the phrase at him. 'It is not the first time I have seen you drunk. Do up your buttons and don't disgrace the Red Army.'

The *katsap* was confused. He opened his mouth as if he wanted to say something, but only exhaled hot air as he tried to fasten his overcoat, but he kept missing the loops with the catches.

So, we continued proudly and without looking back.

'You warble so well in the Muscovite tongue, I could listen with pleasure.' I smiled at the 'educator' of the abhorrent military we had just encountered.

'In what other language could I warble to them?' Tina asked in surprise. 'Is it time to swap over to Polish?'

'Do you know Polish?'

'And German,' she said.

We went into the field over which Shydlivtsi should have appeared after three *versts*. We headed along a broad path which stretched among the lustreless pastures, remembering the instructions of Father Tymofii, to walk along it boldly in the direction of the border; forgetting the evangelical warning that the broad way leads to destruction. Or rather, let us say that it does not always lead to destruction; this most visible road often leads a person into some delusion, as we saw before us a large, marshy lake that the priest had not mentioned. We could get lost and embroiled in mud here. How could we go further if, instead of Shydlivtsi, we ended up in a quagmire or, even worse, at a border post?

Along the bank were clumps of rust-coloured rushes and

green marsh grass. Further along, on the right hand side, were dark birches. I still had not managed to see as far as the water when a shot rang out and a flock of ducks hurtled into the air above the lake. I must acknowledge that my heart almost stopped because that shot did not presage anything good. Two riders came from the birches and cantered easily towards us. When they halted before us, one of them, who held a bloodstained duck in his hand, asked angrily, in Russian, 'Where are you going?'

'To Shydlivtsi,' I said. 'We are taking our child to the doctor.'

'To Shidlovtsy?' he said, using the Russian name and looking in surprise at his companion. 'I think he is lying. It seems like we've caught some spies.'

We were lucky regarding the other Red Army man. He was a sombre, but not a malicious lad, possibly of *Kuban* Cossack stock because his morose moustache and anxious look showed traces of a human spirit. What is more, this *Kubanets* spoke our language.

'And who do you know in Shydlivtsi?' he asked.

'Who?' I thought here about how it was better to conceal where we were going, but it would have been dangerous to dream up something now. 'We know Nychypir Petrychenko and his wife, Marusia, who is going to take us to the doctor.'

'So you are going to Petrychenko,' the *Kubanets* said, a little delighted with something. 'And why have you headed into this morass when Shydlivtsi is over there?' He gestured towards the left side of the lake, 'Follow the curve of the lake that way.'

'Misfortune led us this way,' I said. 'We know where Shydlivtsi is but we turned back to the lake to seek a Tatar herb whose root provides good medication.'

'Oh that's it.' The *Kubanets* nodded, though it seemed he did not believe our little lie. Then, a little ashamed, he asserted that it might improve the temper of his associate if we could find some victuals for him because they were plagued with hunger. It had come, as we could see, to shooting ducks on the border. Even though it was forbidden to shoot anything here.

Tina took two of the loaves and one of the herring from her bag and the *Kubanets* showed us how to continue in the direction of the willows, where there was a boundary that would lead us to the village. They galloped rapidly towards the birches to devour the duck and fish and we went around the lake to seek the path on the boundary that would lead us to Shydlivtsi, the village that was built alongside the Zbruch, before dusk.

A hare could have jumped the river here. How often had I listened to stories about it and how many thoughts had I about how this thread of cold water had divided Ukraine and become a border? So, without looking back, we came to the edge of the village and saw the house with the red roof, where, like Father Tymofii had warned us, there were some Red Army soldiers before the gate and two, with rifles, sitting on the bench outside the house. Seeing we wished to enter the yard, they stepped aside.

We walked safely to the house and knocked on the door, but no one replied and it seemed as if there was no one at home. We went into the porch and knocked again, then entered the house and saw a grey-haired man on a bed beneath an ancient stove. This was Nychypir Petrychenko, who had long since lost his mobility because of a severe illness. He was large of stature and big boned, with long hair and a grey, indeed almost white, beard. It was clearly illness rather than old age that had made him into a grandfatherly old man.

'We come to you from Father Tymofii in Dunaivtsi,' I said in greeting.

Nychypir Petrychenko nodded, but did not ask anything. I explained that we were taking the child to the doctor's on the other side. He indicated a bench with his eyes, as if to tell us to sit, and I was beginning to think he had lost the power of speech when he said, 'Marusia will come soon.' He looked at the ceiling with an expression on his face as if he was uninterested in this world, not because he was indifferent to everything but because he already knew how it was and how it would be.

We seated ourselves on a broad bench by the wall. Yarko began to move around and cry quietly, bored with being in the same postion in his sling. Tina was going to tend to his needs on the bench but Nychypir directed her to the kitchen, where there was a bunk. When she had taken him there, I found myself alone with this taciturn man whose silence compelled me to be silent. It was tedious to sit like a tree stump, and I was glad when a lively girl with a welcoming face appeared at the threshold and said that she had been forewarned of our arrival. It was not hard to work out who had told her because she held a dead duck in her hand. 'They asked me to pluck it,' she said.

It was clear that she was glad of our arrival, though she only had sour milk with which to welcome us.

When we took out two loaves and a herring, Marusia quickly started to boiled a potato in its skin and we anticipated a good supper.

Nychypir Petrychenko raised himself in his bed, put the pillow under his back, and asked for the fish head on which he crunched with such relish that it sounded as though he was crunching a boiled sweet. He took a cloth from under his pillow and, wiping his hands in a wholesome way, suddenly said, 'If I could walk I would also go to that doctor and not return.'

'Yeah, right,' said Marusia. 'You lie around and keep me tethered here. Half our great Ukraine is over the other side, but I have to stay here and clean ducks for the Muscovites.' She threw the duck angrily into the pan, poured hot water over the bird, and set about cleaning it.

'It would be better if they didn't clean you out so much,' Petrychenko returned.

'Oh, it begins,' Marusia said, as if menacing, but without malice. 'Silent all day, then you pipe up. Was it me who called them hither? You have to be nice to our visitors now, I have ended up organising the transport for such as them.'

She cleaned the duck and went outside with it before returning with some straw that she placed on the corner of the bench and said that the gentleman would sleep here. Mother and child would sleep in a warm bunk, and she would lie on the bench on the stove and would wake us in the night.

I did not sleep and only lay on the drab bench and straw. How could I sleep when such a decisive moment approached? A moment that might mean destruction. What if this wretched Marusia led us straight to those who not only hunted wild ducks? I also missed my little sparrow. I had grown used to sleeping next to her and there was no greater happiness for me than feeling her by my side and inhaling the scent of her hair while she slept. Tina loved to sleep like that and I was certain she would not sleep now, she would be looking into the night, into the obscurity of the next day and perhaps the days after.

A silence like the grave had settled on the house of the Petrychenkos. Such an oppressive, crushing silence that it pressed on my forehead and temples, muddied my skull and dispelled sleep more than any sound would have done. In the middle of the night I heard a muffled voice from above me, 'What troubles your spirit, man? Pass bravely over the water and do not look back, for your land is on both sides of the river.'

It was Petrychenko who had spoken and who, apparently, was also having trouble sleeping. I did not know how to reply to him, or if he needed a reply from me but, after being silent for a while responded, 'The land is ours, but it is a foreign country. I also see that there are many Reds watching the crossings.'

'There are easily persuaded men among them,' Petrychenko said. 'Show them money or food. Marusia has already set to work and knows what she is doing. Sleep now.'

Quiet nocturnal conversation is always calming and I was sleeping with my eyes half open when I heard a voice say, 'It's time.'

Marusia was standing over me.

Without kindling a light, and groping around, we gathered our things quickly and as I said farewell to Nychypir Petrychenko, I left a wad of roubles on his table and ventured into the cold night. Stepping after Marusia, I caught sight of her fisherman's wellingtons, which stretched a long way under her dress.

We had barely time to see the curved slope of the river bank before we came to it and were on the point of almost tumbling into the water when it seemed that this devilish young lass had led us into the arms of a border guard.

'This is your acquaintance, Mytia,' she said quietly. 'Hello.'

'Aah, it's the people who are going to the doctor's,' said the guard delightedly, and I recognised the *Kubanets*. 'I would go with you myself but the Polish catch such as I and send us back here where they shoot us.'

I gave the *Kubanets* a slice of *salo* and some money though, from his sombre expression, it was clear he was waiting for liberty rather than food.

Marusia led us further. She instructed me to give her the

child, take off my pants, and take my woman on my shoulders before following in her steps, if I did not want to get drenched to the waist. Tina began to object and said that she could wade the depth herself, but Marusia rounded on her so my little sparrow became quiet and looked with wonder as our guide who, holding Yarko in one hand, gathered her skirt in the other, so that her high wellingtons, which reached to her backside, were exposed.

'Less of that. Well, let's go then.'

I took Tina on my shoulders, like one might take a small child, holding her under her buttocks, and I followed Marusia. The water was so cold that it pierced me to the bone, but, thank God, it only reached to my knees and in a few seconds we were stepping onto the opposite bank. This was such an emotional moment that instead of getting dressed, I looked back and waved at the *Kubanets*. He waved back, either to say farewell to us or exchanging greetings with liberty. Leading us to the nearest house, Marusia, without explaining anything to the drowsy owner, quickly said farewell and almost ran back home because it was growing light. And that was it.

Now we could be glad that we had so easily jumped out of the Bolshevik paradise. However, truth to tell, something did not please me. The worry from our leap across the Zbruch had not settled before our benefactor looked at us very suspiciously instead of trying to make sure his new arrivals were warm and calm. A chilling thought flashed through my mind. Might he yet call those people hunters who return fugitives to the Bolshevik paradise?

I put four wads of money on the table, five thousand Polish Marks in total, and again he looked at me askance, smiled in an unwholesome way, and said that this money was worth nothing because here it was not possible to buy bread or even a broken match for twenty-thousand marks. They were not Austrian Crowns, so it was not worth hanging around for long. What good would it be if we were caught by the border guards and taken for spies? He told us how to get to Probizhna where people did not pay strangers much attention. It was safer there. From there we could go to Kopychyntsi, where we should either report to the elders, or possibly directly to the police, who would transfer us to a home for migrants in Ternopil.

'Thank you and good health,' I said, and we went on our

way.

It is now unpleasant for me to describe our path through the villages on the other side, which although they seemed Ukrainian, were so foreign to me, I cannot talk about it. I will just say that these people were not like our people. They spoke our language, but did not have the goodness and sincere kind heartedness of our folk.

I realised how kind hearted our people were several days into our journey to the border, when we were met at every house as though we were emissaries from God. We were always allowed to stay in the house with the owners, who often slept on a bench and let us have their bed. They would ask us if we were hungry, give us supper, and heat water so we could bathe the child and wash ourselves. However, here in the free world, people looked at us askance, like we were limping oldsters. More than once they closed the door in our faces or, before refusing us, murmured to their family, 'Where indeed! Maybe they are Gypsies who will leave the child here, or embezzlers, speculators, scum who have ended up here.'

This was the first time we were forced to tend to Yarko outside on a road through the fields, but we were fortunate enough to sleep in the barn of a benefactor to whom I had given the rest of my truly worthless Polish Marks. He, this charitable fellow, even brought a coat for us and said, 'So that mother and baby don't freeze.' When I thanked him respectfully, saying that we would have needed to sleep outdoors were it not for his kindness, he said simple naturedly, 'Yes surely, surely. That's how it is. Our people only talk of Christianity.' He went to the house and brought us some bread and two boiled potatoes, 'So that mum's milk does not dry up.'

We had a similar experience in Kopychyntsi where, like old beggars, we wandered from house to house. It was the first time in my life that I had known such humiliation. I had lost all hope when a slender woman, dressed in black, came out of one of the houses and asked us to stay the night with her. We crossed the threshold of her home and, as usual, cast our eyes towards where the icons would have been, to cross ourselves and thank the house for shelter, but there were none.

'You have entered a Jewish dwelling and we have no icons.

You should bear God in your heart or he might be stolen from you,' the mistress of the house said, noting our confusion.

I suddenly remembered the prophecy of old Yevdosia and the severe principles of the Order of the Hand of John the Baptist.

'If you're not too proud, give me the child,' she said, as if guessing my thoughts, 'and take off your coats. I am called Yeva.'

'How can we thank you Miss Yeva?' I said, already accustomed to the fact that kindness costs money in this land.

'You will do something. I have some work for you.'

'Work?' I asked in surprise. 'Yes, however, it mustn't take too long because we have to continue on the road soon Miss Yeva.'

'I see. I am also from fugitive people and I feel for you and still more for this child.' She took Yarko in her arms. 'The work will only take a minute. I want you to cut a chicken because my faith forbids me. That's if you're not afraid of course.'

'No, of course not.' I could not restrain a smile and thought that if only she knew how many 'chickens' these hands had cut it is unlikely she would have let me into her house.

All is well, Miss Yeva, the young chicken will be cooked soon and we can bathe and feed our child. The anguish in your eyes will tell us of the unutterable woe that has tormented you in a foreign land, for you certainly had a man and a child, but the plague has taken them from you forever. Veys mir, why did you leave this woman alone in the world and on what paths will she return to her Jerusalem? She will never return, for these paths are plaited into the scourge of the Lord that whistles over the heads of the scattered tribe.

At supper time Miss Yeva poured us some cherry brandy, thick and as dark as blood; so sweet it made my lips stick together. She told us that she was also not in her own home. This was her temporary dwelling, the accidental resting place of a fugitive, and let us drink to each of us returning to our Jerusalem.

'So,' said Miss Yeva, as she ladled out the golden broth with the choice slices of chicken, making them an offering for all wanderers and exiles who may return, who knows when, to their country.

6

What pleasure could we derive from a liberty over which hovered the spectre of our impending separation? We tried not to think or speak about it, as if the moment when we must say farewell was in the very distant future, but it suddenly came upon us. Even when Tina entered the sombre premises of the police station, we still did not have an inkling of how soon we would be apart. I waited for her in the yard, a little distance away, anxious in case they arrested her for crossing the border. I placed my faith in the fact my sparrow could warble in Polish.

Maybe her linguistic gifts had captivated the police because I had barely finished my third cigarette when she emerged onto the street, conducted by a cheerful officer, and waved her hand at me to indicate that all was well and I could walk boldly up to them. It appeared they had provided a document allowing us to travel free of charge to Ternopil, where we were allowed to approach the immigration home only.

The officer led us to the train station and our goodbye. Having gone some distance away, he suddenly turned and bellowed, 'The train will arrive in twenty minutes.'

He went on his way and we came to the platform slowly, uttering strange words to each other, frightening and inane, knowing that Tina had to continue her travels with Yarko and without me, and not knowing when we would meet again. There was one chance in a thousand that some ephemeral miracle would bring us together and I did not know if the cards would fall in favour of such improbable happiness. I looked at Tina and was stunned for the moment. What words would he have spoken if he were frozen thus, this whistling officer with his twenty minutes? How many? Two hundred, two thousand?

Again, Tina repeated those inane words, 'The train will be here in twenty minutes.'

Slowly, the importance of those words sank into me. A dense fog covered my eyes and through that dense fog I saw, with great clarity, her pale face, her grey eyes, with their crushed expression, and her lips, drained of colour.

'You could come with us,' she said.

'Forgive me.'

'That's everything then.' She tried and failed to smile.

'Not everything,' said a stranger speaking with my hoarse, unpleasant voice. 'If I survive I will find you. Give me a year or two.'

'Okay,' she said. 'You will survive. You are able to because you are strong. I will wait for you.'

'Tina.'

'Don't torture yourself, you have done everything correctly. Only, when you can, remember me. You promise?'

'Something isn't right here Tina. I imagined this happening differently.'

'Everything will be okay. Don't worry about us. I won't go into a camp with the child, I will find work and rent a flat in Ternopil. If fate drives me further away, I will always leave some information for you at the main post office of any town we pass through.'

'Yes, of course,' I said, expressionlessly.

'Let's agree, in what name shall I write to you?' whispered Tina. 'So that you can acquire the document.'

'Name? But what?' I was confused, 'Maybe Rave ...'

'Cruk, Bohdan Cruk, that's what it would be in Polish. You won't forget?'

There was a long, drawn-out rumble and suddenly, from around the long curve of the railway lines, it seemed that the train crawled straight towards us, exhaling steam. It screeched and hissed loudly, swallowing our voices, and then stopped. We went to the carriage where a conductor, with an Austrian moustache which was fantastically twirled up at the ends, appeared. Tina presented the paper to him and he looked at us and said that the train would be waiting for a further two minutes. I, barely conscious and not knowing what to do, gave him the child. He took him mechanically as he gathered tickets from the passengers and only stared at me in surprise when he realised I would not be travelling on the train.

I took Tina's face in my hands and drank it tenderly with my eyes as I wondered what would become of us. The train huffed and squealed again. I tore my sparrow from me and seated her in the carriage. It was as if I had ripped the heart from my breast and given it to the conductor and I began to fall apart into an infinitely deep, barren place.

The train rolled away, gathering speed. The wagons swam past me and I fell deeper into my personal abyss, unable to utter a word. My throat was so crushed that I could barely even say that one small word, 'Farewell.'

Chapter 3

1

In November the banditry in the Chyhyryn, Cherkassy and Zvenyhorodka districts was subject to heavy losses. The larger groups were finally being reduced to smaller gangs. Individual bandits who fell into our traps were killed and some surrendered. Our squad has dispersed these groups so they are now thinly spread across the area.

In early November a new gang, previously unknown to us, appeared and passed the night in the village of Byrky, about 15 versts from Kamenka. On 3 November the gang was at Fundukliivka Station, where the Kamenka ChON, with part of a cavalry squadron, were about to depart on a journey. It seems the bandits disarmed a number of Red Army soldiers. Eventually, operating under the strictest secrecy, we were able to establish that this is a fictitious gang, consisting of Red Army troops, and operates under this guise to catch bandits. This information was given personally by the head of the district unit of the G.P.U., Likhachev. It is extremely secret and is not to be made public.

In the Zvenyhorodka district there is an outstanding issue that is not a subject for disclosure in our accounting documents because it is strictly within the competence of the G.P.U. The only thing it is necessary to establish, from the incident mentioned above, is the presence on this site of Raven's gang of approximately 20 men. There is evidence the ataman was not killed, which had been testified earlier, and still appears in his favoured locations of the Lebedyn and Shpolianskyi forests, having changed his appearance. There is a plan to capture this gang.

Chief of the headquarters of the ChON
304

Kremenchuk government district, Glazunov
Chief of the strategical-combatant division, Semenov
Certified as correct: Clerk (signature)

From the report of the ChON headquarters of the Kremenchuk government district, 22 November 1922

When an otaman has been separated from his men for a long time some of his Cossacks wander off. That is what always happens and if we consider this autumn, one could not have reproached some for suffering from exhaustion and yearning to leave the forest.

Now there were only twelve Cossacks left in Raven's Lebedyn Forest nest. He had realised the band would diminish thus and thought that he should let it be so. Let those who want to, go without compulsion, while fortune will select for you those on whom you can rely in the darkest hour. Let there be a handful left, those steadfast ones who would not shoot you in the back or run to the secret police to save their skin at the cost of your head.

Indeed, the twelve men who had stayed over the winter were a force to be reckoned with. Vovkulaka, Sutiaha, Bizhu, Zakharko, Khodya (where would the poor wretch have gone?), Viun, Kozub and five lone wolves who could not see a life beyond the boughs of the forest. The rest of the boys had dispersed here and there. Some had turned in themselves for amnesty, some had gone afar, others had left early for their winter quarters, promising to return in the spring.

However, regarding Shvaika, his recent history was rather unpleasant. Without warning anyone, he had fled stealthily, you may say he deserted, but not before getting hold of Kozub's rifle and a packet of his Kremenchuk No. 8 Makhorka tobacco. It was fortunate that Kozub awoke quickly afterwards and that he and Vovkulaka pursued Shvaika to Mokra Balka, where they found him seated on a wall and sorting out his footwear. It was interesting because, even though he had fled on horseback, something did not feel comfortable in his right boot and he was trying to change it. He had not thought about the boys who were hot on his tail.

'The *Chekists* will put on your shoes,' said Vovkulaka.

'What's this about *Chekists*, I am joining with Byk,' said Shvaika, in a frightened way, before falling silent when Vovkulaka drew his sword.

'Was it Byk who taught you to steal?' Kozub asked.

'Think. I was just borrowing it,' whimpered Shvaika. 'Take it, if you love it so much.' He stretched his hand towards the Colt but Vovkulaka was ahead of him. They had not chased Shvaika to teach him how to live. He noted an evil glint in the fugitive's eyes that did not give him time to reflect as, almost without being aware, his sabre swiftly severed the head of the deserter.

'You can only envy such an easy death,' he said, sliding off his horse and taking the Colt from Shvaika, together with the tobacco, a Shtaer and two grenades. Then he went to the well, drew some water using the pot that was provided, and asked Kozub to pour it over his hands.

'Shall we dig a grave?' Kozub asked.

'No,' Vovkulaka replied, 'such as he are 'buried' by hungry foxes.'

'I knew who to leave in charge of the unit,' said Raven, as he listened to Vovkulaka.

The wolfish soldier clearly felt he was to blame for so many Cossacks leaving the unit, but Raven calmed him by saying, 'You have done everything correctly.' He caught himself repeating the very same phrase Tina had used to reassure him, but surely those words were just comforting ones.

Vovkulaka softened a little in response to this praise and smiled his broadest, warmest smile. 'I didn't recognise you without your beard, Otaman, and because there is a rumour you are no longer in this world, should we let it seem to be the truth?'

'Yes. Let people think I am dead until my beard grows back.'

'How did you find the journey?' asked Vovkulaka guardedly.

'Bad.'

'Why was that?'

'I only severed one head during all that time, and that was a chicken's.'

'A chicken's?' Vovkulaka said in surprise. 'The kind that lays eggs?'

306

'That kind. You decapitated a traitor and I beheaded an innocent bird.'

'Well, we were bored here without any work to do, maybe that's why some went.'

'Like grandmother from the cart,' said Raven. 'If they went, they went. Winter is almost here.'

'That's why the commune has forgotten us. Their newspaper writes that we are kaput. That's good?'

'And what is good about it? We need them to be afraid of our spirit and the scent of us.'

'Perhaps it's so, but if they let their guard down because of it, that's also not bad for us.'

Raven realised that Vovkulaka was thinking of a complex idea, but was approaching the suggestion of it in a careful and roundabout way. Eventually, he took out a folded issue of the newspaper, *Red October*, from his bag, opened it and handed it to Raven. He pointed at the first page.

The Case of the Bandit called Tuz

The bandit, Ataman Tuz, known for his bloodthirsty and bestial work, will stand before a judge on 9 November. The case was due to be heard in Cherkassy, however, at the request of the workers in Zvenyhorodka, an extraordinary session of the D.P.U. has transferred the hearing there, the place where most of the bandit's activity occurred. Two of his henchmen are also sitting in the dock with him, Bosyi, from Zhurzhynets, and Harasko, from Hanzhalivka.

Let us remember some of the details from the biography of the bandit: He comes from the village of Zhurzhyntsi, in the Zvenyhorodka district, and is 26 years old. He finished agricultural school in Uman and, during the imperialist war, served in the Tsarist Army, completed training as an ensign and served as a corporal. He calls himself a free spirit. He battled against the Workers' and Peasants' Red Army while in the Petliurite military, and after the defeat of the yellow-blue nationalist forces, continued his blood-soaked path in the gangs of Tsvitkovskyi, Hryzlo and Dereshchuk until he organised his own gang. He has occupied himself continually with terrorising Soviet Union power, killed activists and workers, plundered sugar refineries, destroyed the people's goods, burned poor peasant buildings and village councils, and instilled fear in the peaceful population.

There is not enough space here to list all his crimes and innocent victims, which include a squadron commander, a chief of the district militia, a chief of a punitive search squad, and many, many responsible workers, Red Army soldiers and peaceful citizens. Tuz's band made assaults on the towns of Lysyanka, Pochapyntsi, Vereshchaky, Maidanivka, Khlypnivka, Hanzhalivka and many other villages, whose inhabitants can now come to the court and see with their own eyes how the inglorious path of the enemies of the Soviet Union comes to an end. The path that has already led to oblivion for Hryzlo, Tsvitkovskyi, Zahorodnii and Raven.

The moon has set forever over the forest wolves. The October sun will rise yet higher in the bright heaven of revolution!

Kalenyk Hrusha

'Hold on,' said Raven as he tore off a strip from the *Red October* and began to roll a cigarette, 'Otaman Tuz was killed a year ago.'

'Yes,' nodded Vovkulaka. 'In Khlypnivskyi Forest, but that was Stepan Tuz, this is a different one, also from Zhurzhyntsi; all the men there are Tuz, as though they are all from the same family. It is like in Murzyntsi, where every other man is a Momot, so in Zhurzhyntsi they are Tuz.

'Aren't you aiming too high?' Raven asked directly, having guessed where Vovkulaka was heading. 'Security will be tight there and the work will have to be undertaken in daylight before quite a few people.'

'That's why it's good the commune has forgotten us. No one will dream that we might carry out such an action in daylight. It will be so busy there that nobody will even think about such 'dear guests' as us.'

'What an actor,' said Raven, exhaling a cloud of smoke. 'You can't live without your public and really should be in the theatre with a flag in your hand as you enter the stage.'

'Maybe it is so,' agreed Vovkulaka, 'but, Otaman, you are forgetting that this display will be in Zvenyhorodka and I can't go there. I am avoiding it, you know why. Furthermore, they may recognise me in daylight.'

'That's idiocy. I don't believe that an actor such as yourself couldn't be transformed into one of those Red demons. Even I have pretended to be a beggar, a monk and a commissar. Okay, your mug stands out, but if you don't open your mouth unless you need to we can mask your appearance a little. Don't be angry Vovkulaka, this is how it is done now. You have planned something like this and want to sit in the bushes? No Brother, it won't just happen, you need to take responsibility for planning the work right to its conclusion, down to the last detail. This is the kind of play where even the broom fires bullets.'

'What broom?' said Vovkulaka uncomprehendingly.

'The kind that witches use,' said Raven, winking at Vovkulaka.

2

The bandits had not yet been transported from Cherkasy and already the People's Home, the institution where the trial would be held, was bursting with such a crowd that they were trampling on one another's feet. Quite a sizeable throng stretched out in a column from the entrance because it was no longer possible to pass into the building. There were no seats left. The people outside would be the first to see the prisoners and whether they were in chains or tied with ordinary ropes.

The townsfolk were gathered, along with quite a few villagers, mainly the usual village men in their grey tunics, who had to know everything. It was clear they came from villages and areas far and wide because they were strangers and therefore did not gather in groups to converse. They were standing in ones and twos, looking fearfully at the road. An old grandmother, gripping her walking stick and bent almost to the ground, was standing alone. She had limped there with her last strength and was watching for the prisoners. Perhaps one of her grandchildren might be among them.

'Give way! Give way!'

Four militiamen bustled towards the door. They pushed aside the agile individuals, who were outside and trying to not to miss what was going on, and forced their way, as quickly as possible, into the building.

'Who am I speaking to?' one said in a mixture of Russian and Ukrainian. 'And you, old woman, stand to one side. You will get crushed here.'

A roar of motors was heard and a cry of, 'There they go,' was heard as a black car rolled up to the building; behind it, a wagon bounced up and down on the uneven road. The guards were sitting in the compartment with the prisoners, who were not visible because they were bound and on the floor of the vehicle. Three men got out of the car. They were dressed in green worsted and tall, heavy-peaked caps. They held briefcases at their sides and went straight to the front door, with their long boots glittering, as if they had been ironed. They looked ahead as if they saw nothing, when in reality they saw everything. The first had such a large stomach it was as if he had swallowed a young alfalfa plant and it had swollen inside him. This was the representative of the chief of the Cherkasy district division of the G.P.U., Comrade Volskyi. Behind him was the ramrod-straight appointed representative, Kandyhin, a tall man on slender legs, and behind him, a man with bushy moustaches who smiled to himself.

When the trio snaked into the archway of the main entrance, six armed guards streamed out of the wagon and even the grandmother noticed that one of them was Chinese. The Chinese man threw open the back of the wagon and cried in Russian, 'Get out.'

The prisoners, whose hands were harshly tied, slowly rose to their feet and jumped onto the ground. It was obvious they had been repeatedly tortured. They were dressed in tatters and were starved and unkempt. Only one of them was dressed in a warm greatcoat, which was so worn and dirty it was impossible to make out from which army it originated. It was probably from Petliura's army and had not been removed so people could see the symbolic humiliation of the Ukrainian state. The wretch had a quality about him that could not have been named as anything other than an innate pride. As if

310

he was ashamed of the fetters on his hands. He swept his eyes over the crowd with a subtle look of dissatisfaction and a barely noticeably nod, perhaps in greeting or perhaps excusing himself for having come here with such an unpleasant appearance. No one doubted that this was Otaman Tuz.

Without delay, he walked at the head of his men into the 'People's Home'. Behind him followed his brethren, Harasko and Bosyi, who stared into the crowd to see if any of their kin were there so they could say farewell, at least with their eyes, for the last time.

Otaman Tuz was seated on the central bench, which was near to the stage, so the accused would be visible to the three judges and the public. Harasko was at his right-hand side, Bosyi at his left, and on either side of them, two guards were standing with the stocks of their rifles resting on the floor. Two other guards were standing near the door to watch the accused and the entire hall. Order was being kept outside by the militia and two soldiers, one of whom was Chinese. Volskyi, Kandyhin and Holubchyk, who was still smiling to himself inside his bushy moustache, seated themselves at the table on the stage.

The crowd crammed into the hall, wheezing, squealing and groaning. There was such a diverse range of types in attendance: from the tearful woman, to the stale man; from the sympathising villager, to the angry activist; from the thoughtful functionary, to the crazed Communist Party member. There were soviet leaders, military chiefs and respectable guests from neighbouring districts, such as the Matusiv district military commissar, Semenov, who had permission to carry revolver No. 44956 and to use the village vehicles financed by working people's taxes. He was sitting in the third row among the guests of honour, at the end near to the exits. He seemed bored when Volskyi talked at length about the implacable struggle of power against banditism, until, at long last, the time came for the otaman to answer the judges' questions.

Tuz spoke with a level, quiet voice that penetrated the room, so everyone heard him. He spoke simply and directly, without hiding his hatred of the commune. It was as if he were speaking to his boys about the struggle with the enemy, rather than the judges. He said that he regretted nothing except that because of his actions, members of his family would be persecuted by the occupying power.

'So that means you didn't just go astray but consciously fought against soviet power?' Volskyi asked.

'There's no other way,' said Tuz, in surprise.

'Fought for an idea?'

'Of course. I fought for an independent Ukraine and for my people.'

'For these people who are seated in the hall?' Holubchyk asked, indicating to the public with a wave of his hand. 'Have you asked these people if they need your protection?'

'I accept that there are many people who are not inclined to think of a better fate for themselves,' the otaman replied, 'therefore, I have laid down my life for an idea.'

'Do you consider yourself to be Tuz, which I understand means ace?' Holubchyk sniggered, wanting to rouse the hall to mirth, but only a fair-haired lad laughed loudly, then hurriedly began writing in a brown note pad. This was probably the correspondent or the editor of *Red October*, Kalenyk Hrusha.

'Yes,' said the otaman, 'I regard myself as Tuz, for that is who I am. That's my surname.'

'Do you agree that this is the end of all bandits and aces? They are like beaten dogs. They came to us and repented.'

'No. I was caught alive because I was overcome by smoke in a house that was burning. Otherwise I would still kill those such as you.'

In a moment such silence had fallen that the Matusiv military commissar heard Volskyi's stomach rumble. He opened his clenched fist in which his watch was held and saw that it was 1.55pm.

'Bring this *Petliurite* propaganda to an end,' said Kandyhin, leaning towards Volskyi, who asked his last question, 'Do you acknowledge your guilt?'

'Before the commune - Yes,' said Tuz. 'I only struck at it in a small way. Before Ukraine - No. And before the people - They themselves said who I was and where I acted.'

'Ask them.' The cry tore out of Volskyi. 'Ask them. They are here in front of you, your people.'

He cast his eyes around the hall where the community's

312

accusation was due to have been prepared, for this was the time when the well-rehearsed 'voices of the people' would speak.

A Chinese man entered the hall as Volskyi was looking around. He joined the guards near the door.

'I will tell him, the viper.' A female voice, burning with indignation, was heard, and the old woman, who was leaning on her stick, limped from the back rows. In spite of her years it was clear her tongue was sharp enough to draw blood from water. Without thinking too much about it, she climbed the steps at the side of the platform where the judges were sitting and bowed low to them. When she straightened to her full height, the height of a powerful man, the public gasped when they saw she was holding a grenade in each hand. They were of the kind that would explode if you tapped them gently.

At that moment, the Matusiv military commissar jumped out of his seat, brandishing a grenade and a revolver. Everyone thought he was going to shoot the crazed grandmother, but he aimed at the guards who were standing by the accused. A young lad, extraordinarily light on his feet and with a lustre of lamb-like innocence, darted up to disarm them, 'I'll run,' he cried. 'You run.'

Yet another hot-headed lad, with a red trim on his waistcoat, who resembled a young communist knew what to do, even without the command. He menaced them with his Colt as he ran to the guards by the doors. The Cossacks now realised something they had not been aware of earlier as Kozub grabbed the rifle from one guard and the Chinese man threw himself on the other. If the Chinese man had not cried angrily, 'Here you.' Kozub would not have recognised him as one of his own men.

Khodya had dressed as woman and concealed his eyes with a headscarf, but he was now wearing a Red Army uniform with a tall, military hat, under which his pigtail was hidden. It would have been possible to spend longer looking at this Chinese Shaman if it were not for the old witch on the stage, who was holding a bomb in each hand and grinning to reveal her fangs.

'We don't have time to waste on talking to you,' said Vovkulaka in his own voice, as he ripped the scarf from his head. 'That's why this trial will be very brief.' He turned to the transfixed Volskyi, Kandyhin and Holubchyk. 'Perhaps you will see this trial as banditry, but justice is on our side. We did not go into your country to murder, kill and rape, like you did ours. Therefore, I sentence you to death in the name of the Ukrainian People's Republic.'

Holubchyk suddenly laughed raucously. A hysteric could have easily held up the execution of the judges, so Raven shot him first. Holubchyk's head jerked sharply and he slumped back into his chair with his mouth hanging open. Raven fired two more bullets into the heads of Volskyi and Kandyhin. Kozub's, Khodya's and Bizhu's revolvers fired as they took out the guards before they could recover and try to resist.

The Cossacks, Zakharko Momot, Viun, Sutiaha and two of the lone wolves, all outside and disguised as villagers, took their cue and, having no option, shot the guards. Two other rebels were guarding the horses on the ruins of what had been a nobleman's factory, and the one-eyed Karpus was looking after things at the forest camp. Sutiaha even had a cigarette with the guards and asked about how to join the militia, which might have been an option now the devil had created four vacancies in their ranks.

They had to finish off the car driver because he was behaving shoddily and had started up the vehicle and tried to flee on his own, leaving his 'comrades' to their sad fate. They spared the driver of the wagon, who immediately raised his hands and said, 'Lads, I am not a soldier really. I was forcibly mobilised.'

Raven ordered the public not to leave the court or a bomb would be thrown, and ran outside with the other Cossacks. There was no work left for them. All the wasters had scattered and those who were on duty were now laid out before the People's Home. Only the Chinese guard had been lucky enough to escape death when Khodya had earlier compelled him to go to the granary and advised him not to poke out his nose.

'They are all for it here now,' Khodya warned him, relishing the opportunity to speak his native language.

Khodya persuaded his compatriot to undress and he put on the Red Army uniform and, as a precaution against any misadventure, bolted the granary doors. Now Khodya could release the poor man if he wanted, but he was not sure if his countryman might be better off in the granary.

The otaman commanded them to board the wagon quickly and the Cossacks unbound the hands of the prisoners, Tuz, Bosyi and Harasko. They placed them in the back because they were weakened by their ordeal. Raven's gang were leaping around themselves in such a lively manner it seemed as though they went to work on a truck every day. Raven looked with fascination at Khodya. 'How did you do this?'

Khodya stuck out his tongue and touched it with his finger, as if to say, to swap your clothes like this you need to know Chinese.

Vovkulaka sorted out something with a stone in the car and then went to sit in the cabin of the truck. 'Let's get moving while the wind is at our backs,' he said, as he nodded merrily at the driver, who was glad that the boys had not finished him off.

They drove out of the town and stopped on a road which ran through the fields near to the factory. They released the driver and Vovkulaka tended to the wagon because, although he did not want it, he did not want anyone else to have it. They went on foot in single file to the ruined factory where the horses were tethered. Tuz, Harasko and Bosyi could barely walk.

'You bore yourself well in the court Otaman,' Vovkulaka said to Tuz. 'I had to force myself not to applaud your words.'

'But why would you stand with your tail between your legs before them?' Tuz thrust his hands into the pocket of his coat to conceal the marks left by the tightly-bound ropes. 'They'll shoot you anyway.'

There were still some walls, which had been built from a single slab of concrete, standing at the ruined factory, but the other, less enduring parts, were scattered in the overgrown tangle of weeds and heaps of bricks, broken boards and shattered glass. There were the remains of rusted metal farming machinery thrust in the earth and, though it was late autumn, waves of rye, which had sown themselves, respired around it. The horses were standing behind the wall because the lone wolves, Ladym and Fershal, had not let them out to pasture. They held them so they were ready to be ridden away.

Fershal, a short-sighted man with glasses, the frames of which he had made himself from wire, came out to meet them with a doctor's bag and asked if anyone needed help. Ladym was sitting on the rusted machinery and looking at the three strangers, two of whom, Harasko and Bosyi, fell on the overgrown heaps of clay as they approached. Bosyi tore a few grains from the stalks of wild rye and, without cleaning them, put them in his mouth and began to chew. Fershal took a stale bread bun from his antiseptic-scented doctor's bag and broke it apart so that each of the fugitives could have a portion. Harasko and Bosyi ate immediately, to stifle their hunger. Their otaman thanked the Cossacks for the food and asked if he could have a smoke. Kozub proffered him the Makhorka tobacco and after one drag Tuz swayed as if drunk.

'Do you know what the worst thing is about hunger?' he asked, as he began to recover. 'It's when you are hungry but don't want to eat.'

Having caught their breath a little, they mounted their horses. Tuz was so emaciated that Mudei barely moved when he seated himself behind Raven. Vovkulaka took Harasko on his mare, Tasia, and the lightweight Bizhu took Bosyi on his horse. They went over the field to a nearby clump of trees, to hide and check if anyone was on their trail, before heading for Lebedyn Forest.

They kindled a fire in the trees, fried up some old, yellowed *salo* and baked some late autumn mushrooms which grew among the oaks.

Otaman Tuz warmed up and began to excuse himself suddenly, 'We thank you for salvation, for the bread and salt and the arms, but we have to head in the other direction. We won't give you any trouble. We will make our own way home, where work is waiting for us and perhaps at least one free Cossack who hasn't buried his flintlock in the earth.'

At the words of the otaman, Harasko and Bosyi also rose and straightened their shoulders, as if the *salo* and mushrooms had revived them, or as if they drew power from the oaks that smelled of leaf mulch and liberty. Raven did not voice his sympathy or ask them to go further with him because he knew such men as them would return to their own place, even from the other world. If God had saved them, it followed that they had His blessing to exact revenge.

Tuz only asked for matches and a handful of tobacco for the journey, and refused any bread. There were still people on the farms that would take them in, let them warm themselves and feed them.

He shook the hands of the Cossacks in a noble fashion and when he came to Raven, held his hand for a moment longer and said, 'Farewell Otaman, the times are such that perhaps we will not see each other again. However …' and a sad smile trembled on his lips, '… history will say who we were and where we fought.'

Tuz, Harasko and Bosyi walked in the direction of Tarasivka. Emaciated, dressed in beggarly rags, bare-headed, and with rifles on their shoulders, they walked slowly, swaying from side to side, but with that springy, regular step that the forest had accustomed them to adopt. All three merged into the forest so swiftly and imperceptibly it was as if they had become trees.

Chapter 4

1

They were cut off from the entire world when winter arrived with such snow and ferocity that they were forced to sit and wait for it to abate, almost never leaving their home. The remaining Cossacks built their new underground home three *versts* from the Lebedyn Monastery of Saint Mykola, which stood, like Motryn, on a hill in the forest. On this occasion the horses were entrusted to good hands on the farms because the Cossacks had difficulty finding sufficient fodder and so no stable was excavated.

They celebrated Christmas in a dignified fashion. There was even the traditional sheaf in the corner, but it was fashioned from bulrushes gathered from the lake in the forest where they took their water, rather than the traditional rye; water that was now a little insipid from the thawed snow. Their chef, the Cyclopean Karpus, who had lost one of his eyes when they had taken Cherkasy, prepared the appropriate Christmas meal of twelve courses without meat or milk, as was the tradition. The table was laden with fresh bread rolls, fruit compote, wheat gruel, onions, baked potatoes, gherkins, tomatoes and cabbage. There was dried roach, which was prepared especially for today, for what was Christmas dinner without fish? There were dishes of oil for dipping the bread, potatoes and, of course, *kutia*. They lacked the poppy seeds for this traditional dish but made a variant of *kutia* using barley flavoured with compote and honey. They had plenty of the latter because they always stocked up on honey for the winter.

They waited for the evening star to appear before sitting for dinner, said the Lord's prayer, tasted a spoonful of the *kutia* and raised their glasses, although in reality these were a range of different types of crockery, and stood to honour the memory of the fallen. Pouring a further measure, Raven, who was seated at the end of the table, raised his glass to all who had stayed at the camp for the winter in the order they were sitting down both sides of the table. Vovkulaka, Sutiaha, Bizhu, his brother Zakharko, Kozub, Viun, Ladym, Fershal, Karpus, Tsokalo, the unbeliever Khoma, whose name meant doubting

318

Thomas, and Khodya, who had joined them impulsively when he was about to be executed by Raven. Khodya had brightened up with the sacredness of the moment, but modestly lowered his head and gazed at the twelve meatless courses. He could not understand what was so wonderful about this holy day if Karpus had not been allowed to cook the wild goat he had tracked and shot with an arrow when they were gathering water from the lake.

Khodya had fashioned himself a well-crafted bow and arrow because the otaman had forbidden shooting in the forest, and it made no sense to go hungry when they were surrounded by animals. Khodya had quickly worked out what to do. He cut himself a suitable length of dogwood, dried it out and made it into a bow. He made the bowstring from a length of cured hide and then crafted such fantastic arrows that he could also battle with them. The mouths of his colleagues had dropped open in amazement when they saw the 'Mongol warrior' with a real bow. When he had hunted the wild animals just before Christmas the Cossacks were ready to swing him aloft on their hands in delight. Only Khoma, the unbeliever, suspected that the slain creature might have slipped on the frost. He checked it from all sides to ensure it was dead by Khodya's hand. No, it had fallen due to the arrow. Karpus would cook it tomorrow because the rebels' rations did not allow them to fast. Christmas dinner, with the absence of milk and meat, was held to steadfastly.

The only one who permitted himself to eat game on this day was Ladym, a devout pagan who prayed to the old gods, Dazhboh, Svarohov, Perun and Mokosh, and, interestingly, more than once received what he needed from them with his prayers. He had not become a pagan out of a particular caprice, but was that way when he appeared in this world.

Ladym had been born in a ravine which stretched out of the village of Hanzhalivka. It was such a deep gorge that people from there never went 'on high' and no one ever went to them 'in the depths'. The nature of the people there was special and so were their tastes. They were not tall, but they were sturdy and slow moving; they never hurried anywhere, were never noisy and only spoke reluctantly. They were sunburned, almost to the point of being black, because they prayed to the sun. Ladym was also sturdy and sunburned and spoke of his ravine monotonously and repetitively. He used to go 'on high' once every six months, to buy salt and matches, but otherwise lived on his own produce.

They had more than enough bread in the ravine until the horde from Russia had ventured 'into the depths' and taken not only his bread, but his young wife whom he had just married. So Ladym had beseeched Perun to slay the rapist with thunder. After which he was compelled to flee to the forest and had lived there for so long that he could not imagine anything else. He was closer to his gods there and, even now, before supper, he went to the sheaf in the corner and, raising his hands, prayed quietly and slowly. After which, he returned slowly to the table and equally slowly listened to what the otaman said.

'Boys, let us thank God,' Raven addressed them, 'that we are alive, unbroken and battle on. And if it falls to us to perish, Lord, let us meet death ...'

'In battle,' bellowed the Cossacks with the unity of a choir.

'In battle. For even the greatest warrior is not always granted that felicity. The *Cheka* are wrapping everything in their slimy, sticky nets and I ...' he said in his thoughts, without voicing the words aloud, I am not sure that one of their agents is not among us, 'and I,' he continued aloud, 'want to remember our otamans, Zahorodnii, Holyk-Zaliznyak and Hupalo, who foolishly fell into those nets. Now we can neither pray for the dead nor drink to their health, for we do not know what fate has befallen them. What ...'

Raven was silent for a long time. How could he know that the otamans were not alive and ready for battle?

***

It is tedious to be without work. They had cleaned their weapons, mended their clothes and told each other all they knew. Vovkulaka worried about his horse, she was a girl with character and not everyone could tend to her. There was one occasion when Vovkulaka had been bathing her in the River Tiasmyn and, when he had caught her under the tail, she had suddenly lashed out and almost taken off his bollocks.

'Well, your bollocks, that's only half a misfortune,' said Ladym ponderously. 'It's good that she didn't catch your teeth.'

'Is that what passes for a joke in your ravine?' Vovkulaka seemed offended.

'Listen, Ladym,' Khoma interrupted, not wanting to miss the chance to talk about something new. 'What did you do in your ravine during those long winters?'

'We embroidered,' said Ladym, as he released a yawn.

'The peasant lads?' Khoma did not believe it, though he knew Ladym embroidered enthusiastically. He always had a needle and crimson thread and when he had slain a Muscovite he would embroider a cross on the ribbon of his cap. There was more than one there; in fact the ribbon was reminiscent of a piece of patterned embroidery. There were some white crosses as well because Ladym had fought against Denikin's army.

'There are no peasant lads in our ravine,' said Ladym ponderously.

'Who lives there then?'

'Lords and masters live there.'

'Oh right, listen.' Khoma directed his incredulous gaze to Vovkulaka. 'And how do you know that your Tasia is a girl?'

'She has bright eyes.'

They also talked about girls and to listen to them one would think they all had sweethearts, but they only believed Kozub. He talked so much about his Yaryna that all fell quiet and looked at him with enchanted eyes. The severe, even harsh, face of Kozub softened with bashfulness. He had not seen Yaryna for a long time, but there was one occasion when they had both sojourned in paradise. 'Ivas,' said Yaryna, as she accompanied him back to the forest, 'you will return to me. It would be a great injustice if you did not leave me with a child. Your son.'

Even the incredulous Khoma believed Kozub. He would have asked someone else, how was it there in paradise? But now he just nodded his head in a dignified manner.

They played cards while they talked and one pack had already become worn out by the coarse cloth on which they played, so they drew up another. Raven had provided six reams of paper, taken from the notebook he had 'borrowed' from the correspondent of *Red October* as they were leaving the court. The reams were cut up into thirty-six playing cards and they were as happy as children might have been with their home-made pack.

It is well known that when a group of people live together in cramped, confined conditions they will eventually start arguing. This is because each has their own customs and dislikes. One snores, one is so talkative that they make another's head ache, and another is annoying only because they are constantly moving around. Raven noted that most arguments flared up during card games. At first they played 'fool with epaulettes', then various little gambling games; flicking each other's heads like children when they won.

When Viun lost his Shtaer to Kozub, the otaman became seriously angry. He put aside his volume of Knut Hamsun's work, which he was reading for the second time because he had not stocked up on books for the winter. Apart from *Kobzar*, his field library included a collection of the dramatic works of Lesya Ukrainka, a gift from Tina, whose hand had underlined the lines, *Messiah - what does it mean, woman, to give your spirit? Miriam - It means to be ready to die for love.* A little book about Moses, Christ and Buddha called, *Three Deceivers*, 'borrowed' from the Bolsheviks, had also fallen into his possession. Raven now put aside Hamsun, having heard what this game of cards had come to.

'Everyone, whosoever they may be, is subject to a court martial for such criminally irresponsible behaviour regarding your weapons,' he said. 'The appropriate punishment is for you to be pronounced an outlaw.'

This meant that Viun would have to leave them forever, without the right to enlist in another unit. They all looked in confusion at the otaman, who was not accustomed to changing his decisions. The difficulty was that none of them could leave, even if they really wanted to; at least not until the spring. Therefore, he who was now pronounced beyond the law would be shot. Viun became pale and looked as cadaverous as a mummy. Kozub wanted to return the revolver as quickly as possible, but caught the harsh glare of the otaman.

'And don't move, you,' said Raven to Kozub, 'rifling through your own plumage. You wagered a Colt against a Shtaer, rather than gambling for counters?'

'Yes, Sir Otaman?'

The lads exchanged glances because they knew Kozub had wagered his trophy Suta watch against the Shtaer.

'So, first you wager your revolver, then a horse, then what next? All of us? Did we sanctify our weapons to gamble them away in a card game?'

'This revolver wasn't sanctified,' said Viun, ' I took it from a Red myself.'

'That doesn't mean anything,' said Raven. 'None of us has the right to trade our arms.'

'We didn't trade them,' murmured Viun.

'Exchanging, laying aside, reselling. It is one and the same. Then, instead of keeping silent at the right time, you try to justify yourself. You are both fitting to be shot. But if it's one revolver lost at cards then we will show you a little mercy.' Raven narrowed his eyes. 'Let just one of you die.'

Vovkulaka had already realised that Raven had decided only to frighten these devilish children. Perhaps two years ago there might have been an execution, but not now when only a handful remained. He decided to play along with his chief by saying, 'The only one.'

The stunned Cossacks were silent. Each of them felt something was not right here. The otaman's judgement had been severe in the extreme, especially with regard to Kozub, who had taken half of the guilt on himself. And what kind of a decision was that, to let just one of the two die?

The otaman explained, 'If you are such ardent card players that you don't need revolvers, gamble with your lives. One of the parties, the one who wins, will live and execute the verdict.'

The Cossacks stood sombrely, absorbing the realisation of what things had come to. Kozub and Viun were the first to realise what they had to do and sat at the table opposite each other. Vovkulaka took the home-made pack and began to shuffle. The tattered cards flew from his hands and fell onto the table. Vovkulaka picked them up and again tried to mix them. Then he proffered the pack to Kozub and asked him to deal, but Kozub bowed his head in refusal, as did

Viun. So it was left to Vovkulaka to slowly deal six cards and show the trump card. The ace of spades. The Cossacks held their breath as they stood behind the players.

Kozub took the cards. He carefully spread them into a fan and saw he had no trump cards, so said to Viun, 'Your go.'

Viun looked at his cards slowly, then cast his glance over to Kozub, the otaman and the Cossacks who were standing behind his adversary, and threw the cards onto the table. 'And what is there to play for when we've already played?' He rose from the table. 'My cards were already beaten in the previous game. I am ready.'

'Otaman,' interjected Vovkulaka, who was standing behind Viun. 'It seems to me that there are circumstances in which we might soften the verdict.'

'Say what they are.'

'First, Kozub did not gamble his Colt. Truth to tell, he wagered his watch, but he took it on himself to share the punishment with his comrade.'

'And furthermore?' Raven asked, narrowing his eyes.

'Well, Otaman, Viun is so aware of his guilt that he has condemned himself to death. I speak the truth, look.' Vovkulaka threw Viun's cards on the table face up and everyone saw six trumps from the eight to the king of spades. This was a truly wonderful hand.

'Hmm,' said Raven pretending to hesitate.

'Otaman,' said Sutiaha quietly, 'the boys were getting hot-headed.'

'Hot-headed,' said Ladym and Karpus in unison.

'Hot-headed,' said Khodya regretfully.

'Well then, the verdict may be softened,' said Raven, bending a little. 'In so far as the guilty parties have repented without trying to save their own skin and held, above all else, the principle of Cossack fellowship. I decree the following - To cleanse their conscience they will receive twenty lashes with the ramrod of a gun.'

'Uuuuu.'

The softening of the verdict eased the Cossacks and their faces, stretched taut like drum skins, relaxed.

'They will each lash the other,' the otaman continued. 'Give them a nice long one with plenty of heft. I'd like them to use the one from the Arikasa so their arses are nice and blue.'

The Cossacks were smiling now but Viun of course was not amused. It was his turn to drop his trousers and lie on the bench.

Kozub took to the task of cleansing his conscience with total sincerity. He raised the ramrod high over his head and, whipping Viun on the backside with it, asked at every blow, 'Will you? Will you?'

Viun writhed like an eel and bit on his shirt sleeve. He did not scream or moan, he only roared through his gritted teeth. After twenty blows he rested a little on the bench, then rose and, swaying drunkenly, began to grope for his trousers that were hanging around his knees, revealing to everyone his double-wheeled weapon. Having recovered a little, Viun thrashed Kozub saying, 'Will you?' But his colleague did not cry or moan, he only whistled through his nose like a marmot.

Viun struck his last blow and turned away from Kozub with drops of sweat glittering on his forehead. Kozub remained on the bench. He had lost track of the blows and was still waiting for the last one. Finally, he rose, took out the Shtaer from his pocket and handed it to Viun. He looked at Raven with cloudy eyes and said, 'Thank you, Father, if you will pour us a glass.'

2

In February 1923 there was an unusual event that the rebels remaining in the forest did not know about. How could they have any knowledge of it? It happened in Kyiv, behind the high walls of the Lukianivska *Tyurpod*, to use the horrible jargon of the Soviet Russian language for the Lukianivska secret police prison.

To: The Chief of the Special Division of the K.V.O.
From: The arrested atamans Larion Zahorodnii, Mefodii Holyk-Zaliznyak and Denys Hupalo

Testimony

We, the atamans of Kholodnyi Yar, blinded by national chauvinism, believed the provocative rumours and falsehoods for which we battled. We were unaware of the just order that the soviet government brought to our people. Now we see that we did this in error because we were rebelling for a national idea under the harmful influence of the adventurer, Petliura. Now we finally recognise the essence of soviet order and its strength that is directed towards the liberation of the oppressed people, among whose ranks we Ukrainians belong. We acknowledge our guilt and repent sincerely for all those crimes we committed against the important process of liberating the working masses from the bourgeois government.

We swear on our lives before the leaders of the revolution and the proletariat, that from now onwards we will become honest citizens of the Soviet Union and, in the event of war with the bourgeoisie, we will join the ranks of the Red Army and devote all our force towards the liquidation of the rebellion.

Let the government of the Soviet Union thrive! Let the October Revolution thrive!

They had been tormented for four months in the Lukianivska prison and the only reason they had not been shot was because they had not yet provided the interrogators with the names of all the partisans and rebels who remained at liberty. The otamans were not totally silent; they gave the names of fictitious people or of those who had already perished or been amnestied.

The official of the third section of the appointed representation of the G.P.U. on the right bank of Ukraine, Volodymyr Mykhailovych Kurskyi, interrogated the forest rebels in a chilly basement room. It contained only a table, a Viennese chair for the interrogator, and a hard, backless stool for the prisoner. The small, barred window, which was just below the ceiling, only cast a little leaden light into the room.

The empowered representative, Kurskyi, had began to wail quietly to himself when Larion Zahorodnii, for the hundredth time, named Colonel Hamalii and Sergeant Zaviriukha as being among the partisans known to him and the greatest enemies of soviet authority.

'Take these insects by their gizzards,' he said, with an unchanging smile in his eyes, 'and you will expose the entire army. Hamalii himself made me aware that the entire Red Army staff in Kharkiv is already in our hands, along with half the Kotovsky

Division. Prymakov's Red Cossacks have also gone over to the rebels, and Dybenko's corps has long been in our hands. And you, instead of plucking these eagles, have set to catching mice,' Zahorodnii said, shrugging his shoulders.

Kurskyi could no longer endure his smiling face. He was chewing up his nerves with the devious *Khokhols* who had presented themselves as Zaporizhia Cossack Otamans. Even with him, a man with roots in Kharkiv, they spoke their own village dialect, which was how he viewed the Ukrainian language. He had tolerated enough; from now on he would operate in a much simpler fashion. Yes would be yes, and no would be no.

Volodymyr Kurskyi spoke in Russian, 'Alright Larion Zakharovych, we will listen to your advice, but we have made the last offer to you. Your life is in my hands.' He took a sheaf of paper from the table. 'I will not try to persuade you any more. I'll say it directly. If you sign this testimony, I will guarantee your life, if not, your death sentence. But think before you answer. Don't be hasty.'

Kurskyi gave Zahorodnii the proclamation of repentance in the name of the three otamans, which for the sake of authenticity was written in their rural dialect. Zahorodnii read it slowly and the rascal even smiled. He usually smiled continuously, but on this occasion he looked at Kurskyi with an assertive and even loyal smile

'Why is this written in such a primitive manner?' he asked. 'This isn't serious. Anyone would sign a piece of toilet paper to save their life and guilt can, in my opinion, only be expunged, if not with blood then by some serious work. Even more so if it is guilt before soviet power.'

'Give me an example of what you mean,' said Kurskyi, becoming tired.

'For example, if you released me into Kholodnyi Yar with five Cossacks we could catch all the lost sheep there within a month.'

'Sheep?' said Kurskyi, blinking his fat eyelids like a sheep himself.

'I mean those who wander lost there,' said Zahorodnii.

But Kurskyi was already thinking about something else. 'Five of your Cossacks?' he asked.

'Five would be enough.'

'And those would, to be clear, be atamans Holyk-Zaliznyak, Hupalo and your three adjutants, Kompaniyets, Dobrovolskyi and Tkachenko?'

'It could be them. I need lads who know Kholodnyi Yar well and have authority there.'

Kurskyi laughed raucously. He laughed for so long it was as if he wanted to pay back all of Zahorodnii's smiles. Then, snorting loudly into a rumpled handkerchief and dabbing away his tears with it, he asked, 'And who will then catch you? Your eagles? Your mice?'

'I'm serious,' said Zahorodnii.

'And I am serious. You will sign the proclamation.'

'After my return from Kholodnyi Yar.'

'So you think you are already returned from there.'

On 16 January Volodymyr Kurskyi concluded his prosecution report in case No. 446/7971 that concerned citizens Larion Zakharovych Zahorodnii, Mefodii Fokovych Holyk-Zaliznyak, Denys Musijovich Hupalo, Tymosh Arkhypovych Kompaniyets, Vasyl Fedorovych Tkachenko and Oleksa Trokhymovych Dobrovolskyi, who were accused of banditry and in organising and participating in rebellion against soviet authority.

Volodymyr Kurskyi wrote with passion and inspiration:

All the individual mentioned people, from the moment the soviet government organised itself in Ukraine, and without regard to their proletarian and semi-proletarian origins, joined the camp of the enemies of the workers and peasants. They actively led an armed struggle from 1918 to 1922, inciting mass rebellions, massacres, robberies and destruction of property.

The three most prominent warriors of gangsterism stand before the court of the revolutionary tribunal, with three rank and file, but no less active, bandits. They all operated in the well-known Kholodnyi Yar district, conducting a continuous guerrilla struggle against the government of workers and peasants. Due to the terrain, the area referred

328

to was, for a considerable time, a bandits' nest for people inclined to be Petliurite protégées. The guerrilla movement here had such an organised and effective character that Ukraine became the Vendée of the Russian Revolution. The notorious Kholodnyi Yar was, in the eyes of counter-revolutionaries, until now, the brightest symbol of the struggle against soviet power, and there were times when, having huge armed forces, it represented a yellow-blue nationalist island among the stormy sea of civil war.

It is clearly impossible to list all the evil acts of the atamans, Zahorodnii, Holyk-Zaliznyak, Hupalo, and their closest henchmen. Although they may desire to, they cannot recollect and describe the countless quantity of the feats they achieved over such an extended period. These crimes are within the scope of articles 64 and 65, parts 1, 75 and 76 of the Criminal Code of the U.S.S.R. As a result of their actions, the people accused, Zahorodnii, Holyk-Zaliznyak, Hupalo, Kompaniyets, Dobrovolskyi and Tkachenko, are to be handed over for trial and the determination of punishment on this account.

The report was signed by three other *Chekists*, Nikolaev, Horozhanin and Yevdokimov, along with Kurskyi. On 2 February there was a closed judicial meeting held at an extraordinary session of the court, which was chaired by Vasilii Ivanov, who was known as the 'open-hearted lad from Smolensk'. He was assisted by tribunal members Mikhieienko and Horozhanin, and the secretary was Mykhailo Frinovskyi.

They adopted a decision not to summon any witnesses and the sitting was held behind closed doors without the accused being present. The only people who had access to the court were those who were personally trusted by the judge. The verdict indicated by the prosecution report did not change. All six rebels were sentenced to death without the entitlement to the amnesty previously announced by the authorities of the Soviet Union in honour of the fifth anniversary of the October Revolution.

If there was anything positive about the verdict, it was that the Kholodnyi Yar rebels were brought together again, albeit in a chamber for those condemned to death, cell number one at the Lukianivska *Tyurpod*. There were eight other condemned prisoners in this cell. The most senior of these was Captain Zdobud-Volia or 'Grasp-liberty', a forty-eight year old *Kuban* Cossack with a well-groomed Cossack moustache. He continuously demanded a pen, paper and ink from the guards because he wished to write a play about the calamitous defeat of the rebel movement, but they ignored him.

3

To the plenipotentiary representative on the right bank, Ukraine
The Chief of the Kiev Division of the G.P.U.

Report

At 08.30hrs on 9 February this year, the Red Army sentry provided hot water, as usual, for the prisoners in cell number one. There were 14 individuals who had been sentenced, by an emergency session of the Kiev Revtribunal, to the maximum punishment allowable, the death sentence. One of the prisoners tore the vessel with the hot water from the hands of the guard, poured it over him, grabbed his revolver and ran out of the cell. The guard followed and sounded the alarm. Other prisoners simultaneously escaped from the cell into the corridor and then into the office of the tyurpod where they armed themselves with five rifles and opened fire from the top and ground floors of the prison. There was an exchange of fire between the guards and the wrongdoers.

Having arrived on the scene with the purpose of dealing with the emergency, I gave the order to shoot prisoners if they attempted to flee the prison. Two of the prisoners fled through the top windows and into the prison courtyard before trying to run. They were shot on sight. As a result of the incident, a Red Army soldier of the 99th Division, Comrade Abrosymov, was killed and Red Army soldiers Lysyn, Semediankyn and Bespamiatnyi, also of that division, were wounded. The supervisor of the P.P. and K.O.H.P.U., Comrade Shcherbak, was wounded.

Thirty-eight prisoners were killed as they attempted to escape. Among them were the Kholodnyi Yar atamans, who had been sentenced to death, Zahorodnii, Holyk-Zaliznyak and Hupalo.

Chief of the O.A.C.H., Frinovskyi
Correct according to the original (signature)
10 February 1923

From an anonymous letter to the Head of the G.P.U. of the U.S.S.R.(written by hand with printed letters):

I write, not so much due to indignation and insult but because I want to see the re-establishment of workers and peasants, justification for which I, without regard to my own life, shed blood on the battlefields of the Civil War and even in more peaceful times. However, the altruism and bravery of the revolution's devout sons is exploited by those deceivers who take credit for the achievements and merits of others. Now that the revolt of the prisoners in Lukianivska Tyurpod has been crushed some people are being presented with honours, even though they did not fire a single shot. Some of them were not even near the incident. That is perhaps why the facts were distorted.

Also, it was suggested that all the condemned men involved in the uprising from cell number one were shot by the Chief of the Guards, Levytyn, and that the commandant of the tyurpod beheaded the rest. Yes, Comrade Richter might have beheaded some, more than one, among the wounded and the dead, but only in his cellar that he calls 'the slaughterhouse'. He did not participate in crushing the revolt. For the sake of the honour of justice, I find myself compelled to testify to facts that might not be to the liking of many people, but about which I can no longer be silent.

The fact is that the prisoners, Zahorodnii, Holyk-Zaliznyak, Hupalo, Zdobud-Volia and the other bandits, who were in the cell for the men condemned to death and initiated the revolt, were not killed by the heroes mentioned above. Seeing the guards had quickly sealed, with maximum effectiveness, the exit to the courtyard, all the Kholodnyi Yar prisoners returned to the second floor, barricaded themselves in and commenced firing from the top windows. When the ammunition was about to run out, friend turned against friend. They had, in turn, embraced in farewell, then each shot his own cell mate. They turned on each other and so fourteen men fell down dead at once.

There were other prisoners, criminals from other chambers, who, having neither weapons nor chance to flee, had charged boldly into the courtyard and were shot dead.

No, I do not admire the bandits in the least, they deserved death for their vicious crimes against soviet power, but I cannot be silent, as one who is an opponent of injustice and deceit, when Jews trample on our worker and peasant brothers and take all the credit. Why are medals for combatant distinction presented to Richter and Levytyn, who have not spilled their own blood, and not to the Red Army men, Lysyn, Bespamiatnyi, Semediankyn and Supervisor Shcherbak, not to mention the victim, Abrosymov? Clearly, by showing such a scornful attitude to people, we may cause them to distrust the benefits gained from soviet authority.

A Soldier of the Revolution

4

One evening, when they were relishing some fried goat (Khodya had been reborn as a hunter) the otaman noted that Vovkulaka gathered the gnawed bones and crept quietly from the dug-out. Well, if he went out, he went out, perhaps he wanted a little something. Raven waited for half an hour and Vovkulaka did not return, so he went to look for him. It was becoming dark and as dusk drew in there was a frost that sank its nails into him and the snow crackled underfoot.

Raven followed the trail of his comrade, sliding on his heels as if they were skis. He did not have to go far through the branches because, just after the first bush, he was transfixed by what he saw. Where the footprints ended, the otaman saw a huge, ash-grey wolf crunching on the bones of a wild goat. Sensing danger, the animal stopped gnawing and swung its head towards the bush behind which the otaman stood. His hackles rose and he opened his maw to expose his gleaming, white fangs.

The otaman returned to the dug-out, but could not see Vovkulaka. What the devil! If Raven had been superstitious he would have thought that he had turned into the wolf. He remembered the wolf cub Vovkulaka had fed a year ago. Perhaps the cub had tracked down his benefactor to this new location. But why did Vovkulaka sneak out secretly to see the beast and where was he now?

The Cossacks drank blackberry tea with relish after their meal of game, and praised the hunter, Khodya. When Vovkulaka returned, an enigmatic smile played over his frost-gripped, reddened face. Rubbing his hands in a satisfied manner, he sat by the otaman, who felt as if his nose was struck by a sour, acrid scent of wolfishness.

***

At the end of February the frost retreated and the forest smelled tantalisingly of spring. As the ground thawed, a mist settled and the snow almost faded, except for white islets here and there between the trees. At the beginning of March the first snowdrops appeared from under those islets, buds sprouted on the trees and sap oozed from the birches. It was already spring. No one waited for spring like the Cossacks did and no one loved it more passionately.

One morning, from beyond the small lake where a dense forest of pine trees began, strange sounds were heard. Someone murmured, wheezed and whistled piercingly. An entire flock of brightly-coloured grouse strutted from the clearing behind the bushes and trees. They stretched and flexing their wings, stippled their tails and swaggered around each other from side to side, circling and clucking menacingly. That is how male grouse, who love the dense stillness of the forests, begin their mating games. They half leap and fall on each other, extravagantly bustle and squabble, strike their chests, lose feathers and peck fiercely, but do not kill their opponents. It is just to show the females how strong and handsome they are.

Drunk on these mating games, the grouse did not hear the whistle of the arrow that flew suddenly into the biggest brawler and only when he rolled over dead did the others flap their feathers in fear, and flee blindly among the trees, beating the dry branches downwards with pine cones and leaf mulch. After a while, they gathered to resume their tournament and again an arrow whistled through the air.

The lads did not believe their eyes when Khodya carried five grouse into the dug-out just as Raven had told them it was time to mount their horses.

Part Four

Chapter 1

1

In the winter the boys became so listless through our lack of work that by the spring of 1923 we entertained ourselves in any way we could. It was disappointing that of all those who went home for the winter, the only one who returned was Vasylynka. He was a boy without facial hair, whose face resembled that of a girl's. That is why he was called Vasylynka and not Vasyl. Judging by his stature he was sixteen or possibly younger, but would you have asked his age? Vasylynka was stubbornly silent, the same as he had been last year. I had tried to dissuade him from the life of a forest rebel. I told him he should preserve himself for the future, but he threatened to wage war on his own if I did not accept him into the squad.

He came to us like a true Cossack on a well-groomed, grey horse. He was armed and wore a striped *Kuban* Cossack's hat that was too big for him, so the peak kept slipping over his eyes. Vasylynka was an irreplaceable agent and news gatherer for us. He could thrust his nose unobtrusively into the smallest trifle. Lamenting that, 'They had stolen his cow from him, a poor man,' or enquiring after work, or on some other pretext. He would enter a soviet establishment near a sugar refinery or a railway station and find out everything we needed to know. If he went too far with his enquiries, instead of arresting the devious lad, he was just waved away, 'Hey you, snot-nose, sling your hook.'

This time Vasylynka returned to us, not only on his horse and in the *Kuban* Cossack's hat but with a list of communist cooperatives and a train timetable for Tsvitkove-Shpola-Syhnaivka-Khrystynivka-Zavadyntsi.

As early as March, we robbed the safes of the Lebedyn and Nosachiv cooperatives. At the beginning of April we held up two trains and found many quality products in the post wagons. We especially liked a large canvas bag containing blue, military breeches with red piping, sadly without the accompanying jackets, destined for a police unit. But even without the jackets my boys liked them enough to take them. So, the militia will have to forgive us.

We were not that lucky in Shpola, when we checked out the postal building at night. Sutiaha and Kozub set fire to some storage buildings by the station as a diversion. When the armed staff at the unit ran towards the flames with the firefighters, we checked out the post. We requisitioned the safe, destroyed the telephone and telegraph equipment, and ran to the banks of the Shpolka where Fershal and Ladym were holding the horses for us. However, shots thundered to our rear. The guard, who had been hiding somewhere in the granary, had regained his breath after emerging from the smoke. He leaped into the yard and fired after us. He fired at will and sometimes a careless bullet strikes more accurately than one you aim. Viun, who was running ahead, threw up his hands as if he were slipping, but I knew that kind of gesture because I had seen it more than once. Without hesitation, I threw a grenade in the direction of the shot, and in the light of the flames I saw a twisted human shape spiral into the air, head over heels. Viun fell onto his back on the damp, spring soil. Lowering myself to my knees, I leaned over him as he looked at me with his eyes wide open.

'That's how the cards fell, Otaman,' he said. 'It's all right ... Farewell ...' Viun still looked at me, but I saw that the spark of life had faded from his eyes and I closed them gently, bore the corpse in my arms and went quickly to the riverbank.

We buried Viun in a ditch by Shpola Forest. I took a silk cloth from my bag, tore it in half and covered his eyes. We shovelled soil onto the body and then covered the grave with branches. The nocturnal forest was fragranced with the white flowers of fumewort as we rode our horses through it; all except for Kozub, who remained alone with his comrade. When he caught up, I proffered him the Shtaer.

'Why me?' Kozub asked tersely.

'You know.'

Two days later they came to Lebedyn Forest to hunt us. It seemed that we had rubbed salt in the commune's wounds. That morning Bizhu and Vasylynka, who had been standing on guard, ran into the camp and told us that as many as one hundred people were heading our way. The 'responsible villagers' walked in front of a long row, with the militia and a police attack group in their wake. I ordered that we should gather all our goods and go to Hrafskyi Forest.

The next morning we saw that the hunt had not abated and, having spent the night at the Bohun farmsteads, they were now heading for the area around Hrafskyi Forest, so we were compelled to hurry to Kapitanivka. On horseback we could lead them by the nose for as long as we needed, but I did not like this at all. Vovkulaka proposed that we should, almost wantonly, circle around behind them and, without harming the hostages, crush the *Chekists*. A similar arrogant thought had come upon me but I had cast it aside. You could not select your targets carefully in that kind of skirmish.

Everything indicated it was time for us to find a new territory in which to operate, far away from here, because they would not leave us alone. Furthermore, I was filled with a desperate yearning to see Kholodnyi Yar again. How was it there? Would the fire still gleam, albeit in its secluded caves? Would any of the remaining Cossacks be there to greet us? I was sure that it would be so. However, I could not have had an inkling that when I got to Kholodnyi Yar I would be summoned to a meeting by ... Otaman Veremii.

A sixty strong group, including a strike force of the district G.P.U. and militia, and sixty of the villagers who can be held to answer for the bandits, have been involved in an attempt to capture Raven's gang. During the three days that the bandits were pursued, there were some blows struck against them, but they escaped the impact. We need to give credit to our people, who were on meagre rations. They were exhausted but persistently, and with resignation to their task, searched for traces of the bandits. Sometimes they had to nourish themselves with shoots and leaves instead of food, and even some of the seasoned fighters fainted.

In this regard, the reproaches addressed to the divisional G.P.U. that we temporarily stop courses in the Ukrainian language should be moderated. These had very little impact because almost all our employees are natives of the Central Russian government district. They complained that the courses are too formal for this action and say that it is possible to communicate with people and that not all will manage to acquire the language at a suitable level anyway. However, we emphasise once more that the temporary interruption to the courses has occurred because of a conflicting priority of the struggle against political banditism.

Chief of the Shevchenko Division of the G.P.U.
Adamovych
Secretary Orlov

From an explanatory record of the government district G.P.U., 23 April 1923

2

Before they journeyed to Kholodnyi Yar, the otaman wrote a letter home and requested Vasylynka to dispatch it to Tovmach.

Good Day My Dear Family,

I bow low to you Dad, Mum and my beloved sister, Maria. I write this letter with a sad foreboding that we will not see each other again. You surely know there is no way home for me now. I beseeched you and I beseech you now to forswear me, even if only before the Bolshevik government, so that they do not persecute you all your life because your son and brother was a bandit. Their word 'bandit' burns me all the more strongly, for I know it was a stone placed on your spirits when I became one, which I did only because I had a sincere and loving heart. I love my country and my people above all and therefore, without hesitation, went to their defence against the Muscovite occupant.

      Do not worry too much about me. I do not regret

my young life, for I sacrificed it for our sacred idea that will never die, even in an enslaved Ukraine. One of my comrades, one such as I, said some simple words to me not long ago, which still warm and comfort me, so I will repeat them to you - History will say who I was and where I fought. However, I deeply regret that you, my family, suffer because of me. So I hasten to say to you, my father, that when I depart from this life I will carry a huge love for you with me into the next life and there I will remember how you wore yourself out to give me an education and how gratified you will be that I became someone in this life. I have an expectation, Father, that you will never be ashamed of me.

Forgive me Mother, for I know the burden is hardest for you. I wish you to know that in my darkest hour I remember how, when I was little, you led me to a clearing in the forest which was covered with strawberry plants, and did not touch a single fruit until I had gathered them all. Maybe you have forgotten? I often remember that strawberry holiday. Now, from a distance, I fall and kiss your hands that swung my cradle. Do not weep Mother, for I am still alive and, God willing, will live long in spite of our plight. My one regret is that none of my paths will lead to your door.

And you, my dear sister, my Gold Marusenka. I know the worst misfortune will fall on your head because of your brother. You are yet young and this foreign power will not forget whose sister you are and the disgrace will fall, not only on you but on your children. If you can forgive me, whisper to your children that their uncle was never a bandit but fought for Ukraine. It is hard for me to remember how I raised my sabre to you when you urged me to leave the forest, but, Marusenka, know that I would never raise a finger to you, that I would sooner cut off my own arm than hurt you. I know that you regretted my life in the forest only out of pity for me. I thank you, my golden one. Do you remember how you cried over me and ran after the wagon, almost all the way to the station, when I left to study in Moscow because you thought I would not return. So see, that's how it is. I have returned, but not under my own roof. Your heart knew this before it happened.

I thank all of you, my family, for your understanding. I kiss you with the warmth that is in me.

Farewell and do not worry about me for I consciously chose this cross.

Your son and brother
19 April 1923

3

As they drew closer to Kholodnyi Yar they fell on the warehouses in Mykhailivka to stock up on food and tobacco. They didn't wait to cool down before striking at Zhabotyn and made some revisions to the stock of the subsistence cooperative there. They seized flour, groats, sugar, matches and tobacco. In the market, Zakharko waved a gramophone at them and, after a second's thought, tore the horn from it. Somewhere he had heard that if you attached it to a gun barrel the shots would roar with a sound like canon fire.

It was three leaps of a horse from Zhabotyn to Kholodnyi Yar, and before dawn they plunged among oak trees and decided to rest there, at the edge of the forest. Raven wanted to feel the breath of the place and check whether there would be a pursuit from Zhabotyn, which had previously been swarming with Reds. But no, the oak trees exhaled calm and stoic endurance, and the ground was woven with rugs of wild onion shoots. In April Kholodnyi Yar was covered as densely as a lush head of hair with the tangled flowers and shoots of periwinkle and bear's onion. You could always draw strength from their clawed, green stalks so long as you did not venture to sniff anyone. Although the plant was called bear's onion its scent was more akin to garlic. It was clear the bear had made a mistake here. Khodya had a particular passion for these plants and crammed them into his mouth in heaps, sometimes confusing their shoots with the similarly curved stems of lily of the valley.

On this occasion none of the boys left to meet with their girls, but they did enjoy a hearty breakfast of *salo* and wild onions. I smoked fresh tobacco and observed with interest how Zakharko measured the gramophone horn against his rifle to see if it would fit.

'Well, great,' his brother, Bizhu, said to him. 'If it sticks, you can leave it there, you don't need a great intellect for that. How will you aim, you silly head? It will cover up the gun sights and will hide
342

whatever you are shooting.'

'No worries.' Zakharko wrinkled his nose. 'The aim is to scare people. When some of the Red mob are heading for us, they will be met by the roar of a canon.'

'Well, you will scare me,' said the incredulous Khoma. 'When it's blown off the barrel and bashes your head, you'll know about it. Just ask Sutiaha how he was struck by the cover of his Lewis.'

'And what is there to ask about? The largish dent in his forehead,' said Tsokalo and everyone looked at Sutiaha as if they had never seen his dent before. He was sitting under an oak tree, leaning against the trunk and snoring quietly. His head had fallen onto his chest and his sheepskin cap hung over his eyes.

'Where's that mark then?' Khoma asked, even though it was him who had mentioned Sutiaha's scar, and now looked at Tsokalo with incredulity.

'Beneath his cap, that's where.'

'Well?'

'Hah.' Tsokalo made an angry smacking sound with his tongue. The sound made Sutiaha stop snoring, but he did not wake. At this moment Zakharko managed to fasten the horn to his barrel and aimed it in the direction they had come. Then he saw Kozub, who had been wandering through the forest, running towards them.

'Wagon,' he bellowed, drawing on the reins so that his horse reared upwards.

Even Sutiaha jumped to his feet in a flash, as if it had been his cap rather than him snoring beneath the tree.

'A good one?' asked Raven calmly.

'I don't know, but they are heading from Kamyanka to Zhabotyn.'

'Follow me.' The otaman leaped on his horse and before he had ridden far, halted next to an old, dead oak tree from where he could see the wagon on which three men were seated. One was in a military greatcoat, one in a lightly-coloured overcoat and the third ... was a woman dressed in men's clothes.

Stopping these travellers and asking who they were was not convenient because fleeing from the forest was risky and opening fire and lobbing grenades might result in being fired on from who knows where. These might also be their people in disguise. The wagon, swinging on its axles, approached and the Cossacks waited tensely for the command.

'Let me talk to them, Otaman,' said Vasylynka quietly.

Raven looked at him in surprise and Vasylynka guessed what he was thinking - Just look, don't get excited.

Vasylynka jumped from his horse, threw his *Kuban* Cossack's cap on the ground, took off his gun belt, stashed his grenades in his pockets and transformed himself from a partisan into a herdsman. He reflected for a moment in case he had forgotten anything, bent over and picked up a seasoned stick of oak.

'What's he about? Is he planning to beat them with it?' asked the incredulous Khoma in surprise, but no one replied.

Vasylynka had already run across the field to the wagon and, waving his oak stick, shouted as if warning of a fire, 'Stop! Stop! There is a gang in the village.'

On hearing him, all three turned their heads and clearly understood nothing because the wagon rolled onwards.

'Back! Go Back! It's overrun by a gang,' screamed Vasylynka, running to the wagon and waving his stick in the direction of Zhabotyn. 'They have destroyed the cooperative, burned the village council, and hacked up the poor peasants' building.'

'What are you saying?' asked the fat man incredulously. He was wearing a greatcoat. 'What gang? From where?'

'I don't know where they are from, only that Uncle Ivan sent me to Mykhailivka to warn them because the gang has destroyed the telephone exchange and killed my father.'

Vasylynka cried in despair, tears really rolled down his cheeks and this did not allow him to look at the beautiful lady in the leather cap. She was so respectable and proud. It almost seemed as if she were in charge of these men and not in the least afraid of what was happening in Zhabotyn.

'How many are there?' asked the wagon driver, drawing the reins towards him.

'Maaaa-ss-es.' sobbed Vasylynka.

'Hold on boy. Don't cry. Calm down,' said the beautiful lady, looking at Vasylynka with big, dark eyes. 'You mean to say that there are bandits in the village right now.'

'Where else?' Vasylynka bellowed angrily. He was annoyed that this *Chekist* trash was so beautiful and had called him boy. 'Look what they have done to me.'

Throwing his stick on the ground, Vasylynka produced the grenades with a flourish. 'Hands up. This is your death.'

All three were confused and forget where their hands were. Perhaps one of them might have been tempted to reach for their revolver, but Vasylynka had locked his finger on the firing pin of the grenade so that even if he fell down dead, it would still explode and kill them. The fat man was the first to raise his hands. Then, lowering the reins, the wagoner followed. Looking at them, the leather-hatted beauty shrugged casually and, as if it were a game, raised her hands.

'Well, what now?' she asked mockingly. Her twisted smile aggrieved Vasylynka. It showed that the vile woman did not take him seriously, even as she was about to die.

'You want to know where the gang is?' he said with a smile that stretched to his ears. 'The gang is here, Madam.'

Madam did not doubt him when she saw riders galloping towards them from the forest. To make as little noise as possible, Raven had only brought Vovkulaka and Bizhu with him. They swiftly disarmed the trio and searched them before leading them to the forest on foot. Vovkulaka drove the wagon in their wake, carrying three revolvers, a brown, waterproof portfolio, a briefcase and a leather field bag on the back seat.

The trio were met in the oaks by a guard of nine Cossacks. After inspecting the accreditations of their guests, the otaman's face brightened. They had netted quite a large fish. Raven interrogated them simultaneously and found that the fat man was the representative of the district executive commission, Fedor Ivanovych Kasatonov. He said that he was a native of the Smolensk region and had been sent to Ukraine to strengthen soviet power. He had done no wrong here. He had not even killed an insect, but was raising the quality of rural agriculture. He was going to Zhabotyn to organise the spring sowing campaign. If they let him go, he would use his health as a pretext for returning home and would never return to Ukraine.

'You don't look like a sick man,' said Raven, nodding his

head. 'That coat is even too small for you. Have you gained all that weight eating our *salo*?'

'I don't eat *salo*,' said the fat man. 'It brings me out in a rash.'

'It seems that our *salo* is to blame,' said Raven.

'You won't shoot me, I ... am a peaceful man ... occupied with rural agriculture. I love Ukraine.'

'And do you love Russia?' asked Raven.

'Well, of course,' he said. 'I'll go there straight away if you let me go.'

'That will be decided by Vovkulaka.'

Vovkulaka, without taking his eyes of Kasatonov, swallowed his saliva. He had already decided who to send, and how to send them, to the soil committee.

The wagoner in the light-coloured overcoat was called Samokhin. He was a work supervisor in the same executive commission and was also 'raising the quality of rural agriculture'; in other words, taking bread from the villagers. He also began by saying that he had not stayed here of his own will after he had been demobilised.

Raven interrupted him. 'Tell us, who is this lady travelling with you?'

'Who? An appointed officer of the G.P.U. Isn't it obvious?'

'It's obvious. However, I am interested to know what women are doing in the *Cheka* now?'

'Honestly?' Samokhin's face assumed a scornful expression. 'Having sex with the big bosses, especially those who come here from Russia.'

'And this also?'

'Full-time whore. That which they call agent's work now. Do you understand me? Let's keep this to ourselves,' said Samokhin, so trustingly that Vovkulaka almost choked on his saliva.

The supervisor did not comprehend that it was of no significance for him now whether this secret was kept between them or shared with everyone. However, he was not lying about the lady. She bore herself so wantonly, even towards the otaman; as if she could call on the help of the boys. Her accreditation was in a silk wallet, it reeked of perfume and confirmed that before them was the appointed official of the Kamyanka G.P.U., Ada Mykhailivka Libchyk.

'I just want to let you know,' she said playfully, 'I don't have the slightest connection with the unit that struggles with banditism. I like the idea of the forest warriors, it is so romantic.'

'Why are you going to Zhabotyn?'

'For fun. Kasatik has persuaded me to go there and breathe some fresh air.'

'Kasatik - that's Kasatonov?' Raven conjectured.

'Well, it's not Samokhin.'

'Well, how was your breath of air?'

'It was terrible. I am not a man to be treated like this.'

'Then why are you dressed like a man?'

'Because I like it?'

'Did you also like to work in the *Cheka*?'

'Why not?'

'We shoot *Chekists*,' said Raven.

'But clearly not women?'

'Sex doesn't have any bearing on it.'

'Are you joking?' Ada Libchyk wanted to smile but couldn't. 'I'm a woman first and I like to work with men. Whether it's with them or with you, it's all the same to me. We could talk about it. I find it hard to understand what it's like for you without women in the forest.'

She stretched her hand towards the otaman, but Vovkulaka had not fallen asleep. 'Take your pitchfork back or I'll slice it off.' He waved his sabre.

'But I'm ready to agree to anything.' Ada Libchyk pulled off her hat and dark waves of hair tumbled down to her shoulders.

'That's good,' said Raven. 'Good that you are ready to agree to anything.'

'What is the decision of the judge, Otaman?' Vovkulaka could endure no more.

'The two raising the quality of rural agriculture, raise them on the oak.'

'Done. And what about this bitch?'

'Give her to Khodya. She requested it herself.'

Raven gave the command to move on and all, apart from Khodya, mounted their horses. Madam Libchyk looked in their wake with amazement. When Khodya went to her, flaring his nostrils, the *Chekist* officer unfastened her blouse herself, afraid the savage would undress her with his sabre.

'Can Khodya do this?' asked the incredulous Khoma, who was riding alongside Tsokalo.

'He'll learn.' Tsokalo made a deeply meaningful smacking sound with his tongue. 'Do you hear the screams?'

Khoma cupped his hand around his ear, though the cries were now smothered by the forest. It was indeed hard to tell if someone was crying out from pleasure or from fear.

It was a weight off everyone's spirit when Khodya followed them with a naked sword.

The Cossacks only now became aware of how the forest around them was full of the voices of birds, who sang with delight at the sunny day. The further they travelled into the depths of the forest, the more their eyes were gladdened by the expanse of the mighty trees, which imperceptibly passed from the dark masses of hornbeam to the marbled trunks of the ash. Kholodnyi Yar fell away into the depths before them, falling still lower into terraces of trees and branching into crevasses and gullies. At each twist, turn and angle, they paused and listened to see if they could hear human voices, horses snorting, or any suspicious sounds. They looked to see if there were any traces of hoof prints or the ash from extinguished fires. Occasionally they stood and sniffed the air for a waft of smoke, before they continued towards the east between the Motryn Monastery (How was it at their Motria now?) and Skarbovyi Yar.

One year ago, Raven had stayed there with his Cossacks for a week and he liked the defensibility of the location, the proximity to the lake and the invisible magnetism. A force was interred in the depths of Skarbovyi Yar and it seemed as though it wished to keep you there. Maybe that magnetism really was the *Haidamak* rebels' treasure buried there by Maksym Zalizniak, which old people had murmured about for at least half a century. From where else would the name Skarbovyi Yar or Treasure Ravine have come?

Not far away was the natural boundary of the river where the living witness of the *Haidamak's* secret had stood for a long time:

A giant oak, which people called the Zaliznyak Oak, though other Cossack chiefs had rested there more than once, such as Nalivaiko Pavliuk and even Hetman Khmel himself. Raven had reminded the boys about the sacred nature of the location, where they had stopped many times, and Kozub said they should stock up on shovels and good rods for probing the soil quickly. To give 'Treasure Ravine' a good going over.

'I will bring a spade,' said Karpus reassuringly. 'And as for rods, we can use the ramrods of our guns.'

'Och, somehow I don't believe that we'll dig it up.' The incredulous Khoma bowed his head.

'Why?' said Tsokalo with interest.

'It is impossible that it hasn't been found after so many years, so it's not here.'

'It is here and they haven't found it,' said Raven. 'I know it for sure.'

'How can you know this?' said Khoma, still disbelieving.

'Because it isn't precious gold there.'

'What is there then? Silver?'

'No.'

'Well, what else could be here?' Fershal looked at the otaman through his dusty spectacles.

'Figure it out.'

'I know,' bellowed Vasylynka. 'What is there to think?'

Everyone turned towards him. Vasylynka, to annoy them, was silent for a little while, then pushed his *Kuban* cap back on his head and got to the point. 'There are sacred knives buried here by Maksym Zaliznyak. Knives sanctified by Melchizedek himself.'

'No.' Raven shook his head, although he liked this idea. 'You bury knives to make peace and Zaliznyak wasn't preparing to make peace with anyone.'

'Then what?'

Now they were all seized by such curiosity as to what this strange treasure was that they began to conjecture in front of one another in a childlike way. They named all kinds of precious stones, costly weapons, maces, old books and kings' and tsars' charters. They even went as far as considering vintage wine and mead that the old

Cossack characters might have drunk. The otaman, like a child himself, laughed at their conjectures.

Suddenly, Vovkulaka struck himself on the forehead and said they should be silent and listen to him, 'I understand what this most priceless treasure is.'

'What is there then?' Eleven Cossacks asked him with one voice. Even Khodya enquired more expressively than ever before, 'And What?'

Vovkulaka, catching his breath, said, 'A legend.'

The Cossacks were stunned into silence for a moment then, also catching their breath, said with one voice, 'Oh, we know that the legend is obviously the main thing, but there also has to be gold there? Is it not so?'

'Is it so?' Khodya asked, craning his neck.

'Obviously there is a chest full of gold, and not only gold,' agreed Raven. He stopped talking and, reining in Mudei, looked towards a point in space visible only to himself. The sudden tension of his figure compelled them all to pause and hold their breath. They cast their eyes warily in the direction of the otaman's glance and saw what he had seen, a broken branch on a young maple that had been damaged recently. Sap was oozing from where the branch had been snapped.

***

On 21 April an unknown gang robbed a food product requisition station in Mykhailivka and a subsistence cooperative in Zhabotyn, before heading in the direction of Kholodnyi Yar. On the same day, while on the road from Kamenka to Zhabotyn to assist with the sowing campaign, Kasatonov, work supervisor, Samokhin, and G.P.U. Officer Libchyk were brutally despatched. It is ordered that this incident be investigated. The villagers who can be executed for bandits' crimes have been acquired from the villages referred to. The operation will be personally supervised by the representative of the district military,

Commissar Comrade Astrakhnatsev, who has been sent to the area. The necessary measures to establish the character of the gang have been approved. The tense mood of the Kulaks has increased, but no undue agitation among the population is observable.

Head of the district G.P.U. Unit, Berhavynov
Chief C.O.Y. Lenskyi

From the weekly report of the Cherkassy District G.P.U. of the government district, 17 - 24 April 1923

Chapter 2

1

Eventually we would find the treasure, so we dug here in Kholodnyi Yar, where we had camped on a wide, protruding slope covered with a mixture of trees. White maples, ash and birches stood on this balcony, which had previously been clothed with the young leafage of oaks and hornbeams, and from afar seemed wrapped in green smoke. The lower level of the forest had a dense growth of hazel that also had light green branches, dog roses and hawthorn blooming with soft, white, downy buds.

Having slept and rested by the camp fire, the next day we went in pairs towards different areas of Kholodnyi Yar to find out things. Were there still some fraternal forest rebels here (there must be) or were there horned devils hiding among the twigs? After all, someone had broken that maple branch.

I sent Sutiaha and Kozub in the direction of Hrushkivka village, Khodya and Bizhu to Holovkivka, Khoma and Tsokalo towards Lubentsi, and Zakharko and Ladym to Buda. I asked Vasylynka the 'herdsman' to make enquiries at Motryn about the monastery, the bandits and their hunters, and indeed the dreams of the dappled mare. Leaving one-eyed Karpus and Fershal at the camp, Vovkulaka and I headed in the direction of Melnyky. We went almost as far as Kreseltsi Farm, but there was no one anywhere. No human footprints and no hoof prints or horse droppings. We wanted to look at the Kreseltsi forester's lodge, but did not risk it. If Vasyl Chuchupaka had been tracked there in the spring of 1920, what might await us there now?

We turned to the right and went to Zhyvun Spring, but saw no signs of any rebel presence there. The birds deluged us with song; the nightingales warbled and the cuckoos did not fall silent. If it is true they count the summers, why did they coo so much? How many times did a wild goat or a hare run across our path? But there was no sound of any human soul. All that was visible were the flowers called cuckoos' shoes, which shone yellow here and there, alongside violets, lungwort and the golden flowers of the 'night blindness' plant.

Blindness had fallen on us also because, near Zhyvun, we saw a huge fallen tree, which looked recently felled, and did not realise at first that it was the work of beavers.

In the evening we returned home with nothing, unless you took into account the capful of spring mushrooms that Vovkulaka had gathered. The boys had also seen nothing, although Bizhu had run through several ravines and gullies and even discovered a mine and Vovkulaka's tracks, which led him to Zhyvun and then back to the camp. Sutiaha and Kozub had headed towards Hrushkivka and come across a collapsed dug-out. Here they found the rusted ramrod of a Mannlicher, but everything indicated that the 'home' had been left over a year ago.

The incredulous Khoma, who had been with Tsokalo to Lubentsi, had not believed they would find anyone. Their path led towards Zhabotyn and Khoma could not restrain his curiosity, so decided to see if the two corpses were still hanging there? No, they had been found and cut down.

'There was no sign of the bitch either,' he said, looking with suspicion at Khodya.

Zakharko and Ladym passed Buda Farm twice and reached the Zaliznyak Oak. 'There stands our oak,' Ladym said, enthusiastically, 'but no one sits under there now, not Nalivaiko or Pavliuk or Khmel.' He was speaking nonsense, God knows what had happened to his head. There was no one there so Zakharko sat with Ladym. They did not go to the farm.

The only one who had not eaten his bread in vain that day was Vasylynka. Having enquired after work in the monastery, he had found out everything he could there, even the dreams of the dappled mare. It seemed that the Bolsheviks had closed 'Motria', but at the tearful request of the nuns had handed over the goods and the building to a religious community. The sisters were able to lease the Ivano-Zlatoustivska and Troiitskya churches, though they were kept under observation by the Medvedivka district executive committee. Motryn looked the same as it always had from the outside, but everything had changed. The commune had taken over the land. There was nothing to live on and the sisters were compelled to hire themselves out to the villagers for various kinds of work. People were saying that a haberdashery and tailors had opened there and they sewed blankets and many other things.

'Maybe we will be able to stock up on blankets for the winter,' added Karpus, in the manner of a man ordering his household.

'Yes, you stock up,' grumbled Khoma. 'Would you seize them from those devout women?'

'Why seize them? Perhaps they will give them to us.'

'They'll give them. Just wait.'

'Quiet. How many sisters are there?' Vovkulaka interrupted their nonsensical conversation.

'Not many,' said Vasylynka. 'Not long ago there were twelve and a new one has recently been sent from Cherkasy.'

'So there are thirteen now,' said Tsokalo, unable to keep quiet. 'The same number as there are of us.'

'No,' said Vasylynka seriously, as if not understanding the bitter jest. 'Besides the sisters, there are five novices and the Mother Superior, Rafaila. The church is under the auspices of ancient Father Ivan and there's a madman bustling around there in a black mantle. He made me jump out of my skin.'

'Is it Varfolomii?'

'Yes, it's Varfolomii.'

'He is alive?'

'Probably, if he is bustling around,' replied Vasylynka blandly. 'Although you can't see his face below the hood.'

'It's unbelievable.' Raven slowly looked at the incredulous Khoma.

'I haven't yet said the main thing,' said Vasylynka, pushing back his cap on his forehead. 'There are no guards at the monastery, but there are *Chekists*.'

'*Chekists*?'

'Certainly.' Vasylynka nodded. 'And in the vanguard of them all is that young sister from Cherkasy. She came to me ...'

'Alone? To you?' said Khoma.

'Why not?'

'Nothing. It is simply strange that the sister came herself.'

'If it's not interesting, I won't tell you about it,' said Vasylynka offended.

354

'Don't interrupt him,' Vovkulaka joined the conversation. 'He is telling the truth. Who would simply send a sister from Cherkasy if the monastery is practically closed down?'

'Well, you will see what kind of mare she was.'

'Well, okay,' said Khoma, placatingly. 'What happened next? She went up to you ...'

Now Vasylynka was irritated because they had all looked at him for long enough. As he told his story, it was as if he did not want to tell the tale but then he was carried along with it. When the nuns had gone for their supper, Vasylynka, not having any work, set off on his own way. He headed towards Melnyky in case anyone was following him with their eyes, but by the *Haidamak* pond he turned left before he heard someone tracking him. He looked around stealthily and, seeing no one, rapidly turned towards the Melnyky path and lay in a ditch by the road. He heard someone rustling along the track he had followed and then they came to the ditch. As they jumped over him he saw a nun's habit and caught a waft of perfume. Vasylynka could no longer hold back, he jumped up with a gasp and the nun almost fainted with fear. As Vasylynka continued, he blushed, fell silent and lowered his head now and then so that his cap fell over his eyes, but he could not stop himself.

'The nun explained her curiosity away by saying that she liked me very much and she could not live by prayers alone, for her sinful nature demanded its own ... Well, you follow me,' he said, lowering his head yet further.

In a word they went into the bushes and here the most interesting thing happened. Vasylynka, though occasionally quiet, told everything so tastily that it was hard not to believe him. When she had undressed and removed every last thread, there was a red mark on a thigh where a strap had dug into her skin. 'Do you know what?' he asked them before explaining that was where she hid her pistol.

Twelve pairs of eyes glittered at Vasylynka, though they saw, these ram like eyes, not Vasylynka but that indentation in a smooth expanse of white skin.

'But what next?' Khoma licked his lips.

'But what next? Everything that happened next is obvious,' said Vasylynka weightily.

Silence fell. Only Tsokalo made a meaningful smacking sound with his tongue.

'So, how did you notice the pistol?' Kozub asked finally.

'Very simply. When she took off her habit, she didn't throw it onto the grass but instead she very carefully laid it by her side. I saw that something was wrapped in it and later, when all was ...' Vasylynka reddened still more, 'When her ... eyes rolled and she wasn't aware ... I felt that bump in her habit and realised it was a pistol.'

'Perhaps it was something else,' Khoma said doubtfully.

'What?' said Vasylynka, uncomprehendingly.

'Well, some little thing, for example money. Women often hide money in their bosom or lower down.'

'So, I can't tell a pistol from money.' Vasylynka was offended.

'Well, well,' Bizhu shook his head. 'See what he has run into.'

'Yesterday Khodya, today Vasylynka.' Zakharko threw in. 'If this keeps going on we'll have slept with all the *Chekists*.'

'Did you kill her?' Vovkulaka asked, unable to endure.

'You what?' Vasylynka looked at him in surprise. 'So that then they would send an entire squad here? The sisters are so poor there.'

'Well, what did you do with her?'

'Nothing. We said goodbye. I promised that if I was hired for work nearby I would come again.'

'And her?'

'She said to come back. But you haven't realised the most important thing. She didn't follow me out of an itch for sex but because the bitch's nose smelled the partisan in me,' said Vasylynka, finally straightening his shoulders.

'Well, that's obvious from a long way off,' said Vovkulaka, and twelve pairs of eyes looked merrily at each other.

'So, she caught the scent and wanted to follow wherever I went and when it panned out that she wouldn't be going anywhere she played the fool by saying she loved me.'

'Nonsense, like a dappled mare's dream,' said Vovkulaka, smiling broadly as two red spots played on Vasylynka's flushed cheeks.

'Such a dappled mare,' he said in his amazement. 'She was covered with freckles, like someone in a fever, even her breasts.'

356

Twelve pairs of eyes again glittered at Vasylynka, though they did not see Vasylynka but those dear breasts freckled to their mauve nipples.

'I'll beat that bitch out of you with a ladle,' said Karpus, butting into the game. 'The gruel has been over cooked.'

Supper was ready and the gruel, though over cooked, was nice and thick, like broth. Karpus had flavoured it with *salo*, bear's onions and mushrooms. I gave the lads permission to raise a glass and raised one myself. We lay down to sleep on heaped branches close to the extinguished fire, which still held some heat. We tethered the horses so they were closer and could warm one another and us. It is always quiet by horses.

I posted Sutiaha and Khodya on sentry duty but I did not sleep for long and decided to venture further up the slope where we rested. There was no moon and the pin pricks of the stars peeped through the branches. It seemed as if this vast, overwhelming silence covered the earth, but Kholodnyi Yar did not sleep; it lived its own nocturnal life. It was unbelievable that there was no one here apart from us and the inhabitants of the monastery. The forest did not hurry to reveal its secrets.

2

They had wandered to the various ends of Kholodnyi Yar for two days, vainly seeking intelligence, when Khodya returned to the camp with a wild man under his guard. It seemed they need not have gone far because he had been right under their noses and watching everything that happened.

Khodya, having prepared his bow, had gone on his quiet hunting expedition before dawn. He was yearning for meat and previously, in the foliage of a ragged tree, which grew aloft with three trunks, he had seen such a huge bird's nest that his knees shook. If there is such a massive bird in Kholodnyi Yar, thought Khodya, no arrow would bring it down. Perhaps he would not manage to kill it with a rifle. Khodya thought that because it was forbidden to shoot, it would be better to call the boys and let them see this marvel, but then he thought again about calling them because he wanted to look in the nest first. If there were eggs in the nest they would be as big as a man's head. Khodya took off his shoes, took his revolver in his hand, and quietly climbed the tree.

As he reached the nest he saw a sleeping man swathed in branches. His beard almost covered his face and he was so shabby it looked as though he probably never left the forest and lived like an animal. A rifle was next to him, by a squashed, almost empty, ammunition belt. Khodya's eyes glittered as he watched this man, cut off for so long from humanity, for quite a while before his eyes opened. Seeing the narrow-eyed visage of a Chinese man above him, the wild man blinked as if he were chasing away the remnants of a dream, but he was not afraid. 'Who are you?' he asked Khodya.

'A Cossack,' Khodya replied.

'If you are a Cossack, then who am I?'

'And who?'

'You are probably a Chinese man?'

'A Chinese man,' agreed Khodya, 'and a Cossack. And who are you?'

'A Cossack, that's me,' said the feral man.

'Come with me,' Khodya commanded and, taking the rifle, descended the tree. The wild man also climbed down and went compliantly ahead of Khodya. He knew the route they had to follow.

Seeing the wild, isolated man, the Cossacks did not know what to think. Was he an informer or not? A *Haidamak* rebel or not? A lost villager or not? Why had he been hiding near them?

The new arrival's footwear was very interesting, so torn and worn that the upper parts were tied in place with bits of rope. He stood before the otaman, so sombre, wild and wretched that it seemed his spirit was barely able to hold onto his body. Looking at him more closely, Raven understood this was not an old tramp but a young lad who had swallowed more than his share of misfortune.

'Who are you?'

'Hryts.'

'What do you do here?'

'I live here.'

'In the forest?'

'Is that forbidden?' Hryts drew himself upright. 'Animals can live here.'

'But you are not an animal.'

Hryts stared at the otaman, his glaring eyes suddenly grew round and filled with tears, 'Raven? Is it really?'

'Do you know me?'

Hryts fell onto Raven's breast and roared like a baby. 'How would I not know you? You perhaps do not remember me, but I have seen you more than once, Otaman. You came to us when Derkach, Simon Chuchupaka and Panchenko were still here. There were many of us then. You won't remember us all.'

'That's true,' said Raven. 'Why didn't you come to us now instead of hiding in the bushes?'

'Why?' Hryts wiped away tears with his dirty sleeve. 'Because I did not recognise you from afar. I had to stare at you close up for a while.'

'It's good that you didn't recognise me, you don't need to. But didn't you see what we are. Why didn't you approach instead of continuing to hide?'

'Why didn't I approach?' stuttered Hryts. 'Don't you know, Otaman, that *Chekists* disguise themselves as rebels. So I thought I would take a look at you before I made myself known. Then I saw, as I see now, there was a Chinese man among you.' Hryts looked at Khodya. 'Well, I thought, Chinese people aren't natives here.'

'Okay,' said Raven, 'that seems like the truth. And how has it come about that you are in Kholodnyi Yar waging war on yourself?'

'It came about ...' Hryts again crumpled, his nerves were shot to pieces, but he gathered his strength, frowned and explained in such a way that some of the Cossacks also wiped away tears. 'Though some otamans and many Cossacks had handed themselves in for amnesty, there were more than a few who stayed, and the enemy was still afraid of us. We avenged ourselves as best we could and when the enemy is afraid he is not yet the victor, because if not today, they will come tomorrow and ask who has been despatched to the heavenly chancellery and who to the soil committee. They were chasing us like hares. We perished, one after another. We fell in battle, died from our wounds, or fell into the enemy's nets. Some could not hold out and left the forest by using false documents. They went to the Donbas or

Kryvyi Rih mines because they said the enemy would not look for them beneath the earth. Some, in despair, went for amnesty, though they knew there was a catch. However, being trapped in a situation is sometimes worse than death. Death, though you are afraid of it, you never see, but a hopeless situation is always in your face. There was nothing to eat because the Bolsheviks held the villages in such a harness that they could not help us even if they wanted to. Only those things we could capture by force were ours. We lived through one or two winters and finally there were three of us, me, Shamrai and Mykytas. We were already driven mad by hunger. By the end of winter we were cooking bark and grubbing in the snow for acorns, or looking to see if a bird had died in the frosts. When the snow came, Shamrai and Mykytas went to Hrushkivka to seek food and never returned. I did not know if they had fallen into the hands of the Bolsheviks or died of hunger on the road. I waited for them for a while because our dug-out was not far from here. I watched out from morning to evening with my eyes wide open, and still the boys did not return.'

The Cossacks hung their heads in despondency. Was this not the fate that awaited them all?

'You are bearing up well enough,' said Hryts, 'and even on horses …'

Karpus handed him a morsel of stale rye bread. Hryts looked at it for a long time, then sniffed and again crumpled up in sorrow, 'It smells of cornflowers,' he said.

'Well cornflowers grow in the rye.' Raven replied.

Small tears, like little insects, crawled down Hryts's beard. He tore off a small piece of bread, placed it in his mouth and held it there.

'So you were going to carry on as a lone outlaw here?' Raven asked.

'Whether I can fight, I can't abandon Kholodnyi Yar. I can't and that's it.'

'So, you have nowhere to go?'

'That's not it.'

'You were holding on to you last pride?'

'If it had been that … or for the spirit, oh to hold out thus.

But that's not it,' he repeated. 'I could not leave here and take the greatest secret with me. Believe me, I was glad when you appeared, but I had to inspect you carefully, especially when I saw the Chinese man.' Hryts again looked suspiciously at Khodya, then at each of the Cossacks.

Raven suddenly asked, 'Do you have a spade?'

3

Hryts led them to an old, almost dried-up, oak tree, which had revived a little this spring and two branches were in leaf. The trunk was about four and a half metres thick, fissured with heat and hollow in places. Some areas were bereft of bark and the top was burned to charcoal. It was clear the massive tree had been struck by lightning many times. About eighteen metres away there was another old oak, quiet a bit younger than the first. It had begun to expand and was surely the descendant of the original oak. Somewhere between these two oaks Hryts moved aside a small heap of branches.

'Dig to a depth of two metres. Then you will see.'

One-eyed Karpus, who gripped the spade with all his strength as if afraid someone would take it from him, spat on his palms and started to dig. Thirteen pairs of eyes and his solitary eye looked tensely at the black hole in the earth. Fourteen hearts jumped whenever the spade struck a tree root.

'Rest, let me dig a while,' Vovkulaka proposed politely, but Karpus did not even react with a twitch of his eyebrows. Two metres was a stupid trifle for him. If Vovkulaka was so wise he would have taken the spade himself. He was tiring a little but Karpus did not feel it; he only sensed a small twitch in his body and how his missing left eye itched. He was down to a depth of half a spade handle when the digging got harder, but his spirit still did not falter.

'Maybe you could widen the hole,' suggested Vovkulaka. 'It will be more comfortable to dig then.'

'It's unnecessary,' said Hryts. 'He's almost there.'

Karpus sank to his knees, cast some of the excavated soil from the pit with his hands, then set to work with the spade again. Ting! Metal rang against metal. The Cossacks all stepped to the edge of the pit and, bumping their foreheads, peered in. Karpus was on his knees, thrusting his arm in the soil that reached his shoulders, feeling in the dark interior of the pit, clawing for the thing that had rung against his spade. When his fingers had grubbed deeper and they felt the upper part of a smooth, metallic object Karpus had no doubt what it was. He worked more rapidly with his fingers, scraping aside the soil and, at last, bore the weight of a metal pipe into the light of God's world. The pipe resembled a small cannon barrel, but the openings were fastened shut and dark with soil. The Cossacks momentarily fixed their eyes on the object, then looked at Hryts.

'That's it,' he said. 'Pass it here.'

Karpus swivelled his eye to the otaman. Raven nodded as he handed it to Hryts, who took the barrel, produced an Austrian bayonet, and began to break the ties of old copper-zinc alloy. The covering fell away easily, revealing the opening of the pipe. Hryts peered in like a magpie looking into the hollow of a bone, then graciously passed it to the otaman, who also peered in. His heart began to beat faster as he pulled out a bundle of black linen.

The Cossacks' eyes widened. Khoma bit his lower lip to stop himself making any stupid remarks. Raven unfurled the cloth on which a *tryzub* was embroidered in silver thread, amidst a silver wreath and the chief motto of Kholodnyi Yar, *A Free Ukraine or Death*. The other side of the cloth was adorned with the prophetic words of Taras, *A new flame will shine forth from Kholodnyi Yar*. It was like a summons. This was the battle standard of the rebel platoon of Kholodnyi Yar. It was not the first time Raven had seen it, but now the words, *A Free Ukraine or Death,* pierced him with a different, new significance. Perhaps the other Cossacks felt this as they looked at the flag with silent anguish.

'We bore it with us for a long time,' said Hryts. 'We concealed it in our clothes, in the hollows of trees, in the recesses of the forest and in old crows' nests. Last winter, when there were only three of us left, we decided to bury it.

Raven offered his thanks to Hryts for preserving the flag on behalf of the Lebedyn unit. Hryts again wept like a child, for this meant the otaman was accepting him into their ranks.

'If we have a flag, then we need a standard bearer.' Raven

swept his eyes over the faces that had shown the marks of their suffering but were now revived.

'Let it be Vovkulaka,' bellowed the Cossacks with the unity of a choir.

'Great.' The otaman ceremonially handed the flag to the new standard bearer. Vovkulaka, who was profoundly moved, took the flag and, unable to find any words, bowed low to his comrades. Then he carefully folded the flag, kissed it and held it to his breast.

So, their unit became a little larger. The otaman said it was time for them to separate into threes and try their fortune in the villages. Fortune for some, truth for others, he winked at Vovkulaka, and a horse for someone else. He looked at Hryts, at the rags in which he was dressed and thought that his tattered boots would not fit in the stirrups. It was only then it occurred to him that Hryts had tied his boots with rags, not only so the soles and heels did not fall away but also so he did not leave any footprints.

The raven, who was sitting in the old oak tree and almost seemed fused to part of its charcoal trunk, looked idly and with surprise at the humans as they dug up the old metal pipe. If he had been able to converse with the tongues of men, he could have told them where to dig. He would have willingly told them where the pipe was buried because he was not afraid of the forest rebels. Neither were the easily scared magpies, who raised their commotion whenever a stranger stepped into the forest. They never screeched at the rebels and the raven was grateful to the white-sided birds for that because he could not endure their noise. Their sound made his head ache, as any racket would, and that was why he had lived alone for so long, even forsaking the flocks of his own kind. The raven did not love to caw but he had such an itch in his throat now that he could not hold back. He had such a premonition, such foreboding, that an inauspicious feeling tingled through his body with its voice as he opened his mouth and cawed in the ancient fashion.

Chapter 3

1

On 8 May three riders with rifles were seen
coming out of our forest and there are rumours
among the villagers that a new gang has appeared
in Kholodnyi Yar. This is supported by the
unfortunate event which occurred on 9 May
by Strylytsia Hill. There, near the village
of Ivkivtsi, the head of the comiacheika,
Stotskyi, was slain as he returned on horseback
from Ivkivtsi to Holovkivka. Strylytsia Hill
is bereft of trees and is frequently struck
by lightning. Neither trees nor bushes grow
there and the grass is so yellow that people
avoid the place. It was here the bandits who
had slain Stotskyi discarded the corpse and
took his horse. We request you adopt measures
to uncover the bandits for all the activists
of Holovkivka and the nearby villages are in
fear and the Kulaks are rubbing their hands.

The head of the Holovkivka village council,
Trukhnii

From an explanatory record of the representative of the Chyhyryn
division of the G.P.U., 12 May 1923

After they had roamed around Kholodnyi Yar, the otaman decided
to head to the Irdyn Marsh. Let everything lay quiet here. Let the
Chekist strike squads battle with the empty air, they would seek
fortune elsewhere. His intention seemed to be in accord with their
fate. Sutiaha, who together with Ladym and Tsokalo, had travelled
almost to Sokyrne, returned with amazing news. A unit commanded
by Otaman Veremii had appeared near the Irdyn Marsh and wanted
to contact Raven's men.

Raven was unsure what to think. Laying his massive fingers
on the shoulder strap of his rifle, he looked long and hard at Sutiaha.

'Maybe it's not that Veremii,' he said finally.

'That ... who,' Sutiaha echoed emptily, as if speaking into a barrel.

'But he was buried long ago.'

'That was Chort and Veremii himself who organised everything.'

It seemed that when Veremii had been seized, Chort cleverly played a game by pretending to bury the otaman to deceive the *Chekists*. While incarcerated in the Cherkasy interrogation unit, Veremii deviously mingled with the criminals and, not only evaded execution but waited for the right moment to escape. He had gathered twenty of his most faithful Cossacks and was butchering the communists from Nechaivka to Biloziria. He fought with renewed fury, avenging his lost wife and son, who had vanished without a trace. After each attack Veremii and his Cossacks crept back to the Irdyn Marsh, where they knew the paths and the firm islets of ground, to rest and wait for a while before again striking suddenly, in a place where no one expected them.

Sutiaha had by chance met Veremii's adjutant, Chort, whom he had known for a long time, in Sokynyi Forest. Chort, delighted by this meeting, assured Sutiaha that it was not yet time to give up, that the rebellion might still burn anew and rouse everyone. The Blazhevski brothers were smoking their pipes by Horodyshche and Mliiv Otaman Kurinnyi had replaced Zahorodnii at Zlatopol. In the Moshny area, Shpyliovyi was roaming and here, Veremii had risen again. Returning, you might say, from the other world and looking to make up for the time he had been in jail. He was trying to reach other otamans, to revive their work and bring back the good times. He was hoping they could band together and make a combined assault on Bobrynska Station to crush the Bolshevik cavalry unit there before purging Smila, which was swarming with Red wretches now.

If Veremii's resurrection had not been expected by Chort, it had been wished for by Raven. Now he no longer had the right to delay setting off for the Irdyn Marsh. He had to tell Veremii about Yarko's fate. He had to tell him all that had happened, but he could not guess how Veremii would look on what he had done. What could be said? Instead of being glad the otaman was alive Raven looked faintly at Sutiaha.

'And how did he approach you, this Chort?' he asked suspiciously.

'He didn't approach me, I approached him.'

'You?' Raven asked. The question of who approached whom was often significant in their operations. 'You are certain of this?'

'I approached him,' reiterated Sutiaha, and he told Raven how he had entered Sokynyi Forest and gone to a forester they knew, called Hudyma. Raven had known him for a long time; it was Hudyma who had warned him that the *Cheka* were providing the foresters with strychnine with which to kill him.

Sutiaha had left Ladym and Tsokalo on guard and entered Hudyma's place, where he found Chort, Veremii's adjutant. He would have recognised him from a *verst* away because of his owl-like face and beakish nose.

'Well, we talked a little,' Sutiaha continued, 'we had lunch and then Chort said it was time we joined forces and made a united strike on Smila, so that the Tiasmyn River flows with blood.' Sutiaha had agreed that the moment had come long ago. Chort then softened curiously, nodded with his beakish nose, and led Sutiaha to understand that there was a lot for their otaman to talk about.

'Where and when do they want to meet?' Raven asked.

'Sir Otaman,' said Sutiaha in surprise, 'how could I have arranged that on my own authority? Chort is our contact. We can contact him through Hudyma.'

That night Raven's squad headed towards Biloziria. They were no longer unlucky thirteen, wild Hryts had become the fourteenth member. It was wonderful to see how vigorously he rode the horse he had acquired from the wretch struck by their lightning at Strylytsia. The stallion was the least famished of their horses, all of which had not been in a warm fold for a long time. Raven had been unaware of how Mudei, fed up with the fodder of useless journeying, yearned for some action.

'Leap on my old friend, maybe a real battle awaits us ahead.' Raven said to him. 'We are going to Bobrynska, there will be somewhere for you to warm yourself there.'

Chort had surely been exaggerating when he had talked about a fire burning into the heavens because who knows what harbinger of apocalypse needed to appear for these people to awaken; perhaps the few of us would have to stand alone to the end. I thought we would find a common language with Veremii. Our paths had not met earlier. They had twisted over each other, around us, and crossed closely, and you may say, bloodily. We were now like siblings and I did not believe Veremii would reproach me with a single word for what I had done. I was more concerned for Tina. Tina do you remember me, my companion, my grey-eyed sparrow? She, who was now so far away that I could not sojourn with her or call to her. There was not a day or a moment that passed by when I did not remember her with a unique pain in my spirit.

2

Having passed through Sokyrne, I sent Vovkulaka to Hudyma's and led the rest of the squad to the Irdyn Marsh, where we stopped at a place called Vidmyna Pazukha or Witch's Bosom. Though it had such an unwelcoming name, this was a quiet location among the dense and watery marshland, where we had sojourned more than once. The last time we had been here was when we had struck at the warehouses near Ivanova Hata to get our hands on some goods. It was mainly bushy willows growing here, and among them ancient red alders and birches, even some black poplars, which are able to thrive on marsh ground. All around grew the low shrubbery of perpetual green, watery marsh that now bloomed with white, star-like flowers, filling the air with a sweet, yet tormenting fragrance.

Vidmyna Pazukha pleased me because there was only one route into there through a dry gully; elsewhere its little islet was surrounded by marsh where, among the stagnant quagmires, we had traced several possible escape routes. He who knew them would be able to get from Witch's Bosom to dry land if there was danger. He who did not would find himself being the guest of a watery abyss. Here, even an expert could fall into a quagmire from where he would never return. I placed my faith in Mudei, who traced the paths with his hooves rather than his eyes. The problem with the place was the mosquitoes, but what could you do? If you wanted warmth, you had to put up with them.

In the morning Khodya had brought Karpus two wild ducks and two chickens for the kitchen. Meanwhile, Vovkulaka returned and told me about his meeting with Hudyma. Everything was as Sutiaha had said. Veremii had been raging through the area, without pity or compassion, since the beginning of April. His work sometimes seemed bizarre and he continuously wore a black mask to strike terror into the activists. In Zahreblia, he had burned a Communist Party committee member alive, along with his entire family. In Biloziria, he was responsible for hanging a young, unmarried, pregnant communist activist. In Malyi Buzuki, he had cut down a priest agitator, who was turning parishioners against Ukraine's independent church. Not long ago he had held up a train that was taking four members of a punitive search squad from Cherkasy to Smila. He had mutilated the corpses to such an extent that people's hair stood on end when they saw them.

Hudyma waited until Vovkulaka had asked him how they had been mutilated, after which he bellowed enthusiastically, 'The wheels. That's how. Very simply.' He continued to explain to Vovkulaka how Veremii had decapitated the Muscovites with the wheels of the train. After that 'wheeler dealing', the government, in exchange for Veremii's head, had promised a cow, a horse and five hundred grammes of rye.

Seeing that the hair on my head did not stand on end, Vovkulaka quelled his enthusiasm and got to the point. So, he had let Hudyma know we were ready to meet with Veremii on the strip of firm ground leading to Witch's Bosom. He would come with Chort at seven in the evening, Vovkulaka and I would wait for him there and we would discuss everything.

'What do you think of our Hudyma?' I asked. 'He hasn't weakened?'

'It seems not,' said Vovkulaka, shrugging his shoulders, 'but you can't look into his spirit.'

Although I knew the forester well, and Sutiaha vouched for Chort, we prepared for the meeting in case it was a trap. I traversed between the marsh once more to assure myself that the path to 'the witch' was not engulfed by mud. I waited with Vovkulaka, concealed among low-hanging tresses of willow, near the meeting place. At seven o'clock the undergrowth rustled about thirty paces from us and two men emerged onto the bare patch of ground just outside the forested area. I almost whistled with amazement when I saw that one of the riders did not have a face. His head was covered with a straw hat, beneath which the visage was just a black blob. Although Vovkulaka had told me about Veremii's new custom, I had not anticipated that he would appear in a mask. I recognised the other rider immediately, although I had never seen him before; the owl-like face and long beak of a nose meant it could only be Chort.

We went to meet them and as we approached we greeted each other with the word, 'Glory,' as we looked at one another. It was only then that I saw it was not a mask on Veremii's face but a fine, black mesh, like beekeepers use to protect themselves. It fell loosely from under his hat and wrinkled up over his neck. Lower down, from beneath the fastenings of the otaman's tunic, peeked the red and black edging of a traditional embroidered shirt. I admired his mount, which was a thoroughbred Arabian mare.

Looking into the pinpricks of his eyes, which glittered visibly from under that black mesh, I asked him, 'Who are you hiding from Otaman?'

'From mosquitoes. If it makes you uneasy I can uncover my face.'

I had not managed to say anything before he reached his hand towards his neck to unfasten the cord that tied the mask there.

'That isn't necessary.' I stopped him. 'The bugs here are bad, all of us could do with such a mask.'

Mudei shifted restlessly from foot to foot, snorted, and suddenly ran towards the beautiful mare. I pulled sharply on the reins, but he was not messing about and neighed lustily again as he darted towards the Arab.

'He likes the lass,' laughed Chort. 'See how he wants her. I have a lump of sugar somewhere.'

He reached under his clothes, but instead of sugar, suddenly and calmly, he started to draw out a revolver, although he had a wooden holster with a Mauser on his belt. A shot thundered and Vovkulaka's bullet blew away the top of Chort's skull. His horse reared and Chort tumbled onto the ground like a threshed sheaf. I fired my revolver and the bullet hit the 'beekeeper's' wrist as he reached for his weapon. The terrified Arabian mare tore off blindly into the undergrowth.

I turned Mudei and went onto the approach towards Vidmyna Pazukha. After about one *verst* the sound of a shot echoed deafeningly and I recognised Kozub's Lewis. This meant the 'beekeeper' and Chort had not come alone. The Bolsheviks had come in force to the Witch's Bosom. In the wake of that shot, two grenades exploded and rifles fired. I ordered Vovkulaka to hurry towards the boys and, if there was a serious threat there, to retreat by one of the reserve escape routes.

The 'beekeeper's' horse had disappeared into the undergrowth, but I was sure Mudei could track her down. He, the good boy, had been strutting his stuff in front of the Arabian mare and giving me a signal. I had longed with all my soul to believe in the otaman's resurrection, but was on guard against treachery. Hudyma, Chort and Veremii could have sold out, but his possible betrayal seemed the hardest to believe. If the *Chekists* had embroiled the otaman in their plans, they would not have troubled his family. Let that be as it may.

I had chosen Vidmyna Pazukha to meet because they could not surround us there and, long before seven o'clock, I had stationed my lads there in secret. Vovkulaka and I had been prepared for anything as we waited for our guests. When I saw them close up, I was alerted by the cleanness of the 'beekeeper's' embroidered clothes and his mare, which showed no signs of the fatigue that cast its shadow on our horses. Could that beautiful Arabian mare really have spent time in the marsh?

Mudei's hooves scuffed up chunks of hardened mud as he bore me to the edge of Vidmyna Pazukha where the swamp began, and I saw the 'beekeeper' between clumps of marsh grass. His Mohammedan mare struggled in the quagmire, trying to reach firmer ground, and was writhing like a snake. Lunging around in the watery marsh, she managed to reach the shallower area, then dry ground, and headed right for me. I swung the revolver and aimed at the depression in the neck that Mohammed had ordained on steeds of Arabian stock. I did not get the chance to shoot. The Arab caught her front hooves on a weak patch at the edge of the quagmire as she leaped along the dry ground and the earth beneath them collapsed. With a wild neighing, she toppled onto her side. She fell so quickly that the rider could not escape from the saddle and was caught in the stirrup as the full weight of the horse's body pinned down his leg. He twisted like a grass snake, but could not break free. The mare did not rise up because she had clearly broken a leg, and she moaned painfully.

I leaped from my horse and without emerging from the bushes called, 'Throw your revolver aside or I'll shoot.'

He remained still, as if reflecting on my proposition, then he fired in my direction, one, two, three shots ... He fired rapidly and blindly like people do when they are afraid, as if aiming at their own death while it approaches from an unknown angle.

'Aren't we going to talk?' I asked.

The son-of-a-bitch understood that I wanted to take him alive and was therefore behaving with wanton arrogance. He tore his leg from under the horse's body, jumped up, fired twice in my direction, and ran, limping, into the marsh. He knew he would not be able to flee through dry ground but thought that heading through the quagmires might provide a lucky escape. I pulled up a young marsh birch and quickly stripped off the branches. Going into the marsh without a stick was suicide. The 'beekeeper' had already gone about forty steps, leaping from islet to islet and tussock to tussock. I followed in his wake. The moist earth squelched underfoot, the black slime bubbled with the poisonous stench of stagnant places, and it became harder and harder to advance. His revolver thundered again and the bullet whistled over my head. The 'beekeeper', placing himself by a broad birch that was partially submerged in water, was aiming to my left, but he only had one bullet and would only fire at close range.

Hiding in the bushes, I approached him from the side, bending over so that my chest was almost touching the water. I stopped twenty paces away and when I straightened up saw a tense figure looking at me through a black mask. The 'beekeeper' had heard me creeping towards him. You cannot move quietly in a marsh, but he had anticipated that I would draw closer, to within a range where he could aim more accurately.

'Throw your weapon aside,' I ordered him again, 'or I will finish you off.'

I aimed the revolver and shot him in the leg. The bullet hit him below his knee and he again tried to flee, but while limping he tripped over the tail of his coat, which was hanging down heavily with the moisture. The water reached his waist as he forged ahead with brute force, but he sank up to his chest. The marsh had seized him by the legs and was beginning to drink his body avidly. Putting his revolver down and forgetting about the pain in his wrist the 'beekeeper' began flapping both his arms in the marsh. When it reached his shoulders he understood that this was the end. Now only the black mask in its tilted straw hat poked above the quagmire and it evoked the image of a wondrous head; perhaps that of the evil spirit of the waters, or a strange marsh creature.

'Help me,' he said in a voice filled with anguish.

I stretched out my stick to the marsh creature, who grasped it with his left hand.

'Remove your scarecrow mask or I will let you sink into the depths,' I said.

'I can't,' he moaned, 'my hand is broken.'

'You can,' I said, jerking the stick towards me and out of his left hand. The quagmire slurped him in further, with a contented sound.

'Well, throw off your mask before it's too late.'

With a sharp jerk he loosened the fastening on his neck, tore the hat and mask off and cast them onto the undulating morass. I saw a long visage, deformed with fear, similar to another mask.

'Wow. What a meeting, Sergeant. Such a delight!' It was the chief of the headquarters of the Black Sea Insurrectionary Group, Sergeant Zaviriukha. 'Didn't I say that I would follow you when you deceived me about going to Zvenyhorodka?'

He looked at me with his eyes wide open, like the image of fear itself.

'But where is the captain?' I asked. 'What is his name?'

'Hamalii.'

'I'm asking for his real name.'

'Trokhymenko ... Petro.'

'And yours?'

'Yukhym Tereshchenko.'

'I will chase Petro,' I said. 'Where is he now?'

'I don't know.'

I poked him with the stick so that he slurped some of the stagnant water.

'Get me out of here,' roared Tereshchenko-Zaviriukha, spitting it out. 'Then I'll tell you.'

'You don't have anything to bargain with.' I poked him under the water up to his ears again, then pulled him up so he could speak.

'Trokhymenko can be found,' the murderer said, snorting out black slime. 'His father, mother and sister live in Yelysavetgrad.'

'Where?'

'Number nine, Pishchana Street.'

Shots ran out from the path through the marsh and a gun stuttered.

'What a shame,' I said, 'if you hadn't brought the Muscovites with you we could have talked for longer. So, excuse me, it's time I left.' I jerked the stick out of his hand.

'Come back,' he cried. 'You don't know everything.'

'Excuse me. We could do this another time, okay?'

The black water slurped with relish as it swallowed his head and then huge bubbles burst onto the surface. As my heart smiled I ran quickly to Mudei and then, hearing someone chasing me, looked around. It was another marsh creature, his face was dripping with slime and running water.

'You've made me speechless,' I said to Vovkulaka when I could eventually speak.

3

Leaping onto our horses, we hurried towards our men and soon stumbled across three Cossacks, Vasylynka, Khoma and Hryts, who had gone among the marsh birches first. Fershal and Karpus were waiting there with the horses so we could ride out of Vidmyna Pazukha. Vasylynka said that a unit of maybe one hundred Reds were after them but they had managed to hold them back. It was a good thing we were defending a narrow route through the marsh because the Bolsheviks would not be able to fan out into a line and advance.

'Go,' I said. 'Go to the other end of the path away from the battle. Vovkulaka and I will head towards the enemy.'

From the chaotic, heavy fire, I understood that the enemy was firing at us, both to demonstrate their strength and to try to force us out of a good defensive position. We would abandon it, but not all at once. Before long I saw another trio of my Cossacks. Two of them were carrying the third man in their arms. It was Khodya and Bizhu bearing Zakharko Momot. When they saw me, they laid him on the earth. I leaped from the horse and leaned over Zakharko.

'Are you wounded?'

'From all of us brothers, Otaman, only Bizhu remains,' said Zakharko quietly, without opening his eyes. 'Look out for him, he is the smallest of us.'

'Zakharko don't you dare die,' said Bizhu quietly. 'Do you hear me? Don't you dare ...'

But Zakharko did not hear him.

When Vovkulaka and I reached the path, the Bolsheviks were advancing. Kozub's machine gun stuttered again, Ladym's and Tsokalo's rifles fired and one of them threw a grenade. The Bolsheviks retreated, leaving over one dozen corpses in the clearing behind them.

We tethered our horses in the undergrowth and I cawed twice to let them know I was there.

'Take Ladym and Tsokalo,' I whispered to Vovkulaka, 'and go quickly. We are behind you.'

I took the rifle from my shoulder and, hiding among the trees, advanced stealthily towards the left side. I stood among some willows, about thirty paces from Sutiaha. He was lying low by a crooked stump, but he was not looking into the clearing where the enemy could appear at any moment. He twisted his head like a woodpecker searching for someone. At last he found him. He saw Kozub, who held the stock of the machine gun against his shoulder, and left his position. Sutiaha rose suddenly and, after taking off his cap and placing it over the barrel of his rifle, ran straight at the enemy.

'Don't shoot.' A cry in Russian came from the side of the trees. 'You are ordered not to shoot.'

After this, a silence dense enough to touch wrapped itself around everything, among which it seemed Sutiaha blundered clumsily. He was caught in its fine mesh and he appeared to fall. He had run to a dense growth of birches where the Reds had gathered and a rifle shot echoed. Sutiaha crumpled and looked slowly in my direction, as if before death he had a burning urge to know who had shot him and, as he looked, he folded to the ground.

The rifles stuttered, the command, 'Forward!' was heard and the Reds entered the clearing. A short burst of fire spurted out of a Lewis gun to my right. Kozub was firing as he ran, but it was not enough to halt them. The Bolsheviks flocked into the clearing. I hopped onto my horse as one of them thrust his ugly mug right out of the willow branches in front of me. I jerked my body to the side and heard how his pistol clicked and did not fire. I did not give him the chance to try again and I hit him with my rifle butt between the eyes with such force that I tore open a third eye. I turned Mudei and flew towards Kozub, who was running towards me clutching the Lewis. As he ran and the horse galloped I stretched out my arm, Kozub took it, stepped onto my boot, as if it were a stirrup, and swung onto the croup of the horse. Mudei sagged briefly, but broke into a gallop. Bullets flew overhead.

'Kozub, you're a good lad!' I bellowed. 'All the clearing was covered in corpses.'

He was silent and I thought he wanted to ask something about Sutiaha, but Kozub remained taciturn, as if he had not seen anything. I only felt how the cover of the Lewis bumped against my ribs.

'It's been a long time since you've bitten them like that, eh?'

He did not reply. I thought that he could not hear because that often happens after a good battle, especially if you are a gunner. We flew to the marsh birches where Fershal was waiting for us with three horses. Vovkulaka had led the other Cossacks along a 'reserve escape route' through the marsh and I looked at Kozub. 'We're here,' I said and suddenly saw how he leaned to one side. It was only then that I understood why he had not replied. He had been wounded just after he had leaped on Mudei, taking a bullet that would have killed me. Kozub stayed on the horse until we had reached the trees where he fell into Fershal's arms. We saw two large, red patches on his back.

'Nothing to worry about,' bellowed Fershal encouragingly, but he looked at me sadly. 'It will heal very quickly, like a dog's wound.'

I understood that Kozub was dying.

Fershal went to his own horse and produced the doctor's bag. Kozub suddenly seemed to regain consciousness and, with a weak hand, took his trusty Colt, which had never refused to fire, and put the barrel against his head.

Kozub moaned. 'Let Yaryna know ... Say that I ...' He squeezed the trigger before he had finished his sentence.

Would I have been able to stop him? I don't know. Perhaps.

Everything suddenly grew dark around us and dusk fell on Vidmyna Pazukha. We had to hurry, so I laid Kozub on the horse before me and Fershal grabbed the Lewis as he looked at me through the frames of his glasses, damp with sweat.

'Where is Sutiaha?'

'He died,' I said, 'I couldn't bring him.'

We hurried to the reserve escape route, bringing the riderless horses with us. There was no sound from the direction of the Reds. It was obvious that they also wanted to live. We passed over the marsh and reached dry ground where Vovkulaka, Bizhu, Khodya, Ladym, Vasylynka, Khoma, Tsokalo, Hryts and Karpus were waiting. There were now only eleven of us. I told the lads the same thing about Sutiaha that I had told Fershal, because before telling them the truth I had to check out something.

Now we could get some rest. The Reds, even if they tried to pick up our trail, would not venture on the track through the marsh at night. We buried Kozub and Zakharko here in a single grave. It was hard to look at Bizhu, who was about to bury his last brother. He sat by him for a long time, not letting us lower him into the grave, which was already beginning to fill with water.

'Boys,' I said, 'today we gave the commune a real battle. But what price did we pay for our victory? Two true Cossacks perished ...' Then I told them how the sell-out, Zaviriukha, had died. Let the news bring some pleasure to those murdered by Cain. When I told of the glorious end to Kozub and Zakharko I saw, for the first time, how Bizhu wept. The Cossacks bowed their heads lower to hide their eyes. I do not know if anyone noticed that I did not refer to Sutiaha.

That night we went to Sokynyi Forest and before dawn we visited our old friend, the forester Hudyma. I regretted that I did not have the beekeeper's mask to show him, to appear before his eyes as the image of that Veremii about whom he had woven a few fables. I went to him with my own face.

Hudyma fell on his knees and babbled something about a wife and children, but I was more interested in Sutiaha. Hudyma said that Sutiaha had been persuaded towards treachery by Chort, who had convinced him that this was his one chance to gain absolution for his sins in the eyes of the Bolsheviks.

'That's true,' I said. 'You both had a chance to live.'

The knife pierced him below the left rib and Hudyma died quickly.

Chapter 4

1

There have been some remarkable examples of banditry during the period covered by this report. For instance, on June 2, in Sosnovka, three bandits attacked the commander of the Cherkassy battalion, Comrade Karpukhin, who was travelling with an orderly. As a result, he was severely wounded and the bandits stripped the orderly of his uniform.

The bandits engaged in an insolent political prank on 3 June. Eleven horsemen, reportedly from Raven's gang, armed with rifles and one Lewis gun, dared to pass through the village of Sokyrne, 15 versts to the south-east of Smila, early in the morning. The bandits sang loudly, 'Ukraine has not yet perished', and the rider who led them held a fluttering black flag with the inscription, 'A Free Ukraine or Death'.

We are undertaking the systematic removal and execution of those peasants from the villages whom we have deemed to be accountable for assisting banditry, or leaders who do not adequately struggle against it. Measures are also being undertaken to locate the hidden caches of weapons that supply the gangs.

On 17 June, in the Chyhyryn district, a group of the 1st Regiment, based near Rebedailivka, seven versts to the north of Kamyanka, seized three bandits who did not offer resistance and, in their own words, came to surrender.

Chief of the district unit of the G.P.U., Berhavynov
Chief C.O.I., Lenskyi

From the monthly report of the government district of Cherkassy District G.P.U., June 1923

She cast the mantle from her head, unwrapped the habit, threw aside

378

her dress and, instead of a nun, Raven saw a naked sinner by the bank of the lake. At first he thought that he, thick-head, was dreaming because he had been lying for an hour beneath the low-lying bushes of Pontian azaleas, which bloomed with huge, yellow flowers alongside the lake, and had drunk in their bitter-sweet fragrance. Raven was ashamed that he kept looking, but did not avert his eyes. What kind of fascinating nun was this who, even in this abandoned spot, so freely and fearlessly uncovered her body? Was it the wanton *Chekist* who had tempted Vasylynka to sin?

The sister was standing against the sun, she stretched her sweet body, entered the lake and swam straight towards him. She swam like a snake, so swiftly and fluidly, that before he realised her intention it was too late to hide. She had seen an azalea in bloom on the side of the lake. Falling to the earth, Raven peered at her face from behind the bush and thought that this nun did not resemble the freckled *Chekist* sinner. On the contrary, she was very beautiful. He languished here in the devil knows what kind of situation. She came out of the water, slender but strong of body. Her nipples were erect in the golden water, and aimed directly at Raven. He did not let himself look lower down but gazed at her face that bore no freckles. It was a face pure and bright. She reminded him very much of someone. If the long, beautiful tresses of hair had still swung over her body Raven would have recognised her from afar. She stepped carefully between the bushes, the azalea was so prickly that it could catch the skin, and he did not know what to do. He did not want to frighten her to death. He wanted to call out, 'Dosia don't be afraid, it's me,' but his throat was so desiccated he could not make a sound.

When she saw Raven she did not cry out but only curled up a little and instinctively placed her hands to cover up what she could, but her eyes showed more surprised delight than fear. She was confused but clearly thinking about the situation. She stood before him as naked as a new born baby. Who knows what she would have done if Raven had not turned away. He took off his linen shirt, it was no longer possible to tell what colour that well-worn shirt had been, and gave it to Dosia. It covered her to her knees and was like a dress for her. When she had fastened it and rolled up the sleeves she allowed Raven to look at her. He still saw everything it was supposed to hide, the nipples, erect from the cold water, seemed more visible beneath the fabric.

'Sit. We will talk,' said Raven, a little concerned that in taking off the shirt he had exposed his old scar which made the left side of his chest look as if his heart had been removed.

She sat on the lush, spring grass, pulled the linen over her knees, hugged her legs to herself, and a little fearfully, even stealthily looked into his eyes. 'We will talk,' she said quietly.

Even though they had not seen each other for some time, they had nothing to talk about. So much had changed since they had last met and there was not even a fragment of anything good in those changes. There was no uplifting news they might share. Why squander the spirit and sow the seeds of sorrow? There was only the past between them and maybe because the fragrance of the azalea maddened him, the image of that distant, almost forgotten night, rolled over his mind with the intoxicating fragrance of datura, wild orchids and fumes of incense.

'Come to me,' he said.

2

We concealed ourselves in the recesses of Kholodnyi Yar in June. There, beneath Velykodna Hill, wild Hryts showed us a cave where there was a good stock of ammunition, including ten machine-gun belts for a Lewis gun and two chests of Mills grenades. The entrance resembled a fox's hole beneath a heap of dried branches, but further inside it was a genuine grotto. Who knows who had dug it or when, but this was at the edge of an ancient system of subterranean catacombs that spread under Motryn Monastery. The cave ended with a wall of collapsed earth, beyond which it was certain there were more underground thoroughfares.

It was good to have this 'home', where we all, admittedly without horses, could hide from the rain and inclement weather, even in the summer. But what inclement weather in summer? Summer is our ally. Then there is no cold or hunger. The boys wove traps from reeds and caught tench and gathered berries and mushrooms in the forest, and Khodya brought back some game almost every day.

We traded the horses that had been left after the deaths of Kozub, Zakharko and Sutiaha and exchanged them for provisions and clothes from the farms. But the villagers had been transformed into cunning, avaricious people who, knowing our hopeless situation, would not pay a fair price. They said that buying our horses was too big a risk for them and they might have to pay with their lives. But they did not worry too much about their own skin when they gained a horse for only one or two sacks of barley or an old coat. That is how they behaved. What is there to say now?

Fate turned its back on us more often now. In the middle of June, Tsokalo, Fershal and the one-eyed Karpus fell. One day, all three headed towards Rebedailivka and did not return. It is hard to say what happened to them but I was sure they had been overtaken by some misfortune. As a precaution we left the cave for a while, which was fortunate because a little later some armed foresters appeared. They were the villagers who could be held accountable and shot for our crimes and were therefore searching for our trail, hoping to find and kill us. We waited quietly, not far from the cave, ready to move at any second. Everyone held his horse tightly by the bridle to prevent them from neighing. The foresters passed one hundred paces away from us and did not see anything. If anyone had seen a trace of us, they were silent. These press-ganged squads of accountable peasants did not worry us, we called them wooden tops, but if there was a skirmish with them we would have to relocate.

There were now only eight of us. Vovkulaka, Bizhu, Khodya, Vasylynka, Ladym, incredulous Khoma, wild Hryts and myself. That was our entire Lebedynskyi squad. After our three boys did not come back, the spirits of the remaining lads fell. Bizhu was the first to grow listless. Having lost his brother, he had become taciturn, as if locked within himself. I did not know how to cheer him up. 'Maybe you could visit your Murzyntsi,' I suggested to him once because I thought that maybe he wanted to leave us and, if so, I would let him go. I was ready to make it easier for him to take this step, but he only bowed his head. There was no way he was going back home. I wanted Vasylynka and Bizhu to leave the forest because they were so young and could start their lives afresh, but it had to be their choice.

I knew I needed to lift the mood of the Cossacks now. Only a sharp, successful operation could renew their faith in their own power. Our courage had not tasted the sweet mead of success in a while. I sent Vasylynka to spy on what was happening near Fundukliivka Station because the railway always aroused a particular interest in the boys. Burning the village council, the action commission, or the poor peasants' committee was all one kind of work, but tackling a railway station and holding up a train was an exit into a wider world. An exit to Rostov and Moscow, whose unstoppable population flooded through our railways.

Vasylynka came to me after a couple of days and told me there was a railway defence unit of twelve men at the station. Furthermore, the transport militia patrolled Fundukliivka. There was also, of course, the representative of the G.P.U. sitting in a room with a sign that read, *Officer On Duty at the Station.*

That night, we ventured into some fir trees adjacent to the station, ready to visit 'Grandmother Fundukliivka', as we called her, when it grew light. It would have been safer to do this in the dark but then our visit would not have seemed as official.

While the boys disarmed the guards in the reception office, I looked in at the officer who was taking his turn to be on duty and told him not to be alarmed because our gang was fictitious. 'We are only pretending to undertake an assault to get people talking,' I said. 'We need the trust of the bandits hiding in the woods around. We will certainly catch them. Our special unit was formed by the G.P.U. organs, but not a soul must know about this apart from the G.P.U. officer on duty at the station. Unfortunately, I have to disarm you.' I liberated his holster from the kilogram of metal weighing it down. A Luger with all its bullets. 'Your documents please.'

The officer seemed like a smart enough *Chekist* but I did not like his looks. I never trust people whose jaws are wider than their foreheads.

'Why didn't anyone warn me about this?' His eyes twitched comically and at first it seemed to me that the son-of-a-bitch was winking at me.

'This is a great secret. No one should doubt the genuineness of our band. Do you understand me?'

'Yes.'

'Then listen to me carefully.'

So everything I had said would seem like the truth, I aimed a revolver at him and asked him to call the station chief and the cashier, 'Tell them to bring all the money in the office.'

His eyes twitched comically again, but the son-of-a-bitch opened the door and bellowed, 'Ledyayev! Kapula! Come here!' They entered the room together and when they looked at the 'bandit' with the revolver, they understood everything. The cashier, Kapula, swiftly fetched the waterproof bag with the cash. 'Could you provide a receipt to prove who has taken the money?' asked the *Chekist*.

'Certainly,' I said, 'give me a pencil and some paper.'

I completed the paperwork with great relish. I certified in writing that the money had been requisitioned by Sergeant Zaviriukha because, even in that world, graspers traded money.

Having read the receipt, the *Chekist* looked at me like a dog at the entrance to a mill.

'Are you making fun of me?'

'Forgive me, yes,' I said, taking out an Austrian carpenter's axe from my boot and severing the telephone wires.

'You are a redoubtable bandit,' said the son-of-a-bitch, winking at me.

'Did you doubt it?' I plunged the axe blade into the left side of his chest where the breast pocket was. He slithered clumsily from the stool and onto the floor as the station chief and the cashier raised their hands.

'We don't trouble functionaries,' I explained. 'If you don't show your nose outdoors, you will live.'

Once outside everything transpired swiftly and in order. The Cossacks disarmed the guards and the militia. They managed to undress them and drive them like sheep to the station granary with the barred windows. They did all this without firing a shot, but there was a puddle of blood by the wall, left by the Russian commander of the defence unit who had not understood Vovkulaka's order.

Seizing some provisions, we went through the forest towards Nova Osota. There, like we had done in better times, I lined up the squad and gave them my thanks for taking the station at Fundukliivka. The Cossacks took heart, but before long a dispute broke out. Bizhu could not come to terms with the fact we had not killed the station guards because he was driven by a thirst for revenge after the death of his brother. He was supported by Ladym and the incredulous Khoma.

'Lads,' I said, 'it's a different war now. Courage is not required to gorge itself only on blood.'

Ladym, as if hearing nothing, sang slowly:

Oh, what is that Raven,
Who alone
Calls his comrades
Into the forest of Lebedyn?

When I first heard this song from Ladym I was convinced he had made it up, but he said that the song was one hundred or maybe even one thousand years old. So, it seemed it was possible that the unknown writer, across a gap of centuries, whispered to me to tell me what I should do now. 'Go to Lebedyn Forest,' he ordered. 'It will be the harvest soon and the Bolsheviks will set about thieving from the villagers. Go and disrupt their plans as best you can.'

Ladym knew what and for whom he was singing. That is why he did not sing the song to the end. There, it spoke of what had happened all those years ago:

Oh, we buried the otaman
Deep in the grey soil.

We were soon in Lebedyn Forest. In July and August we burned the offices of several district executive committees, where there were lists of people's tax obligations. Like the hairs on your head, every last ear of grain, from every villager, was reckoned and over every soul stood a requisition squad. Therefore, whenever the occasion arose, we taught these vampires how to eat our sacred soil in place of bread. Ladym alone sewed seven red crosses on his ribbon. But it became oppressive for us in the forest, the strike squads pursued us from place to place and it became harder and harder to slip out of their encircling forces. Sometimes we were only saved by God coming to our aid.

Nothing presaged evil on that August evening. The trio of Raven, Vovkulaka and wild Hryts crossed the dam by a pool in a broad depression, not far from Krymky village. It was so quiet and calm that Vovkulaka suggested they bathe. He had already undone the buttons of his police tunic, a gift from 'Grandmother Fundukliivka', and he wanted to freshen up in the pond after a long day of patrolling the roads.

Raven did not have the chance to argue with him before they heard the sound of a horse neighing in a small clump of woodland on the other side of the depression, which was followed by the sound of shots and, one after another, riders jumped out of the trees. There were at least twenty of them. Raven, without a second's thought, shot the lead rider, but the others, with a wild hollering, flew onwards and the rebels had no choice but to flee. Raven, Vovkulaka and Hryts ran towards the forest half a *verst* away. They could see the dark wall of trees as they were running out of the depression, but their pursuers did not slacken. Their cries grew louder and the shots drew closer. When they were about two hundred paces from the forest (oh, this had happened before) Vovkulaka's horse tumbled. A bullet had struck her white sock and she fell with such momentum that she pushed into the grass with an agitated neighing for quite a while. Vovkulaka flew out of the saddle and rolled ahead of her. Raven pulled up Mudei sharply and the horse reared.

What happened next was like a nightmare when you can do nothing and change nothing. Vovkulaka jumped to his feet and straightened. Although he was dazed, he turned his face towards the enemy. Raven saw how a red patch was growing on the white tunic between his shoulder blades. The bullet that had struck him in his breast had flown out of his back. Vovkulaka staggered and grasped at a tall thistle, he squeezed a handful of the sharp, thorny branches, for he no longer felt any pain, and fell on his back with a dark pink flower in his hand.

This was one occasion when they were unable to carry their slain comrade from the field of death. The enemy riders were so close that if it had not been for a grenade stunning the lead one, they would not have been able to seize the chance to flee.

Raven let Mudei gallop to where Hryts was waiting for him in the forest. It was only a short distance and the otaman would be hidden in the trees. The Reds knew they could not catch the Cossacks in the trees, so, as if on command, they quickened their pace and opened fire. The bullet caught Raven across the forehead, tearing the skin from the bone, just as he made it to safety.

'Otaman.' He heard Hryst's terrified voice. 'Are you alive?'

'What do you think?'

'There is blood on your face.'

'Don't be afraid,' said Raven, 'I have a hard head.'

He tore the sleeve from his linen shirt, bandaged his head and listened to check if he could he hear the pursuing unit, but there was just a quiet sobbing sound.

'Hryts, what are you doing?'

'There is no Vovkulaka.'

'He is no more.'

'Our standard bearer has gone ... How will we manage without him? He was ... he was the spirit.' Hryts remembered how Vovkulaka had kissed the flag that he, the last isolated soldier of his unit, had preserved in Kholodnyi Yar, and cried even more.

'Weep Cossack,' said the otaman, gulping his saliva. 'Weep. Don't be afraid.'

In the forest it grew dark quickly. Raven sat beneath a tree as he smoked his third cigarette.

'What are we waiting for?' Hryts asked.

'You will see.'

Hryts understood. They waited until night came and then quietly left the forest. It was lighter over the field and the Reds had clearly left to celebrate their victory. It seemed black on the spot where the battle had taken place. Clearly the dead horse was there but a small flame of hope that he might find his dead comrade flickered in Raven. He left Hryts in the trees and went on his own into the field. No, they had taken Vovkulaka. They would be honoured for the death of this forest rebel. There were two dead horses, the lively steed that had jumped onto Raven's grenade and ... Raven leaped onto the earth and saw Tasia was still alive. She was on her side and moaning quietly, 'Tasia ... my little Tasia.' A star was reflected in her huge, dark eyes, a tremulous equine tear. Raven took out his revolver. This was all he could do for Tasia. When he laid the revolver against her ear, she understood and screwed up her eyes. 'Chase after Vovkulaka,' said Raven, 'it will be good for both of you.'

He squeezed the trigger and the shot echoed more deafeningly in the night than in the day. Mudei jumped sideways with fear.

4

What led him once more to Liashchiv Farm?

Raven and Hryts went there in the night and the otaman thought that neither wind nor rain would extinguish the spirit of fire there. They led the horses to the barn and, plagued with fatigue, fell to the straw-covered floor.

Raven rested in the same spot where he had once placed his coat for Tina and himself. Was it a dream or a vision of the recent past that swirled before him? The dark pink flower ... the horse's violet eyes ... the white breasts ... the world, that other world, entire with its forests, valleys, lakes, aromas and roads. He saw a foreign country. In that country, in a cathedral festooned with gold and coral, he would marry Tina. It was full of strange people, men in long-tailed coats and women in long dresses. He was late and ran into the church in his rough, woodland clothes, adorned with grenades. 'Kruk, Kruk,' murmured the voices all around.

Father Oleksii married them. Tina was wearing her rose-coloured dress and was as fragrant as a flower. She wanted to place the ring on his finger but it was too small and would not slide on. It slipped from her hand and fell to the floor. That is a bad omen, thought Raven, but it did not frighten him. He knew it was a dream, but he awoke with a heavy spirit. The church was an inauspicious omen.

The morning light pierced the gap between the doors and was accompanied by suspicious sounds coming to them from outside. Raven touched Hryts lightly on the shoulder and when he opened his eyes, he placed a finger to his lips. Then he went to the door and looked through the round hole that had been created when the branch it was made from fell.

Damn. A Red herd had surrounded the farm.

***

Early in the morning of 19 August we received a report that two bandits had been detected, having spent the night in the barn at an abandoned farm. Our unit was directed to the location and surrounded the farm. They were intent on waiting to apprehend the bandits alive. These warriors of the forest usually engage in a protracted exchange of fire and only take resolute action when their ammunition is exhausted. On this occasion we did not have time to put the barn under guard before two horsemen suddenly jumped from it and, having wreaked chaos with two grenades, fled swiftly. One was successfully knocked off his horse when he was subsequently wounded, and then we were compelled to witness an unusual and terrible event.

A very mundane bandit raised a revolver to his temple, intending to commit suicide. Our soldiers were ready to seize him but the bandit fled and jumped down a well so deep that we could not haul out the malefactor. So, as a precaution, we threw a grenade after him.

What happened to the other bandit was something unforeseen. After our initial shots, he fell out of the saddle, but did not land on the ground, instead he dangled from the stirrups. This is often the case with killed or wounded riders. His hands dragged lifelessly along the ground. The soldiers waited until he either fell out of the stirrups or the horse halted. When he was almost in the woods the bandit moved in an amazing manner, like a Caucasian rider or circus performer, and resumed his place in the saddle. By the time we realised his ruse he had disappeared into the wood. Further

pursuit appeared to be futile.
In connection with this episode I request that an additional group of cavalry cadres be sent to capture the bandits and authorisation be given for a more severe uptake of hostages from nearby villages.

From the report of the commander of a strike group of the anti-banditry unit, Orlov, to the chief of the Cherkassy district division of the G.P.U., 9 August 1923

Chapter 5

1

The raven had lived for almost three hundred years, but he had never seen such a wet autumn until now. It rained from mid September onwards and for two months there was neither heat nor sunshine. Although he could hide from inclement weather in caves, the hollows of trees or, as he was doing now, within the roof above the porch of a vault, the dampness saturated his feathers through to his bones. It rained everywhere, over Kholodnyi Yar, the Irdyn Marsh and Lebedyn Forest. It was good that the water drove mice out of their niches and drowned them, otherwise he would have died of hunger. He had become as emaciated as a marsh lark or perhaps that man in a black mantle who had wandered these parts since time immemorial.

Sometimes it seemed to the raven that he had known Varfolomii for two hundred years. But people did not live that long, and never would, the raven thought, with a little malicious pleasure; though he had a good and sensitive heart. It was rare that female ravens lived to such an age, though they were granted the chance to do so. One year, one hundred, three hundred years pass as swiftly as a single day, the raven reflected while sitting on the mossy roof of the monastery vault, where no one had entered for a long time. Why would they? The ancient structure could collapse at any time, for nothing lasts eternally.

Even the Svyato-Troiitskya Church had burned and fallen before his eyes more than once. The raven remembered a time when it had been a wooden edifice with blue domes adorned with silver stars. When he looked down from far above in the night it seemed as if the heavens were beneath. One hundred years passed and when it was rebuilt in stone it fell and was made anew. All that is not here now is in the past, whether it be stone, a raven, or a star in the sky. All that is eternal is eternity. The vault, which stood against the wall, was far older than either the monastery or church, so it had outlived its own kind. It was strange that it had not collapsed.

The raven could not believe his one good eye when a human silhouette flowed out of the night and to the door of the vault. He almost fluttered his feathers in surprise but managed to restrain himself. The doors squealed open and a nun slithered into the vault.

2

There were now six of us. Bizhu, Ladym, incredulous Khoma, Vasylynka, Khodya and me. Not many, but we could still show ourselves. It was a pity that even the weather did not smile on us. We had never known such a rain-sodden autumn. The damp ate into us, the timber was soaked, the village council did not burn well, the roads were wiped out, and our ammunition became saturated too. Things went so badly with us after we had crawled out of the forest that we had no other clothes to wear. There was of course the 'Sunday-best clothing' but we were saving that for a special excursion. The lack of provisions was arduous and the horses' ribs showed through their skin.

While it rained and rained, the pagan, Ladym, raised the palms of his hands to the heavens every day, beseeching Mokosha to stop the flooding, but his deity did not listen. The incredulous Khoma was surprised that Ladym believed in this female deity. Vasylynka lamented that he could not go and 'hire himself out' in this terrible weather. Khodya was worried the rain would hamper his hunting because the animals and birds were hiding and would not venture out into the forest in these conditions. He was sitting in a corner of the dug-out, bored and humming his persistent, monotonous melody, which I had first heard during our negotiations with Dybenko and Kuziakin. Bizhu had not run for a long time. He did not bustle around at all and it seemed he was indifferent to what was happening outdoors, whether it rained or whether stones fell from heaven.

I racked my brains as to what we could do next when we lacked Vovkulaka. It was like an empty desolation had been created behind me, into which I was walking slowly. How well Vovkulaka could inflame the lads to action. How aroused he was by the aroma of Muscovite blood.

I was tortured by my guilt over Hryts's death. However much I told myself that danger followed us at every step, it was me who had led him to Liashchiv Farm. That is how the cards fall.

It was necessary to look after the few Cossacks who remained.

When spring came, the new season would whisper to us about how we should proceed. After much persuasion, I succeeded in sending Vasylynka home. I told him that there was no work in winter and, even though the rains would abate, we would have to rest up like bears until spring. So, he gave way.

'Sit on your grey horse, ride until his shoes fall off, and go home. You are a quick-witted lad, tell a few white lies and hire yourself out.' I gave him some money and stuck his *Kuban* cap on his head, but it slipped over his damp eyes.

'In spring, if you don't take me back, I will wage war myself.' He furrowed his brows.

'Of course.'

When I embraced the emaciated Vasylynka it seemed as if I could feel every bone. The pagan goddess, Mokosha, made my eyes water.

Vasylynka said farewell to Ladym, Bizhu and the incredulous Khoma, then, as he embraced Khodya, his cap fell off his head. He picked it up and put it on Khodya's head. 'This is a gift for you,' he said.

We all went into the rain and looked after him as he left in silence; Khodya waved the cap at him in farewell. We returned to the dug-out with a silence that was worse than any argument. A week passed, the rain continued to fall and listlessness settled on my Cossacks. If it had been listlessness alone it would not have been too bad, but there was anguish also. In their short conversations they would remember more often those who had handed themselves in for amnesty. I said that they were already no longer among the living and if someone still was, then he would be hunting us. Maybe we would meet them one day.

There was one occasion when Khoma recollected Pylyp Khmara in whose unit he had served in 1920. He still did not believe that Khmara had perished. The boys said that when Pylyp had been badly wounded they had borne him at night to his sister's house in Tsvitne. It seemed he had died there and was buried in the garden. However, the otaman was not the kind who would die like that. Khoma had heard from the people of Tsvitne that Khmara had revived, changed his appearance, burned off his eyebrows and trimmed his eyelashes, which had been as long as a girl's. He had done something else to change his face and had gone to Crimea where he lived under a false surname, which they said was Filipov. I knew that it was not so but I did not wish to argue with Khoma, for he would never have believed me anyway.

It was good they made up legends about the otaman, but I did not like this tale about Crimea. Those kind of fables sow doubts about the point of further struggle, and once these doubts have sprouted in someone, you cannot dispel them; they grab an individual like an incurable illness.

'I think that Khmara went to Donbas,' I said, encouraging Khoma. 'There are so many dubious people there that it's easier to disappear. It's said that they won't seek you beneath the bowels of the earth.'

Did the incredulous Khoma understand that I was giving my blessing for him to take to the road? Before long I became convinced that doubt is a contagious disease, because Ladym announced he was going to Donbas with Khoma. It would be jollier if they went as a duo.

'Perhaps you could join them?' I suggested to Bizhu.

'And what is there in Donbas that I have not already seen?' he asked in surprise.

I was guiltily pleased because I loved this lad. Let him be around me for a little while longer.

It was sad to watch how Khoma and Ladym prepared for their journey. Ladym spent a long time twisting his head around in his cap and counting the crosses on the ribbon. The last one had been embroidered at the end of August when, at the collection point used by the Reds, he had caressed the head of a requisition squad member with his gun butt. Would that be the last one then? The crosses swam in Ladym's eyes. He could not count them and instead of being proud, he was ashamed of his cap. How could he be proud when he could not take it with him?

One night Khoma and Ladym went to Syhnaivka and agreed where they would sell their horses and how they would travel to the station when they returned in daylight. They came back and cut their hair, shaved and tried on their best clothes. While trying to restrain their stupid agitation, Ladym cut himself twice when he was shaving. At dawn we took them almost all the way to Syhnaivka and said farewell in a nearby field.

'If you don't like it there come back.'

'Perhaps we will in spring,' sighed Khoma.

However, I sensed we would not see each other again.

It was strange, but after this parting Bizhu revived a little, perhaps because there were only three of us remaining. It was as if he had suddenly revived. At last, he gained renewed strength, a last breath. He even suggested that we held up a random train at Syhnaivka.

'Listen, have a conscience,' I said. 'Let them go to Donbas without any trouble happening.'

'Okay,' agreed Bizhu. 'Then what?'

'What are you saying?'

'Let's go somewhere. We are already on horseback.'

It had not yet grown light before we went to the oil producing cooperative which stood outside the village. It was a small, brick building which had been erected where the former lord's factory had once stood. I knocked on the door politely, but no one replied, so I knocked louder; still no one came. Bizhu, unable to restrain himself, banged the butt of his rifle into a small, barred exterior window. The glass rang.

'Who is there?' A frightened male voice was heard behind the door.

'Your own people. Open the door,' ordered Bizhu. 'Do we have to throw a grenade in there to wake you?'

I liked the fact Bizhu took it on himself to act. He was resolute and in some degree wrathful. The oil worker opened the door and Bizhu and I entered and left Khodya by the horses. I told the worker we meant no harm but would not be opposed to having a bite to eat and borrowing some oil.

'What oil?' a voice groaned in the darkness. 'The rain has prevented us from gathering the sunflowers. Everything has rotted to mulch and the press is dry.'

When he lit the gas lamp, I saw a young poor peasant activist in a striped sailor's smock. An uneaten supper was going stale on the table, a slice of rye bread, sliced *salo*, pickled cabbage and three dumplings. Next to these was a large bottle, half a litre of which had been decanted into two glasses.

'Where is the other one?' I asked, looking around the room.

'Who?'

'Your drinking companion.'

He also looked at the table, saw the two glasses and understood it was better not to lie, but instead of being afraid he was nonplussed. 'There.' He nodded towards the door that led to the store room. 'I will give you everything you need, only don't go in there.'

Now even a thick-head would have understood who was hidden in there, but caution is more important than anything. I nodded to Bizhu not to take his eyes of the man and I opened the door carefully. A half-undressed girl was sitting on the bed, she was like a frightened kitten looking at me with wide eyes. It seemed to me that her lips were smeared with sour cream, but instead of fastening her clothes over her breast both hands grabbed a revolver.

'Don't come in or I'll shoot,' she screamed.

'Idiot,' I said. 'You will continue your games soon but it is better to give this toy to me.' I took the revolver from her. 'You are so brave. A young communist perhaps?'

Hiding the trophy Browning in the pocket of my coat, I left the boudoir.

We were lucky because, although the top of the press was dry, the oil commune still milled crops, along with young female communist activists. There were some sacks of grain by the mill and I told Bizhu that he should bring a sack of barley for the horses, but not to be too generous because a horse who gorges after starving might be unable to stand, and told him to come back later with Khodya.

'Forgive me, but we need to breakfast.'

When Bizhu and Khodya entered the oil works I found a large aluminium mug because we did not have time to drink from small glasses. The communist gaped at Khodya in surprise.

'Do you like his plait?' I asked.

'Well, no,' he said, almost panicking.

'What is it then?'

'He is also for Ukraine?' asked the communist warily.

'Yes,' I said, 'and are you not?'

'I'm for the working people.'

'We've seen how you work,' I said, indicating the boudoir with my glance. 'That's why your press is dry and the girl isn't satisfied.'

It was curious but I felt no malice towards the oil worker. He was a ram who wanted to eat and drink with the herd and suck at the slimy teat of the state. This castrated ram looked at Khodya, who was eating *pyrohy* dumplings with cheese and stuffing his mouth with *salo* and cabbage. But that is not everything. Breakfasting and softening up from the alcohol, Khodya sniffed in the direction of the boudoir. Bizhu had probably told him what was hidden there. Or had he sniffed it? Bizhu looked at me enquiringly.

'Have a conscience,' I said. 'Let's go.'

Our horses had revived and we took a sack of barley and two containers of mulled grain. I thanked the communist for the drink and wished that his press was always as moist as the 'poppy' of his beloved. However, it was entirely plausible that we would visit again.

When we reached the forest, it was growing light and we felt something unusual was happening. We all looked as one to where the sun rose.

***

When we returned to Lebedyn Forest I spoke to the boys as if we were a complete unit. I am not fond of fancy oratory, but these words came from the heart. I said that, although there were only three of us left, a trio was an organisation, the military linchpin of partisan units. We would continue to fight for Ukraine, for her freedom and for the honour of our arms.

Bizhu and Khodya stood shoulder to shoulder, as if they were on a parade ground, as I ordered that we would prepare and go to Kholodnyi Yar, where our battle standard was hidden. We would take with us everything we could and hide what we could not carry.

'Machine gun, luws luws,' said Khodya, tapping himself on the chest, and I realised that he was asking to become our gunner.

After Kozub, Ladym had taken on that job, but he was also gone now. I agreed and thanked Khodya in my mind because lugging a heavy Lewis on a military expedition was not a great pleasure.

3

Dosia did not know if she would meet Raven again, but she was always looking for him. She had joined the monastery, God forgive her, because of him. 'If it is not ordained that we will become a couple then I will be a sister to him. If such happiness happens to come my way.'

Good fortune had fallen on her on the bank of Lake Velykodne. Now winter gripped everything and she had heard nothing from him. He had promised to send news when he came to Kholodnyi Yar, but she had not heard a whisper. She waited and prepared. She knew what winter meant for the rebels, so she stocked up on two pots of lard, a vat of honey, some *salo*, a jar of alcohol, a bag of tobacco, and warm blankets, and hid everything in a place where no one else went. This secret brought Dosia the greatest pleasure. It was a secret that had been revealed to her by the holy man, Varfolomii.

She had almost died of fright when he had knocked quietly on the door of her chamber one night. During the day she worked on a Singer sewing machine there. He called her outside, led her to the wall, and almost forcibly dragged her into the vault. The place he showed Dosia stunned her into silence, though she had heard of this secret more than once. Heard and believed, but had never realised it was so near.

Holding Dosia by the hand, Varfolomii led her down some well-trodden steps and only then lit a wax candle. The flame illuminated the half-fallen innards of the vault and its walls deep in the earth. In one of its recesses there was a niche about a third of a person's height.

'There is a world there,' whispered Varfolomii hoarsely, as he got down onto the earth and crawled into it.

Dosia remained in the darkness, frozen to the spot. When she saw a flame appear in the niche, Varfolomii called her to come to him. She hesitated. The holy man would not have called her here for empty amusement, there was some meaning here. She crawled towards the flame. The niche widened and after a couple of yards it led Dosia into a cave. In the flickering candlelight she saw two narrow passages, and Varfolomii was heading along one of them. She followed him and it seemed that she could barely breathe and the subterranean place would bury them alive.

Ahead of them was another cave, similar to a dug-out. Its ceiling and walls were strengthened with columns and beams of oak. Dosia thought that her underground roaming would end here, but there were two more narrow passages and when Varfolomii continued she remembered the tale of a network of man-made underground caves and tunnels here, which extended beyond the monastery. They went well beyond the boundaries of Kholodnyi Yar and one underground walkway went almost as far as Zhabotyn. Dosia could barely keep up with Varfolomii, who, from time to time, repeated a single word, 'Tears.'

They entered a spacious cave where they could breathe freely, and here Dosia could hear the sound of water warbling nearby. This round, stone grotto had once been a pagan temple, in the middle of which stood a sacrificial altar. Varfolomii leaned over it, ignited some soaked rags, which burned with a high flame, and illuminated the massive, oppressive walls, which were covered in rough, hewn stones. Water flowed down one wall into a stone trough, where it was lost in a pulsing, circular gullet of more water. The stone from which the spring flowed was reminiscent of a sorrowful female face carved in the rock. Now Dosia understood Varfolomii's words, 'Tears.'

As if divining her thoughts, he stretched a bony arm, which protruded from the sleeve of his mantle, in front of him and bellowed hoarsely, 'The tears of the Mother of God.'

That was the name of the spring.

***

Later, when Dosia came to the cave by herself, she knew Varfolomii had revealed this secret for some other reason than just to astonish her. She was afraid of crawling into confined spaces and the subterranean place oppressed her, but she quickened her pace and reached the

398

spring again. Though two further passages opened out from this cave, breathing the secrets of one thousand years onto her, she did not go a single step further. When she needed to, Dosia would choke down her fear and explore all the branches of the labyrinth, even if they led to Zhabotyn. However, now she was concerned with something else and was doing everything she could to make sure someone would be able to pass the winter here. Like a beast, who, as winter approaches, prepares its lair where it may keep warm, so Dosia stocked the cave with good provender. Like that beast, she was ready to cut the throat of whoever might find her secret lair.

One night, when she was carrying a bag of flour, Dosia went outside and again headed to the vault. The night was dark and cold, and after the prolonged rain the lower clouds were beginning to swell with snow. She listened to the darkness and, as she reached the door of the vault by the wall, she suddenly felt she was not alone. At first she thought that maybe the omnipresent Varfolomii roamed here at night, but then she realised that it could not be. A cold feeling crept down her spine. It was the chilling breath of danger. She quickly moved away from the doors of the vault and looked, but nothing had changed. If someone's evil eye noted Dosia's presence here then all her plans would be ruined. She threw her hood onto her shoulders so she could hear better. No, there was not a sound. She froze and listened to the silence so intensely that her ears began to ring.

Having assured herself that her fears were groundless and there was no one here apart from her, she still could not move onwards. Then she heard someone breathing and that breathing gradually drew nearer. Dosia clutched the bag of flour to her chest so she could not hear the pounding of her heart. The nun, for that was who it was, came closer and even in the darkness Dosia recognised Sister Olga. Raven had warned her of this spotty informer, but Dosia was already aware and vigilant. Sister Olga was strong and healthy but she pretended to be a mad woman and often wandered the forest, just like now, in the middle of the night. She came to the vault. They stared at each other intently for a while, knowing they could not just pass each other on this path.

'Come and look what I have found,' Dosia said, in a welcoming manner.

She unfastened the tie and showed Sister Olga the bag. When the nun looked closer, she flung a handful of the flour into her eyes. The nun stepped back, covering her face with her hands, and the next moment Dosia kicked her in the stomach. Sister Olga crumpled and fell, but quickly rose again. Dusted with flour and resembling an apparition, she pulled out a revolver from her habit. Dosia did not love revolvers, the Hrushkivka Cossack, Dosia, loved the sabre. Confused, she stumbled and bumped her back against the door of the vault.

Lord, how stupidly things happen, how pointless to die with that secret and at the hands of this degraded woman. Sister Olga drew nearer, but still kept a safe distance.

'Hands up,' she said in Russian. 'And don't doubt that I will add an extra hole to your body.'

In the quietness of the night her deep voice might have awakened the dead. Suddenly a raven flew from the roof over the doors of the vault and wafted his wings over Sister Olga. He flew onwards, but that moment of distraction was enough to give Dosia the chance to leap and punch the nun's head with such force that the informer flew one way and the revolver another. Because Dosia loved sabres, which never misfire, she did not look towards where the gun had flown, instead she leaped towards the informer, who was already on her feet. She struck her on the jaw, but as she fell, the nun grabbed Dosia's robes and they both fell to the ground. They rolled together, first one way and then the other, until they bumped to a halt against the rampart of the monastery. At that moment Dosia was in the saddle and, waving her hand as if it held a sabre, she struck the other nun in the throat. There was a long, tasty sound of air escaping from below the side of her hand.

'Goodbye,' said Dosia. 'And don't wander any more.'

She dragged the body to the rampart, threw it in the ditch and covered it with earth. She found the revolver by the vault and gathered the bag with the flour. Dosia did not venture under ground again that night.

The secret employee that we infiltrated into the Motryn Monastery has vanished without a trace. The fact testifies to the continued operation of the band in this area. I consider it necessary to send an anti-banditry unit into Kholodnyi Yar to conduct an operation to destroy the bandits.

Chief of the Cherkassy division G.P.U., Berhavynov

From the monthly report of the Cherkassy district G.P.U. of the government district G.P.U., 26 November 1923

It is a shame for a Cossack to complain about dark days, but at the end of November truly black times came on us. Returning to Kholodnyi Yar, Bizhu, Khodya and I sat in a cave beneath Velykodna Hill and reflected on which people we could trust to take our weakened horses for the winter. We finally decided to leave them at Melnychanskyi Farm.

I am talking about the famished horses, but what about us? We were so weak with hunger that we bent in the wind. We cooked some barley and groats, and baked loaves mixed with water, and so we lived. Khodya's hunting was disrupted. The ducks had flown from the lake and the tench had dug deeply into the mud. It is not easy to shoot a goat or a hare with a bow and if there is no snow, there are no tracks to follow. We had finished our salt and our last box of matches was too damp to light. We had already stopped smoking. That is a true woe for a Cossack, enough to make him bounce off the walls. Then Bizhu went to Melnychanskyi Farm to buy salt, matches and perhaps potatoes, and to talk with 'our man' about the horses. 'Our people' in the villages and farms had not yet changed, but you could not say they were glad of our visits. Who could be sure that yesterday's brother might not sell out today? After all, that is what had happened to the forester Hudyma and with others.

We dealt with them, the sell outs. I had a truly loyal person, not far from here, who would have brought me salt and cooked eggs for us with her own hands, but I did not wish to trouble her kind heart. I could not show my anguished state to her, so I did not leave any news in the hollow of the willow tree where I had promised I would when I returned to Kholodnyi Yar. It would have gone against my conscience to live off her goodness. Such was our happiness, like the horse shoe that Khodya found in the cave. Drawing it out of the earth he warbled delightedly 'Horsshu, Horsshu,' as if he had found his happy destiny, but when he scraped away the earth it became clear it was a human jawbone.

There was no less curious an event involving Khodya when we were waiting impatiently for Bizhu to return with salt and matches. A day passed, then another, and still he did not come back. A cold foreboding, as stealthy as hunger, crept onto us. Khodya and I often glanced at each other, not daring to speak our fears out loud. On the third day, Khodya, unable to endure the unknown any more, went out with his bow to try his luck. It was not long before he returned with a dead raven.

'Khodya,' I said, 'this is a raven.'

'The bird that goes caw, caw,' Khodya replied.

What happened next was even more curious. He did not clean or pluck the bird, but reached inside and neatly peeled the skin and feathers in one fluid motion, as if unpeeling a stocking from a leg. Then he cut off a drumstick and offered it to me. I took it because I did not want to offend him. The meat was raw but it was clean and fresh and did not smell too bad. I looked at this dish as I listened to Khodya chewing with relish. Then I thought, what difference does it make whether it is a raven or a chicken? People eat wood pigeons, quail, thrushes, tits and oyster catchers, why is a raven worse than them? Well, good, let's eat it. OK, it is not as tasty, maybe the meat is harsher, but what does that matter when you are starving? Finally, I ate the drumstick. I will not say it was appetising, but it was not disgusting either. Here is what is interesting though. Having convinced myself that raven was no worse than many other disgusting things people eat, I did not consider that the meat was raw and unsalted.

After another day, a light snow began to fall and we had to make a decision. It was unlikely that Bizhu would return. If he was alive, he was either wounded or in the claws of the *Chekists*. Necessity compelled me to write a note and stuff it into the hollow of the willow tree by Velykodne Lake. We just needed a single match to kindle the fire, then we could smoke. My sparrow had once said that smoking kills hunger. My sparrow, where are you now?

In the evening our horses snorted warily. Mudei and Khodya's Steppe pony were tearing at their reins. I asked Khodya if he would soothe them and he took their reins. I decided to go further up the slope on foot and look to see if some devil was approaching.

As I stood and listened, I suddenly sensed that someone was looking at me. I swept my eyes here and there, and twenty paces from me I saw a huge wolf staring at me from under a bush. He was sitting on his back legs with his white belly towards me. He looked at me sadly. His small, dark eyes stared into mine. A cold shiver ran over me. 'Is this your sign from the other world?' I whispered. He raised his muzzle upwards in a wolfish way, as if wanting to howl, but did not make a sound. Then he rose and walked, slowly and reluctantly, into the forest. I returned to the cave distracted.

'What was there?' Khodya asked.

'Nothing,' I said, 'something bothered the horses. It happens.'

That night I saw the vision again. The temple adorned with gold and our wedding. It was cold, so cold there. It was nothing to me because I was in my warm coat and sheepskin cap, and my sabre still rattled at my heels. Tina was still in her thin, rose-coloured dress. The ring fell to the floor, but that did not frighten me for I knew it was a dream.

***

When we met Dosia, I was most grateful for the matches and after rolling myself a large cigarette, inhaled avidly. My head spun so much that, at first, I did not know what she was talking about because I was lost in my muddled thoughts, but at last I understood.

'Immediately behind the door,' said Dosia, 'there will be a candle.'

'How wonderful you are.' I embraced her tenderly.

After the strike group had caught a mounted rebel by Melnychanskyi Farm, the commander of the anti-banditry unit, Orlov, had no doubt that a partisan squad was still operating in Kholodnyi Yar. The mounted rebel was the first proof of this. The rebel tried to flee and as he turned his horse and headed for the forest the front legs of his famished steed gave way as he reached the trees. The bandit hit the ground hard and he did not manage to put his revolver against his temple before the best soldier from the strike group, Kukushkin, grabbed his hand and twisted it away. When Commander Orlov grabbed the heavy bag next to the partisan, salt ran out of it from a bullet hole.

'Finally,' said Orlov, delightedly. 'Now we have someone to question. Kukushkin be gentle with him, he is barely alive.'

'Can it talk?' Kukushkin asked doubtfully, as if they had caught an animal.

'There is no one whose tongue cannot be loosened,' said Orlov, crushingly. 'The secret is only in the means by which you achieve this. It would be best to let him revive a little first.'

That day Orlov decided to base his squad in Motryn Monastery and then to disperse into separate groups to comb the forest each day. The sisters were not very happy, of course, but let them keep their mouths shut. Let them be thankful for being permitted to stay here and open up their sewing cooperative. In Orlov's view it was necessary to have swept these black-habited ones away with a shitty broom long ago. After the disappearance of Sister Olga they should have lined up all of them against the wall because they did not know who was guilty.

When the Muscovites occupied the monastery Mother Rafaila did not say a word. The nuns sat quietly in their cells, not daring to stick their noses outside, but their fears were groundless. Orlov had strictly forbidden any harassment of them when, in the evening, he had lined up his men in the monastery courtyard. 'Comrade Orlov's men, I hope that you will not shame the honour of our unit. Anyone who is unable to restrain his desires will be severely punished. Besides, we have to wake early tomorrow,' added Orlov, and they all smiled.

They had combed through the forest ravines for three days but had not found a trace of the rebels. Orlov vented his fury on the bandit who seemed to be really dumb, but beating him did not help. Now he was numb everywhere. They had crushed his fingers in a door and burned him. The rebel screamed, roared and writhed, but did not speak.

'Well,' Orlov smiled at him as he spoke, 'we don't need you any more. Now we will cut off your hands. Isn't that right Comrade Kukushkin? Then we will cut off your legs so you will know how to run to the forest next time. You clearly like to run? So you will run. Kukushkin, bring me an axe and a saw.'

'That's not necessary,' said the rebel suddenly, 'I will tell you.'

Orlov and Kukushkin looked at each other expressively, as if a stone had spoken to them.

'No, you will show us right now. But if you are mistaken ...'

Orlov knew they could not procrastinate any longer because the bandit would think again after the shock had passed. It was necessary to act decisively. That is how it happened, you wore out your legs patrolling the remotest gullies, through all the ravines and channels, and the bandits were half a *verst* away from the monastery.

The rebel walked with his hands bound, while Orlov's men rode. They stole up to Velykodna Hill as quietly as they could, and when they were by the lake Orlov's mare neighed suddenly. It was obvious she wanted a drink, but now they could also hear neighing from below the hill. At first Orlov thought it was an echo, but he was silent and waved his hands to silence his men. The rebel had not lied. On command, the riders fanned out into a line, like a curving wing.

'Flee,' cried the rebel suddenly. 'Flee! I betra ...'

Orlov shot him in the head at point-blank range.

***

When the leading riders came into view, Khodya swept the Lewis over their ranks, but the enemy fire was so dense that it was hard to work out the best direction in which to retreat. They galloped at random. It was either sink or swim. Holding their horses closely, Raven quietened Mudei a little because he was flightier than Khodya's Steppe pony.

'Otaman, have you heard Bizhu?' cried Khodya.

'Khodya forward.' The otaman did not hear his question. Whichever way he looked there was a hail of enemy rifle fire. The bullets ricocheted off the trees, leaving white divots on their trunks. Raven waved at Khodya to stop firing because they did not need to draw attention to themselves. Whichever way they turned hot lead poured out to meet them.

Now it seemed they would have to force their way through.

Khodya's horse neighed again, the first time he had been answering the call of an unknown mare but now he neighed from pain and despair as he fell on his side, writhed over the earth and bumped against tree roots. A bullet had ricocheted off an oak trunk and hit him in the abdomen. When Raven looked over, Khodya had already jumped to his feet and thrust Vasylynka's *Kuban* cap on his head. He grabbed the Lewis and fired a short burst at the enemy.

'Here Khodya,' Raven cried, 'to me.'

But Khodya already knew what he would do next. The otaman would have to forgive him, but on this occasion he had made his own decision. He did not take cover, but stood fearlessly as he fired and advanced.

'Khodya flee!'

But no. Khodya had already decided. He knew that no one apart from him was covering the otaman and when the first bullet struck him he only jerked a little and continued firing. As another bullet thudded into his chest, Khodya staggered and again stepped forward. The third bullet struck his forehead and he still made another step forward before he fell, face upwards.

'Forgive me Otaman.' Blood poured over Khodya's eyes, but Raven saw how his spirit, like a small feather, flew into the heavens, to a place of light and bliss, where there was no pain, anguish or hunger.

Raven flew to his horse and in his breast there was also no pain or anguish, just a gaping, dark hole. Salt welled in his throat, salt that he could not swallow. Turning Mudei towards the slope, he was surprised that his long-suffering horse could keep going. Mudei waved his head and trotted powerfully upwards.

As twilight drew in he brought Raven to the monastery ramparts on which a solitary figure was standing. Dosia had come out when she heard gunfire and realised what it must mean. When she saw Raven she ran down the rampart to meet him. He was not surprised she was here. As he leaped off his horse, he was as dark as the night itself.

'You are alone?' she asked.

'Can't you see? I have a request for you,' he said.

'Just say and I will do it.'

'Give Mudei to a good pair of hands.'

Her voice was black with sorrow, for Dosia understood everything.

'I will do it,' she said.

'Do it at once and get him away from here.' He gave Dosia the reins, took the saddle bag and extracted two grenades from it. 'Don't linger.' He looked at her kindly but firmly.

Dosia gathered up her habit and leaped on the horse. Raven hugged Mudei's head and pressed the hairy, equine face against his face, it was so warm, so warm.

'Don't you linger either,' said Dosia. 'They are swarming here now.'

Closing his eyes, he embraced the horse. 'Farewell…' He combed his hand through Mudei's mane, touched Dosia and pressed his forehead against her thigh, 'Thank you. Know that you were always my love.'

She rode away on the horse as he followed her with his eyes. He needed to hurry, but he was unable to tear his gaze from her. He took the rifle and saddle bag and ran swiftly up the rampart and to the vault. He stepped up to the door and he listened.

'Stop,' a voice called in Russian. Three Reds dashed out of the church of Ivano Zlatoustivska and shots rang out. Raven looked down the rampart to where more Muscovites were sprouting. They became entangled in their greatcoats as they ran towards the vault.

'Stop,' another voice called in Russian. 'Don't move.'

Bang. Bang. Bullets whizzed past his ears.

The leading Muscovite dug into the earth as riders appeared on the rampart, and Raven aimed the rifle with one hand. He ran into the vault where he found the candle just behind the threshold. Stumbling in the darkness, he descended the worn steps, which crumbled underfoot. At the bottom he stumbled against a heap of something, went to one side, and lit the candle. There was a cacophony from above and it seemed as if the vault was collapsing. The earth was already pouring onto his head.

'Come outside bandit or we will throw grenades at you.'

Raven crawled into the niche and after a couple of yards the candle illuminated a cave. He looked around, thought and nodded his head. They would not crawl in here, foresight is paramount. Two grenades, one after another, rolled out of the niche and into the vault.

What happened next stunned even the old raven. He was sitting on the cross of the Ivano Zlatoustivska Church and, after the first shot, he was about to fly when he suddenly felt his wings would not let him. He saw how the bearded rebel plunged into the vault. His pursuers gathered around, some even crawled to the vault, but none were stupid enough to enter. Why would they? The rebel had shut himself in a cold place. Then something bizarre occurred, an explosion underground that even shook the church. The vault moved a little and, before everyone's eyes, it sank into the earth.

The old raven felt his heart had stopped. This is death, he thought calmly, and flew diagonally downwards. Hitting the ground, he rolled onto his side and his one good eye looked into the heavens for the last time.

From the Author

This is where we must say farewell to Otaman Raven because there are no reliable sources to allow us to follow his path to the end. It is only known that this journey did not conclude with his flight to the monastery caves, the entrance of which he 'sealed' with two grenades.

From 1924 onwards the *Chekists'* archives are completely silent about the otaman until, in a report from 1926, we stumble across the following information:

`Raven's gang was liquidated on June 6 1925`

So, sealing the entrance to the caves, the otaman managed to find his way in the labyrinth of tunnels under the monastery and make his escape. It appears that he organised a new unit and battled on until at least 6 June 1925. The enigmatic report about 'Raven's gang' being liquidated offers hope because it does not directly refer to the otaman's death.

Moscow, which from time immemorial has pronounced anathema against anyone who fought for the freedom of Ukraine, was extremely wary of the forest rebels. They forbade any mention of their names, even in deprecation, because they did not want to waken the memory of the grey masses for whom they fought. However, a legend that one of them survived remains to this day.

In Tovmach, in March 1964, a tall grey-haired man, dressed in clothes of a foreign make, who they say was Raven, travelled through the town in a taxi. He did not speak with or meet anyone, he just went to the cemetery. This story seems plausible because in March 1964 the Zvenyhorodka region welcomed many guests from abroad when the world celebrated the one-hundred and fiftieth anniversary of Taras Shevchenko's birth. The numerous delegations, one after another, visited Moryntsi and Kerelivka, and Tovmach is not far from there.

I can testify to the truth of the story, for I saw him in the taxi with a beautiful grey-eyed woman. He asked the driver to take them to Shpolianskyi Forest. It was spring. No one saw the spring like they saw her and no one loved her more passionately. He stood for a long time by a ditch near the trees. Was this not where Viun was buried?

When they returned to the car, he took his seat and searched his pockets for a cigarette or Validol.

'Is it your heart?' she asked.

'Everything is okay,' he said. 'All is well, my little sparrow.'

But what fate befell the others? We can only surmise what happened to Otaman Veremii, but it is more than likely he was shot in the Cherkasy prison.

Blind Yevdosia left the Irdyn Marsh for an unknown place. I have been shown the spot where her cottage once stood by the forester, Pavlo Vakuliuk. It was the end of May and I saw for the first time how the Pontian azalea blooms.

Ladym and the incredulous Khoma did not live for long in Donbas. While working below the earth they expropriated the cashiers of the Chystiakivskyi mine offices. During the operation a guard fatally wounded Ladym in the stomach. Khoma was unable to carry his comrade from the 'field of death' and from then on bore in himself the wound of sorrow that would not heal. He married a *katsap* girl, took her name and, as Foma Holikov, returned to the Zvenyhorodka region where he worked in the Budyshche collective farm and stables. In 1934, someone reported him and he was sent to Solovky. Who returns from there?

Veremii's mother and old Tanasykha died of hunger in the spring of 1933.

Dosia married in Hrushkivka, gave birth to seven children, three of whom died, and lived to be ninety. She had a beautiful trunk that she would not let anyone touch. It was only in 1986 that she opened it before her granddaughter, Lida. Some old photographs were preserved in there, and in one of them Lida saw her grandmother, a young Cossack girl with a sabre. She was wearing a stripped, *Astrakhan* hat with a long ribbon. A bearded man, in a white sheepskin cap and with shoulder straps crossed over his tunic, was standing next to her.

'Your Mudei would let no one else saddle him,' Grandmother Dosia spoke happily to the man in the photograph, as tears ran down her cheeks. 'He bit, kicked out with his hooves and reared up. No one could approach him. Unfortunately, when he was yoked to a wagon, wounds and dry scabs appeared on the poor thing and he passed away quietly.'

Kozub's Yaryna gave birth to a boy, but he was brought up by other people because she was driven mad with sorrow for her lost lover. Little Ivash was sent to an orphanage, finished military college and became a Red Army commander. He died at Kursk in 1943 and was posthumously awarded the title of 'Hero of the Soviet Union', for such are the whims of fate.

'Colonel Hamalii', real name Petro Trokhymenko, was shot in 1937 on the twentieth anniversary of the October Revolution. His *Petliurite* past had caught up with him.

1996-2009

Glossary and Information

Babusya - the Ukrainian word for grandmother

Cheka - the shortened form of chrezvychaynaya komissiya or extraordinary commission, the Soviet Security Organisation which ruthlessly suppressed political opposition and carried out crimes against humanity and acts of genocide.

Chekist - Member of the Cheka

Cherkasy - the Ukrainian spelling of the city. The Russian spelling is Cherkassy and it is this spelling used in the reports, which are original Russian secret police documents.

Comiacheika - the smallest structural unit of the communist party

Desyatykhatnyky - villager who could be shot without trial in reprisal for actions carried out by the Cossacks

Embroidered shirt - traditional shirts with ancient motifs, peculiar to their region, worn by Ukrainians.

Haidamak - peasant or Cossack rebel

Halushky - Ukrainian dumplings

Horilka - Ukrainian vodka

Hrechanyky - buckwheat cake/roll

Katsap - slang term for a Russian person

Khodya - slang term for Chinese person

Khokhol - is originally the word used for the 'topknot' worn by Cossacks but became a term used, both affectionately and in a derogatory way, to refer to Ukrainians.

Kholodnyi Yar - (Ukrainian) and Khalodnyar (Russian) is the same place but spelt in different ways in the text to highlight some of the impact of the Russian occupation on the Ukrainian language.

Kobzar - One of Shevchenko's best known works.

Komnezam (committees of poor peasants) - peasant organisations established by the soviets to requisition food and establish control in rural Ukraine.

Kopeck - the equivalent of a penny

Kuban-Cossacks - ethnic Ukrainian Cossacks from Kuba, the Ukrainian speaking region of the North Caucasus.

Kulaks or Kurkuls – wealthy peasants

Kutia - traditional Ukrainian dish eaten at Christmas

Kyiv – the Ukrainian spelling of their capital city (Kiev is the Russian spelling)

Lesya Ukrainka (1871-1913) - real name Larysa Petrivna Kosach-Kvitka, classic Ukrainian author

Melkhysedek - Znachko-Yavorsky Melkhysedek (1716-1809) prominent Ukrainian churchman

New Economic Policy - a policy that ran from 1921-1928 and allowed a degree of small scale capitalism, thereby disarming resistance to soviet power.

Otaman – the leader of a Cossack unit. (Russian spelling - Ataman)

Odesa - The Ukrainian spelling of their seaport (Odessa is the Russian spelling)

Patronymic - Slavs sometimes refer to someone by their patronymic, e.g. Ivan son of Denis (Ivan Denisovich), as a polite form of address.

Petliurite - follower of Shymon Petliura, a Ukrainian Nationalist leader and military commander.

Pood – Russian word, originally from Norse, 1 Pood =36.11lbs

Potaptsi – a Ukrainian dish made from dried bread, sometimes eaten with tomato and cheese or sour cream.

Shelmenko-Denshchyk – a popular comedy play

Shevchenko - Taras Shevchenko is Ukraine's national poet.

A new flame will shine forth from Kholodnyi Yar is the last line from Shevchenko's poem, Kholodnyi Yar, which from time immemorial was a centre of resistance to Russian power and the haunt of Cossack leaders. The poem is a prophecy of the resistance movement that would awaken there time and again and ensure that the nation eventually gained its independence.

Shulyavskyi dialect - a joke, because Fania is really speaking Russian

Sich - Ukrainian word for fortress.

Solovky - archipelago in the White Sea. Site of a first soviet labour camp.

Spirit of Kerensky – Alexandra Kerensky (1881-1970) Russian democratic politician and prominent leader before the Russian Revolution of 1917.

Tryzub – the trident symbol on Ukrainian military uniforms and flags.

Varenyky - Ukrainian dish similar to ravioli

Verst – obsolete Russian measurement, 1 verst = 1.668 kilometres
Volhyniaka-Viking - The term Volhyniaka refers to a native of Volhynia in Ukraine.
Zaporizhia - the Ukrainian spelling of this group of Cossacks

Although the text sometimes refers to 'dug-outs', these were a network of underground tunnels and living quarters constructed by the rebels to avoid detection. A similar method was used by the Ukrainian Insurgence Army (UPA) during, and in the years immediately following, the Second World War. This method went on to be used by the Vietnamese Communists, who had studied UPA's techniques, during the Vietnamese War.